The Village Online

Lily Hayden

Copyright © 2018 Hayden Woods Creative

All rights reserved.

ISBN: 9781983206733

The Village Online by Lily Hayden is published by independent publishers Hayden Woods Creative.

For rights, books, news and contact details, follow us on Facebook, Twitter, Instagram and LinkedIn at Hayden Woods Creative.

We're excited to bring you news of upcoming titles and look forward to meeting you online! Your feedback and reviews mean everything to us. Thank you for reading!

Acknowledgements

This book is for:

My own lovely community & especially my Cedar Wood family

The Real PC Parker- any policing inaccuracies are purely creative license. Thanks for keeping the streets safe!

Mike, Ethan, Grace, Lila & Max as always

But mainly for Livvy and her love of a community page ;)

Love, Lily

March 2017

Tina Cleary had been away all weekend, visiting Robbie in Plymouth. The coach journey seemed to take forever, and she'd only just made it back to The Crown in time for her Sunday evening shift. She had the foresight to text her boss to tell him she might be late, but luck was on her side and she ducked through the heavy wooden doors with minutes to spare.

Tina swung her backpack from her shoulder and underneath the bar for safe-keeping. She took off her leather jacket and knotted her hair into a ponytail; securing it with the elastic from her wrist. The lounge was empty now after the lunch period and the bar had not yet started to fill up with the usual evening crowd. Tina busied herself with a few odd jobs, making the most of the quiet time, not daring to pull out her books until she'd done some work.

The door opened as Tina was wiping down the tables, sending a blast of cold air into the small bar. A voluptuous blonde woman moved through the narrow doorway, her husband holding the door chivalrously for her. Tina looked up, surprised to see Barry Simons and his wife, Dana. They both looked fraught and, instead of making his way straight to the bar, Barry settled his wife at a corner table, helping her to remove the dark-coloured shawl she was wrapped in.

Tina pasted on a cheery smile, addressing Barry. "We haven't seen you for ages! We were about to put up 'Missing' posters!"

She expected the usually jovial couple to laugh at this, but Barry looked embarrassed and Dana just smiled politely.

Tina tried again to engage Barry in conversation as she took his order at the bar.

"Are you ok?" She asked solicitously.

Barry shook his head. "It's awful, awful news."

"What's happened?" Tina asked in concern. She finished pouring the drinks and gave Barry his change, waiting for him to reply.

The door opened into the bar and Barry turned towards the noise, distracted from Tina's question. Kelly Russell and her husband shuffled into the room, closely followed by another couple. Kelly's face was devoid of her usual make-up and Tina could see her eyes were red and puffy as she navigated her way around the tables to the bar. Her husband, Evan, followed her and Tina was surprised to see Barry hug Evan in an unusual display of affection.

"We can't stay long," Evan was muttering to Barry. "My mum is with the kids. We just needed to get out of the house."

Tina turned her attention to Kelly. "What's happened?"

Kelly opened her mouth to speak but her lip wobbled, and her eyes filled with tears. She waved a hand at Tina, indicating that she needed a moment.

Tina turned her eyes towards the other couple. Darren and Steph Rees wore identical strained expressions to Barry and Dana, and Steph was sniffing into a crumpled tissue. Dana was up out of her seat and had pulled Steph into her arms. Darren stood, a little awkwardly, next to his wife and her friend. He glanced over at Tina and Kelly at the bar before looking away sharply

"Kelly?" Tina asked again, ignoring Darren, panic rising in her chest. "What's going on?"

"Jim Burbridge." Kelly managed to choke out, her voice breaking. "He's dead."

October 2016

Chapter 1

It all started with a condom. An innocuous little square foil packet. Looking back, Laura couldn't believe that something so ordinary could trigger such a sequence of events but, as they always say, hindsight is a wonderful thing.

Jim Burbridge had had an awful day at the office. It started when Keeley missed the school bus and Jim ended up executing a last-minute school run, leaving him stuck in the awful traffic along the single carriageway. Laura had predictably already left for her own office job in Birch Grove which was conveniently, for her, travelling against the rush hour traffic. Jim arrived twenty minutes late to the council offices, flustered and irritable. He was running a safe-guarding course for the newest batch of parent governors that day and had been stuck with a particularly annoying bunch who'd asked questions all day and thrown him off schedule. Jim joined the same rush hour traffic at 5.30pm, travelling in the opposite direction along the only road to Birch Grove. By the time he got back to his four-bedroomed semi in Oak village, it was 6.30pm. His shirt was sweaty and crumpled from sitting in his car for an hour to crawl what should have been a fifteen-minute journey.

Laura had been home for well over an hour and was perched on a stool at the newly-fitted breakfast bar; a glass of water in hand as she leafed through the mail, one eye on the pot bubbling on the hob.

"Hello Jim." Laura glanced up through her thick-rimmed glasses at her husband as he dropped his keys and wallet on the counter. Jim leaned across and gave his wife a dutiful kiss on the cheek in greeting.

Laura was an attractive woman, even more so now they were in their forties. When they had met, at college, Laura had been a serious-looking thin girl, with sharp, angular features and a heavy dark brown bob. Jim had been athletically-built with a thick mop of sandy brown hair that fell across his forehead. The athletic build had faded away to what Keeley called a "dad bod" and the glorious hair had slowly retreated to a slightly greying, receding hairline. Laura, however, still maintained the thick chin-length hair, her features were still as sharp, not yet giving in to the sagging of age, and her figure was an athletic tribute to the hours she spent running and at the gym.

"Keeley missed the bus." Jim said frowning at both the memory and the kitchen worktop littered with plates and glasses.

Laura nodded, putting the handful of mail down and attending to the large pot that was now sizzling. "She said," Laura stirred the pot and added a pinch of herbs. "Bless her."

"Bless her?" Jim snorted derisively. "I was the mug late for work because she can't get herself organised. Where is she?"

"Netball." Laura ignored Jim's statement of annoyance at their teenaged daughter. "I'll pick her up."

"You'll have to," Jim tutted. "Kate is coming over at 7 to discuss the carriageway proposal."

"You should have said," It was Laura's turn to frown. "I've got a class!"

Kate Evett was a local community councillor for Little Cedars, the small suburban area made up of Oak Village and several other small housing developments. Jim was an avid supporter of Kate's and had developed a keen interest in all local affairs. Laura hoped that this was just a phase and Jim would be back to his previous hobbies of badminton and golf soon as she was already finding the meetings and the constant networking irritating. Jim had recently started an online group for the community on social media and Laura was mortified at the type of nonsense that grown adults posted about, although she was also secretly fascinated by it and would spend hours scrolling through passive-aggressive comments chuckling to herself.

"Dinner will have to wait." Jim announced, glancing at the clock. "What is that anyway?"

"Garlic chicken and rice." Laura gave it one last stir, turned the hob off and replaced the pot's lid. "I'll pick Keeley up and I'm off to Boxercise. I'll eat later."

Laura dashed off to change into her workout clothes and Jim followed her upstairs to their bedroom. They had lived in this house in the village since they had got married fifteen years previously. Back then, there'd been just three little cul-de-sacs branching out from a central avenue, a mile from the top road that went to Birch Grove or Little Cedars, depending on whether you turned left or right. The hub of the village had been an independent newsagent, a little post office and a traditional pub that did cracking Sunday lunches. Four years ago, the Oak Fields estate had been built on the edge of the village; a few hundred houses on a parcel of land that hadn't looked bigger than a football pitch. Jim had said at the time that this would cause chaos for traffic in the area and he'd been right. It wasn't just the fault of the Oak Fields estate of course. This development was just the straw that broke the camel's back in a long line of housing developments along the stretch from Birch Grove to the motorway. The congestion was awful until approximately 9.30am every week day as cars bottlenecked trying to access the junction at Little Cedars. Jim wished he'd been more interested in local affairs back in his thirties as a strong voice during the public proposal meetings may have made all the difference rather than any concerns being swept under the rug until traffic reached its current tipping point, driving commuters to despair. Nevertheless, he was awake to his community's needs now and he was determined to help shape the area for the better.

Jim stripped off his pale blue shirt and balled it up before tossing it in the direction of the laundry basket. He didn't have time to shower and settled for a blast of deodorant spray, a splash of musky aftershave and slipped into jeans and polo shirt that he thought was the right combination of smart and casual.

Laura picked up the shirt and dropped it into the missed target of the wicker basket designated for any dirty clothes. She unzipped her own tailored grey dress and deftly dropped it on top of the pile, adding her tights and underwear. She quickly redressed in Lycra leggings and a matching top, sliding her feet into her trainers and throwing on a hoody. Jim had time to give her body a quick appraising glance before she was covered back up. Not quick enough though that she didn't notice, and she rewarded his attention with a judgemental eye roll.

Jim felt a prickle of annoyance at her reaction. She should be grateful that he still desired her. Jim knew of a few of his friends who'd stopped finding their wives attractive. In fact, most of his close friends were already divorced; either in the honeymoon periods of second marriages or negotiating the minefields of online dating. Jim was a firm believer in the importance of marriage, to the point where he blamed a lot of the anti-social behaviour and economic problems in society on the downfall of traditional values. He held this steady belief even when he felt a little envious of the bragging of some of his acquaintances.

"'I'll drop Keeley outside, but I won't be back in or I'll be late," Laura told him as she left. "Don't bang on at her about being late. I don't want to come home to a massive row again."

Keeley was being very difficult lately and Jim was often getting caught up in blazing arguments with his previously sweet daughter. Laura was always making excuses for Keeley; blaming hormones and the difficulties of being a teenager. Jim didn't have time to get into an argument this evening with either his wife or his daughter, so he nodded his agreement.

"Do you have time to tidy away downstairs?" Jim asked hopefully.

"It's tidy." Laura waved a hand dismissively. "Tina's been today. It's just a few plates and glasses out from Keeley and her friends after school. I forgot to pay her, by the way. She said she'd pop past later but if I'm not back there's money in the top drawer."

"Tina?" Jim frowned, not following the conversation.

"The cleaner." Laura shook her head in exasperation and darted out of the house before Jim had any time to ask any more questions.

Laura hopped into her Kia Sportage and made the short journey to the Comprehensive school. Luck was on her side and Keeley and her friend, Ellie, were waiting at the gates. Laura delivered them both back to the village, made it in time for her fitness class and was back home at a little after 8pm.

To her annoyance, Kate Evett, who had also been running late, was still at the house. Laura dropped her own keys onto the counter.

"Hello Kate." She smiled politely at the short, slim woman sat at her kitchen table pouring over some plans with her husband. Kate was still dressed in her charcoal grey skirt suit and looked up to give Laura a weary smile.

"Hello Laura." Kate replied. "We won't be much longer. Will you be coming to the proposal meeting? We've got a date?"

"Oh," Laura was caught off-guard. She couldn't think of anything worse but, obviously, she couldn't say that. "What date is it?"

"November 9th." Kate confirmed. "It's a Wednesday."

Laura glanced at the wall calendar, not wanting to turn to the next month in case it was empty, and Kate was witness to this. At that moment, there was a knock at the door. Laura gave an apologetic smile and darted off to answer.

Jim turned back to Kate and they resumed their conversation where they'd left off.

"As much as I empathise with the plight of those that may be impacted," Jim brayed in the grand tone of a man who really knew what was best for the local community. "One cannot expect the tax payer to bear the brunt of higher costs when, if you really think about it, we've already put our hands in our pockets to subsidise the "affordable" housing that's now bloody mandatory on every new development. It's not fair that people like you and I work our socks off to pay a premium to live in a lovely area just to have it opened up to all and sundry when these new estates spring up."

Kate flushed a little. "Right, well, that's a little off subject."

Laura was also flushing with embarrassment in the hallway. She could hear every word Jim was saying clear as a bell and so could Tina, who happened to live in one of the apartments on the Oak Fields development that had been added to meet the developments' quota of "affordable housing".

Laura hurriedly paid Tina the money she owed her and thanked her profusely before closing the door. Kate was getting to her feet and gathering up her paperwork.

"What's the affordable housing got to do with the road?" Laura asked Jim, too annoyed to care that Kate was still there.

"Oh," Jim looked surprised that neither his good friend nor his wife had been quick to agree with his perfectly reasonable aside. "Nothing really except potential concerns from some of the residents if the top road is turned into a dual carriageway as the apartments are closest to the road."

"I wish you'd keep your voice down," Laura tutted, pushing aside a stack of coats and replacing her purse back in one of the handbags hanging underneath on the banister. "Tina lives there, and she could clearly hear what you were saying."

Jim flushed a little. "I wasn't to know. Anyway, thank you for your time, Kate."

Kate said her goodbyes and hurried out.

"Honestly," Laura shook her head at her husband as she ladled out a plate from the pot of Garlic chicken. "I was so embarrassed when you were bloody braying on like that. I bet she thinks we're stuck up idiots now!"

Jim ignored Laura and reached for a plate to dish himself up some of the dinner.

"There's a lot of garlic in here," He commented, sniffing at his forkful of chicken and rice. "The whole house stinks of it."

"Light the candles then," Laura slammed the lid back down and carried her plate over to the table. "That's what they're for."

Jim, still reeling from his dressing down, searched through the cupboards and drawers looking for matches to light the fragranced designer candles. Laura picked at her meal purposefully ignoring his fruitless hunt.

"There are no matches." Jim gave up and looked to his wife for guidance.

"There might be a lighter in my bag." She shrugged. "Call Keeley down for dinner please."

Jim rooted around underneath the jumble of coats and fumbled in both leather handbags dangling by their straps.

"Keeley!" He called up to his daughter, and then again louder when he had no response. "KEELEY!"

His fingers closed around something and he pulled it out to inspect it closer. Keeley came crashing down the stairs, sounding like a herd of elephants despite being a petite fourteen-year-old, at the same time as Jim registered the little square foil packet in his hand.

"What the hell?" He stared at the condom in confusion and disbelief.

"What's the matter, Dad?" Keeley asked as she brushed past him into the kitchen.

Jim closed his hand hurriedly around the offending object.

"Laura!" He hissed, ignoring Keeley's question.

Keeley shrugged off her father's strange behaviour, gratefully accepting the plate her mother offered. Laura caught Jim's eye and stuck her head out into the hallway to see what he wanted.

"What is this?" He opened his palm and flashed the shiny contraceptive packet at his wife.

Laura shook her head, looking genuinely confused. "Where's that from?"

"Your bag!" Jim spat out furiously.

Laura shook her head again, her eyes widening. "Are you sure?"

A look of horror dawned on her face and she shot a look over her shoulder in the direction of her daughter. "You don't think...?"

Jim frowned. "It was in *your* bag."

"I honestly have no idea." Laura replied bewildered.

Jim closed his palm around the condom; his mouth opening and closing as he weighed up what to do with this incriminating evidence and Laura's protests of innocence.

"Just put it in the bin!" Laura exclaimed.

"What's the matter?" Keeley repeated, from the kitchen.

"Nothing." Jim and Laura replied in unison. Laura snatched up the foil packet and tossed it into the bin, slamming the lid down. Jim followed her into the kitchen and stood silently; still unsure of what to do.

The doorbell went for the second time that evening and they both looked at each other surprised. Laura, seeing that Jim was making no move to answer it, moved to answer the door.

"Hi!" Their next-door neighbour, Dana Simons, beamed a cheery greeting and, without waiting to be invited, stepped across the threshold.

Dana was as voluptuous as she was talkative. Barely pushing five feet tall, she made up for her lack of height with her personality and her volume. Today, she was squeezed into a low cut red silky top and a black pencil skirt in a clingy jersey material. Her stilettoes click-clacked across the wooden floor and she breezed into the kitchen, brandishing a piece of paper.

"We're having an extension!" Dana announced, handing the paper over to Jim ceremoniously. "The builders say we need to do this party thing agreement, just a formality, of course!"

Jim took the paper, still flustered from his discovery, and scanned his eyes over it.

"You just need to sign it." Dana waved her hand dismissively at the document. "We're in a rush to get started. I've instructed the builders to not start too early, so we won't disturb you."

Laura smiled at Dana's insistence. They had only moved in the previous year, but Laura had already grown fond of their larger-than-life new neighbours. She rummaged in the drawer for a pen and handed it to Jim.

Jim frowned at Laura, refusing to take the proffered pen. "We'll need time to digest this, Dana."

Dana looked surprised. "It's just a standard agreement. There's really no need…"

Jim folded the paper decisively. "We'll get back to you within the timescales."

Dana flushed at his frosty tone. "Right, well, the thing is…"

Jim cut her off again and Laura wanted the ground to swallow her up. Keeley slid from her seat and smiled apologetically at Dana before darting back up to her bedroom.

"We'll be in touch." Jim said firmly and walked to the door, throwing it open in a discourteous request for their neighbour to leave.

Dana looked at Laura, throwing her a silent plea to intervene.

Laura grimaced at Dana apologetically and mouthed "Tomorrow?"

Jim caught Laura's gesture and his face turned almost puce with rage.

"Shall I ask Barry to come around?" Dana asked hopefully. "He can probably explain it better than me, being in the trade and all."

Jim shook his head and looked down at Dana, a touch condescendingly. "This type of contract will need to be looked over by our solicitor."

A flicker of irritation flashed across Dana's face, but she tried to mask it. "Jim, I'll just send Barry over. We're meant to be starting work tomorrow."

Jim's nostrils flared in anger. "Well, you won't be. We'll be in touch."

Dana's mouth dropped open and she marched through the open door. Jim pushed the door closed behind her rudely.

Laura put her head in her hands. "Oh Jim! Did you need to be so rude?"

Chapter 2

Dana Simons burst through the dark grey composite door into the tiled hallway of her four-bedroom semi.

"Barry!" She shouted, her heart still racing from the confrontation with next door. "You'll never bloody guess what's happened?"

Dana slipped her feet from her stilettoes, sending them skittling across the floor, and lent against the doorframe to catch her breath.

When there was no reply, she ventured into the living room. Barry was tucking into a takeaway supper; feet up, television blaring.

"I was calling you." Dana frowned. "He only won't sign the agreement."

Barry glanced up from the TV. "He wouldn't sign it?"

"No!" Dana sunk down onto the plush black and grey sofa next to her husband. "He said he wanted his solicitor to look at it first."

Barry rubbed his hand across the dark stubble on his jawline for a few moments as if digesting this information. "That's a nuisance. I'd better go around and speak to him."

Dana nodded. "He was very rude to me."

Dana waited for Barry to jump to his feet and heft his burly frame across the herbaceous border between the two houses to defend his wife's honour, but Barry went back to his Chicken Bhuna.

"Barry?" Dana nudged his thigh with her toe. "Are you going?"

Barry barely glanced in her direction as he replied, "Not now. Tomorrow. I'll speak to the boys and see if they can push it back a few days. We don't want to fall out with the neighbours or I'll end up forking out for a different surveyor for them. Let him cool off."

Dana drummed her manicured red nails against the glass surface of the coffee table in irritation at Barry's lack of action. She'd psyched herself up to have the work started on the attic conversion and she found it very inconvenient when things didn't run to schedule. It also annoyed her that Barry didn't seem remotely bothered that Jim had caused her offence.

Dana and Barry had only been married just over a year. It was a second marriage for both, and while Dana's son, Jordan, was practically grown-up, Barry's children, Tyler and Chloe, were both still in primary school and spent every other weekend at the house. This was why Dana was so keen on getting the attic converted to a usable bedroom for her and Barry. The house had seemed a great size when they'd moved in, and it was fine when it was just Barry, Dana and Jordan during the week, but it felt a little crowded when they were operating as a family of five. Barry insisted that Tyler and Chloe have their own bedrooms, but this meant there was no spare room for the dressing room that Dana needed for her huge collection of clothes, shoes and make up.

Barry slowly got to his feet and started to collect up the empty foil cartons, balancing them on top of his plate. Dana followed him into the kitchen and watched Barry deposit the loaded plate on the worktop next to the sink. She wrapped her arms around his solid bulk and rested her head against his huge chest.

"What's that for, love?" Barry asked gruffly, but with a smile.

"Nothing," Despite her annoyance about Jim's refusal to sign the agreement and subsequently delaying her dream bedroom, Dana felt a surge of love for her handsome giant of a husband. "It's nice to have you home at a reasonable hour. Shall we watch a film and have an early night?"

Barry gave Dana an affectionate squeeze. "I'd love to, but I need to pop down the pub and see Gary about pushing the work back. I won't be late, so we can still have that early night."

Dana sighed inwardly but flashed Barry a bright, pearly-white smile. "Don't be too late."

Dana set about tidying up the mess that Barry and Jordan had left behind before running herself a hot bath. She lit the fragranced candles and slid into the soothing bubbles, taking a sip from the large glass of wine she'd poured to help her unwind. When the glass was empty, Dana reached for her phone and scrolled through social media to catch up on the day's events.

"Stephanie Rees has invited you to join 'The Oak Village Community Group'." Dana read out before pressing 'join'.

There were loads of posts even though the group seemed to

have only been set up recently. Dana recognised quite a lot of the people and poured over some of the comments' screenshotting a few and sending them to her friend Steph.

"Omg!" Steph replied via message to a particularly passive aggressive post about poor parking etiquette outside the post office. "I can't believe some of the posts. I could spend hours on this!"

"I'm not even halfway through!" Dana tapped out a reply. "I might post a rant about my neighbour. He's making a fuss and delaying the start of our building work!"

"What a nightmare!" Steph empathised. "I know how much you've been looking forward to that. You should set up a bar in the garden and have parties all year to spite them!"

Dana, feeling calmer about Jim's rudeness now she'd had time to relax and a large alcoholic beverage, laughed at the thought of this. She was still more than a little annoyed, but she trusted that Barry would deal with it and it was just a minor setback. Like Barry had said, no point falling out with neighbours. No matter how rude they were. Laura had always been very pleasant and lovely, in Dana's opinion, and Dana decided that she wouldn't stoop to Jim's level. Maybe he was just having a bad day.

Dana sunk deeper into the bubbles, enjoying the sensation of the hot water washing over her, and read a few more of the Oak Villagers' posts.

Kelly Russell was using the page to tout her latest pyramid scheme or whatever the technical term for her endless cycle of 'new business opportunities' was. Kelly was a lovely lady, but Dana knew, via the school mum network, that she wasn't the only one who'd blocked any of her endless online promotions from showing up on her feed. Dana moved further down the page to look at what else had been going on in the neighbourhood.

Ooh, the new estate had a mystery criminal mastermind who hadn't been scooping their dog poop. Dana devoured the comments on this thread, trying to work out which residents were seriously furious at the mucky pavements and which posts were taking the mick. Barry's friend, Gary, had posted a few memes which were clearly aimed at inciting the fury of the original poster. Dana was pretty sure he had a dog and he lived on the estate. Dana didn't know Gary that well but, in her opinion, he seemed exactly the type to not scoop his poop.

Dana put her phone down and reached for a fluffy pink towel. Once she was dried and changed into a slinky nightie, she flopped down onto bed. She was exhausted after a long day at work, but she wanted to try to stay awake until Barry got back from the pub. He'd been away all last week and the kids had been here all weekend, so they'd hardly spent any time together. Jordan was staying at his father's tonight, so it would be nice to have some quality adult time.

Barry worked for one of the biggest building firms in the country and oversaw the contracts for this region. He'd started out as labourer after leaving school at sixteen and had done extremely well for himself; working his way up to foreman and then into managing the contracts. Dana had first met him when she worked in the office for a local Traffic Management company years ago when Jordan was just a baby and she was, at the time, happily married to Dave. They'd reconnected on a dating app two years ago and it had been a whirlwind romance with them tying the knot within twelve months of their first date. Dana now worked in admin at the hospital and had been doing early shifts for the past few months. She'd never been an early bird, but Barry was always up and out by 6am and she figured that she could have more time in the evenings at home as well as miss the awful traffic in the mornings by keeping these hours.

Dana rested her head against the stack of decorative pillows piled up on the bed. Her eyes already felt heavy and she fought the urge to close them; knowing if she did she'd be out like a light. She browsed the community page for a little longer, sending an invite to Barry to 'like' the page. Barry rarely used social media, but Dana thought he might get a laugh out of Gary's dog poop post. She rested her phone against a heart-shaped cushion and decided she'd just close her eyes for a moment.

When Dana woke up, it was 4am. She was freezing cold and her neck was aching from the unnatural angle of the pillow pile she was led on. Groaning, she pushed the pillows to the floor and struggled to climb under the tightly tucked covers. She closed her eyes again, trying to welcome sleep before she lost the 'tired' sensation as she knew, from a fleeting glance at the digital display of the clock, that she only had another hour before her alarm sounded. In the split second before sleep could wash back over her, Dana's brain registered that Barry wasn't tucked into the bed beside her and suddenly she was wide awake.

Dana grabbed her fleecy dressing gown from the bottom of the bed and her phone to check for any missed calls or messages. A tiny flutter of panic started to knot her stomach as she saw the lights downstairs still blazing. Dana hurried down the stairs, trying to suppress any wild irrational images of Barry lying dead in a ditch somewhere, and felt a surge of relief when she saw Barry sprawled across the sofa; television still flickering and snoring like a train. Irritation replaced the relief and Dana decided to leave him there to sleep off what was, no doubt, too many beers. She stomped back upstairs, stripping off the seductive sleepwear she'd wasted and climbed into her bed to spend the last hour before her alarm tossing and turning.

At some point, she fell back asleep and, in her confused half-slumber, managed to silence her alarm, waking up disorientated and groggy to realise she was now thirty minutes late for work and would have to contend with the rush hour traffic. Barry had managed to wake up, despite his no-doubt hungover state, shower, dress and get off to work without rousing her. Dana had no choice but to forego her usual primping and preening. The only advantage to the stop-start crawl to the motorway was she was able to apply a semi-decent layer of make up in the rear-view mirror and fluff up her flat, lifeless hair so she looked half-human when she finally arrived at the hospital nearly an hour and a half after her shift had started.

Barry, on the other hand, had managed to spring to life at 5.30am as he did every Monday to Friday as if he'd been programmed to do so. Barry's morning routine was as low maintenance as Dana's was not and, with a quick wash and a change of clothes, he had jumped into the Mitsubishi Outlander and had arrived at the office to check in before heading back out to a meeting about a potential new contract all before 8am.

Barry enjoyed the hustle and bustle of his job as well as the pays and the perks but there were times when he missed being hands on. One thing he still found difficult to get used to was wearing a shirt to work.

Barry Simons was a big man; over six foot three and built like a rugby player. He had been more of a football player, back in his youth, and still played a regular game of 5-a-side with his mates but now he was the wrong side of forty, he was no way as fit as he had been. Barry was aware that all the takeaways and pints were causing his shirts to feel that little bit tighter and vowed that he'd start looking after himself. He'd been a lot more active before he'd met Dana but, then again, he had been single for a few years and going to the gym had been a way of staving off the boredom of going home to a lonely house after his marriage to Lindsey had broken down. Barry was much happier being married as he hated being alone. He knew he was lucky to have met someone as bubbly as Dana, especially as she had made such an effort to welcome Tyler and Chloe into the home they'd set up together. Barry had always had a bit of an eye for the ladies, hence his break up with Lindsey, but he was making a real effort to stay on the straight and narrow; not fancying being thrown back into the nightmare of online dating. Before he'd landed the jackpot with Dana, he had not enjoyed the whole dating game; much preferring the comfort of knowing there was someone waiting at home for him. Barry thought that he had maybe got too comfortable though, judging by his growing beer belly. His mate, Evan, still went to the same gym. Maybe he'd give him a call later and join back up. There were a few too many temptations at the pub. An hour throwing around weights and a little bit of cardio would do him the world of good plus there'd be the bonus of knackering him out, so he wouldn't be tempted by the call of The Crown.

Barry arrived early to the council office and sent Evan a quick text while he waited in the reception area. He was just pocketing his phone when he noticed his neighbour walk into the building. Barry raised a hand in greeting. He hadn't had much to do with the new neighbours, but they had always exchanged pleasantries in passing.

Jim Burbridge raised his own hand in an identical greeting and paused at the seating area next to the reception desk.

"Good Morning." Jim looked a little nervous and tugged at the knot of his maroon tie.

"Morning!" Barry boomed cheerfully, not noticing Jim's apprehension. "You work here, do you?"

"Yes," Jim nodded, still looking a little uncertain. "I'm in Education. Are you here on business?"

Barry nodded and then remembered the party wall agreement that Dana had taken over yesterday.

"Dana said you had some questions about the work we're having done," Barry decided to take this opportunity to try to smooth over whatever misunderstanding Dana and the Burbridges had had. "I should have come over myself to explain but Dana was keen to get the work started. Are you around later?"

Jim shifted his briefcase from one hand to the other. "We're running the agreement by the solicitor today. We'll get a recommendation for a surveyor and be in touch."

Barry fought the urge to grimace. Jim was well within his rights to appoint his own surveyor at a cost of both time and money to Barry. It would be so much easier if he'd just agree to using Barry's surveyor. Typical council types.

"Of course," Barry nodded, deciding to put Jim at ease before he turned on the charm that had got him this job in the first place. "I'd feel more neighbourly if you'd let me show you the plans and a draft of the schedule. Maybe we could grab a quick pint later?"

Jim shook his head. After yesterday's grim discovery, despite Laura protesting her innocence, Jim certainly wasn't in the mood to be coerced by the pushy neighbours into signing over his consent for them to do God knows what with his property.

"I'm afraid I've got something on." Jim replied coolly and turned to leave. "I'll be in touch."

Barry gave what he hoped looked like an understanding smile and watched as Jim got into the lift at the end of the corridor. He let out an audible groan as soon as Jim was out of earshot. Barry hadn't got this far in life by giving up that easily. He'd have been happy to swallow the cost and the time delay, but Jim's bad attitude had now made this a personal challenge.

Chapter 3

Jim just about managed to get through the excruciatingly tiresome final day of training the Parent Governors. He made his way back to his desk at the end of the day to gather up his belongings. Most of the staff in the open-plan office had already left for the day and he loitered at his desk for a few moments savouring the quiet.

Jim removed his reading glasses and rubbed his aching eyes. He'd barely got a wink of sleep last night; consumed with the anger and hurt that Laura could be cheating on him. Laura had continued to protest her innocence after Jim's discovery had been rudely interrupted by next door and their arrogant demands. Jim, not usually one for confrontation, didn't know what to think. On one hand, Laura had never given him any reason to worry about her fidelity and their relationship seemed to be just as satisfactory as usual. On the other hand, she was an attractive woman and she wouldn't be the first person he knew of to do something out-of-character in their forties.

Jim sat down heavily on his upholstered swivel chair and rested his elbows on the desk. Everything had been such a blur since he'd found that item in Laura's purse. Dana had taken him by surprise and he knew, in his heart, he would have dealt with the situation in a more civil manner if he hadn't had such a shock. As much as Laura seemed genuinely bewildered, Jim wasn't naïve enough to believe it had just appeared in her bag out of thin air. Laura had asked Jim whether he believed her as they were getting ready for bed and her concern had seemed so authentic that he really felt torn on what to believe. He had replied with a non-committal grunt and muttered something about talking about it tomorrow before feigning sleep. His mind was working overtime and it had almost tipped him over the edge to come into the sanctuary of work to be confronted by that awful woman's Neanderthal of a husband. Jim had never fallen out with neighbours before. He liked to think that he was a courteous and civil citizen, but he was not a push-over and would not be railroaded into signing an agreement to allow any old cowboy builders to mess about with the structure of his property. Laura had taken the agreement into work to ask one of the solicitors for advice. Even this had bothered Jim though as if Laura was indeed having an affair then the likelihood was that she was carrying on with someone in work. Laura had only been at this office for the last two years and Jim hadn't paid much attention to any of the colleagues she'd spoken about. It was a large firm, with several branches, and Laura managed the office. Laura reported directly to the partners, Chris and Jane. As far as Jim was aware, Chris was happily married but he couldn't for the life of him recall names of any other staff.

Jim slid his glasses up onto his head and put his head in his hands despondently. It had been less than twenty-four hours since the discovery and he felt like his whole life was teetering on the precipice. He would be heartbroken to lose Laura. They had had a few more disagreements than usual lately but that was just down to how difficult Keeley had been. Laura had always been too soft with her parenting, in Jim's opinion, but even where they had clashed slightly, there was no huge argument that would justify Laura seeking out another man.

Jim gathered up his belongings. He would have to go home and face up to the situation. He couldn't just hide away at his desk all night. His phone vibrated, and Jim fished the phone out of his pocket. It was a notification for his group. Jim clicked on the link and approved the various requests that had come in throughout the day. He scrolled through some of the posts; basking in the comradery of the neighbourhood.

Mark O'B had found a set of car keys while out walking his dog along the river and these had been reunited with their owner, thanks to the online group.

Amanda Holland had been looking for her cat. Trixie was suspected to be hanging around a few streets away and Amanda was currently on her way to River Way to see if this was her kitty.

Jess Reilly had privately messaged him to complain about Kelly Russell over-using the page to promote her latest new business opportunity.

Jim frowned at this. It wasn't the first complaint he'd had about posts on the page although the most complaints had been from Angela Hanigan, the lady who lived at the end of Conifer Lane. Unfortunately for Angela, her house was on the corner before the pathway down to the river and she was experiencing an ongoing issue with dog owners not picking up after their pets. Angela posted quite regularly on the subject and, while many residents empathised with her, there had been a few replies to her posts which were mocking in tone and Angela had been bombarding Jim with requests to have some of the commenters banned from the page. Jim was a firm believer in free speech and didn't want to have to police the page, however he had had to serve a warning to residents reminding them of the expected conduct. It would be a shame to lose such a useful medium of communication due to the minority. The online page had been particularly useful for raising awareness of the traffic issues and would hopefully drum up support for the upcoming consultation on the proposed road improvements.

Jim decided to send a polite request to Kelly Russell that she cease promoting her business as the three consecutive days posting on the group was sufficient for all residents to have seen it. He hoped that he came across slightly more diplomatic than he had done with Dana Simons, but he had been caught off guard and hopefully he would be able to resolve this now Laura had spoken with a solicitor.

By the time Jim had been through all the posts, he had been at his desk for approximately half an hour. He hadn't thought that there'd be so much work involved in running a page for the local community when he'd started it, but it was certainly taking up a fair bit of his time. Jim had considered adding another admin, but nobody stood out as the right person to help moderate the group. Kate would have been perfect, but as a local councillor it was important that she remained impartial. Jim would have to rack his brains for the right candidate. Just as soon as he'd got to the bottom of Laura's handbag contents and resolved the party wall nonsense.

Kelly Russell was navigating the aisles of her local Tesco when she received the message from the admin of the Oak Village Community group.

Kelly's phone was never far from her hand and she was

reaching for a bottle of wine when the phone pinged. Kelly paused to read the message and dropped the bottle into her trolley with a little more force than she intended.

The bloody cheek. She thought to herself angrily wheeling the shopping cart away from the Beers, Wines and Spirits aisle. Kelly was so annoyed that she almost missed the special promotion on fruit ciders but, luckily, she caught herself in time and heaved a crate in for her husband. Kelly should have been used to being on the end of other people's negativity by now; this current venture was the latest in a long line of Kelly's entrepreneurial career.

Kelly Russell was thirty-six years old and she'd been a passionate representative, or partner as was the term now, since she'd gone back to work when Sophie, her youngest, started school five years ago. Kelly had dabbled in cosmetics, health supplements, been a weight loss representative, done a Personal Training course and was currently delighted to be helping her friends and neighbours save money on their utility bills. Verity, Kelly's upstream partner, had even mentioned the importance of objection handling the cynics in her latest web event. It still rankled Kelly though that there was so much negativity in the world that people couldn't be happy for the success of others.

Kelly caught sight of her reflection in the mirrored dairy display and smoothed back a strand of auburn hair that had escaped her meticulously-styled messy bun. She had just been to the gym and was still dressed in her work-out gear. Kelly was extremely proud of her size-eight figure and spent her spare hours at whatever classes she could fit in. It was a shame her Personal Training career had never really taken off. The course instructor, Nick, had said Kelly was a natural motivator but Kelly hadn't had a lot of luck filling her classes at the local leisure centre. This was because she wasn't available during the peak hours people wanted to train because her husband's job and hobbies meant she was restricted to working during school hours.

Kelly felt the corner of her lips turning up into a smile at the thought of Nick, distracting her momentarily from her irritation at pompous Jim Burbridge. Kelly bumped her trolley into a checkout queue and, while she waited, updated her social media profiles with an inspirational quote about people's negativity that she'd had saved in her camera roll and been dying to use. Feeling better now she'd vented, Kelly loaded her shopping into the boot of her BMW hatchback and spun out of the carpark to pick the kids up from her mother-in-law's.

She dialled her husband via the handsfree system and tapped on the steering wheel impatiently as she waited for him to pick up. His voicemail kicked in and Kelly ended the call, annoyed. It was after 6pm now. He had taken his gym bag this morning and told her he was going straight from work, but he should be done by now as he used the gym just around the corner from his office. He could be so selfish sometimes.

Kelly braked sharply as she joined the traffic, still queuing, along the top road in the direction of Birch Grove. The traffic around here was ridiculous. Kelly lived in Oak Village, on the new estate, which was the next turning, but her mother-in-law lived another couple of miles along the road. Kelly twirled the dial on the central console until she found Pam's number. Pam answered after a few rings.

"The traffic is awful," Kelly lied. "I'm stuck back at the motorway junction. Any chance you can give the kids dinner?"

Pam was more than happy to keep her beloved grandchildren for longer and even offered to drop them back to Kelly at about 8pm.

"Oh, Pam!" Kelly gushed. "You really are an angel."

Kelly really did think Pam was an angel and felt lucky to have such a lovely, helpful mother-in-law. At times, Kelly wondered whether Pam was so nice to her and the kids to make up for how useless her son was as a husband. Not that Kelly was ever unhappy with him; he was loving and provided financially for his family. He was just never bloody home.

Kelly turned left at the next junction but drove straight past her own turning and pulled into the carpark of the village pub instead. There was nothing frozen in her shopping bags, so she figured she'd use the time constructively and pop in and see who was around. If Tina was on shift, Kelly might even have something to eat.

Kelly strutted into The Crown and was pleased to see Barry Simons and his friend, Gary, propping up the bar. Kelly flashed Barry a flirty smile.

"Look out!" Barry called, getting up to greet Kelly with a hug. "Here's trouble."

Kelly gave a throaty chuckle and hugged Barry back before sliding onto the stool next to them, taking care not to disturb Gary's sleeping German Shepherd that was sprawled, snoring, along the length of the bar.

"Where's him-indoors?" Barry asked, angling his body away

from his friend and towards Kelly.

"God knows!" Kelly replied airily but smiled to show Barry she was joking and wasn't the type of woman to keep tabs on her husband.

Barry Simons wasn't really Kelly's type. She preferred the clean-cut athletic types but even she had to admit that there was something sexy about Barry's bulking build and raw masculinity. Not that she would ever "go there", she reminded herself. Barry was great friends with her own husband but that never stopped him having a good, old-fashioned flirt with her whenever they bumped into each other at The Crown.

Tina appeared from the door to the kitchen and smiled welcomingly at Kelly.

"Hiya Kelly," Tina beamed, wiping her hands on the tea towel slung over her shoulder. "What are you having?"

"Just a small wine, please," Kelly reached for her purse. "Got to be back for the kids in a bit."

Barry ordered two more pints and insisted on paying for Kelly's wine. Tina completed the transaction and darted off back to the kitchen.

"How's everything with you?" Kelly asked the two men as they sat enjoying their drinks.

"Good, good," Gary moved his stool back slightly, so he was facing Kelly and not Barry's back. "I see you're doing that money-saving thing."

"Are we friends online?" Kelly asked, pleased that Gary had brought up her business venture.

"No," Gary looked a little embarrassed. "I saw you posted it on the Community Group."

Kelly felt a burst of satisfaction. She knew that it had been a great avenue for marketing; shows how much bloody Jim Burbridge knew about what people wanted to see on his boring group.

"I'll add you!" Kelly gave him a solicitous smile, which she usually saved for closing deals. "What's your surname?"

Gary gave her his last name and she searched for him and added him quickly.

"I bet I can save you a ton of money!" Kelly told him confidently

"Really?" Gary looked interested. "What do I need to do?"

"Have you got half an hour now?" Kelly asked, feeling the familiar buzz of adrenaline that she got from a sale.

Barry, not one to be left out, jumped in quickly. "You're meant to be having a pint with me, Gary! Not chatting up young ladies."

Gary flushed slightly, and Kelly laughed delighted.

"Oh, Barry!" Kelly rested her hand, just for a second, on his bare wrist. "I can save you a ton too. There's enough of me to go around!"

Barry grinned, looking pleased with himself. "What do you need from us, young lady?"

Kelly opened the diary on her phone. She could tell Barry would be a tough sale and didn't want to lose Gary's interest.

"Tell me when you're free," She hopped down from the stool and moved over to Gary's side. "I'll come over to you and talk you through the quick and easy switch. Just have your current bills to hand so I can show you the amazing savings! Just pop your address in there."

Gary keyed in his details and Barry gave Kelly a cynical look.

"Don't be looking like that, Barry," Kelly wriggled past him back to her bar stool, purposely brushing against him. "When can you fit me in?"

Barry shook his head. "Dana sorts all that stuff out."

"That's very unfair!" Kelly protested. "I had you down as a modern man! How about you pop over to mine and you can surprise your lovely wife with a few savings. Use the money to treat her. Get in the good books?"

Barry took the phone from her hand and regarded it thoughtfully. "Oh, go on then. I have some time to kill between meetings this week. You better give me extra mates-rates, or I'll post bad feedback about you on the page!"

Kelly giggled, feeling delighted that she'd just secured two leads. She knew she could convert Gary into a sale, but she could tell Barry would require some convincing.

"I'll get you banned," She winked. "Freedom of speech is not permitted. I had a shitty message from the admin already. Do you know Jim Burbridge?"

Gary laughed. "We were just talking about him. He messaged me giving me a warning about my comments."

"Oh!" Kelly leaned her body across Barry to look at Gary. "About the dog poo? I saw that! So funny!"

Gary looked pleased. "I thought so too! Miserable sod, he is."

"He's my neighbour," Barry told Kelly. "He kicked off at Dana last night when she asked him to sign a formality for our attic conversion."

"What's it got to do with him?" Kelly asked, feeling pleased now that it was apparent that it wasn't other residents complaining about her adverts but just one grumpy busybody.

"We're in a semi," Barry explained. "We need consent as Gary'll have to cut into the wall to stick a joist. The neighbours are being awkward, and I've got a feeling they're going to insist on using their own bloody surveyor to spite me rather than just agree to use the one we've got."

"Nightmare," Kelly gave him a sympathetic smile and finished her wine. "Right, I need to get home before the hubby reports me missing!"

"He told me he was working late!" Barry exclaimed in mock-offence.

"Did he?" Kelly flushed slightly at that, hoping she hadn't dropped him in it with his friend. "What did you want him for? I'll give him hell for you."

Barry patted his beer belly affectionately. "I need to get myself back down the gym. Married life is agreeing with me too much!"

"You could come with me!" Kelly gestured at her trainers

and Lycra leggings. "I live in the gym!"

Barry waved his hand dismissively. "You do all that running nonsense! I couldn't keep up with you plus you'd distract me in those little crop tops you wear!"

Tina walked out at that moment, catching the tail end of the conversation, and shot Kelly a bemused but non-judgemental look.

"You know what he's like, Tina!" Kelly exclaimed. "You need to ban these two."

Tina leaned against the bar and smiled good-naturedly. "If I banned people for inappropriate remarks, I wouldn't have anyone to serve!"

Tina gathered her shoulder-length dark hair into a ponytail using the elastic band from around her wrist to secure it.

"Kelly's been harassing us into making appointments with her for her newest load of nonsense." Barry winked at Tina.

Tina flicked Barry with a bar towel. "Be nice, Barry, or you'll be banned."

Kelly smiled gratefully at Tina. Tina Cleary was such a nice woman. Kelly had never heard her say anything negative about anyone since she'd first met her when they'd both moved onto the new development a few years back.

"You going already?" Tina turned her attention back to Kelly.

"Got to be back for the kids." Kelly sighed. "Are you working this weekend? If not, let's have a girlie night!"

"I'd love to," Tina smiled apologetically. "Robbie's home from Uni though. Text me though, we'll go the weekend after if you like."

"I will do!" Kelly promised. "Is he getting on ok?"

"Yeah," Tina nodded. "He loves it. Hardly hear from him so it'll be nice to see him this weekend."

Kelly thought it was lovely how Tina's face lit up when she spoke about Robbie. She stuffed her purse back into her bag and dug out her car keys.

"Don't forget to give Evan an earful from me!" Barry called out as Kelly said her goodbyes and left the pub.

Why was he telling Barry he was working late and telling her he was at the gym? She wondered to herself, pursing her lips as she slid into the car. He better have a good reason or he'd be getting an earful alright.

Chapter 4

Laura Burbridge was exhausted by the time she eventually left work that day. Jim had been furious about the condom and they'd gone to bed without any resolution being reached. She *knew* it looked bad. Laura absolutely got that. She was adult enough to know if the shoe was on the other foot, she'd be just as upset as Jim was about it. Laura had told him that she had no idea where it came from and that was what was concerning her. Jim had brushed off her concerns as if she was just trying to pass the buck. At one point, Laura had felt so overwhelmed that she wanted to scream at Jim to try to get through to him.

If Laura had to choose between her marriage ending or her daughter being sexually active at not even fifteen years old, she knew which one she would choose. Any day of the week. Calming Jim down after the discovery had been the priority yesterday; especially after the neighbour's bad timing had raised his blood pressure to dangerous levels. This evening, Laura knew she'd have to raise the subject with Keeley.

Laura was late leaving work as one of the solicitors had promised to have a look at the Simons' agreement at the end of the day. Laura was sure it was all fine and above board. Barry Simons managed building contracts for a huge nationwide company. He was hardly going to allow some amateurs to endanger his own property. If Laura hadn't been on the back foot at that moment, she would have stepped in and signed the agreement then and there. Laura knew in her heart that Jim probably would have too. It was just bad timing.

Evan Russell opened the door to his office and gave Laura the thumbs up.

"Ready when you are!" He called cheerfully.

Laura thought Evan was lovely. He'd been at Ricer & Wallis about the same amount of time as Laura and specialised in conveyancing. Evan was a few years younger than Laura. She only knew this because he'd celebrated his fortieth birthday earlier that year and they'd all gone out for drinks after work. He was quite quiet but always friendly and good-natured. Evan was very handsome in a clean-cut way but there was nothing 'flash' or attention-seeking about him.

Laura finished filing the stack of papers in her hand and locked the cabinet before walking into Evan's office. Four solicitors were based at the Birch Grove branch and so the office was little more than a cubby hole. Evan had a stack of work still spread over his desk and his PC still turned on.

"Are you still working?" Laura asked concerned. "Honestly, if you're busy don't worry about this. It's nothing major."

"No," Evan gave her a reassuring smile. "I'm just getting a head start on tomorrow, so I can leave a bit earlier. Sophie's got a netball match and I really want to be there to watch."

"Ah, that's nice," Laura smiled and picked up the framed photo of Evan's two children from his desk, turning it over in her hand as she regarded the young girl and her older brother; both who were the image of their father. "How old is Sophie?"

"She's ten," Evan smiled fondly at the photo. "She's in her last year of primary school so I just want to make the most of all the nice bits before I'm banished from her life."

Laura laughed at the truth in what Evan was saying. Keeley had used to love her coming to watch her play netball when she was still in Junior school. Laura said as much to Evan.

"How old is Keeley?" Evan asked leaning forward in his chair.

Laura perched on the edge of the desk, careful not to disturb the paperwork.

"Fourteen," Laura replied. "And you're right to enjoy these years. It certainly gets a little challenging. She does still play netball though."

"My son is in the second year," Evan said wryly. "We're definitely there with the attitude with Jacob."

"Is that why you hide out at the office?" Laura teased, referring to Evan often being the last to leave in the evening.

A look of surprise flashed across Evan's eyes and Laura immediately felt embarrassed that maybe she'd crossed a line or touched on something personal, but Evan recovered himself quickly and grinned at Laura.

"I usually go straight to the gym around the corner after work," He admitted. "I meet a friend there, so I usually just hang around here rather than go back home first. Although, sometimes I am just hiding."

Laura laughed at his honesty. Sometimes she didn't feel like going home so she could relate.

"You should use the leisure centre by the High School."

Laura told him. "It's really convenient and the opening hours are great."

"Is it?" Evan looked interested. "I've been thinking about changing gyms, to be honest. How often do you go?"

"Most days." Laura said. "The classes are great, but I doubt you'd be interested in classes. If you just want to use the gym its even cheaper."

"Why wouldn't I be interested in classes?" Evan looked at her and frowned.

Laura flushed. "Sorry! I just couldn't picture you doing boxercise or Zumba."

Evan laughed, and Laura realised, with relief, that he was teasing her. She laughed as well and swatted a hand at him for winding her up.

"I don't think I'd be any good at those classes," Evan smiled. "I just do weights then cardio. You?"

"Same." Laura nodded. "I run a lot too."

"I've just started!" Evan looked genuinely excited. "I bet you do marathons though. You look the type."

"What's 'the type'?" Laura asked trying to imitate his own stern look from earlier.

It was Evan's turn to flush slightly. "I meant fit."

Laura couldn't help but blush at his flustered response.

"I've only done half-marathons." She said modestly.

"That's five more miles than I can run." Evan admitted.

"That's really good for a new starter!" Laura looked impressed.

"You live in Oak Village," Evan stated. "We should go for a run some time."

"Yes definitely," Laura nodded, thinking that it would be nice to have some company. "I usually run on the days I don't have classes. Wednesday and Sunday."

"Either work for me." Evan looked pleased. "It's a date. Now, let's look at that paper. I've taken enough of your time."

Laura slid the agreement across the desk and Evan glanced over it.

"Right," He sat up straighter, slipping automatically into professional mode, despite the fact he'd already shed his tie and unbuttoned the top of his shirt. "Basically, your neighbour is going to cut into the party wall for a joist for their attic conversion. You can't stop them doing it, but you can have a say in how and when they carry the work out. It's a bit naughty that they've just told you as they are obligated to give you between two months and a year's notice. If you can't come to an agreement with them, you can appoint a surveyor together or separately. They would usually have to pay your surveyor costs; hence most neighbours try to agree on these things."

"That's pretty much what I thought," Laura sighed. "I'm fine with the work being done whenever as long as they're not banging around early or late at night. I don't care if they start tomorrow to be honest. Thank you for your help."

"You're welcome," Evan stood up and started to tidy his

papers away. "If you need any more advice, just let me know!"

Laura finished tidying away her belongings from her desk and gathered up her own bag. Evan followed her out to the car park, pausing to set the alarm and lock the door.

"Don't forget our run!" Evan called as she opened the door to her car. "Or I'll turn up to Zumba!"

Laura was still smiling from this exchange as she took the right turning to Oak Village. As she pulled into Sycamore Street and saw Jim's Toyota on the driveway, her good spirit faded a little. She was not looking forward to her tasks this evening.

Keeley was sat on the bottom step of the stair, dressed in a khaki hooded jacket and skinny jeans tying the laces of her Nike trainers.

"Where are you going?" Laura asked as she walked into the hallway and hung the straps of her bag over the pile of jackets.

"Out." Keeley replied shortly.

Laura cringed at her daughter's tone. It was as if she had two different personas and it was clear that today she was going to be difficult. Laura could hear Jim pottering around upstairs and wondered whether he and Keeley had had an argument.

"Have you had dinner?" Laura asked, deciding to ignore Keeley's attitude.

Keeley shook her head and made for the door.

"What time will you be home?" Laura tried again.

Keeley made an exasperated noise and shrugged.

"Keeley!" Laura barked in frustration. "You need to tell me where you're going and what time you'll be home."

"I'm going out with my friends," Keeley drew every syllable out sarcastically. "And I'll be back at 10."

"9." Laura countered standing firm.

Keeley glanced in Laura's direction and seeing her mother's expression decided against arguing and nodded. Jim chose that moment to come banging down the stairs.

"Where's she going?" He asked, addressing Laura instead of Keeley.

"Out." Laura repeated, feeling a little petulant herself.

"There's been complaints about anti-social behaviour down by the river," Jim frowned. "Don't go down there, Keeley."

"No there hasn't!" Keeley protested. "Who said that? Your ridiculous group?"

"Yes," Jim replied incensed. "My "ridiculous group". Any more of that attitude and you can forget going out."

Keeley pursed her lips but said nothing and closed the door a little harder than necessary on the way out.

Laura looked at her husband, trying to determine whether he was still harbouring suspicions about her or whether he'd moved on.

"Good day?" She tried tactfully.

Jim snorted. "Not particularly. Did you get advice on that building work?"

Laura relayed what Evan had told her, wondering whether to omit the part about the two months' notice to save the hassle but deciding that now was not the time to get caught out in a lie.

"Evan?" After all the information Laura had given Jim, this was what he chose to query.

"Evan Russell. He deals with conveyancing." Laura explained, feeling uncomfortable loitering in the hallway having this conversation. She moved into the kitchen and started to tidy up for something to do.

"You haven't mentioned him before." Jim said suspiciously.

Laura felt a flare of irritation. Was he still accusing her of cheating? Laura sank into a chair and put her head in her hands.

"I probably have," She replied as calmly as she could muster. "What do you want to do about giving the Simons an answer?"

Every spare moment in Jim's day had been taken up by the fear and the anger that Laura had been unfaithful. He knew that maintaining good relationships with neighbours was important, but he felt blindsided by his emotions and these were clouding his judgement. He had always taken pride in how rational they were as a family. They rarely raised their voices in temper (except for lately now Keeley was a difficult teenager) and there were never any discussions of 'feelings'. Jim pondered on Laura's question for a moment.

What he wanted to say was that he didn't care: he didn't care about the Simons' attic conversion. All he cared about was getting to the bottom of why there was a condom in his wife's bag. But, he couldn't say that. He couldn't bring himself to show Laura the hurt it was causing him. Instead he lashed out again at the Simons.

"If the law states that we must be given two months' notice," Jim replied in a pompous tone. "Then I'll let them know that that is what we expect. I'm not going to sink to their level and demand to use an independent surveyor. I'm sure they have enough costs to deal with as it is."

Laura opened her mouth, wanting to protest that what difference did it make to them if the Simons started tomorrow or in two months, but she could see by Jim's expression that he was not going to back down. Laura's main objective now was to save herself, not to fight the battles of the neighbours.

"Do you want me to go over and let them know?" Laura asked, her mind already racing to think of excuses she could give for demanding the required two-month period without looking pedantic.

Jim shook his head. "I'll go on my way out."

"Where are you going?" Laura asked surprised.

"A meeting about the road improvement proposals." Jim replied, avoiding eye contact with Laura.

He gathered up his wallet and his car keys and she watched him, wondering whether she should bring up their unresolved impasse. It was clear to Laura that they were both consumed with their own feelings since the mysterious condom had been unearthed; Jim full of hurt and anger, Laura on edge, empathetic but frustrated.

"Do you want to talk about last night?" She asked finally.

Jim looked taken aback by her directness. A flash of something that looked like hurt shadowed his face, but he turned away abruptly.

"What's to talk about?" He asked bitterly. "Unless you're ready to confess?"

"Oh Jim!" His tone felt, to Laura, like a knife through the heart. "I swear to you that I don't know where it came from! I would never!"

Her voice trembled a little as she protested her innocence and, for a second, she thought Jim was going to reach out to comfort her.

Instead, his mouth turned up into a sneer. "I don't know what you've got to be hysterical about."

In a perfect replication of his teenaged daughter, Jim turned and left the house with no further comment; just the hard pull of the door behind him, more civilised than a slam but with enough force to convey his annoyance.

Jim stormed down the driveway, taking the long way to the Simons' home rather than hopping over the neat borders that separated their lawns. He noted that both cars were on the drive indicating that they were both home and he rapped sharply on the door.

Dana answered, looking flustered and wearing a fleecy dressing gown over her clothes.

"Hello," Jim tried to smile politely, aware that they hadn't parted on the best terms the previous day. "Is this a convenient time to talk?"

Dana tightened the gown at her waist and looked hesitant, but she stepped aside. "Sure. Come in."

She gestured for Jim to go into the living room. Jim looked around, taking in the décor; oversized sofas, glass-top coffee tables teeming with ornaments and candles and a huge feature fireplace that resembled a television.

"Barry's not home yet." She said, and Jim could tell from her tone that she was a little nervous.

"Should I come back?" Jim asked. "I saw the cars and assumed you were both home."

"No, it's fine," Dana hovered in the doorway. "Would you like a tea or a coffee?"

Jim weighed this up and decided that it would look more neighbourly if he accepted her offer. He sat awkwardly on the edge of the sofa and waited for Dana to return with the drinks.

Dana sat back on the opposite sofa; almost being swallowed up by the voluminous cushions.

"Thank you for getting back to us so quickly," Dana started. "Sorry it was such short notice. Gary, the builder, had a last-minute cancellation on a big job and could get started straight away."

Jim felt his resolve to insist on the lawful notice period dissolve a little at Dana's reasonable explanation and at her deferential manner. She'd seemed brash and forceful yesterday but here, in her decadently-decorated house, she seemed polite and respectful.

Jim opened his mouth to speak at the same moment as the front door flew open.

A voice boomed from the hallway and the sound of something like shoes being dropped to the ground. "Nah, mate! She's my neighbour. Ollie's been there."

Dana's face dropped in embarrassment and she shouted out to the new arrival.

"Jordan!" She called. "I'm in here with Jim from next door."

Jim frowned as a strapping young man, dressed in the grey blazer and trousers of Little Cedars Comprehensive School strode into the living room; his phone still attached to his face.

Dana's son, Jordan, was as tall, lean and dark as his mother was short, curvy and blonde. He raised a hand in greeting to his mother and to Jim but turned on his heel and continued his conversation as he bounded up the stairs.

"Sorry about that," Dana apologised. "I'm not sure if you've met Jordan before. He stays with his dad a lot."

"I think I've seen him around." Jim nodded. Jordan's conversation was still playing in his mind. There weren't many teenagers on Sycamore Street, but he surely couldn't have been referring to Keeley, could he? From what Jim had heard, the conversation sounded very derogatory.

"Were there any questions you wanted to ask?" Dana went back to the conversation. "I'll try to answer as best as I can."

Jim felt immediately on the back foot again. The crude phrase Jordan had used had brought the previous day's events flooding back to Jim. Laura had tried to raise concerns that there was a risk that the item may have belonged to Keeley, but Jim had dismissed it; preferring to believe that it was Laura's than to even fathom that Keeley would have any need for such thing. She wasn't even fifteen until June. The thought of Laura cheating filled him with hurt, but it felt like the lesser of two evils. Did he even know what Keeley got up to? He didn't even know where she was now! He felt almost overwhelmed with panic and his chest tightened uncomfortably.

He realised he hadn't replied to Dana and she was looking at him with an expression of concern. Why was she looking concerned? He wondered, paranoid. Had she also assumed that her son was talking about his daughter. He tried to focus his mind on the reason for his visit, but it was all too much.

"We have no objections to the work," Jim managed to say finally. "We're happy to use the same surveyor as you but there is a two-month obligatory notice period. My concern would be whether the lack of rule-following could potentially cause problems if anything untoward were to happen."

Jim stood up and placed his coffee cup down on a spare square of space on the coffee table.

Dana's face fell in disappointment and Jim felt a miniscule sentiment of pity for her.

"The thing is," Dana pleaded. "Gary's got a space now and he'll not be able to do it until the new year otherwise. He's turned down a job and everything to do this."

Jim almost faltered. There was something endearing about Dana that made him feel bad for disappointing her, but he stuck to his guns. He had bigger issues than Dana having to wait a few months to fill another room with tacky decorations and plastic chandeliers, he reminded himself.

"I'm sorry," Jim said firmly. "I must insist that we follow the law on this."

Jim left the house hurriedly, again taking the long route down the drive and back up his own to his car. He glanced at his phone to check for any new messages and saw that Angela Hanigan had posted again about anti-social behaviour at the river. She'd uploaded some blurry photos this time and Jim peered at the images. He could make out several teens in khaki jackets and jeans, but the picture wasn't clear enough to pick out individuals. There had been an influx of comments on the image and like most things, there were clearly two camps: the law-abiding citizens horrified by the behaviour and the let-them-be protesters, who probably didn't even have children or were just trolling the page. Jim saw the same troublesome names cropping up again and again. His inbox was full of messages and he glanced through them; they were all regarding this post and offence that had been taken. Jim's chest tightened again, and he knew that he needed to appoint at least one other person to assist in moderating this page before things got out of hand. He just had too much going through his mind and he was now running late, which would put his whole evening out of sync. Jim made a spur-of-the-moment decision to ban the few who'd been mentioned more than once in complaints and in a few clicks, it was complete. He shot off a quick, courteous reply to a few of the complaints and sent Laura a message urging her to check Keeley wasn't at the river. Laura could deal with that. He couldn't face the added stress right now on top of everything else going on.

Chapter 5

Dana relayed the bad news to Barry when he got home from the pub later that night. Barry, easy-going as always, had forgotten his earlier intention of winning the Burbridge's over already. He had bigger fish to fry.

Dana, however, looked devastated.

Barry wrapped his arms around Dana and gave her a consolatory kiss on the cheek.

"I know you've been looking forward to this, love," He said gruffly. "But it makes more sense to do everything properly. I promise we'll get it done after Christmas."

"You were adamant you wanted it done," Dana sniffed trying not to cry. "What's changed?"

"It's not worth falling out with the neighbours over," Barry said, and then added the real reason his mind was elsewhere. "There's a possibility I might land a huge contract in work. Massive road improvement piece, possibly even a new dual carriageway, here in Little Cedars. This will be massive for so many businesses and contractors down here. And the bonus I'll get will pay for your new bedroom and a holiday. Maybe even a new car for you."

Dana smiled up at him, genuinely pleased for her husband. "Well done, Barry. I'm pleased for you."

"It's not set in stone yet," He warned her, taking his wife's hand and leading her into the living room. They curled up together on the huge sofa. "They'd rather go for road improvements for the top road. Possibly widening it to two lanes. It's certainly doable, and it'll be cheaper, but they're envisaging complaints due to how close some of the new estates are built to the road. I'm confident I can win that. The real earner would be if there are enough protests, they'd fork out for a bypass. Realistically, they'll need one the way the area is growing in the next ten years. The only protests to that'll be the loss of a big chunk of woods."

Dana frowned at the last bit. "That's a shame for all the little animals."

Barry knew that she would say that.

"Don't go chaining yourself to the trees and stopping my contract!" He joked, smiling affectionately.

Dana laughed at this. "I won't. It had better be a good holiday then."

"Oh, it will be," Barry promised. "Thank you for being understanding about the building work. I know it's hard for you with us all squashed in here when the kids are over, but I just want you to know I really appreciate you."

Dana felt her heart melt a little at his words. She was so lucky to have him.

"Shall we have that early night?" Barry asked hopefully. "I can't believe I fell asleep down here and missed out last night."

Dana regarded him regretfully. She had meant to stay in a mood with him over that but the whole business with next door and Barry going straight out after work had made her forget.

"I'd love to," She replied. "But Jordan's here tonight, and I said I'd pop over Steph's."

Barry looked disappointed but nodded understandingly. "Where you off? The Crown?"

Dana nodded. "I don't want to go but Steph's having a bit of a hard time. I'd better get a move on."

Dana was still dressed in her work clothes underneath her fleecy dressing-gown and she shed the robe, sprayed herself liberally with perfume and slid her feet back into her stilettoes.

"I won't be long." She called back to him as she left the house. "Make sure Jordan has something to eat when he gets in please!"

Dana quite fancied having more than one drink so she set off on the short walk to The Crown. She texted Steph on her way to tell her she'd left. As she crossed the road on the end of the street, Dana could make out a group of youths congregated at the bus stop. There was a lot of noise coming from that direction, but she knew most of the teenagers in the area, so she walked on towards them unperturbed. Dana could make out a few familiar faces as she got close enough.

"It's Jordan's mum." She heard one of the boy's hiss and the mass of skinny-jean-wearing teens parted to allow her to pass without having to step off the pavement.

Dana smiled gratefully at a few that she recognised. "Hi

Ollie, Keeley. Where's Jordan?"

Keeley opened her mouth to reply and Dana caught Ollie giving her a nudge to be quiet.

"Think he's just gone to the shop." Ollie replied quickly.

Dana knew instinctively that he was lying but she didn't press him for any more information.

"I'm just going to see your mum," Dana told him. "Tell Jordan to text me."

Dana made her way onwards to the pub. She wasn't overly concerned as Jordan was a good boy and she knew kids would be kids. There wasn't a lot for them to do around here in the evenings, so it was only natural they'd get into a little bit of mischief. She walked into the bar of The Crown, paid for a bottle of wine and settled down in the corner to wait for her friend. Steph was running late. She'd sent Dana a message to say she'd be there as soon as her husband got home from work.

Dana sent Jordan a text as she waited and then browsed the latest posts on the Oak Village Community page. She rolled her eyes at the latest of Angela Hanigan's complaints. She was now moaning about the kids congregating in the evening down by the river. A few parents had commented assuring her that they'd speak to their children but there were equally as many villagers who were calling her out for her constant complaining. Dana wondered if these complaints had been why there were so many kids hanging around the road outside. They'd probably moved up from the river on warning from their parents.

Steph finally rushed in twenty minutes late, looking

flustered.

"I'm so sorry!" She said, shedding her coat. "Bloody Darren was 'working late' again."

She used her fingers to make quotation marks around the words 'working late' and rolled her eyes. Steph sank into the chair opposite Dana and used her hands to comb her shoulder-length red hair to one shoulder then the other shoulder before giving up when her wavy hair wouldn't sit right and knotting it into a ponytail. Dana watched her friend as she fidgeted and waited for her to tell her what was wrong.

Steph took a big sip of the drink Dana had poured her and then leaned forward. "I think he's cheating again."

Dana could see the sadness in Steph's huge blue eyes. "Oh, Steph. I'm so sorry. Tell me everything."

Steph sighed, and Dana felt her heart ache for her sweet friend. Steph Rees and Dana had been friends ever since their sons, Jordan and Ollie, started nursery together over eleven years ago. Dana had fallen in love with the ditzy, forgetful Steph and they'd struck up an instant rapport that surpassed the surface-level friendships they had with the other parents. Steph had supported Dana through her own rock-bottoms: redundancy, the deaths of her parents and her divorce. Dana had been there for Steph every time she had caught Darren in one of his frequent affairs. Each time Steph vowed that she wouldn't put up with it any longer, but each time she took him back; claiming that he would change but Dana knew that Steph didn't believe it any more than she did. Dana secretly thought Steph stayed for the security and for the children. Steph hadn't worked since she'd had Ollie, now fifteen. Steph's younger child, Kendall, was now ten and Dana felt Steph should at least be thinking about getting back into work, so that she had the financial freedom and didn't rely so heavily on her selfish husband.

"Just the usual," Steph confessed. "The hiding his phone, working late, acting shifty."

"Have you said anything?" Dana asked diplomatically. There was no point asking Steph what she was going to do. Dana had been here so many times with Steph, she could write the script.

"No," Steph admitted looking tearful. "I'm too scared he's just looking for an argument to give him the excuse to pack up and leave."

"Oh, Steph!" Dana's own eyes filled with tears of sympathy for Steph. Dana had heard Darren's infidelities openly discussed, years ago, in the school yard by other parents. After the first few became public knowledge, Dana had watched as any sympathy for Steph died away and was replaced by self-righteous, judgemental comments by some people that they'd once called friends: "It's her own fault for staying", "I would never put up with that" and most hurtfully, "What does she expect? She's practically told him it's fine by putting up with the last ones.".

Steph swiped at an escaped, lone tear and shrugged. "Can we talk about something else? I don't want to cry here."

Dana glanced around and saw that there were a few people she recognised in the bar area of the pub. Kelly Russell was draped over Gary, Barry's builder friend, and the local councillor, Kate Evett, was sipping a wine thumbing through some documents on her own. Dana raised a hand in greeting to them and turned back to Steph.

"What do you want to talk about?" Dana plastered a cheery smile on her face, resolving to get Steph laughing this evening. "That community page is possibly the most entertaining thing I've seen for years."

Steph managed a smile. "I knew you'd find it hilarious. Some of the people on there make your blood boil though!"

Dana filled Steph in on the latest dramas and explained that she'd seen Steph's own son, Ollie, on her way here this evening.

"I think he's going out with Keeley," Steph nodded. "She's been to the house a few times. Is she in the year below? I don't really know the parents."

"They're our neighbours," Dana told her. "Jim is a bit of an arsehole but the mum, Laura, is always really nice."

Dana filled Steph in on the drama about the attic conversion and Steph shook her head in disbelief.

"How petty!" She exclaimed. "I'd be so embarrassed to be that uptight about such a little thing."

"He's a bit of a busybody," Dana agreed. "He's the one who set up the ridiculous community page."

"Too much time on his hands!" Steph joked. "Although it is good for the traffic updates."

"Those updates!" Dana rolled her eyes. "People are obsessed with moaning about the traffic. It's rush hour. The clue is in the name!"

"People are obsessed with moaning." Steph laughed, and Dana felt pleased that she'd taken Steph's mind off her marriage temporarily.

"I can only have one more," Dana said apologetically when she realised it was almost 9pm. "I'm still doing early shifts in work to miss that traffic."

They had finished the wine between them, so Steph volunteered to get the drinks in and Dana watched as she chatted to Gary and Kelly at the bar. Kate Evett had been joined now by Jim. Dana had watched Jim notice her as he entered the pub, but he seemed to be going out of his way to avoid eye contact, angling his chair so he was facing away from her. Dana tried not to let his presence annoy her. She prided herself on rising above other people's pettiness.

"Was Kelly trying to sign you up for one of her pyramid schemes?" Dana joked as Steph came back with their drinks.

Steph grinned. "She did mention her latest business opportunity, but she was working on signing Gary up, so she didn't go in hard on the sales pitch. She'll probably get me on the way out."

Dana could see Gary was lapping up Kelly's attention. "I wonder if his girlfriend knows this is where he is."

"Probably not," Steph shook her head. "She's always in here flirting with different men. Mind you, I don't blame them. Look at her figure; she's gorgeous."

Steph, like Dana, would never be a size eight nymph like Kelly. They were both naturally curvy. Dana dressed to accentuate her curves whereas Steph hid hers away under floaty dresses and layers. Dana wished Steph had more confidence and could see that she was a beautiful woman. Darren should think himself lucky to have her.

Dana, not wanting to get back onto depressing subjects, quickly steered the conversation back to the community page. "That's Keeley's dad over there. He's avoided looking at me since he got here."

Steph swivelled around to have a look. "They look like a very boring couple."

"That's not his wife," Dana shook her head. "That's Kate Evett. The councillor."

"Oh!" Steph squinted a little before turning back to face Dana. "I do recognise her now you mention it. She was talking to Darren the other day when I dropped Kendall up to him in work. She wanted to book a meeting room for something-or-other. "

"Looks like they're on official business," Dana commented, regarding the documents spread out between them. "Oh, look! What's going on?"

As soon as Steph had turned her back to the pair, Dana had noticed Kelly slip from her bar stool and make her way over to their table. Gary had followed her and they both looked like they'd had too much to drink. Kelly was wearing jeans so tight they looked like they'd been sprayed on and she wobbled on her high-heeled ankle boots unsteadily. Gary had an expression of amusement on his face and Dana had heard enough tales from Barry to know that he was capable of being a little lairy at times.

Steph swivelled around in her chair to watch the exchange.

At first, Kelly looked friendly as she spoke to Jim animatedly, with a smile on her face, her hands moving quickly as if to illustrate her point. Dana watched closely. She had always been a lover of people-watching. Dana could tell from Jim's closed off positioning that he wasn't enjoying this conversation. He started to respond and, while Dana couldn't see his face or hear his words, she could see Kate was growing uncomfortable and Kelly was starting to shift her weight from one foot to the other like she was warming up for a fight. Kelly opened her mouth, pausing as if drawing enough breath to release a torrent, but Gary stepped forward. He was a stocky, muscular man and he put one hand on Kelly's shoulder and angled his own body, so he was between Kelly and Jim. Gary started to speak now, and his expression had changed from amusement at Kelly's monologue to annoyance. Jim was shaking his head and trying to turn his back to the pair, but this seemed to be aggravating Gary even more. Dana began to fear that there was a chance that this would turn nasty and wondered whether she should step in. Gary reached forward and put a hand, in what looked like an aggressive gesture, on Jim's shoulder. Jim shrugged it away and, before Dana had chance to react, Kate was on her feet between the pair. Gary took a step backwards but continued with his rant; his voice now rising to be heard across the bar.

"You're not the supreme leader of the community," Gary sneered, prompting Kelly to laugh. "All I want is for you to apologise to Kelly and me for your censorship."

Jim held up both hands defensively and replied to Gary in a level tone. Kate said something to Jim and started to gather up the documents. There was a back and forth exchange but in quieter, more civil tones before Gary nodded and stuck his hand out for Jim to shake. Jim paused. Dana and Steph exchanged glances both wondering if he was going to refuse but were relieved to see Jim accepted Gary's gesture before he and Kate left the pub.

Kelly was beaming from ear to ear, which Dana thought was a little childish of her. She squeezed Gary's huge bicep and led him back to their seats. Gary and Kelly finished their drinks before Gary got to his feet and made to leave.

Dana waved Gary over as he started to leave the bar.

"What was that about?" She asked, hoping she looked concerned and not just nosy.

"Kelly was annoyed that he'd told her off for posting about her business on that community page," Gary had the decency to look a little embarrassed about the scene. "He was a bit rude to her, so I told him off. He bloody well banned me from the page too, but he's apologised for that now."

Dana shook her head, half-amused but half-horrified at the behaviour of grown adults over an online group. "I'm glad you've got it sorted."

"Do you want a lift home?" Gary asked politely, smiling at Steph so she knew she was included in the offer.

Dana shook her head. "No, thanks. You probably shouldn't be driving either."

Gary shrugged. "It's only around the corner."

Kelly was hovering at the door clearly waiting for Gary and she gave Dana and Steph a friendly wave. Gary said his goodbyes and joined her.

"Do you think there's something going on with them?" Steph asked wide-eyed.

"I don't think so," Dana frowned. "Kelly wouldn't be so

blatant, surely."

Dana changed the conversation again, not wanting to be hypocritical and get caught up in neighbourhood gossip. Steph looked more relaxed and happy by the time they were both ready to leave. They wrapped back up in their coats, against the October chill, and walked out into the night, running into Steph's son and his friend, Keeley.

"Ollie!" Steph exclaimed looking pleased. "You can walk home with me."

Ollie, on the other hand, looked mortified to see his mother when he was with a girl. Dana hid a smile at both Ollie's typical teenage embarrassment and at how oblivious Steph was to his discomfort.

"I'm walking back with Keeley." Ollie spoke in a voice two chords lower than his usual tone.

Steph frowned at this. "Have you got a sore throat?"

Ollie flushed, and Dana could see Keeley Burbridge hide an amused grin. They fell into an awkward silence for a moment.

"Go with your mum," Keeley said politely. "I'm only around the corner and I'm late."

Ollie glanced at Keeley through the curtain of dark hair that fell across his forehead and mumbled something that sounded like a goodbye.

"I'll walk with you if you don't mind." Dana said picking up her pace to match Keeley's strides.

"Do you mind if we walk fast?" Keeley asked politely,

glancing at Dana's stiletto heels. "I'm half hour late and my dad is going to go nuts."

Dana raced along, trying to keep up with the pretty, dark-haired girl who was taller than Dana even in her flat trainers.

"Been anywhere nice?" Dana asked conversationally.

"Just out." Keeley glanced at Dana suspiciously and then added politely. "What about you?"

"Just to the pub." Dana said. "Did you see Jordan after?"

Keeley nodded. "Yeah but he's gone home now."

They fell back into silence as they entered Sycamore Street. Keeley saw that her dad's car was missing from the driveway and breathed a sigh of relief.

"My dad's still out." She grinned. "My mum is so much more chill about things."

Dana laughed at this. "I doubt Jordan would say that."

"No way!" Keeley rewarded Dana for her self-depreciation with a wide smile. "All the boys say you're the coolest mum."

Dana smiled with pleasure at that. "You better get in quickly then!"

Keeley hovered at the end of the driveway like she wanted to say something. Dana looked back at her and paused to allow her to speak.

"If you see my mum or dad," She said nervously. "Can you

not mention I was hanging around the bus stop? Or that I was with Ollie?"

Dana frowned at the strange request. She knew Jim was a bit pretentious but surely, he wasn't that prehistoric that he didn't know what kids got up to. Dana assumed they were around a similar age to her and Barry, and she'd hung around many a bus stop and a park back in her time. Dana saw the earnest expression on Keeley's face and took pity on the well-mannered girl.

"Of course," Dana gave her a conspiratorial wink. "Good night, Keeley!"

Keeley waved her hand in thanks and skipped up the driveway. She shut the door behind her and leaned against the wood to catch her breath. She felt like she was in a movie; all starry-eyed and happy. She sighed with pleasure; it felt like she was floating in a bubble and nothing could bring her down.

Chapter 6

A few days passed, and Laura still couldn't bring herself to raise the subject of the condom with her daughter. Laura knew she was being ridiculous, but she felt constantly on edge at home and Keeley had been quite cheerful and pleasant. Laura already had one person in the family furious with her; she could do without falling out with Keeley too.

Jim had said nothing more on the subject, but Laura knew from his cold, distant attitude that he had clearly not forgotten. The atmosphere in the house was frosty but civil on the rare occasions they were both home at the same time. His meetings about the road improvements seemed to be taking over his life as he was out almost every evening.

Laura tried to make a joke about it when he appeared in the kitchen Saturday morning dressed to go out.

"Where are you going?" Laura asked politely.

"Kate's meeting with a journalist from the local paper." Jim replied curtly. "We're looking to engage the public to take part in the consultation."

"You could have built that road in the time you've been talking about it." She commented flippantly as she laced up her trainers. She felt a little stab of irritation at Jim referring to Kate and himself as "we". It seemed hypocritical that he was furious at her for her alleged infidelity, despite her innocence, yet it was fine for him to be spending every evening with another woman.

Jim ignored Laura's remark and left the house.

Laura sighed with frustration. They weren't an argumentative household and all this bad atmosphere was starting to get on top of her. She called up to Keeley, who was predictably still in bed, that she was going out and decided that today, as soon as she'd been to her spin class, she'd face up to the conversation with her daughter and with Jim.

Laura was early to her class and could see there was another class in session. She took a seat in the reception area to wait.

A larger lady with red hair bustled in, looking agitated, and went over to the front desk. Laura smiled politely, recognising her from the school. The woman seemed agitated and didn't seem to notice Laura.

"I'm looking for Darren." She said to the young girl manning the till.

"He's off today," The girl smiled politely. "Can I help?"

"Oh." The woman was visibly taken back. "He said he was working."

"Can I help?" The girl repeated, her polite smile still in place.

"Are you sure he's not here?" The woman chewed her lip nervously. "I'm his wife."

Laura shifted a little in her chair; not wanting to pry but feeling drawn to the scene. She could see the girl redden and start to panic.

"Oh!" She exclaimed. "Right, yes. He's around but he's really busy."

"So, he's here?" The red-haired woman looked relieved but confused. "So why did you say he wasn't?"

"Oh," The girl looked away and started to fidget with a pile of papers. "He didn't want to be disturbed, that's all. He might have just popped out somewhere, but I'll check his office."

"I know where his office is," The woman insisted. "I'll have a look."

The blonde girl shook her head quickly. "No need! I'm pretty sure he's popped out. Just give me five."

The girl didn't wait for a reply and snatched up her mobile phone from the desk and dashed out the back.

The red-haired woman looked around and saw Laura watching her. Laura smiled politely, unsure of the etiquette when you've just been caught eavesdropping.

Fortunately, some people arrived at that moment for the 9.30 Spin class. They hovered at the front desk waiting to pay. Laura seized the opportunity to get up and walk over to wait at the doors to the studio. Laura felt mortified for the woman at being blatantly lied to by her husband's junior staff in front of an audience and didn't want to hang around to hear the second instalment when the girl returned no-doubt empty-handed.

Laura was glad to see the woman had left when the Spin class was finished. She said goodbye to her friends in the class and made her way out to the car park. Laura saw a

Nissan Qashqai pull up into a Disabled space and the errant Leisure Centre manager, Darren, jump out. Laura wondered if he really had been working or whether he'd been summoned here by the girl on reception. Laura used the facilities here regularly and she knew Darren to say hello to. He wasn't a bad looking man; a bit on the short side for Laura's taste but quite muscular. Laura noticed that he didn't look remotely hurried or panicked; maybe he was innocent. He waved a hand to her in greeting. She waved back and continued to walk to her car.

"Laura!" A voice called suddenly, and Laura turned, thinking Darren was calling her but he had his back to her and was disappearing through the reception doors.

"Over here!" The same voice called, and Laura realised it was coming from a parked car near her own. She peered at the driver; not able to make them out clearly without her glasses. The door opened, and the driver got out. It was Evan.

"Hi!" Laura felt her face lighting up into a genuine smile. "Sorry! I didn't see you there."

"I've just dropped Sophie to swimming," Evan told her. "I was just leaving when I saw you."

"Have you thought any more about joining?" Laura asked, referring to their conversation the other day in work.

"I still haven't got around to it," Evan said. "I'm still waiting for you to text me about running."

"I don't have your number." Laura smiled.

Evan pulled his phone out of his pocket and held it out to

Laura to type her number in.

Laura flushed at his forwardness and typed in her number. Evan was dressed in shorts and a t-shirt despite it being late October.

"Aren't you cold?" She asked, more for something to say as she felt a little tongue-tied for some reason.

"I was going to go for a run now." He told her and then added. "Fancy it?"

"I've just done an hour's spin," She grimaced. "I don't know if I've got many miles in my legs."

"Quick one then?" He asked. "Sophie's class is only forty minutes, so I wasn't going far."

Laura felt flattered that Evan wanted her company and she nodded. "I promise I'll turn back when I start to flag rather than hinder you though, ok?"

"You won't need to! I'm rubbish at running." Evan gave a self-depreciating laugh. "Ready?"

"From here?" Laura asked. "Let's go!"

Laura didn't need to drop out and was pleased that she managed the quick run with ease. They chatted easily for parts of the way and Laura felt upbeat as they parted ways back in the car park. Darren was getting back into his car and Laura waved at him for the second time that day.

Darren Rees waved in response to one of his customers and pulled his own car out of the parking space. He drove the short distance home and parked on his drive behind his wife's Citroen. Work had been manic this week; two people had been off sick and there was still a stack of outstanding paperwork to be completed. Steph had called him home; stressing about a leak that was coming through the ceiling.

"Steph!" He called out as he entered the three-bedroomed townhouse. "I'm home."

He was a bit annoyed that she'd come up to the Leisure Centre when she couldn't get hold of him this morning. He couldn't be on the end of his phone twenty-four hours a day; he had work to do.

Steph came out from the kitchen. "Sorry I disturbed you in work. I didn't know what to do and I panicked."

Darren peered at where the water was dripping from and made his way up to the bathroom. His brother was a plumber so, worst case scenario, he'd call him over rather than fork out to have something fixed. Darren was quite handy though and managed to locate and stem the flow.

"Are you going back to work?" Steph asked, when it was done.

"I might just go tomorrow now," Darren said. "It's my own fault for getting so behind but Colleen and Jessica's absences haven't helped. I just need a few hours more to catch up on everything."

Steph nodded but didn't say anything.

"Where are the kids?" Darren asked, wanting to fill the awkward silence. There were a lot of silences lately and Darren suspected that Steph had something on her mind.

"Ollie's in bed," Steph told him. "And Emily's mum has taken Kendall to dancing."

Darren sat down on the sofa and started to flick through his phone.

"Did you have a word with Ollie about hanging around down the river?" Darren asked. "They're all bloody moaning about it in that internet group again."

"They were all hanging around down the road from the pub last night instead." Steph told him.

"I might post on the page moaning about that." Darren joked.

Steph laughed. She was still feeling a little sheepish about turning up to Darren's work and disturbing him about the leak. She hoped he didn't think she was checking up on him. He hadn't seemed defensive at all and his explanation that he'd had to drive over to Finchester, the neighbouring leisure centre, was perfectly reasonable.

Steph wondered whether she was too dependent on Darren. All her friends and acquaintances worked. Maybe she had too much time on her hands and was imagining things that weren't true.

Darren made a loud noise of surprise and this jerked her out of her thoughts.

"What's the matter?" She asked.

Darren was staring at his phone. He shook his head and put his phone away.

"Nothing," He said quickly. "I just remembered something I needed to do today. I'll text Gemma on reception now."

"You made me jump!" Steph laughed. She reached for her

own phone. "I haven't read those comments. I'll have a look now."

Darren reached out for her hand, stopping her from picking up her phone.

"Why don't we go for a walk?" He said. "Take the dog down the river?"

"Oh," Steph was surprised at this as he never usually suggested doing anything together. "That would be nice."

"Go and tell Ollie," Darren urged her. "Then get your wellies on. I'll just text Gemma now."

Steph made her way up the stairs to let Ollie know they were popping out. Kendall was going back to Emily's after dancing, so they wouldn't have to rush back.

Downstairs, Darren frantically messaged the page admin of the Oak Village Community Group. Some interfering busybody had posted a picture of his car double-parked and up on the pavement behind the apartments. He couldn't have Steph seeing that. He had a personalised number plate too, so everyone would know it was him, including customers from the Leisure Centre. It had only been posted in the last five minutes so hopefully not many people had seen it.

He could hear Steph pottering around in their top-floor bedroom and he wondered how long the admin, Jim, would take to respond. The longer the picture was up, the more chance of people seeing it. Frustrated, he went outside and dialled Gemma's mobile number. Her phone was always in her hand so there was more chance of her answering that than the work phone.

"Hiya!" She chirped pleasantly. "Sorry about earlier! Hope I didn't drop you in it."

Darren frowned at her familiarity. "I was at Finchester. Anyway, I need a customer's number. I know he had a badminton court this week. Jim Burbridge."

"Ummmm." Darren could hear Gemma typing into the computer. "Did he definitely book the court?"

"I think so," Darren said, racking his brain. He knew who Jim was. He booked the court on Wednesdays most weeks. He'd come in on more than one day this week though and with someone else. "Try Wednesday. But last week?"

"Got it!" Gemma replied triumphantly. She read out the number to Darren. He thanked her before hanging up and dialling the number. Before he pressed call, he headed back into the house to check where Steph was.

"I'm just phoning work a minute!" He called to her. "Can you have a look for my blue coat? I think it's in my wardrobe."

It wasn't. It was in the boot of his car, but this would buy him a few more minutes.

Luck was on Darren's side and Jim answered the call.

Darren, used to thinking on his feet, introduced the call as work-related and, feigning a system problem, asked to double-check whether Jim had booked the court Wednesday.

Jim confirmed that he did, and Darren launched into his real reason for calling.

"I noticed that you're the admin on the Oak Village Community group," Darren started. "My wife has double-parked my car, and someone's posted a picture of it. It's a bit embarrassing for me and she's really upset. Any chance you can take it down, mate?"

Jim paused. "I don't like to police people's rights to free speech. It's not illegal unfortunately so there's not a lot you can do about it."

Darren felt a stab of panic. "Please, mate. My wife is really upset."

Jim would usually have refused to out of principle, but he was in the middle of something and just wanted him off the phone.

"I'll have a look," He said tentatively. "I'm a little busy so if you'll excuse me."

He ended the call without saying goodbye and Darren felt his blood boiling. He didn't believe, for a minute, that Jim was going to remove the image. Darren walked back into the house and called up to Steph.

"Don't worry about my jacket!" He yelled, feeling irritable that he'd now agreed to wasting his time on this walk. "Let's go!"

Chapter 7

Kelly had seen one of the village busybodies snapping a photo of the badly-parked Qashqai from her bedroom window. The back of Kelly's three-bedroom detached faced the carpark for the residents of the twin apartment blocks at the end of her street. It was a dead-end and only used for parking, so Kelly suspected that the nosy neighbour had purposely walked up the street with their mangy mutt to take the photo to name-and-shame the driver.

Kelly shook her head in disgust. She would put a week's commission on that picture ending up on the village online group. What the hell happened to people minding their own business? She dropped the curtain and hopped back into her unmade bed.

It was still early, for a Saturday, and Kelly had no intention of getting dressed before 11am. Evan enjoyed running the kids around to their various clubs and social activities on the weekend. They were all up and out at 9am every Saturday. Jacob had been selected to train for a youth academy which took Evan over half an hour to get to and then he dropped Sophie straight to swimming lessons. After swimming, it was a race to Finchester to Sophie's Performing Arts group and Evan usually headed to the gym before going back to pick Sophie up and then making the hour round trip to pick up Jacob. Kelly was grateful that Evan enjoyed his Saturday bonding time with the kids as she resented spending her Saturdays driving them around after doing this almost every weeknight.

She could almost set her watch to Evan's routine; week and

weekend. Kelly led back against the pillows as she reflected on this. They barely spent more than a few hours together each week except for when they were asleep. Despite the predictability of Evan's comings and goings, Kelly knew she was taking a lot of risks lately. The smallest event could cause him to come home early at any moment; Evan could forget his gym bag and come straight home from work instead of strolling in at about 7.30pm as usual, Sophie could forget her water bottle on a Saturday, Jacob could finally insist on quitting football (as he kept threatening to do) to spend all his spare time hanging around the shop on his bike like all his friends seemed to do. Kelly knew that she was recklessly brazen at times. She'd been seen getting into Gary's car, in a clearly inebriated state, at the pub this week by quite a few people that knew both her and Evan. Everybody in the village knew that she networked as part of her business but being drunk and borderline disorderly with a man that wasn't her husband was bound to get tongues wagging.

She checked her phone and, sure enough, the car in the back lane had been posted on the village page, accompanied by a condescending rant. The incensed resident had been careful to take the picture at an angle to take in the pavement it was mounted on, the Qashqai's registration and a sliver of the BMW hatchback parked opposite it to demonstrate how it would "obstruct emergency services". Kelly was glad she'd taken care when parking her own car at the back of the house last night. She'd have been livid if some interfering villager criticised her parking publicly. Kelly refreshed the post and read some of the holier-than-thou comments. Jim had kept his word and allowed Kelly back into the group after their conversation at the pub. Kelly hadn't pushed her luck and posted anything about her business, but she fully intended to next week. She'd had quite a few leads last week and Gary had already signed up.

Kelly glanced at the time and decided that it was about time she got up. They were going out this evening for a meal for Pam's birthday . Kelly wanted to nip into town and buy something new to wear. She showered quickly and dressed in tight jeans and a bardot-style bodysuit. She scrambled through the pile of clothes that had dropped to the bottom of her wardrobe, searching for her leather jacket. Kelly vowed that she'd sort out the jumble of clothes this week. She couldn't find anything in this mess. Kelly frowned trying to remember when she'd last seen the jacket. It came to her that it was when she'd last had a proper night out with Tina. Tina had been wearing an identical jacket and they'd both laughed over the coincidence when Tina had met Kelly after her shift at The Crown. Kelly had hurriedly taken hers off and carried it for their bar crawl through town. Kelly had been quite merry that night and prayed that she hadn't left it somewhere. Kelly pushed through the racks of clothes and was relieved to eventually find it hiding underneath another coat. She slipped it on, pleased that it hadn't been left for dead in a lost-and-found box somewhere.

Kelly bounded down the stairs, feeling cheerful and upbeat at the prospect of a few hours retail therapy. She exited through the back door, grabbing a packet of gum from the counter as she went. She shoved the pack into her jacket pocket as she locked the door and then frowned when she realised the small pocket was already full. Kelly pulled out a branded gym card and a handful of hair ties. She stared at them for a moment, confused. She used the leisure centre gym by the High School, and she only wore her hair up at the gym. The elastic bands were what triggered Kelly to realise she must have mixed up jackets with Tina in the taxi home. Tina was never without a hair tie, either around her wrist or in her pocket. Kelly's jacket had been a birthday present from Evan and had cost about £200 from All Saints whereas Tina had bought hers on eBay.

Kelly drove the twenty yards to the top of the street and turned left into the carpark. Each apartment had an allocated space with the number sprayed onto the ground. Kelly pulled into the space marked number 8 and hurried over to the entrance to the closest building. She leaned on the buzzer for Tina's apartment for a few moments but before Tina could answer, a man juggling a baby in a car seat came out. Kelly caught the heavy door and held it open for him.

"Thanks." The man smiled gratefully at her.

Kelly ducked into the block and took the two flights of stairs up to the second floor. Kelly rapped on the door of the middle of the three top floor apartments. She could hear music playing from behind the door and finally the sound of keys turning in the door.

Tina pulled the door open a fraction so only her face and shoulders were visible. She looked surprised to see Kelly.

Kelly held the jacket out. "We've mixed up jackets. I've only just realised."

Tina's arm snaked out from behind the door and she took the jacket.

"Thanks," She looked a little uncomfortable. "I'm just rushing to get ready. Do you mind if I drop yours over later?"

Kelly pulled a face. "Sorry to be a pain but I need it now."

Tina hesitated for a second but then pulled the door open. She was wrapped in a towel as if she'd just got out of the shower, but her shoulder-length dark hair was styled in loose waves and her face was made up.

"You look nice." Kelly complimented her. "You off out with Robbie?"

Tina frowned. "Robbie?"

"You said he was home this weekend." Kelly reminded her, wondering if Tina had lied to her to get out of going out drinking. Kelly wouldn't take offence if she had. It was probably because she was skint and didn't want to cry off due to low funds. Kelly completely understood.

Tina flushed. "He couldn't make it at the last minute. Work to do."

Kelly nodded. "That's a shame. You up to anything nice?"

"Just popping out," Tina replied, turning away quickly. "Let me grab your jacket. Sorry, my wardrobe is a mess! It might take me a few minutes."

Kelly followed Tina into the apartment. The door opened into a narrow hallway; to the left was the doorway to the open-plan living room and kitchen, and to the right were three doors to the bathroom and two double bedrooms. Tina pulled shut the door to the second bedroom as she walked past it and walked into her own room. Kelly waited politely by the door as Tina opened her mirrored-door wardrobe and started searching for the jacket. After a few moments, Tina held up the jacket triumphantly.

"Thank you!" Kelly took the jacket and slipped her arms into it. "Sorry to disturb you."

Tina smiled apologetically. "I'd offer you a coffee, but I really am rushing. I'm in The Crown Tuesday and Thursday- come in and we'll have a drink."

"Definitely," Kelly smiled to show Tina she wasn't offended by Tina rushing her out. "Are you still free to do mine on Monday?"

"Yes, of course," Tina nodded. "It'll have to be in the afternoon."

"That's fine," Kelly nodded. "I'll have to get you a key at some point. Can you just not mention it to Evan if that's ok? I want to keep up the whole Domestic Goddess thing."

Tina gave a genuine laugh. "Your secrets are all safe with me."

Kelly hurried back down the steps and out of the building. She really liked Tina, even if she could be a bit sketchy at times. Kelly put her own hands into the pockets of her lovely jacket and pulled out a crumpled object. It was a few pound coins wrapped in a ten-pound note. She sent a quick text to Tina to check whether it belonged to Tina and then dropped her phone into her lap to set off to town.

It didn't take her long to find something to wear and she was strutting back to the multi-storey carpark, swinging her carrier bags triumphantly when she almost bumped into Barry Simons as he walked out of The Friendly Fox.

"Barry!" Kelly held her bags up to steady herself as she came to an abrupt stop to avoid a collision.

Barry looked up sharply and Kelly watched as his expression changed from mild panic to relief.

"Bloody hell," He laughed. "You're everywhere!"

Kelly laughed good-naturedly. "You cancelled on me! I'm going to follow you around until you let me save you some money."

"As long as you don't attack me in the pub like you did to my neighbour!" Barry joked.

Kelly covered her face with her free hand in mock-embarrassment. "News spreads fast. Or should I say malicious gossip!"

"The miserable folk of Oak Village will think twice about complaining about you now they've heard that you're up for a scrap in the pub." Barry grinned. "You off home?"

"Yes, just popped in to get a top." Kelly nodded her head in the direction of the pub he'd just come out of. "Are you having a break from the shops?"

"Dana's been in Debenhams for an hour," Barry rolled his eyes. "Just been reading the paper with a pint like the old man I am."

Barry gestured to the rolled-up local paper under his arm.

"I remember when you were wild!" Kelly teased. "You and Evan are both like a pair of pensioners these days."

"You've got to take an interest in local affairs," Barry replied with a playful smile before adding. "Actually, there's an informal meeting for Oak Village residents at the Leisure Centre this Thursday that I want Evan to come to. And you if possible."

"Sounds exciting." Kelly deadpanned. "What's it about? The bad parking or the dog poo?"

"It's for the local councillor to gather any questions or concerns from residents to take to the public proposal meeting about the plans to improve the road between Birch Grove and the motorway." Barry explained. "There's a piece in the paper about it."

"I'll probably give that a miss." Kelly made a face. "I'll pass that on to Evan though."

"Please!" Barry urged her. "How about I'll listen to your sales pitch and give you a few leads if you come."

"Why does it matter to you?" Kelly asked amused. "However, you've got yourself a deal. I'll be there."

"I've got some insider info," Barry told her. "It'll impact the village if they make the top road a dual carriageway: noise, possible accidents and the traffic will be much worse while they complete it. There's another option of a bypass which would run over the other side of the river and would take traffic from Birch Grove and Finchester, on the other side, away from the top road. They'd rather upgrade the top road though as its loads cheaper. My thoughts are if enough people complain, there's more chance of them going for the bypass."

"You'll have to remind me what to say!" Kelly joked. "Evan would definitely be interested in that though. He loves a cause!"

Barry promised to text Kelly his availability for a full utility bill review that week and they parted ways. Barry headed back to Debenhams, hoping that Dana would be ready to leave soon. Tyler and Chloe were with their mother this weekend and Barry had been hoping to have a lazy day around the house, but Dana had had other plans. After the disappointment of the delayed conversion, Barry would have gone along with anything she wanted to cheer her up, but after half an hour browsing the same rack of dresses, Barry had made up an excuse about needing the loo and nipped off to the pub for twenty minutes. He was glad he had now as he'd seen the miniscule article about the meeting.

He would have been furious if he'd missed the opportunity to gather some voices to be heard. It was ridiculous that Kate Evett expected residents to read a tiny write-up buried on page ten between the enthralling reports of a chip shop changing its opening hours and police involvement over a row about an umbrella at a charity shop.

Jim Burbridge should be using his ridiculous community group to raise awareness of this, Barry thought to himself as he dialled Dana's number to track her down in the huge store.

Dana answered his call and directed him up to Lingerie on floor two. Barry rubbed his hands together with a grin. That was a bit more promising than workwear.

Barry found Dana quickly and took the armload of clothes off her to free up her hands to browse. There was a chair outside the fitting room and he laid the clothes over his lap and browsed Jim's online group as he waited.

Barry rolled his eyes at the latest post that had generated over thirty comments. Some poor man, called Dazza judging by the personalised license plate, was having his character assassinated over his inconsiderate parking. Barry considered making up an account for the sole purpose of trolling some of these nosy parkers. He was surprised Gary hadn't already done so after the to-do at the pub. He opened a post of his own on the page.

"Apologies that this post is not about poor parking or poop," He typed, deciding to go for a humorous angle to hook as many readers as possible. "I would like to bring to the attention of Oak Village an informal meeting with local councillor Kate Evett on Thursday 27th October at Little Cedars Leisure Centre ahead of the public consultation re local road improvements (planned meeting, open to public, Wed 9th Nov). The proposed 'improvements', while very much needed, will bring noise and disruption to the area and I urge as many residents as possible to attend to ensure your concerns are heard. There are alternative plans but unless we come together and speak up, we will have no say in this. The full details are in Saturday's Gazette (page 10). Alternatively, if you are unable to attend due to the short notice, I am happy to act as a spokesperson if you would like to inbox me your questions/ queries."

Barry pressed the button to publish the post and, once this was completed, drafted a message to his mates in the area to convince them to attend.

Dana reappeared finally with something black and lacy which had Barry reaching for his credit card.

After he'd made the hefty purchase, Barry convinced Dana they deserved lunch out and a few glasses of wine.

"You have can have a few if you want," Dana offered. "I'll just have one glass and I'll drive us home."

"Are you sure?" Barry's eyes lit up at the prospect of a boozy lunch. He'd already had a pint with his paper, but Dana didn't know that.

"Yes," Dana smiled affectionately at him. "You deserve a few after treating me!"

Barry filled his wife in on the informal community meeting that he'd read about in the paper, bumping into Evan's wife and his online post. Dana looked impressed as he told her how he was rallying the troops and opened her phone to have a look.

"I can't see your post." Dana frowned.

Barry leaned over the table to show her. He'd had a few comments already that he'd noticed while he was queuing to pay for Dana's shopping spree. He scrolled down the page, but it was gone. Barry noticed the car parking post seemed to have been removed too.

Puzzled, he reached for his own phone. Dana might have bad signal and it hadn't refreshed. He had several private messages and at the top was a message from Jim Burbridge.

"Listen to this!" Barry exclaimed angrily. "It's from Jim Burbridge. 'Hello Barry. Apologies for removing the post. I fully intended to post about the meeting later as admin of the group. It's great to see that you're taking an interest in local events, but I feel the post was negatively biased, referring to noise and disruption. The road improvements will be crucial for the local economy and for the convenience of not only our village but those in neighbouring areas. I will add your offer to bring any concerns to my post and look forward to seeing you at the event. Thank you again for your comments and I sincerely hope that you understand my reasons for the post removal. Kind Regards. Jim'."

"What an arsehole!" Dana gasped. "Who the hell does he think he is?"

Barry shook his head slowly. His blood was boiling. First Jim had upset his lovely wife and now he was trying to censor Barry. He was done with being civil. This meant war.

Chapter 8

Jim was pleased to see Kate's interview with the local paper had made it into Saturday's Gazette. He had got up early and taken a walk to the local shops to buy a copy. He'd picked up some bacon and eggs too, and had enjoyed a hearty, cooked breakfast alongside his morning paper.

He'd felt a little bad about being rude to Laura this morning when she'd asked him where he was going but he was still upset with her. He couldn't keep avoiding the elephant in the room. He'd purposely made excuses to be out all week; citing interest in the upcoming road consultations as reasons to see Kate as well as booking in extra badminton sessions with some colleagues but he was quickly running out of places to go to avoid being in the house at the same time as his wife.

Kate Evett, who had been a good friend for years, had been quite short with her replies to his messages since the commotion at The Crown. Jim was still extremely embarrassed by the incident and it had put him off going to the pub since. Not that he was a big drinker, but they regularly went there for Sunday lunch.

Not that they were likely to go out as a family any time soon, Jim thought to himself. Not with the current bad atmosphere.

Jim finished his breakfast and tidied away the dishes. He had called up to Keeley to offer her some, but she had ignored him. He had felt his temper start to flare at his daughter's lack of respect but had bit his tongue. Jim was exhausted after a week of confrontations and couldn't face another one this morning. He poured himself a cup of tea and carried it out to the Orangery. Kate had had plans last night, so he hadn't seen her, but he had sent a quick text this morning inviting her over for a cuppa and to discuss how best to engage the community ahead of her informal meeting next Thursday. It was great that they had coverage in the local paper, but Jim thought it was wise to utilise other methods of communication; like the social media group. He had been hoping that they could spend the day brain-storming their approach to maximise engagement. Jim's phone beeped to alert him of a text message. He opened the message and was crestfallen to see Kate had declined.

Jim sipped his tea and wondered whether the incident in the pub had anything to do with Kate's sudden distance. Kate had insisted they cut their drink short after Kelly Russell and that Gary had made a scene, and they'd driven over to Kate's cottage, on the other side of Little Cedars, to finish their discussions instead. Jim had thought that they had been getting along extremely well up until that point. She was a lovely woman and extremely fascinating, in Jim's opinion.

It was almost noon by the time Keeley surfaced and Laura returned home from her class. Jim had enjoyed the peace and quiet and was feeling slightly refreshed and in better spirits. His phone started to ring, the display declaring an unknown number, at the same time as Laura came through the door. Jim shut the door of the Orangery for privacy. When he returned from fielding an inappropriate request from the manager of the Leisure Centre, Keeley and Laura were deep in hushed conversation in the kitchen. They both looked uncomfortable and Keeley hurriedly got to her feet. Laura reached out to touch her arm and Keeley brushed her away.

"I'm going out." Keeley announced. She shot a look at her mother, as if waiting for her to stop her but Laura just nodded her head.

"Ok," Laura looked and sounded weary. "What time-"

Keeley cut her off before she could finish her sentence. "Not late. I'll text you."

Keeley shoved her feet into her trainers but turned back at the last minute and glanced at Laura guiltily. "Love you."

Jim noted how Laura sat up a little straighter and rewarded her daughter with a bright smile at this. It was ridiculous how a tiny crumb of affection changed Laura's body language immediately; no wonder Keeley was running wild.

"What was that about?" Jim asked, folding his arms across his body.

Laura rubbed her fingers in circles around her temples, which annoyed Jim. He was the one with a potentially-unfaithful wife and a queue of disgruntled neighbours harassing him.

Laura could sense Jim's hostility and sat up straighter, turning to face him.

"I asked her," Laura looked Jim directly in the eye and spoke in a steely tone. "About the condom. I can't live with this atmosphere between us. Keeley claims it was nothing to do with her, which is, of course, a huge relief but it still brings us no closer to resolving this."

Jim felt his chest tighten. What the hell did she expect him to say? How could they resolve this?

He turned away from her; unable to bear her pleading stare.

"This is very difficult for me." Jim said, struggling to keep calm. "Do you just expect me to forget it and be back to normal overnight?"

"No!" Laura exclaimed. "But I expect you to believe me when I'm telling the truth."

Jim's heart was physically hurting, and he wondered, for a moment, whether he was having a heart attack from all the stress he'd been dealing with. He leaned against the kitchen worktop and tried to catch his breath.

"Jim?" Laura was up on her feet; her arm around his waist in concern.

Jim shook her off with a little more force than he meant. "I'm fine!"

"What are we going to do?" Laura sat back down now that she could see he was physically fine.

She looked close to tears and Jim suppressed the urge to reach out and comfort her.

"I just need time," Jim finally said, regaining his composure. "Can you understand?"

Laura nodded sadly. "And until then?"

Jim frowned, not understanding what she meant.

"And we just live like strangers until then?" She clarified but there was no malice in her voice, just sadness.

Jim felt his annoyance spark up at this.

"You're not the victim." He snarled.

"I'm not the guilty party either!" She cried, throwing her hands in the air in frustration.

The conversation ended there. They weren't the kind of people that went around raising their voices; this was new territory for them both.

Laura had felt energised and positive following her morning of exercise but, after tackling the dreaded conversation with Keeley and this confrontation, she felt the dull ache of a tension headache pressing behind her temples. She showered, changed and stayed in her bedroom for longer than necessary to give Jim some space. She glanced out of their bedroom window and was half-relieved, half-anxious to see Jim's car still in the driveway. Laura had expected him to storm out. It hadn't gone unnoticed the amount of time he'd been spending outside the house; usually with Kate.

Jim had been friends with Kate Evett for years. Laura had never seen this friendship as a threat to her marriage, even after Kate's divorce; but now she wasn't so sure. Accusations aside, Jim had been spending a lot of time with Kate over the last few months. Laura wondered whether maybe Jim had been looking for a reason to argue. She shook away these thoughts.

"You're being ridiculous." She muttered aloud to herself.

Laura wandered back down to the kitchen and helped

herself to pain killers before the headache took hold. Jim was making a fresh pot of tea.

"Fancy going to the garden centre?" Laura asked civilly. "We could get a late lunch out."

She fully expected Jim to decline but he nodded.

"Half an hour?" He replied politely. "I've just got some admin to do."

Laura felt a little of the tension dissolve and realised how much she wanted things back to normal.

Jim took his tea back into the Orangery. He'd had time to process his conversation with Darren and, after the saga at the pub, he didn't wish to get involved in another confrontation. There had been quite a few notifications on the post too, and Jim didn't want poor parking etiquette detracting attention from the important event he was about to share with the Oak Village community.

Jim was annoyed to see that Barry Simons, of all people, had already posted on the page about the event. He was completely missing the point, Jim realised. Traffic improvements, while inconvenient, were vital for the local economy. Barry's post was utter scaremongering; firstly, he'd made a condescending comment about the topics discussed in the group "poor parking and poop" and rather than highlight the benefits, he'd highlighted the negatives like noise and disruption.

Without a moment's hesitation, Jim deleted the post alongside the scathing review of Darren's parking. Jim replaced Barry's notice with a more informative and unbiased notice of his own. He then sent a private message to both Barry and Darren. He had learned, from Kelly Russell, that not all residents were able to take constructive feedback and he was both polite and courteous in his messages to both.

Feeling quite proud of himself, Jim gathered up his belongings. He didn't particularly feel like spending time with Laura, but he didn't want to appear churlish and he didn't have anything better to do.

As it happened, the day wasn't too painful. By the time they had browsed the Garden Centre and sat down for a light lunch at the adjoining café, a sense of normality had returned. There was still a little underlying tension and Jim could tell that Laura's quiet politeness was her way of not rocking the boat.

Over lunch, Jim filled Laura in on the latest regarding Kate's informal meeting prior to the consultation.

"Why is there an informal meeting?" Laura asked politely. "Shouldn't people just attend the council proposal?"

Jim regarded Laura, wondering whether she was insinuating that the meeting was pointless.

"As Kate represents the Little Cedars community," Jim decided that he would give Laura's question the benefit of the doubt as her tone sounded genuine. "It's important that she is prepared to take residents queries and concerns forward at the initial meeting. It's often a case of speak up now or forever hold your peace. She's hosting several different informal chats to ensure every village along Little Cedars can be heard."

"I'll definitely come along." Laura told him.

Jim knew that this was Laura's attempt at a peace-offering but rather than feel pleased that she was finally taking an interest in the same issues he was passionate about, he experienced the familiar pain in his chest as he was reminded of the reason why she was so keen to please him.

Jim tried to brush this feeling aside, but he could already feel his mood start to darken and he remained quiet for the rest of their meal, answering Laura's attempts at conversation with short, one-word responses until she gave up and sank into an uneasy silence.

Laura gazed out of the window on the journey home, blinking back tears of exasperation. Jim's eyes were pointedly fixed on the road ahead of him and his jaw was set tight. Laura's headache was returning, brought on by the frustration of the failure of the attempted 'quality time'. Her head felt like it was in a tightening vice and she knew that she would have to go to bed and try to sleep it off once they were home.

Keeley's bedroom faced the back garden and it was only when she heard Jim's keys in the door that she was alerted to her parents' return.

"Shit." She hissed to Ollie. "They're home."

Ollie had been lounging on her bed, watching a video on his phone as he waited for her to change her trainers and get some money. Keeley had watched her parents drive out of the village less than two hours ago and knew, from experience, if they were out together on a weekend, they'd be at least three hours, usually longer, as they would have lunch out. Bloody typical that the day her mother decided to have an embarrassingly awkward sex conversation, Keeley was about to be caught with a boy in her bloody bedroom.

Ollie shrugged. Keeley felt annoyed at his reaction.

It was alright for him, she seethed to herself. His parents weren't old-fashioned and prudish like hers. Despite Laura and Jim being the same age as most of her friends' parents, they were so straight-laced and overbearing it was painful. Not that she didn't love them, she did. Keeley wished, sometimes, that she had a brother or sister to take the focus off her. It just felt like they were so obsessed with knowing everything about her life. Her friends had so much more freedom than her. Keeley had to tell her parents where she was going, who with, what time she'd be back. Her mother still insisted on checking with other mothers whenever Keeley slept over a friend's. It was embarrassing to be treated like a child.

For a moment, Keeley considered letting her parents know Ollie was here. She wasn't doing anything wrong. Her trainers had got covered in mud when they'd all walked along the river this morning and she just wanted to change them before a group of them met back up to head into town to watch a film at the cinema.

Keeley weighed this up, tired of lying, but the risk was that her parents would go off on one in front of Ollie. She would risk not only looking foolish in front of her boyfriend but if they were particularly furious, which they probably would be, she wouldn't be allowed back out and she'd have to miss out on the rest of the day.

Keeley could hear them in the house now. They'd already stopped at Ollie's and he had clean trainers on, which he hadn't taken off to come into the house. Keeley had left no sign downstairs that she was even in the house. She'd used the back-door key and locked the door behind her. The key was lying on the end of her bed, alongside her purse and her phone.

Ollie opened his mouth to speak and Keeley shushed him hurriedly. She needed to think.

"What do you want me to do?" Ollie whispered, looking amused. "Climb out the window."

Keeley's eyes lit up. Yes! She'd done this before several times and had never got caught. The only risk would be if her parents were in the Orangery that spanned the width of the house. She had two windows in her bedroom; one facing the garden and one facing the side. The side window was slightly narrower but opened above the garage roof. From there, it was just a few feet drop to the roof and then a careful clamber over to the wall. Ollie wasn't much bigger than her. He would fit.

Ollie regarded Keeley with a mixture of horror and awe as he realised this was exactly what she planned to do. He pocketed his phone and followed her tentatively to the window sill. Keeley scooped up the ornaments on the windowsill and quickly stuffed them into a drawer. She could hear footsteps on the stairs and held her breath. She exhaled in relief as she heard the door to her parents' bedroom close and quickly pushed the window open as far as it would go.

She pointed out the route wordlessly to Ollie and he nodded to show he understood. He climbed onto the sill, with his legs dangling from the window. He hesitated, and Keeley felt herself growing impatient. She held a finger to her lips and pointed again.

Ollie lowered himself carefully onto the roof and assumed a crouching position. Keeley hopped up onto the window herself and gestured for Ollie to use his hands to scramble across the roof.

"Slowly!" She hissed at him. "Just be careful not to slip."

She recognised that she was taking a risk. Not only was she risking Ollie falling off the roof and hurting himself, but her parents could glance up and see either of them at any minute. While she could have explained her innocence if she'd called out the minute she heard them come home, Keeley had to admit that sneaking a boy out of her bedroom window looked very incriminating.

Keeley held her breath again as she watched Ollie make a crab-like crawl across the roof. He paused at the end and Keeley immediately knew the reason for his hesitation. She should have explained this part more clearly. She could hardly shout out to him now across the rooftop. She signalled for him to wait there and, praying that the roof was sturdy enough for them both, she dropped effortlessly onto the roof. She stood up carefully and, when she was confident of her balance, pushed the window shut behind her. She scrambled across the roof with more grace and ease than Ollie had managed. He was crouched awkwardly on the corner, looking down at the solid garden wall with trepidation. Keeley brushed past him lightly and, not taking any time to pause, assumed a sitting position, with both legs dangling over the side of the garage. The easiest thing to do was to drop down from the lowest part of the garage into the back garden. Keeley wanted Ollie to climb from the middle of the roof onto the wall, despite the risks, as it meant she could eliminate the risk of being seen from the Orangery. She knew this part was a little awkward as there was a narrow path between the garage and the wall. She had to swing her hands forward like a trapeze artist to hook onto the wall, taking care to not bang her face against the solid bricks, as she transferred her weight to her arms and then used her feet to stop her body hitting the wall, before dropping lightly to her feet.

Ollie watched her descend with ease and he shook his head at her.

"I can't do that!" He hissed. "You're loads lighter than me."

Keeley looked up at him from the safety of the ground. She wanted to be annoyed at him for wasting time and increasing their risk, but she knew that what she was asking him to do was quite dangerous.

"Drop from the end?" She pointed to the back garden and he nodded. It was still over six foot, but it was a simpler landing.

Ollie scrambled lower down the garage roof and Keeley indicated that she'd check to see whether the coast was clear. She crouched down and edged around the corner, peering to see if anybody was visible through the windows. She couldn't see anyone, and she just wanted this over with. Her heart was pounding in her chest and she quickly gestured for Ollie to jump down. Ollie pushed himself from the roof, landing awkwardly.

"Are you ok?" Keeley asked concerned.

Ollie ducked around the corner quickly, pausing to rub his ankle.

"Yeah," He nodded and then grinned at Keeley. "I can't

believe you made me do that."

Keeley laughed and took his hand in hers. "Come on, we've got to get past the house next!"

Inside the house, Jim had thought he heard a thud from the garden and walked through to the living room to check. Some of the neighbourhood cats used his flowerbeds as a toilet and he was forever shooing them away. He couldn't see anything, and he went back to the kitchen to finish making another pot of tea. Laura had retired to bed with a headache, which Jim secretly thought was an excuse to be in a different room after the atmosphere had turned sour again earlier. He told himself that he was glad of the quiet time. He had a whole heap of notifications on social media, as well as private messages with questions about the road improvement proposals to answer, and when he was finished with this, he had a few programmes recorded on TV that he still needed to catch up on.

Laura resurfaced at about 5pm, when it was starting to grow dark, looking pale and tired.

"Has Keeley not come home yet?" Laura asked as she carried a glass of water into the living room and sat down on the chair opposite Jim.

"Not yet." Jim barely glanced up from his programme.

"I tried to phone her," Laura looked concerned. "I wonder if I should go out and have a look for her."

"It's only 5 o'clock." Jim said, a little exasperated at Laura's dramatic behaviour. "She's fourteen, not four."

Laura didn't answer but Jim could see her fidgeting

nervously out of the corner of his eye.

Jim found himself growing irritated with her presence and distracted from the programme he was watching. He was considering turning it off when he heard a thud and a shout from the direction of the back garden. He was reminded of the noise he'd heard earlier, and he got to his feet and opened the Orangery door to take a closer look.

"What's going on?" Laura got to her feet and followed him, looking over his shoulder.

The noise was coming from the Simons' garden. Barry was pushing a wheelbarrow into his garden, calling out noisily to someone.

"What the hell are they doing now?" Jim wondered whether Barry was going ahead, illegally, with his building work after all. Was this the start of the materials being dumped in the garden? Would he come back from work Monday to see the scaffolding erected? Jim felt incensed with fury and hurried to open the door to the garden.

"Jim!" Laura could see that her husband was angered by the interruption and she knew what conclusion he'd jumped to. She just didn't want him rushing out there and getting into an argument.

Jim ignored Laura and called out over the fence.

Barry had emptied one wheelbarrow of what looked like concrete slabs and was making his return journey to the garage. He stopped in his tracks at Jim's interruption. Barry lifted a hand in greeting.

"Hello, Jim!" He called in a friendly tone.

"Busy building?" Jim called back politely. "I could hear you inside. What are you up to?"

Laura cringed at Jim trying to sound friendly when it was clear that he was checking up on the neighbours.

"Yeah," Barry nodded in agreement before purposely not answering the question. "Building."

Laura watched Jim's agitation grow and felt her own headache start back up.

Jim was outside now, leaning over the fence as Barry turned his back to him.

"What are you making?" Jim called, and Laura could hear the stress in his voice.

Barry turned back to Jim and tapped the side of his nose. "None of your business."

The tone Barry used was jovial and playful, but Jim felt his indignation give way to pure rage and fury. Before Jim could reply, Barry had disappeared around the side of his house. Laura watched as Jim's mouth opened and closed in frustration. Jim turned and marched back into the house.

Laura observed him with horrified fascination as she realised he was about to go storming next-door to confront Barry.

"Jim!" She grabbed on to his arm. "You can't go marching around there! This won't get us anywhere."

Jim shook her hand away, but he stopped before he got to the front door.

"It looks like he's doing something in the garden," Laura tried to reason with him. "I think he's trying to get a reaction out of you."

Jim didn't turn around, but Laura could tell that he was listening to her.

"If he does go ahead," She said, her heart racing but her tone calm. "I'm pretty sure it's a civil matter. We'll get a solicitor. Deal with this the right way."

Laura knew that she was appealing to Jim's law-abiding nature. He was a man that liked law and order, rules and regulation. What Laura wanted to say was what the hell did it matter to them when the bloody Simons started building. This is what she would have said on day one when bloody Dana came strutting over waving paperwork. Laura knew Jim would have gone along with whatever she said to do. But she didn't say anything. She couldn't upset the apple cart while she was still on trial for a crime she did not commit. The injustice of it felt overwhelming.

Jim slowly turned away from the door and walked back into the living room. He took his place in front of the television and resumed staring at the moving pictures until his heart rate returned to normal and the fury running through his veins subsided. Laura sat on the sofa opposite him, silent and anxious, until finally Keeley clattered through the door. Keeley claimed she had already eaten at a friend's and Laura, finding herself with nothing to do, decided that lying in bed alone was preferable to sitting up with Jim in this unbearable silence.

As Laura lay in bed, wide awake but exhausted, she reflected on the conversation she'd had with Keeley that morning. Keeley had seemed genuinely shocked and horrified when Laura had asked her about the "found" condom. Laura had scrutinised Keeley's face for any guilt, but her daughter had seemed like she was telling the truth. Before Laura could explain or discuss anything further, Jim had interrupted, and Keeley had used the excuse to leave. Laura knew that she needed to continue the conversation. She didn't like leaving their exchange open-ended, but, after the events of the day, Laura didn't have the strength.

Tomorrow, she vowed to herself. I'll talk to Keeley.

As for Jim, Laura had no idea when this would reach a resolution. She prayed that it was soon, before she ended up a nervous wreck.

Chapter 9

Tina wiped down the bar for the fourth time that shift, just for something to do. She only picked up two or three shifts on a casual basis, usually on the weekend, but they'd asked her to work a few weeknights this week and she needed the money. Tina had hoped that this would be the start of some more regular work, but the bar was dead this evening.

Tina liked to keep busy to stop work dragging, but there were only so many jobs she could invent to pass the time. Frustrated, she reached into her bag underneath the bar and pulled out her phone to check her messages, even though she'd vowed to herself that she wouldn't look until the end of her shift.

She heard the bar door open as her fingers closed around her phone and she dropped it back into the depths of her bag, standing up straight to greet her customers. She turned up the wattage on her 'customer service' smile.

"Hi Kel!" She beamed as Kelly Russell strutted into the bar, dressed in a bright teal coloured bodysuit and tight jeans, looking like a magnificent peacock.

"Hi!" Kelly slung the bag and leather jacket she was carrying onto the bar stool next to her. "Where's everyone?"

"No idea." Tina admitted. "I've been bored out of my brain."

Kelly ordered a drink and peeled a ten-pound note from a wad of cash in her purse. "Buy yourself one, Tina. I don't like drinking alone."

Kelly then peeled off two more notes.

"Sorry, I forgot to leave you money Monday." She held the money out to Tina and she took it gratefully. "Thanks, by the way. It looked lovely until the kids came home!"

Tina laughed at this and finished pouring Kelly's wine.

"I don't know why you insist on slogging your guts out when you could come and work with me," Kelly continued, raising her eyebrows in disapproval. "Honestly, you could make a killing."

Tina smiled but refused to get drawn into this conversation again. She was a firm believer that there was no such thing as the get-rich-quick Holy Grail that Kelly so ardently sought through her various schemes. The only thing that truly paid off was hard work. Tina was under no illusion, even if Kelly wouldn't admit it, but the wads of cash, designer clothes and sporty BMW were the product of Kelly's husband's salary not the flash-in-the-plan business opportunities that Kelly changed every few months.

"You don't usually work here in the week," Kelly saw that Tina wasn't biting and changed the subject. "Is this a regular thing?"

"Just this week, I think," Tina said, leaning against the bar. "I don't know why they needed me if it's always this dead. It wasn't too bad on Tuesday."

"Oh, I do know," Kelly remembered suddenly, sitting up straight. "It's because of that meeting."

"Meeting?" Tina asked confused.

"About the top road," Kelly shrugged. "Barry Simons has

roped loads of people into going. He asked me, but I couldn't think of anything more boring!"

"Has Evan gone?" Tina asked, turning to refill Kelly's wine without being asked.

Kelly reached for her purse, but Tina waved her money away. "It's on me."

Kelly smiled her gratitude and took the wine. "Yes, Evan went. Barry was insistent. Even Gary's gone."

"What's it about?" Tina asked, looking interested. "And how come I haven't heard about it?"

Kelly shrugged again. "Evan did tell me, but I honestly can't remember the details. Apparently, it was in The Gazette and there was a post about it in The Oak Village Moaners and Groaners group."

"Lucky that you're not still banned then." Tina joked.

Kelly laughed. "You should use that page to advertise, like that Sparkles Cleaning do. I've got loads of leads from the village that way."

"I'm pretty busy," Tina shrugged. "I'm not taking anything else except for here."

"Are you working every day still?" Kelly scowled. "I miss having a gym buddy."

"Every day." Tina confirmed, pulling a sad face in response. "I doubt I could keep up with you anyway!"

Kelly flexed a muscle playfully in response.

"What time does the meeting finish?" Tina asked. "Hopefully we'll get an influx of customers when they're done."

"Not sure," Kelly responded. "I can't see it lasting long. There can't be that much to say about bloody roadworks, surely. They're at the conference room at the Leisure Centre, so hopefully it'll liven up a bit soon."

Tina was actually quite interested and wished she'd known about the meeting. Her apartment was in the block closest to the road so if there were going to be any huge changes, it would nice to have a say in what would be going on. Tina didn't say this to Kelly though. Kelly would just roll her eyes or make a sarcastic comment.

Kelly steered the conversation back around to all the leads she'd been working on this week and Tina made a show of listening attentively. Kelly had knocked back quite a few drinks when the bar started to fill up with people coming from the meeting. Tina was rushed off her feet for the next hour. She didn't get a chance to ask any questions until later when people started to leave and only the hardcore pub regulars were left behind.

Kelly was annoyed that Evan hadn't come inside for a drink with Barry and the others. He'd insisted on going straight back to the house to relieve Pam of her babysitting duties, according to Barry. He had promised Kelly he would come in for one when she'd asked him to arrange a babysitter. Evan had been annoyed that Kelly had left it until the last minute, but she'd been so busy with work she'd forgotten about his stupid meeting.

Barry Simons had been holding court at a large table in the corner, but as the pub started to empty with people making their excuses about "early starts in the morning", Barry moved over to the bar. Kelly moved her possessions up to make space for Barry and his entourage.

"Why weren't you at the meeting?" Barry asked Kelly, flashing her a grin to show he wasn't annoyed.

"I promised Tina I'd keep her company." Kelly gave him an apologetic smile.

"You're forgiven," Barry directed this at Tina. "You had a legitimate excuse."

"I would have liked to come," Tina admitted. "Can you fill me in?"

Barry was more than happy to have an audience and repeated the word-perfect monologue that he had delivered to his fellow residents earlier that night. He was a naturally charismatic man and had a way with words which had aided his success in life. He could captivate any audience and even Kelly found herself drawn in as he talked about the impact the planned road improvements would have on Little Cedars. Tina, who had been worried about noise and pollution, was starting to change her mind about the proposed work when Barry started painting a picture of the downside; highlighting all the concerns Tina had and more.

"It's not a good thing?" She asked, unsure of how to feel.

Barry shook his head slowly. "It's complicated. The infrastructure is lacking, and something needs to be done, but demolishing the top road into a dual carriageway isn't the answer. Yes, it would solve the current traffic problems, but it would split Little Cedars in two. Would you want the kids crossing a dual carriageway to get to school every day?"

Kelly shrugged. "They catch the bus. It's too far to walk."

Barry ignored her. "The impact on not just the Oak Fields estate but all the houses closest to the road would be terrible. Depreciate the value of those homes. Is the council prepared to compensate them? Of course not!"

"Something has to happen though," Tina said thoughtfully. "The traffic is only going to get worse. It's impacting people's lives."

"Surely, you'd be for the road," Kelly regarded Barry suspiciously. "Your company would probably win that contract and that's mega-bucks!"

Barry was impressed by Kelly's nous. The only person who had asked the same had been Evan. Barry had nothing to hide though and he was prepared for this question.

"Oh yes," Barry nodded. "I'm not disputing that the work is vital. It needs to be done. I just think that they should consider other routes and keep the top road as a single carriageway. I know, for a fact, that they could connect Birch Grove via Finchester to the motorway with a by-pass. They'll have to at some point, the way the area is growing. This is just the cheaper, easier option."

Tina tried to get her head around what Barry was saying and Barry, sensing her confusion, sketched a quick map on the back of a beer mat.

"It would take out a chunk of the wood," Tina noticed straight away.

Barry held back from rolling his eyes. That had been Jim Burbridge's objection too which had a lot of residents jumping from Barry's camp back to Jim's. Who knew there were so many tree-huggers in Oak Village.

"They'll do it eventually," Barry told her. "It's inevitable. I just think why mess around with the top road when eventually all the traffic will be directed on the other side of the river. It makes sense."

Tina nodded. What Barry said did make sense. She thought the natural boundary between Little Cedars and Finchester was beautiful; it was one of the main reasons she'd been attracted to the area. Oak Village was one of the nicest housing clusters in Little Cedars, bordered by the top road on one side and the river and the woods on the other. Barry's drawing had shown a road crossing the river out of Oak Village and joining a by-pass closer to town. It would be a shame to lose some of that greenery but if they were going to do it anyway at some point, aesthetically it would look better than a dual carriageway zipping past her bedroom window.

"You don't know that's what they'd do." Kelly argued, tapping a fingernail against Barry's drawing.

"No," Barry downgraded his opinion of Kelly from impressed to irritated. "I don't. However, I've managed hundreds of contracts and I have a good idea of what they tend to do. I'd be happy to put a wager on it if you want to put your money where your mouth is."

Kelly looked like she was considering this.

"No," She said eventually. "You know more about this than me. I'm going to choose to bow out."

Barry rewarded her with a wink and a new drink.

"I'm making this my last!" Kelly announced. "I'm pretty drunk and Evan's going to be furious when I get in."

"I'd better make it my last, too." Barry nodded. "I've been meaning to cut back and get back in the gym."

"You still haven't gone?" Kelly wagged a finger at Barry.

"No." Barry admitted. "I don't like going on my own. I get bored."

Darren Rees had wandered up to the bar and overheard this conversation.

"You can have a free trial at the leisure centre," He spoke directly to Barry. "It's always busy. You won't get bored."

Kelly had watched the group Darren was with disperse but he had waved them away insisting he would finish his drink and be off. As soon as they left, he came up to the bar to buy another drink.

"Thanks, mate," Barry looked pleased with his offer. "I'll take you up on that."

The conversation turned away from the road improvements and Kelly listened as Barry and Darren chatted about the gym. Tina had left the bar, after serving them, and was busying herself clearing the tables around the room.

"It's the best gym in the area." Darren said proudly. "I don't know why anyone would go anywhere else."

Tina arrived back at the bar, at that moment, laden with empty glasses.

"Tina doesn't think so." Kelly cut in suddenly, causing them all to turn and look at Tina.

Tina frowned at Kelly, not following the conversation.

"What's wrong with my gym?" Darren asked Tina with a teasing smile.

Tina flushed, feeling put on the spot. She turned away and started to stack the glasses, while she recovered her composure.

"We always used to go to your gym," Kelly addressed this to Darren. "But Tina doesn't come any more."

"I'm too busy!" Tina protested. "The gym is fine."

Tina realised that Kelly was drunk. She was so cool and calm usually but after a few wines she always had a bit of a mouth on her.

"You don't go to another gym then?" Kelly asked in a challenging tone that made Barry and Darren both turn and look at Kelly warily.

"You're so lairy when you're drunk," Barry joked, hoping to defuse the situation. "Don't you have work in the morning?"

Kelly ignored him and fixed her gaze on Tina, waiting for a response.

"I told you," Tina looked directly at Kelly. "I'm too busy."

Kelly necked the last of her glass of wine and wobbled slightly on her bar stool.

"You've never been to another gym?" Kelly repeated. "Not even, I don't know, the one in Birch Grove."

Tina realised, in that instant, that Kelly had seen the gym card in her jacket pocket.

"One of my customers works there," Tina shrugged nonchalantly. "They gave me a free pass, but I've never used it. It's too far away."

Kelly eyed Tina, trying to assess whether she was telling the truth. Tina held Kelly's gaze until Kelly looked away.

Darren looked uncomfortable, but Barry looked amused at the exchange.

Tina rang the bell for last orders and disappeared to stack the dishwasher. The landlord appeared, from out the back, and offered to take over cashing up for Tina.

"Are you walking back?" Kelly asked Tina, as she pulled on her leather jacket. Kelly had hoped that Tina would have to stay to cash up, but now that it was clear that she was leaving with her customers, Kelly thought it would be churlish not to walk back together.

Tina nodded and retrieved her own bag.

"I'll walk with you." Darren offered.

Barry lived in the opposite direction and they parted at the door to the pub.

"Party at mine next weekend!" Barry called out as he crossed the road and turned right. "Gary's putting up a little bar in the garden. Kids welcome!"

They all laughed at Barry's outlandish plan and agreed to keep the date free. Tina promised she'd pop in after her shift.

"Are you going?" Kelly asked Darren as the threesome crossed the road.

"Not sure," Darren said uncomfortably. "Depends what I've got on."

"Dana's good friends with your wife," Kelly observed. "Surely she'll want to go."

Darren shrugged and said nothing.

The night had grown old and Kelly shivered a little under her leather jacket.

"Are you cold?" Darren asked.

Kelly turned to look at him to respond and felt a flicker of jealousy when she realised he was addressing Tina, who wasn't wearing a coat. Kelly watched Tina smile politely at Darren and shake her head. She had put on a cardigan over the long-sleeved top she was wearing but she was visibly shivering.

Darren chivalrously removed his own North Face jacket and, ignoring Tina's protests, slipped it over Tina's shoulders.

Kelly, not used to not being the centre of attention, pouted silently for the rest of the journey. Her phone started ringing and she fumbled in her bag for it, stumbling slightly on the pavement as she did. Darren caught her arm and supported her as she stopped to retrieve her phone.

"It's Evan," Kelly answered the call, stopping in the middle of the road to do so. Tina had walked on slightly and stopped about ten yards ahead of them to wait. Darren dropped his arm from Kelly's waist as she started to talk into the phone. "I'm on my way home. I'm with Tina and Darren, from the leisure centre."

This seemed to answer Evan's reason for the call and, without saying goodbye, Kelly ended the call and dropped her phone back into her bag. Tina started walking, not waiting for them to catch up.

"This is your street." Kelly announced when they got to the corner of Darren's cul-de-sac.

"I'll walk you ladies home." Darren continued walking towards the end of the estate.

"No, it's fine." Tina shook her head. "I'll see Kelly home."

Tina waited for Kelly to catch up and took her arm to indicate that Kelly was in safe hands and that Tina held no hard feelings over Kelly's inquisition earlier.

"No," Kelly slurred a little, leaning against Tina. "Darren, I insist you see Tina home."

"I'm fine." Tina shook her head and physically turned Kelly in the direction they were walking.

"I think," Kelly had to jog a little in her high-heeled boots to keep up with Tina's strides. "Darren should make sure you get home safe."

Darren laughed at how drunk Kelly was. "I'll just make sure you can handle her."

Tina groaned inwardly. She just wanted to get Kelly home as

quickly as possible before she started mouthing off about something else.

Kelly insisted on going in the back way and Tina felt obliged to wait by the gate to watch her get in safely. Kelly shook her head at Tina.

"No! You go ahead!" She insisted. "Darren, you have to walk Tina now!"

Kelly sat down heavily on the kerb outside her house. "I'm not going in until I see you walking Tina home. It's dangerous!"

Tina felt a flare of annoyance at Kelly. She was so bloody awkward when she got in states like this. Tina was not prepared to argue, and she jogged off in the direction of her home. Darren stood awkwardly unsure of which woman to see home safe.

"Go!" Kelly urged him, pointing in Tina's direction.

Kelly climbed unsteadily to her feet and searched in her bag for a key. She watched Darren obediently follow Tina to the end of the street and, using the fence for support, stumbled towards the darkness of her home.

Darren had hoped that Steph would be in bed by the time he got home. He'd had quite enough of women and their unpredictable behaviour.

Honestly, Darren seethed to himself as he tried to unlock the door to his home as quietly as possible, you try to do a good deed and see two women home and they both end up disappearing without so much as a thank you.

He kicked his shoes off and realised that Tina had left without returning his jacket. He tossed his keys onto the table in annoyance. Not only was that inconvenient but it would also land him in the bad books with Steph if she found out. Not that she would say anything, but she'd get all uptight and quiet, which was worse than a blazing row in Darren's opinion.

In Darren's exasperation, he didn't notice that the lights were still on downstairs until he saw Steph, wrapped in a blanket, watching TV in the living room.

"I didn't think you'd still be up." He said and walked into the room, sitting down opposite his wife.

Steph pressed pause on the TV remote. "I wasn't tired. Did you have a nice time?"

Steph had gone to the meeting too. Ollie was old enough to keep an eye on Kendall, but Steph didn't like leaving them for too long as they'd inevitably argue at some point and Steph was fed up of coming home to World War 3.

"Was ok," Darren replied. "I couldn't get away from the work lot any quicker."

Steph shrugged as if she didn't care but Darren could see the look of hurt that seemed to be permanently etched on her face. Darren looked away guiltily. He knew that he was the cause of it today. After the meeting, Barry and Dana had asked them if they were coming to The Crown for one. Darren had seen Steph's face light up at the prospect of a night out, and he had felt awful when he apologised, telling them he had a few things to take care of at work first.

"I'll try to pop down after." Darren had offered halfheartedly.

"I think I'll just go back for the kids," Steph had given Dana an apologetic smile. "They wind each other up if they're left alone too long. We'll catch up another time."

"Definitely," Dana replied. "I didn't tell you that Barry jumped on your Tiki bar idea, did I?"

"No!" Steph laughed in disbelief. "You never, Barry?"

Barry had chuckled. "It's not a Tiki bar. More of a glorified shed. Party at ours next weekend to celebrate the opening!"

"We'll be there!" Steph promised, then shot a glance at Darren. "Well, I will be. God knows with your working hours, Dar."

"The kids are welcome too," Dana added quickly. "We've got a full house, so it'll be good, clean fun."

"Sounds awful!" Barry joked. "Might see you later, Darren."

"I think I might call it a night," Dana said as the two couples made their way out of the meeting room. She lowered her voice and glanced over her shoulder to make sure they couldn't be overheard. "It'll just be Barry giving a blow-by-blow account of how he defeated every point Jim Burbridge made. I hear enough of that at home!"

Barry and Steph both laughed uproariously at that; both used to Dana's quick wit.

The Simons had jumped into their car and Darren had loitered awkwardly, waiting for Steph to climb into her Citroen.

"I won't be long." He had promised but he had sent Steph a text message at 9.30, explaining that he had just finished up at work and was going to drop into the pub "just to show his face".

Despite it now being 11.30pm, Steph didn't make a sarcastic comment about "just showing his face". Darren felt infuriated at her "niceness" and then guilty for feeling like that. It was like they were trapped in a vicious circle of Darren being thoughtless and Steph saying nothing. Darren would then get annoyed at Steph for not calling him out on his behaviour and the cycle would continue.

Steph held up the TV remote. "Do you want to watch anything? I'm not fussed on this."

"Not really," Darren shook his head. "I might just go up to bed."

"I'll let the dog out and I'll be up." Steph replied, turning the TV off and getting to her feet.

Darren wandered into the kitchen, not taking in the mess that Ollie and Kendall had left for their mum to tidy up. He poured himself a glass of water and made his way up to bed. He plugged his phone into the charger next to his bed and was still browsing the internet when Steph finally came up twenty minutes later.

"You were ages." Darren commented, turning his phone off as he always did during the night.

"Tidying up after the kids." Steph replied, climbing into bed next to him.

"They're old enough to pick up after themselves," Darren

said. "You need to be a bit stricter with them."

They'd had this conversation countless times, but today Steph felt riled by this criticism.

"Or you could talk to them." She countered, and Darren looked up surprised.

"I suppose," He started hesitantly, more interested in Steph's challenging tone than a conversation about their parenting. "I'll talk to them tomorrow."

"And say what?" Steph asked, her tone back to tired and weary.

"Whatever you want me to say," Darren offered. "They should be able to look after themselves now. You've given up enough of your life hanging around the house looking after them."

"Hanging around the house?" Steph repeated quietly. "Is that what you think I do?"

Darren frowned, confused by the cool edge to her tone. "I'm trying to be helpful."

Steph opened her mouth to speak and then closed it again. She was silent for a moment before speaking again. "Sorry. It's fine though, I'll speak to them."

"It's up to you," Darren shrugged. He was only trying to be helpful. "What did you think about the meeting tonight?"

"I don't know," Steph admitted, grateful for the change in subject. "Something definitely needs to be done but I can see both sides of the argument."

"Can you?" Darren hadn't really given it much thought. He would rather the by-pass be built purely as this wouldn't affect him getting back and forth to work via the top road while work was being done, but other than that he didn't really care as their house was one of the furthest away from the road on the Oak Fields development.

"I wouldn't say that to Barry though," Steph laughed quietly. "He certainly seems to have made it his mission to upset Jim Burbridge."

"Do you think?" Darren rolled onto his side. He loved a bit of village gossip; just so long as it wasn't about him, of course.

Steph quickly gave him the back story she'd heard first-hand from Dana about the party wall agreement and the postponed building work, the social media post being censored, and the bar Barry was building in revenge.

"He's never just doing that to spite his neighbour!" Darren laughed at the outrageousness of grown adults acting like children.

"You know Jim is Ollie's new girlfriend's dad, don't you?" Steph informed Darren, enjoying having Darren's full attention for once.

"No!" Darren gasped, recalling the phone call he'd made to Jim with horror. Hopefully, Ollie's relationship would be the typical flash-in-the-pan teenage romance, although knowing Darren's luck, they'd end up married.

Steph laughed at Darren's reaction. "I hope Barry's party doesn't wind them up any more. It would an awful first impression of us."

Darren stayed quiet and Steph looked at him wistfully, adding. "It would be nice if you could come. We never do anything together."

"We went for a walk the other day." Darren protested, feeling the familiar twinge of guilt.

"For about ten minutes," Steph responded, smiling to show she wasn't looking for an argument. "Then you left me to go to the pub!"

Darren had wanted to "pop "into The Crown on the way back from their quick walk along the river. Steph had offered to drop the dog back home and come back to meet him, but Darren had waved away her suggestion claiming he'd only be ten minutes. He'd eventually arrived back at the house two hours later, but she'd said nothing at the time.

"Tom and Gemma were there!" Darren said, defensiveness creeping into his voice. "I'm their manager. You think I want to be hanging around when I could be at home relaxing? I do it to keep up morale. It's part of my job."

Steph regretted saying anything now. Just when they started getting along, she always seemed to say something to annoy him.

"Sorry," She finally said quietly. "I was only joking."

"It's fine," Darren rolled back over and closed his eyes. "Goodnight."

"Goodnight." Steph echoed, turning away from her husband and shutting her own eyes.

In the darkness, she replayed the conversation several times as she often did, trying to identify how to stop herself saying something that would trigger one of Darren's sullen moods. It was only as she was drifting off to sleep that she realised Darren had dodged replying to her comment about wanting him to come to Barry and Dana's party.

What was his problem? Steph wondered as her mind threw up unhelpful suggestions for Darren's reluctance to socialise with his own wife. Was he seeing someone local or could he not bear to be around her at all? Steph felt startled by her own thoughts as she realised that, while she could understand Darren having his head turned by pretty women, if he genuinely hated her company that much then this marriage was pointless to them both.

Chapter 10

Kate Evett was thrilled with the turn out for the informal community get-together she'd hosted. She loved being the Little Cedars Community Councillor. The role had been a blessing following the end of her marriage to Colin. While work had kept her busy during the day, Kate had struggled with coming home to an empty house and her new duties had kept her mind occupied and rewarded her with a sense of purpose.

Kate made herself a cup of green tea and took it into the sitting room of her cottage. She browsed through the notes she had made and decided that she would work on grouping these together into valid community concerns this weekend. Weekends were usually difficult for her and the prospect of having something to do was a relief.

It had been a surprise, Kate reflected as she sipped her tea, that so many locals had turned up and shown an interest. From experience, Kate knew that a lot of people would have opinions but, when it came down to it, people didn't usually care enough to give up their free time. Jim had attributed this to his online announcement. He had said as much to Kate, which had irritated her. Kate had first met Jim years ago when they worked for the Education department of the council. Kate had left years ago, and they had maintained a casual acquaintance until Kate had taken the Community Councillor role. Jim's presence, at first, had been flattering. Kate enjoyed having company, particularly male, but his interest had started to become irksome. Not a day had gone by, over the past few weeks, when she hadn't had a text or a call from Jim inviting her to meet up. Kate cared deeply about the community, but she knew that, realistically, what happened with the road improvements would be decided by the powers that be; her role was to share any concerns on behalf of the community. Jim, in Kate's opinion, was taking the whole matter far too seriously and acting like he had been appointed some decision-making powers. Kate had started to distance herself from Jim, not just because he was irritating her with his calls and messages, but also due to local perception of Jim. Kate was aware that Jim had rankled a few of his neighbours with his lack of sensitivity and judgement on his online group. She had been mortified when she had, inadvertently, been involved in the fracas at The Crown. Kate had a few regrets; firstly, letting her acquaintance with Jim grow from monthly Badminton games with a group of ex-colleagues to more intimate meetings and, secondly, inviting him back to her home on more than one occasion.

If Kate had learned anything from life, it was that dwelling on regrets wasn't constructive. She quickly traced her thoughts back to the meeting and the feeling of pride at the community representation. Jim had credited the engagement to the social media promotion, but it had been clear to Kate that Barry Simons had commandeered a huge group of supporters. He was a charismatic man, Kate thought to herself as she traced a finger along her notes to find some of Barry's points. He was the kind of man that would be an asset to local politics. Kate wondered whether Barry had ever considered representing the community, or even the local authority. He was just what the area needed. Kate would have liked to have accepted Barry's invitation to continue discussions at The Crown, but Jim had been like her shadow at the event and Kate had already lied to him that she had somewhere to be following the meeting.

Jim's wife, Laura, had attended the meeting. Kate had thought she'd sensed an atmosphere between the couple and hoped that it was nothing to do with the amount of time that Jim had been spending with Kate. Kate recognised the tension as similar to the strain between herself and Colin towards the end of their marriage. This solidified Kate's resolve to limit the time she spent with Jim. He wasn't a bad-looking man, but his self-righteousness was grating. Kate got the impression that Laura, despite being a quiet and private woman, was well liked within the community and Kate didn't wish to be gossiped about as a 'home-wrecker'. She shuddered at the thought.

Kate finished her tea, filed her notes away with the rest of her papers for the next Community Council meeting and got ready for bed. It wasn't late, but she had early classes and a few errands to run tomorrow. It was a shame she had missed out on the opportunity to acquaint herself properly with Barry Simons but there would be plenty of opportunity to bump into him in The Crown. Hopefully, Barry would have acquired a taste for championing local causes and Kate could encourage him to invest more of his efforts into the community. She just needed to shake off Jim's persistent attempts to shadow her everywhere she went as it was quite clear that there was no love lost between the two men.

Kate woke up bright and early the next day, beating the traffic and arriving at Finchester college before any of the other lecturers or students. Kate had been fortunate enough to retire in her early forties, but, despite the various projects she always had on the go, Kate missed the routine of working life and had worked on a self-employed basis as a Lecturer ever since. Kate liked the hustle and bustle of working at Finchester college; it was a bigger college than the others that she had worked at. She used the quiet time to open her laptop and put the final touches to a tutorial she had prepared. Once this was complete, Kate checked the time and was pleased to see that she still had twenty minutes before her class began. She packed up her laptop and headed down to the coffee shop to pick up a tea. As she turned the corner, between the stairwell and the entrance to the library, Kate bumped into a slender, dark-haired woman.

"Sorry!" The woman reached out and grabbed Kate's arm to stop her stumbling.

Kate recovered her footing quickly, glad that she had chosen to wear flat boots today instead of heels. If she'd been wearing her heeled court shoes, Kate had no doubt that she'd have gone flying on impact.

"That's ok," Kate responded. "My fault for not looking."

Kate glanced up and realised she recognised the woman.

"Oh, hello." Kate smiled politely, racking her brain to remember how she knew the young woman. "What are you doing here?"

"Just using the library." Tina smiled back awkwardly.

"Very good." Kate nodded, unsure what else to say but Tina removed her hand from Kate's arm quickly and set back off in the direction of the exit without another word.

Kate frowned, feeling flustered by the exchange, trying to place the woman's face. It hit her that she was the woman, from the village, that had cleaned Kate's house once. Kate had noticed a pair of earrings go missing and had decided to terminate the contract rather than risk anything more valuable go walk-about. Kate wasn't a hundred percent sure that she hadn't misplaced the earrings, but once there was a shadow of doubt, Kate didn't feel comfortable continuing with the service. Kate replayed the brief meeting in her mind as she queued to pay for her herbal tea. The woman, whose name completely evaded Kate, had looked slightly unsure when Kate had attempted to make conversation. Was she still harbouring a grudge? Kate wondered. She caught sight of the woman, through the large floor-to-ceiling windows of the coffee shop, waiting in the car park. Her back was to Kate, but she was recognisable from the leather jacket and the dark ponytail.

There was a perfectly good library in Little Cedars, Kate mused to herself as she paid for her tea. Not many non-students used the college library. It was a strange thing to do.

Kate caught sight of a dark-coloured 4x4 pull up next to the woman. She found herself pausing to watch the woman climb into the car. The license plate was obscured by the bollards separating the pavement from the carpark, but Kate caught a glimpse of the driver and thought she recognised him too. He had been at the Oak Village meeting, Kate was confident of that. She couldn't think what his name was though either.

Kate felt a flicker of concern at all these little things escaping her memory. Her doctor had mentioned memory loss as a potential side effect of the sleeping tablets she took. Kate smiled to herself at the irony of remembering this fact. She had a prescription review in a few weeks. She'd mention it then. It was unlikely to be anything to worry about, Kate reassured herself. She dealt with a lot of different people between lecturing and her work in the community; she couldn't possibly be expected to remember the names of every person she had ever met.

She hurried back up the stairs to the room where her first class was being held; taking extra care to give the corner a wide berth to avoid another collision. The day went quickly, and it was lunchtime by the time she remembered to check her phone. She was irritated with herself to see that this was another thing that had skipped her mind today. Kate had purposely turned her mobile off, following the meeting last night. Jim had been keen to debrief with her, despite Kate insisting that she had somewhere else to be, and Kate was certain that he would call or message her regardless.

Kate checked her messages and saw that she had been right. There was a message from Jim and he'd left a voicemail. She ignored both, instead dialling the number for her stockbroker. She had an appointment at 3pm, but she wanted to bring it forward if possible as she'd booked to have her hair cut and coloured at 4.30pm, which would be cutting it a bit fine.

Kate felt uneasy about ignoring Jim. As much as he'd irritated her, he was still a member of the community that she represented, and she didn't want him to harbour any bad feeling towards her. Begrudgingly, Kate replied to his message, apologising that she was so busy and telling him she would see him at badminton Wednesday. Kate re-read the message and decided her wording was perfect: creating boundaries while still coming across pleasant and polite. Satisfied with her diplomacy, Kate returned her phone to her bag.

Jim made a point of never taking personal calls in working hours. Half of his colleagues seemed to waste their days texting and browsing the internet. In Jim's opinion, this wasn't only disrespectful to the rest of their colleagues but demonstrated a lack of self-control and work ethic. He didn't look at his phone until he left the office at 5.30pm.

It had been a long day and Jim was still reeling from the meeting the previous night. Jim had been delighted at the excellent community turn-out. It was deeply satisfying to see so many different residents of Oak Village take an active interest in community matters. Jim had organised a litter picking day along the river, at the end of the summer, after several vocal residents had complained on the online group about the mess left behind along the riverbank and the footpath. Despite the number of neighbours claiming they were "outraged" and "disgusted", relatively few people had actually bothered to show up to help tidy up their village. Jim had half-expected only a handful of residents to attend the meeting to air their concerns, but the room had been full of people from the village, keen to share their opinions. His gratification, at seeing so many keen neighbours, had quickly soured when Barry Simons, in his typical exhibitionist manner, had hogged the session with his tedious monologue. Jim could see through Barry; he clearly had a hidden agenda for trying to persuade neighbours to object to the top road improvements and insist on a by-pass that wasn't even part of the local authority consultations. Jim suspected that Barry had never got involved in anything that didn't directly benefit him and he was determined to get to the bottom of Barry's intentions.

Kate had seemed to lap up Barry's nonsense, which had further infuriated Jim. Jim knew that her role was to listen to the opinions and the feedback of the community and act in their interest, however he felt that she should have been more proactive in stopping him from monopolising practically the whole meeting and encouraging some of the other residents to use their own voices. She was too passive, Jim thought to himself. Kate was constantly being coerced into various meetings and matters. She had been rushed off her feet lately and had barely any time to spare.

Jim had even thought she had been giving him the cold shoulder, after they had grown so close lately, but he realised now that she had just been busy with all the responsibilities that came with her community council role. He had been secretly pleased that she had had to dash off following the meeting last night. Laura had insisted on attending and, despite their relationship being at rock bottom lately, Jim had worried that Laura would automatically assume any invitation extended to her too which would have made conversation between Jim and Kate awkward and uncomfortable. Jim had, however, been hoping that Kate would be free this evening. There was a quaint little pub that served lovely meals out in the country lanes and Jim had been looking forward to a civilised evening of good conversation and food with his dear friend. Jim was disappointed to see Kate's response was a decline and this further worsened his already low mood.

He joined the heavy traffic slowly crawling back towards Little Cedars. For once, he didn't feel irritated at the stop-start journey. He was in no rush to get home to the tense atmosphere and an evening of twiddling his thumbs. He couldn't even enjoy sitting out in the Orangery any more. It was already getting dark but that was beside the point. The Simons had been banging around out there all week assembling a huge shed. Jim had been furious that Barry had childishly led him to believe that the building supplies he'd been carting around were for the beginning of the attic conversion. Jim had been glad that he had kept his cool in the face of Barry's provocation. He was dreading the start of their official building work, but he was determined that he would present a calm exterior and not give Barry the reaction he clearly craved.

Jim pulled into the driveway. Laura's car was already parked on the drive and Jim sat in the car for a few minutes, browsing through the day's posts on the community group. He could have done this in the comfort of his home, but he felt the need to prolong his bubble of solitude before he could face the inevitable tension in the house. He saw that Kate had posted a link to the Little Cedars library page; reminding villagers of the facilities. Jim followed the link and browsed some of the library events. There was nothing posted to suggest Kate was hosting any events at the library, but Jim supposed that this was likely. He decided that he would visit the library in the morning. In his opinion, the library was an under-rated commodity. Jim thought that he might even offer to volunteer there in some way or other. Jim browsed some more of the posts on the Oak Village group. The neighbourhood had seemed to take note of his reminder of guidelines and etiquette as there were no posts and only two comments that required moderating today.

Jim gathered up his belongings and started to get out of the car. It was just his luck that at that moment, Dana pulled up alongside him into her own driveway and Laura came out of their own house, dressed in her work-out clothes. Jim nodded politely in Dana's direction, determined to be the bigger person.

"Hi!" Dana's usual cheery tone had an edge of nervousness

to it. "How are you?"

"Hi Dana." Laura called back from the door step.

Jim grunted a response at his wife and his neighbour.

"I'm glad I caught you both!" Dana continued and made her way across the stepping stones at the top of her lawn to cross onto the Burbridge's property.

Jim sighed inwardly. He had been making a break for the front door and was hoping Dana would continue her address to just his wife.

Laura had almost reached her own car, but she politely turned back when she saw Dana was stood outside their house. Jim stopped short of the doorstep as if he couldn't bring himself to bridge the last few feet to Dana.

"Firstly," Dana cleared her throat. "I wanted to apologise for any upset we might have caused; springing the building work on you."

"It's fine." Laura cut in quickly, glancing nervously at Jim as if she was worried about his reaction to this.

The look wasn't lost on Jim and he felt a surge of irritation at Laura. What did she think he was going to say? For goodness sake, he thought to himself.

"And I wanted to thank you, Jim," Dana continued. "For raising awareness of the road improvements so that we could all have a say."

Jim said nothing but nodded his acknowledgement of her comment.

"That's nice," Laura smiled warmly at Jim. "Isn't that a nice thing to say, Jim?"

Jim reddened slightly; his frustration with Laura rising as she spoke to him like a child.

A look of confusion flashed across Dana's face at Laura and Jim's strange behaviour, but she recovered her composure quickly.

"It's really been great," Dana ad-libbed quickly. "The "Community" page. I've found a new hairdresser, a new cleaner, activities for the kids. It's great. Really great."

It was Laura's turn to regard Dana in confusion. Had she just called them over to tell them about her love of the community social media group?

"Yes," Laura echoed, starting to turn back towards her car. "It's great. I'm just off to pick Keeley up so I've got to run!"

"Oh." Dana's face fell a little and then she remembered her reason for calling the Burbridges over. "Sorry! I've gone off on a tangent! You might have noticed we've been putting up a little cabin in the garden."

Jim almost snorted at this. It was a large shed.

"We noticed." He said, dryly. "I thought it was a shed."

Dana waved her hand flippantly as if the detail was unimportant. "Cabin, shed. Barry's calling it the Tiki bar," She paused here, smiling affectionately as if Barry was the funniest person she'd ever met. "Anyway, we're having a little party next Saturday in the garden if you're free?"

A Tiki bar! Jim would have laughed if it wasn't such a

ridiculous thing to do!

"We're busy." Jim said at the exact same time as Laura replied.

"We'd love to!" She exclaimed.

Jim and Laura stared at each other in horror. Dana looked between the two in confusion.

"Oh yes!" Laura blushed and tapped her head with the palm of her hand in a "Gosh-I'm-so-forgetful" gesture. "We're out that evening. What a shame. Thank you though! I hope you have a lovely time."

Jim nodded his head in Dana's direction, indicating that the conversation was over. He pushed open the door to the house and went into the kitchen, leaving Laura to clean up the mess she'd made with her big mouth. He could hear their voices, as he went into the kitchen, and he turned the kettle on, hoping the noise would drown out their words.

Jim was furious that Laura would even consider accepting an invitation from them. It had been one thing after another with her lately. He made his tea and carried it up to his bedroom to get changed as his mind worked through all the flaws he'd noticed in his marriage. He had considered himself content with their quiet, companionable relationship, but was he? He wondered to himself as he listed all the things Laura did that frustrated him. They didn't have any common interests. Since Keeley was born, they'd stopped doing anything together. Laura had always enjoyed socialising with his group of friends back when it had just been the two of them. She invested all her time now in either running around after Keeley or her exercise obsession. Jim's thoughts fell on the still-unexplained contraceptive. There was no innocent explanation for it, he knew. She was clearly not the person he thought she was. He was capable of perfectly innocent friendships with women; Kate was a prime example of this. He skipped over any feelings of his own guilt as anything that he had done had been caused by Laura's glaring infidelity. He was glad that he hadn't reacted on the spot and had given Laura a chance to prove her innocence, but weeks had passed now, and she had offered him no reasonable explanation. He wasn't a rash or hot-tempered man. He didn't plan to walk out on his family and lose his home and all the things that he had worked hard for. He would have to sit this out a little longer as difficult as it was.

He pottered around the house until Keeley and Laura finally came back just over an hour later. Laura was fussing about around Keeley as if she was a small child and Jim felt the familiar tightening in his chest, which he was attributing to the stress of his home life. Laura caught him mid-pang, steadying himself against the worktop.

"Jim!" She turned to him, her voice full of concern. "Is it your chest? You keep doing that."

He temporarily forgot his pain in exasperation at her tone. She was always fussing about nothing.

"I'm fine." He replied gruffly. "Just off out."

Laura's face fell at his response. "I thought we were going to go out to try that new Indian restaurant."

Jim recalled that she had mentioned the Indian restaurant that everyone had been raving about, but he certainly hadn't agreed to go.

"You never said anything about going." Jim frowned at her. "I'm busy."

"I mentioned it Tuesday," Laura said defensively. "I said we should go Friday and you nodded."

Jim shook his head. "I wouldn't have agreed to that. I knew I had plans."

"Where are you going?" Laura asked, visibly upset.

Jim felt put on the spot. After Kate had declined his offer, he didn't actually have anything to do, but he had just wanted to get out of the house for a few hours. He had planned to go for a drive; maybe stop at the little pub and have something to eat on his own. He knew that it was a bit selfish to let Laura down, but he honestly couldn't recall her mentioning going out and he really didn't want to be around her right now.

"Just going for a pint with some friends from work." Jim replied coolly. "I'll see you later."

Laura felt her heart sink as Jim took his keys and left the house. How much longer were they going to go on like this? She called up to Keeley to ask if she wanted to go for meal but, unsurprisingly, Keeley already had plans of her own. Laura fumbled about in the freezer for a microwavable meal-for-one, cooked it in eight minutes, peeled back the film lid and, realising she had no appetite, promptly tossed it straight into the bin. She poured a glass of water instead and carried it up to her bedroom. Her phone blinked with a new message and she was pleased to see Evan had texted her.

Laura hadn't really spoke to him much since their run. Work

was always so busy, and he'd taken a few half-day's leave this week, but whenever they passed in the office, Evan had referenced their agreement to work out together. Laura felt a little bit uncomfortable, just because of the way her relationship was with Jim. Despite it being perfectly innocent, Laura was mindful that she didn't want to add any more fuel to the fire, but, feeling lonely and rejected, she saw Evan's casual text about when she fancied a run and she replied straight away. Keeley didn't need her, Jim didn't want her, it would be nice to have company for once.

·

Chapter 11

Dana was relieved that Jim and Laura Burbridge had declined her invitation. Dana thought Laura was nice, but Jim made her feel uncomfortable. She had insisted to Barry that they invite the neighbours out of courtesy. As much as Jim had annoyed Dana, they had to live next-door to them and Dana was worried that Barry was going out of his way to wind Jim up after Jim had deleted his post.

Dana carried the bag of shopping through to the kitchen and unpacked the M & S meal deal. She was glad it was Friday. It had been a long week and her early shifts were gruelling. It had been Barry's turn to have his kids last weekend and, as lovely as they were, Dana found these alternative busy weekends exhausting. She was looking forward to a quiet night in with Barry; some nice food, wine and an early night.

She reached for her phone to send him a quick text message. Dana had expected him to be home by now, but, knowing Barry, he'd probably stopped off at The Crown for one. He could look out if he thought he was staying there all night, Dana thought to herself.

Footsteps upstairs interrupted her thoughts and Dana realised Jordan must be home. She called up to him and, moments later, he came bouncing down the stairs in a cloud of aftershave.

"Phew!" She gasped, laughing. "You smell nice. Got a date?"

Jordan leaned down and gave his mother a quick kiss on the

cheek in greeting. He flashed her a toothy grin in response. "With looks like these? Of course!"

Dana smiled. He was a handsome lad, her Jordan. She just wished he would take as much interest in his school work as he did in his social life.

"Who's the lucky girl?" Dana asked, secretly hoping it wouldn't be any of the friends of his latest ex-girlfriend. She'd had bad experiences with upset girls turning up because Jordan sometimes lacked sensitivity when switching girlfriends.

"She's from Finchester." Jordan said, walking into the kitchen and rifling through the items she'd just unpacked. He popped open a packet of prawn crackers and Dana slapped his hand away.

"They're for me and Barry." Dana warned him, reaching into the cupboard and passing him a packet of crisps instead. "Finchester school. How did you meet her?"

"Online." Jordan accepted the crisps and hopped up onto the stool. "We're going to the cinema and for food."

"A group of you?" Dana asked, quickly putting the food away before Jordan saw something else he fancied. "Or just you and …?"

"Felicity." Jordan answered. "Yeah, just the two of us. I'm going to have to go in a minute or I'll miss the bus."

"What time will you be home?" Dana asked.

"Last bus?" Jordan looked questioningly at Dana, but she nodded in agreement.

"Just phone me if you miss it." She said sternly.

Jordan gave her a hug and headed out. Dana smiled to herself. It wasn't often that they had the house completely to themselves. She decided to switch the hot tub on in the hope that Barry would fancy a late-night dip.

He still hadn't responded to her text message, she realised, and walked back into the kitchen to retrieve her phone. Before she could reach it, she heard his car pull up onto the drive and Dana felt a little flutter of pleasure at a night alone with her love. She stretched up to the cupboard to fetch two wineglasses when she heard the front door open.

"Hello!" Barry boomed, and Dana went out to greet him.

"Hey sexy!" Dana called. "Guess who's got the house to-"

Her words died on her lips as she saw Barry was accompanied by Tyler and Chloe. She felt her heart sink, but quickly pulled her lips into a welcoming smile.

"Hi!" She greeted the children. "This is a nice surprise!"

"Hi Dana." Tyler smiled politely, kicking off his trainers and walking through to the living room.

Chloe held her iPhone up to Dana. "Dana, it's out of battery! Can you charge it?"

"Yes, of course, love," Dana took the phone from Chloe. "Where's your charger?"

"It's broke." Chloe followed Dana into the kitchen and climbed up onto a stool. "My mum won't get me a new one. She says I don't look after them."

Chloe pulled a face and looked at her father expectantly.

"I'll get you a new one tomorrow." Barry ruffled her dark hair affectionately.

Dana shot him a look. Barry was always winding Lindsey, his ex-wife, up by spoiling the kids and going against her wishes. Dana was fed up of having to act as a go-between. She replaced the wine glasses back in the cupboard and pulled out some tumbler glasses and a coffee mug instead.

"Are you staying for dinner?" She asked Chloe, assuming Barry had picked them up from afterschool club as Lindsey was stuck in traffic or running late.

Barry took the glasses from Dana and started to pour drinks for the kids.

"Coffee for you?" He asked Dana, before explaining. "Lindsey's away tonight. Last minute invite."

"Oh right," Dana tried to not look annoyed. "You didn't say. I would have got something in for the kids to eat."

"She only texted this afternoon," Barry gave Dana an apologetic look. "Her babysitter let her down or something."

This wasn't the first time Lindsey's "babysitter had let her down", Dana thought to herself crossly. She'd always planned her life around Dave's weekend with Jordan and wouldn't have dreamed of throwing in all the last-minute changes that Lindsey did. Dana thought that Barry should be firmer with Lindsey. Barry never changed his weekends making his plans around the kids, although Dana noted that he did sometimes "nip" to the pub after they'd gone up to bed, leaving Dana in charge. If Jordan was home, Barry would encourage Dana to come, but Dana didn't like to put the responsibility on Jordan and would always decline.

"I thought you said we could go out for dinner." Chloe had hopped down, investigated the contents of the fridge and, finding them lacking, was regarding her dad with her puppy-dog eyes.

"Is that ok with you?" Barry realised that he might have infringed on Dana's own plans and shot her a hopeful look.

Dana regarded the Chinese meal deal regretfully, before turning her attention to Barry. The meal would keep until tomorrow and it wasn't the poor kids' fault. She should be grateful that Barry was a good man, who wanted to be an active part of his children's lives.

"Of course," She pasted on a cheery smile. "What does everyone fancy?"

They ended up going to a local pizza restaurant. Dana gritted her teeth and tried to enjoy herself and the greasy pizza. She kept up a stream of interested chat with Tyler and Chloe. She was well-schooled in their interests and Barry relaxed, browsing through his phone while Dana kept them entertained.

Dana had watched Barry texting on his phone and intuitively knew that he was planning on "popping" to the pub later. She'd seen Gary's name flash up on his screen and there was no way they were talking about work at this hour on a Friday. She felt a knot of annoyance tighten in her stomach, but, being an eternal optimist, Dana decided to confront the issue head on.

"You're not planning on going out tonight, are you?" She reached across the table and touched Barry's hand casually to get his attention.

He glanced up surprised. "Oh, I thought maybe we could pop out for one if Jordan was home?"

Dana pulled a regretful face. "He's out late tonight. New girlfriend. I said he could catch the last bus home"

Barry looked expectantly at Dana. This is where she would usually offer to watch the kids.

"Steph has asked me to meet up with her," Dana fibbed, ignoring Barry's gaze. "Unless you want me to mind the kids?"

"Oh, no!" Barry's face fell, but he would never expect Dana to drop her own plans for him. "You go ahead. I didn't realise you'd made plans."

"I hadn't." Dana fixed him with a smile. "I was going to see Steph tomorrow, but I've got us one of those meal deals you like. We'll have a cosy night in tomorrow instead."

Barry recognised that Dana was firmly telling him that he was forbidden to make plans tomorrow and he grinned at her assertiveness and offered her a jokey salute.

"Hot tub is on, so you and the kids can have a dip when I'm out if you fancy." Dana informed him.

Barry took Dana's hand in his as they walked back to the car. She smiled up at him.

"Sorry about throwing this on you," He said quietly. "I didn't realise you'd made plans for us."

"It's fine!" Dana waved her free hand dismissively. "It can't be helped. I'm just gutted to be missing out on having an empty house with the love of my life."

Barry wrapped his arms around Dana, dipped her theatrically to the floor and kissed her on the lips as he did.

"Urgh! Dad!" Tyler shook his head disapprovingly. "You're too old for that!"

They all laughed at this as they climbed back into Barry's oversized 4x4. Dana had sent Steph a quick text to see if she was free and Steph had responded that she was. Dana asked Barry to drop her off at Steph's house and they would walk over to the pub together.

"Oh!" Chloe looked disappointed when Barry stopped the car at the entrance to Steph's cul-de-sac. "Why aren't you coming home with us, Dana?"

"I won't be long." Dana felt a pang of guilt that she'd made plans when Chloe was looking forward to spending time with her. "I'm just seeing my friend, Steph."

"What if Dad goes to the pub?" Chloe asked, looking concerned.

Barry laughed and playfully tapped Chloe on the legs. "I'm not going to leave you!"

Barry's reaction was quick, but Dana had seen a shadow of guilt cross his face at Chloe's comment. Her heart went out to Barry. He was a good man and a great father, but maybe he did need to hear that from Chloe. It had crossed Dana's mind, on more than one occasion, that Barry spent an increasingly large amount of time at the pub. Not that there was anything wrong with being sociable, Dana thought to herself, as she waved goodbye to Barry and the kids. Goodness, she'd spent enough time at her old local when she lived over the other side of Little Cedars and she'd first split up with Dave. Barry and Dana had spent the best part of their relationship at pubs and restaurants. Dana had just assumed that once they had bought the house together, they would stay in a bit more together, whereas, if anything, Barry seemed to be going to The Crown even more regularly; after work, on the weekends, sometimes even popping in at lunchtime if he was in the area. He didn't drink a lot at home, so that wasn't the problem. Dana thought back to the recycling she'd put out this morning; the three wine bottles were almost all her doing and there were relatively few empty cans belonging to Barry. Dana knew that it wasn't the amount Barry was drinking that was concerning her; she just didn't want to get to a point where they got into the habit of taking each other for granted and spending more time apart than together.

Dana knew that this had been the downfall of her marriage to Dave. They'd spent more and more time socialising separately until eventually they had felt like strangers living in the same house. She would speak to Barry, she told herself as she knocked on the door to Steph's house. She just needed to work out what she wanted to say, so she didn't sound like she was making a fuss over nothing.

Steph's daughter, Kendall, answered the door to Dana. She was a pretty girl with long red curls and big, expressive blue eyes. Dana always insisted that she was the image of Steph, but Steph would wave away Dana's comments.

"She's just got my colouring," Steph would insist. "I was never that pretty. Or skinny."

"Hi!" Kendall swung the door open. "My mum's just getting ready. Come in."

Dana stepped over the clutter of coats, bags and shoes that were dumped in the hallway. Someone (Darren, most likely) had left a box of protein powder at the bottom of the stairs and Dana struggled to squeeze through into the kitchen-diner at the back of the house.

Dana was surprised to see Darren stood in the kitchen, buttering slices of bread.

"Hi Darren." She greeted him. "How are you?"

Darren finished what he was doing and dumped two plates of chips and sausages onto the table.

"I've just done the kids dinner," He said, looking a little flustered. "Come into the living room."

Darren called the children down for their dinner and walked through to the living room with Dana. Dana tried to hide her surprise at Darren being home on a Friday night and displaying any domestic skills at all. In all the years Dana had known the couple, she'd never seen him do so much as empty the dishwasher. Dana glanced around at the organised chaos of the Rees' living room, looking for somewhere to sit.

Darren hurriedly moved a basket full of clean, folded laundry from an armchair onto the floor.

"Sorry about the mess," He grimaced. "You pair off to the pub?"

Dana was puzzled by Darren's behaviour. Firstly, he was cooking dinner and suddenly, after knowing the family for years, he was acting embarrassed about Dana seeing an untidy house. Steph had never been tidy. The house was always clean, but there was always a jumble of belongings everywhere. It didn't bother Dana. Dana had wondered, when she first befriended Steph, how Steph could bear to live in such disorder. Dana liked her own home immaculate, with everything in its right place, but she quickly realised that Steph's home was a comfortable sanctuary that reflected Steph's scatty-but-homely personality.

"Yes," Dana replied, reaching down to smooth the head of the Rees' little terrier. "It was a shame we all didn't get a chance to catch up properly last night. Barry says you managed to pop over after."

Darren nodded his head and continued to fuss about tidying. They fell into an awkward silence and Dana was racking her brain to think of new conversation openers when Steph came into the room.

"Sorry to keep you." Steph smiled at Dana warmly.

"You look lovely, Steph." Dana appraised her friend.

Steph's red hair was loose around her shoulders and she was wearing a cream chiffon blouse over dark jeans and ankle boots. Steph rarely wore make-up, but Dana could see she had accentuated her features with full shaded brows and a brown liner. Her usually pale lips were a creamy shade of pink.

Darren glanced up from the papers he was stacking and did a double-take.

"You do look nice," He agreed, looking pleased. "You've got make-up on."

Steph flushed a little and ignored his comment. "You sure you're not going out?"

"Yes," Darren sounded annoyed now as if they'd already had this conversation. "Ol's off out now. I'm hardly going to leave Kendall on her own."

Steph looked hesitant. "Well, phone me if anything changes."

"Nice to see you, Darren." Dana said politely and followed Steph out of the room.

As they left the house, Dana gave Steph a curious look, waiting for Steph to fill her in on whatever had happened to cause Darren to help around the house and 'babysit' on a Friday night and Steph to wear make-up.

"Good day?" Steph asked, ignoring Dana's questioning stare.

"Same old," Dana shrugged. "What about you?"

"Not bad," Steph replied. "Sorry if Darren was a bit weird."

"Has something happened?" Dana asked, slipping her arm into Steph's companionably.

"Why do you ask?" Steph glanced at Dana, but her lips turned up into a slight smile as if she found Dana's interest amusing. "Because I'm wearing make-up? Or because Darren's actually made dinner for the kids and is staying in on a Friday night?"

Dana laughed at Steph's response. "Yes! Both!"

Steph's expression turned serious. "I went to the make-up

counter in town today and paid a fortune for a stack of stuff I'd never heard of. If I'm going to be a divorced, unemployed, middle-aged woman, I at least want to be a bit less frumpy."

"What?!" Dana stopped dead and turned to face Steph. "You're getting a divorce? What happened?"

"Oh, no, nothing like that," Steph interjected quickly. "We haven't talked about it. I've just had enough."

Dana listened to Steph explaining how Darren had been out until 11.30pm after insisting he had to stay in work, how she felt that he didn't want to spend any time with her and then, the piece-de-resistance, how she'd seen a picture of his car on the 'Oak Village Community' page the other week when he was meant to be in work, solidifying her fears that he was, once again, up to no good.

Steph was still talking as they walked into the pub and Dana let her continue; she clearly had a lot of things that she wanted to get off her chest. Steph paused at the door to The Crown and turned to face Dana.

"I know what you're thinking." Steph smiled sadly. "Why now?"

Dana opened her mouth to deny it, but then nodded.

"Sorry," Dana said, genuinely meaning it. She felt awful, as if she had been judging Steph for staying with Darren. "It's not my business. I just care about you."

"I know." Steph pulled Dana towards her and hugged her friend. When they broke apart, Steph pushed the door to the pub open. "Let's get a drink first."

When they were seated with their drinks, Steph tried to explain that there had been no big argument or confrontation. She had simply seen what she'd been trying so hard to avoid since the kids were small; Darren didn't want to be with her. He was happy to have a mother to his kids and a wife at home, but he didn't care about her. Steph had tossed and turned all night, tormenting herself with 'if's' and 'but's' until she'd reached the conclusion that she could torment herself with the past all she wanted, but it wouldn't change anything. For the first time in years, Steph felt motivated. She had put on a lot of weight after having Ollie and had suffered with awful post-natal depression. Both had dramatically impacted her confidence and Darren had gradually lost interest in her until the suspicion and then the whispers started. For so long, Steph had been so terrified of being on her own that she had buried her head in the sand, but she was done now. When Dana had texted her to ask about going out, Steph had made her first step in her new life by texting Darren and telling (yes, telling!) him that he needed to be home to feed the kids as she was off out. Darren had been so surprised by this out-of-character behaviour that he had agreed without any argument or excuses about work.

"And that's the thing," Steph admitted, sipping her drink thoughtfully. "Darren's not a bad guy. He never argues with me. Anything I ask for, he's always been happy to go along with. I feel like I choose to be a doormat."

"You don't!" Dana cut in defensively.

Steph smiled gratefully at Dana. "Thank you. You are such a loyal friend, but I do. If Darren doesn't enjoy my company, that's not his fault. God, Dana, I don't even enjoy my company most days."

"Well, I do!" Dana said loyally, meaning every word. "You're funny and kind. It's his loss."

Steph shrugged, her face falling a little. "I'm not going to pack my bags and run off. I'm just ready to take my life in my own hands. Starting with getting a life of my own."

"Good on you," Dana clinked her glass with Steph's. "Anyone would be lucky to have you and it's about time you realised that."

Steph felt lucky to have a friend as genuine and supportive as Dana.

"Anyway," Steph picked up her purse. "Let's get some more drinks and we can talk about something else. I'm bored of thinking about myself!"

Dana laughed and gratefully accepted the wine that Steph brought back to the table.

"What else are you planning then?" Dana asked when Steph was sat back down. Dana was delighted that Steph was making a positive step to be happy, after years of prioritising everyone else.

"I need to get a job." Steph said decisively. "I think it'll be good for my confidence and it'll mean Darren will have to take more responsibility for the kids."

"What do you fancy doing?" Dana leaned forward in her seat interested in what Steph had to say.

"I don't know," Steph admitted, wrinkling her nose. "I haven't worked since I was pregnant with Ollie."

"You could always re-train." Dana suggested.

"I just want to get started," Steph told her friend. "While I feel like this. If I think about things too much, I'll end up over-thinking and put myself off."

"That's a good point." Dana agreed. Dana could imagine that it would be overwhelming to go back into the working world after so long out of it.

"I saw some posts online about jobs in the village." Steph said hesitantly, glancing up shyly at Dana.

Dana nodded encouragingly for Steph to continue. She was hoping that Steph wasn't referring to Kelly Russell's network marketing venture. Dana didn't want to pour cold water on the flames of Steph's renewed confidence, but she wasn't sure if Steph would enjoy working on her own or had the resilience just yet for hustling people for leads. Dana knew that there were a lot of knockbacks in Kelly's line of work.

"Definitely something where you're working with people," Dana tried to steer Steph away from the idea of anything that had the potential to fail. "The school would be perfect for you. You're so good with people and you'd enjoy it."

"I'll probably have a look this weekend." Steph trailed off, as if she sensed Dana's reservations. She had seen several posts about self-employed opportunities that seemed to be posted by the same woman, who Steph vaguely recognised, but she knew intuitively that Dana would try to talk her out of this.

Dana took her phone out of her bag. She didn't want Steph to lose her enthusiasm. "Let's have a look."

Dana shifted her chair so that they were sat side-by-side and they scrolled through the "Oak Village Community" page.

"Is this it?" Dana asked, trying to keep her tone upbeat and positive as she found a post from Kelly Russell.

Steph regarded the post and, not wanting to look foolish or naive, shook her head. "No, I don't think I'd be great at that."

Dana scrolled further down the page, but there were no adverts for job opportunities, just complaints about traffic, teenagers and dogs.

"Oh!" Steph pointed to the latest post, keen to change the subject. "What's this one about?"

Dana clicked on the post. It had only been posted within the last hour and was a photo of a large brown and black dog.

"Found! Female German Shepherd running loose in Conifer Way." Dana read aloud. It looked a bit like Gary's dog. She scrolled through the comments and established quickly that it was indeed, and he'd been notified and had collected her. That should have been the end of the post, surely, but Dana saw that several of the serial-posters had commented on how irresponsible Gary was.

"Not the first time!" Angela Hanigan had commented. "These dogs are aggressive. Hope the owner secures this animal properly before someone is hurt."

"Can't comment on the individual animal," Sharon Morgan had replied. "But I agree, Angela. Only a matter of time until somebody gets hurt. I suggest that the next person to find this stray dog calls the warden rather than post, please. Only way irresponsible owner will take heed. Admin- please delete future posts!"

"That's a bit harsh," Dana grimaced. "She's quite a friendly dog."

"I'm glad there wasn't anything like this around when we were younger," Steph shook her head slowly in disbelief at some of the comments. "Could you imagine people actually being this passive-aggressive to their neighbours' faces?"

Dana completely agreed with Steph. "It really does seem to bring out the worst in some people."

"Your party will be on here next week," Steph joked and put on a posh voice. "Please could number 28 Sycamore remember that they live in a middle-class area and therefore turn the music off and return their guests to the drawing room for canapes. Some of us have Pilates and Polo in the morning."

Dana grinned at Steph's impersonation of a disgruntled resident. "Barry would wipe the floor with anyone who dared to complain. He's still reeling about his post being censored."

"I'm surprised he hasn't started his own rival page," Steph said flippantly. "It's not like Barry to take that lying down."

"I'm trying to encourage him to be the bigger person," Dana admitted. "Jim's pushed quite a lot of Barry's buttons. I don't know how much longer Barry will keep schtum. The attic conversion will be the real test."

"Is that still scheduled for after Christmas?" Steph asked.

"Yes, and I can't wait. We seem to be having the kids more and more often," Dana sighed and then added hurriedly.

"Which is great, of course. It's just taking me time to adjust to having a houseful."

Steph tried to draw out Dana's feelings further, but Dana remained tight-lipped on the subject, feeling she was being disloyal if she complained about Barry or the kids at all. Steph gave up, respectful of Dana's privacy and confident that Dana had whatever was on her mind in hand.

"Fingers crossed that we'll both have everything sorted in the new year," Steph clinked her glass with Dana's in a toast. "New job, new life for me and a shiny new bedroom and no more neighbourhood disputes for you!"

"I'll drink to that!" Dana took a large sip of her wine and found herself crossing her fingers under the table for luck.

Chapter 12

Laura couldn't wait to get back to work. The period between Christmas and New Year always felt like living in a limbo, and combined with the over-indulgence of food and drink, Laura usually felt a little out-of-sorts and listless. This year had been much worse than usual though and Laura felt like she was going stir-crazy. It didn't help that all her usual fitness classes were cancelled this week as people spent time with their loved ones in front of festive television or at the pub. Even the leisure centre was running reduced opening hours this week, so Laura was limited to when she could get out of the house.

The atmosphere, at home, had been fraught as always. After two months of living in a perpetual stand-off, neither of them making any progress, Laura felt permanently exhausted and drained. Even the daily exercise that had always kept her feeling upbeat and energised couldn't counteract the overwhelming tiredness that Laura felt every day from the moment she opened her eyes.

Keeley had finally confessed that she had a boyfriend and was constantly out with him or her group of friends. This had been a point of contention for Jim, whereas Laura was firmly on Keeley's side, furthering the divide between them. Laura suspected that Jim was standing his ground purposely to be contrary to Laura. If she said something was black, she imagined that he would insist it were white, such were their differences lately.

The only saving grace had been Laura's increased efforts in her social life. Laura had neglected her friends over the years; pouring all her efforts into her home life, partially due to the guilt of juggling a full-time job alongside motherhood. Laura had reached out to some of her friends and made sure that she accepted any invitations that she would usually have declined. She even had an invitation to a New Year's Eve party at an old colleague's. Jim had never been fussed on the hype of New Year and they had always stayed in together, preferring a nice meal in the comfort of their own home. Laura hadn't even asked him what his plans were this year. The final straw, for her, had been when he hadn't bought her even a token gift for Christmas.

Laura stretched out against the low wall at the end of her drive as she thought back to the hurt she had felt when the day had passed, and it had become evident that he had bought her nothing. Laura felt a surge of anger rush through her veins at just the memory of the humiliation of realising that the cashmere scarf and perfume set that she had stumbled upon while she was looking for somewhere to hide yet another bag of surprise gifts she'd bought Keeley, were either for somebody else or Jim had had a change of heart and coldly returned them.

Laura had felt a rush of happiness when she found the gifts and had quickly tucked them back into the department store paper bag. She had wondered if this would be a turning point; Jim's way of bridging the gap that had grown between them. Laura had rushed back out into the bustling crowds in the town centre. The beautiful, expensive gifts Jim had bought her made her feel cheap and thoughtless for just getting him an impersonal new electric razor (on offer from Boots) and a hardback autobiography of a golfer he admired. She'd spent hours deliberating over the right gift; something that was tasteful and personal.

Laura finished her stretches and launched off into a quick jog, feeling the memory of her embarrassment and her subsequent fury fuel her on.

It had taken her hours of hunting to find a golf sweater, but even that hadn't felt enough next to the effort Jim had gone to for her. Laura had spent hours online, scouring the internet for something that was just right. Eventually, she thought she'd found the perfect gift: a rare vinyl record of a little-known band he had loved when they'd met in college. Laura had been delighted with the find and had been adamant that Christmas would be the day that they were both able to bury the hurt and the distance of the last few months. She'd even developed a thicker skin in the week before Christmas, telling herself that she was being over-sensitive to Jim's blunt, cool responses to her attempts at conversation. It was all going to be fine, she had been sure of it. Those two thoughtful gifts said everything she needed to hear from her husband.

Laura felt her anger build and she quickened her pace; welcoming the stretch and pull on her muscles as she ran the familiar route down to the river crossing.

She could vividly picture Jim's unappreciative glance at the gifts she'd poured so much effort into. He'd placed them quickly on the table next to him, as if she'd presented him with a multipack of socks.

"I didn't think we were doing presents." He'd told her with a cross expression as if she were the one in the wrong and her thoughtful gifts were a passive-aggressive attempt to make him feel bad.

Keeley had seen the fleeting look of hurt and confusion across her mother's face, despite Laura composing herself quickly, and had rushed off to her bedroom, returning with an armload of gifts that she'd lovingly chosen for her parents.

Laura had felt a rush of love for Keeley's thoughtfulness and had expressed her delight at the toiletries and pyjamas Keeley had chosen her. Jim had displayed slightly more appreciation for the mug and socks that Keeley had bought him. Laura thought she might have lost her temper then and there if he'd dared be as rude and unappreciative to his daughter as he had been to her.

It had been a turning point for Laura. She had accepted Gina's New Year's invitation the next day and was biding her time until Jim bought up the subject of a separation. Laura knew Jim well enough to know that if she raised the subject, he would play the victim and dig his heels in over the possession of the house. He needed to be the one to raise this and Laura knew that it was only a matter of time.

She reached the bridge a lot faster than she had intended, she realised, and consciously slowed her pace to prevent her from burning out too fast.

"Hey!"

Laura turned towards the source of the voice calling her; her mouth turning up into a welcoming smile.

Evan Russell, kitted out in brand-new Christmas running gear, lengthened his strides to reach her.

"What kept you?" Laura joked, bouncing on the spot to keep her blood pumping.

Evan glanced at the new fit-bit on his wrist. "I'm on time.

You're early."

Laura's eyes travelled over his outfit and smart new watch. "Wow, you look the part."

Evan usually ran in old football shorts and a t-shirt.

He grinned at her sheepishly. "Santa clearly knew I'd been a good boy all year."

Laura laughed and, without waiting for him, set off on their usual route at medium pace. Evan quickly caught up with her and they ran for several minutes along the riverbank in companionable silence. Laura focussed on her breathing, letting her stressed mind go blank and her senses take over. The branches, overhead, were bare this time of year, but the foliage that bordered the footpath was still an abundance of green. The only sounds, except the pounding of their feet on the mud path, were the chatter and rustle of birds in the thick bushes and the steady gurgle of the river.

"Good Christmas?" Evan asked conversationally after they'd comfortably put away their first kilometre.

"Lovely," Laura lied. "How about you?"

"Yeah," Evan replied, not breaking stride. "Kids loved it. Just got to pay for it now."

"Looking forward to going back to work?" Laura asked, expecting him to laugh.

"Is it awful if I say yes?" Evan grimaced.

They had reached the gate which took them away from the river and up a small incline adjacent to the woods. They both stopped, but instead of quickly hopping over and continuing at a slow jog up the hill, Evan stretched out against the gate; his muscular arm against the top post preventing Laura from climbing over.

Laura turned to face Evan. "No, I feel the same."

"Things still not great?" Evan gave her a sympathetic look.

Laura and Evan had developed something of a companionship since they had started running together in October. At first, they mainly ran in silence and any conversation centred on fitness and milestones. They were now running between two and three times a week together and, as Evan's fitness had increased to allow him to comfortably hold a conversation without struggling to breathe, they had moved on to more personal topics like their children and their home lives. Laura, essentially a deeply private person, had had one too many prosecco's at the Christmas party and had confided, with a little encouragement from Evan, that her relationship was a little rocky. Laura had been embarrassed about mentioning it to Evan when he'd brought it up on their next run, but he was a great listener and Laura had found herself opening-up to him.

"Not the best," Laura gave him a wry smile. "I'm sure it'll all work out."

Evan straightened up from his stretch and touched Laura's shoulder gently. She looked up, surprised at the gesture, and Evan hurriedly dropped his hand back to his side.

"Do you want to talk about it?" He asked.

Laura shook her head. "Not really. Thanks though."

Evan waited for Laura to cross the barrier and followed her over. They jogged up the hill in silence before Evan spoke again.

"Are you going to the New Year's party at The Crown?" He asked breathing a little heavily now.

Laura heeded that he was struggling slightly with the incline and deliberately slowed down. He hadn't been running for as long as she had and, although he was doing great, she was conscious of not pushing him too hard.

"No," She replied. "I'm going to a party at a friend's. Are you and Kelly going?"

"Maybe." Evan said. "My mum has offered to babysit, but she's had the kids every year since Jacob was born. I thought it would be nice if she went to the pub with Kelly or did something with her mates."

"Ah," Laura smiled at his consideration towards his widowed mother. "That's nice of you. She probably likes having the kids and helping you out."

"She loves it," Evan admitted. "I just worry about her building her whole life around the kids. My sister lives in Scotland, so she rarely sees her kids, and mine are growing up that quickly that they won't need babysitting soon. I don't want her sat around feeling lonely."

"Do you think she would be interested in meeting someone?" Laura asked, interested. Evan had talked about his mother before and, from what Laura could gather, she was still reasonably young in her early sixties.

"I don't know," Evan replied. "I want to suggest it, but she wouldn't want to discuss meeting men with her son, would she?"

Laura thought about this for a moment and turned her head to look at Evan. "Maybe Kelly could speak to her. They get on, don't they?"

Evan pulled a face. "They get on, but they're not close. Kelly just drops the kids to my mum and runs off to do whatever she's out doing all day. Kelly doesn't worry about what my mother will do with her time when the kids are both teenagers, as long as she's here right now to suit her social life."

"Is that fair?" Laura asked cautiously. She didn't want to get into the dangerous territory of slagging off another man's wife. Laura still had occasional pangs of guilt about their secret running meetings, and they were perfectly innocent. "Kelly works. It must be hard juggling both, and your mother clearly loves having the kids."

Evan had the decency to look shame-faced. "I'm not having a go. I know that she does the majority of the running around after the kids and it's not that she takes advantage of my mother purposely. It's just hard to talk to Kelly. She's such a whirlwind that she only hears what she wants. I've tried to talk to her about so many things…"

He trailed off as if lost in his own thoughts and Laura felt a pang of empathy for him.

"I understand," Laura said quickly as they simultaneously increased their speed now they had reached the flat. "Jim is the same. I just want to resolve all this, but I swear he hears what he wants."

"It's hard," Evan agreed, sneaking a sideways glance at Laura. "Like all the money she spent over Christmas. I've lost track of the times I've asked her to respect our budget."

Laura was surprised at this. Her keen eye had already appraised that the new outfit he was wearing must have cost a good few hundred pounds, and that was without the top-of-the-range Fitbit he was sporting.

"It's nice that she put all that thought into your gifts though." Laura commented, feeling a twinge of envy that at least he was cared about.

Evan sensed there was something underlying Laura's words and he kept his eyes firmly on her reaction as he replied. "They're lovely. Really thoughtful. It's not that I don't know how lucky I am, it's just we're a little over-stretched financially and I'll still be paying this off next Christmas."

"I see what you mean then," She said. "Sorry if I sounded like I was being judgemental."

"Not at all," Evan waved away her apology. "It was me being whiney. What did you have for Christmas anyway?"

"Just bits and bobs," Laura said casually. "We don't really go in for presents anymore."

"That's probably a sensible idea." Evan nodded.

They reached the top of the road to Finchester, which is where they usually turned back, and automatically slowed to a walk.

"I'm dying of thirst," Evan commented, eyeing up the pub a few hundred yards ahead of them. "Have you got time to stop or do you need to get back?"

"I've got time," Laura nodded, but held up her empty hands to him. "I think you're forgetting that we don't have the means to pay."

"We're runners," Evan winked at her. "We'll open a tab and leg it."

Laura laughed at this and went to turn back, but Evan pulled a crumpled banknote from a hidden zip pocket in his top.

"Oh, go on then." She responded to his infectious grin. It wasn't as if she had anything else to do.

"Shall we have a proper drink?" Evan asked eyeing up the beer pumps, once they were inside.

"We've got to run back!" Laura protested. "Just water for me."

"We don't *have* to run. We could stagger." Evan joked, pausing to see if he could convince Laura. "It's happy hour somewhere. And it's still technically Christmas."

Laura smiled at his persistence. It sounded like he was having a tough time too. Maybe he could do with the company. "Just a half for me, then."

Evan paid for their drinks and they settled down onto a window seat facing the woods.

"I don't think I'll feel like running after this." Evan admitted taking a large sip of his pint.

"Nor me," Laura replied. "I was struggling a little today. I need to get back into my routine."

"You didn't look like you were struggling," Evan insisted. "I was though; that last mile was a killer."

"Did you sign up to any of those races that I sent you links for?" Laura asked, shifting over a little on the bench seat so she could stretch her legs out under the table. Her foot brushed Evan's and she pulled it away hurriedly.

Evan pretended not to notice Laura's foot brushing his and he took another sip of his drink before replying. "I haven't yet. I want to do a half-marathon though. It's going to be one of my new year resolutions."

"What other resolutions are you making?" Laura asked thoughtfully. "Maybe I should make some this year."

"I haven't got anything else yet," Evan grinned. "I thought of the half-marathon and then I was too tired to think of any more."

Laura chuckled at that. "It's making me tired thinking about it. I've signed up for two. The first one is in March, so I really need to get serious about training."

"Is this not serious training?" Evan looked alarmed. "You're the fittest person I know! If you're not ready, then there's no way I can do one."

"No way!" Laura shook her head. "I do a lot of classes, but they're more for fun because I have no life. You've made amazing progress already. You'll be fine."

"Do you think?" Evan regarded her sceptically. "I definitely need to run more."

"Well, you've got all the gear now," Laura smiled. "I was thinking of joining a running club."

"A running club?" Evan repeated. "I like our running club."

"Well, it's very exclusive," Laura deadpanned. "There's one in Little Cedars. Someone shared a post to the Oak Village page. Did you see it?"

"I've had to stop looking at that page," Evan admitted with a grimace. "Some of the self-righteous people on there really wind me up."

"It can get a bit much," Laura agreed, sheepishly hoping he hadn't seen some of the sanctimonious tripe Jim posted in the forum. "There are some advantages to it though. Like I never forget when to put my recycling out and I always know that people heading in the other direction are sat in worse traffic than me!"

Evan laughed. "That's a good point. It'll be a nightmare for all of us though once they start work on that top road."

"I know," Laura nodded, thinking back to the latest community update that had advised that the powers-that-be had given the go-ahead for the road improvements to the Birch Grove to Little Cedars stretch. "That's if they happen. There's been talk of a protest."

"I had heard." Evan said. "It's a difficult one, isn't it? Something needs to be done, but the alternative is to lose all this."

He gestured out of the window to the beautiful green scenery around them.

Laura surveyed the scene thoughtfully. "It would be a shame. I don't really know which side to take."

"Really?" Evan frowned at her indecision. "Your husband

has been a pretty vocal supporter of the original suggestion."

"I thought you didn't read the Oak Village page." Laura teased, wanting to move the subject away from Jim's opinions.

Evan blushed a little and Laura was surprised that she found it oddly endearing.

"I've seen a few posts," He shrugged. "It's all Barry bangs on about."

"It seems to have taken over the majority of the Oak Villagers' conversations." Laura commented dryly. "Shall we both agree to stay neutral on it?"

"That sounds like a plan." Evan agreed enthusiastically. "So, are you going to abandon me for this running club?"

"We can still run together," Laura insisted. "I just need to up the amount I'm doing, and I'd rather not run alone. It's not too bad when it's light, but that's months away yet."

"I can come more regularly," Evan protested. "Just tell me when and I'll be there."

"It's late by the time you finish the gym," Laura tried to let him down gently. "I want to do at least four times a week."

"I can do the gym anytime," Evan shrugged. "Unless you don't want to?"

"No!" Laura exclaimed, a little too quickly. "I like running with you."

"It's settled then," Evan looked pleased. "Or we could even

go running straight from work."

"In Birch Grove?" Laura frowned, trying to get her head around the logistics.

Evan finished his pint and reached for Laura's empty glass. "Let's have another and we'll work out what days are best."

Laura had meant to decline. She liked Evan, but while they were both married, it seemed a little inappropriate to be making regular plans together. Still, he hadn't given her any impression that he wanted anything more than a friendship, and for all Laura knew his wife could be fine with their arrangement. Laura pictured Evan's glamourous young wife and smiled to herself at her own paranoid thoughts. Of course, Kelly Russell wouldn't mind handsome Evan running with a colleague. Laura was nowhere near as attractive as flirty, self-assured Kelly. Laura shook her head and suppressed her ridiculous thoughts.

Neither Evan nor Laura felt up to running after their liquid lunch, and they kept up a light chatter as they managed a brisk walk back to the village.

"Are you up to much for the rest of the day?" Laura asked conversationally as they drew closer to their parting point.

Evan glanced at Laura curiously, wondering if she was going to extend an invitation to him. Laura noticed the look and cursed herself in case she'd made it sound like she was giving him the come-on.

"I'm heading into town," Laura said quickly, not giving him time to answer. "More shopping."

Evan smiled politely. "I've got a few things to do this

evening, so I'll probably just spend a few hours with the kids."

Laura paused as they reached the entrance to Sycamore Street. Am I being weird? She wondered to herself. There seemed to be an awkward tension between them, as if Evan regretted crossing boundaries from running buddies to confidantes over drinks. Laura knew she tended to overthink and she pasted a friendly smile onto her face as she waved goodbye.

Evan broke into a quick jog the moment Laura disappeared out of view. He'd completely lost track of time and it would put his whole day out of sync.

What was I thinking? He thought to himself in frustration. He'd only meant to be out of the house for the usual forty-minute run, but he'd been enjoying Laura's uncomplicated company and had wanted to prolong the relaxed feeling. Before he knew it, their quick run had turned into two hours idling the time away at the River Tavern. He now had to come up with a credible excuse; Kelly would never believe he was capable of running for two hours and, even if she did, it would make his premeditated excuse of going to the gym that evening seem unbelievable. Evan's nerves were frayed with keeping up with the half-truths and fabrications that he'd started, even if he had started them with the best of intentions. Christmas had been strained enough as it was; Kelly developing suspicions about his whereabouts would only cause more stress.

Chapter 13

Darren waited for a gap in the traffic and spun his car across the road. A flashy BMW driver sounded their horn in annoyance at his risky manoeuvre and Darren flipped them a finger in response.

"Darren!" Steph gasped from the passenger seat.

"What?" He shot her an exasperated look of annoyance. "Do you want me to wait there all day?"

"It's hardly all day." Steph muttered quietly and turned her head to look out of her window, signalling that she had nothing more to add on the matter.

Darren fumed silently as he drove along the road to the motorway. Despite it being the Christmas holidays, there was a steady stream of traffic on the single carriageway, preventing Darren from being able to drive above 30 miles per hour.

"This road is a joke." Darren drummed his fingers against the steering wheel in frustration.

"It'll be even worse when the road works start." Steph commented dryly.

Darren thought that she was probably right, but he said nothing. Steph had gone from being timid and diffident to voicing opinions on everything from his driving to their holiday plans. Darren thought back to all the times he'd found himself frustrated at Steph's apathy over the years and wondered on the irony of being careful what you wished for. He couldn't pinpoint a particular change that had brought this on, but he was suffering the consequence as they were headed away to Steph's brother's house to spend the new year.

Ollie was sulking in the back of the car. The thought of spending three nights having to share a bedroom with his eleven-year-old cousin was almost unbearable and, to make matters worse, he was missing a New Year's Eve party at Jordan's. Keeley was still going, and Ollie was worried that one of the boys would make a move on her. If Keeley finished with him, it would be all his selfish parents' fault. Jordan had promised that his mother and step-father would be out at The Crown until the early hours, so Jordan's house party was guaranteed to be amazing. His parents were so thoughtless, Ollie fumed to himself. His dad didn't even want to go to stay with Uncle Andrew and his family. He should have just said no like he usually did to everything his mum suggested. Ollie didn't know what had been going on with his parents lately. His mum's family always invited them to stay, but they hadn't been for years as Darren always used work as an excuse. Ollie had overheard them having an argument about it and his dad had relented. Ollie hadn't overheard the whole conversation, but he'd felt a stab of panic that maybe his mother had finally wised up to his dad's philandering and it was all going to come spilling out. As much as they aggravated Ollie, he didn't want his parents splitting up. Ollie had felt on edge since one of the idiots at school had made a dig about seeing his dad parked up outside the leisure centre with a brunette in his car. Keeley had been with him, much to Ollie's mortification, and she'd urged Ollie to ignore the comment. He was the manager of the leisure centre, Keeley had reasoned, he was probably giving one of his employees a lift. Ollie had pretended to agree with Keeley, but he had already had doubts about the hours his dad kept and his blatant eye for the ladies. Ollie was almost certain that his dad had cheated on his mum in the past. He couldn't bear the thought of his sensitive, sweet mother being heartbroken. She had virtually no social life, other than their family, and Ollie didn't know how she'd cope. Ollie hadn't voiced his fears to anyone, not even Keeley. Keeley wouldn't understand. She was always moaning about her parents, but, then again, Keeley's dad was more embarrassing than Ollie's. It was one thing to be parked up with a woman in your car, Ollie thought, but it was another thing to be publicly falling out with half the village over trivial stuff like escaped dogs and disputes over the rightful owner of a recycling bin. There were a few people who used fake accounts to troll the local community groups that everyone's parents were members of. Keeley had got a fair bit of stick over some of the screenshots that kids in their school had passed around, but luckily, she was friendly with the popular sporty girls and they'd stuck up for her. She still got a little bit of ribbing over posts, but nothing compared to what someone less popular would have had to contend with. Keeley managed to laugh it off; it was fortunate that she was so easy-going. Ollie had felt pure rage when he'd been teased about his dad being with another woman. Ollie was usually quite laid-back, but he had a fierce temper when he did finally lose it. His dad used to joke that he must have inherited the red-headed rage from his mother without the actual hair colour. Ollie thought that that was a bit rich coming from his dad whose temper was a hundred times worse than his mild-mannered mother's. Ollie had seen his dad lose his cool over the most trivial events; he'd even been 'sent off' from spectating by the referee at one of Ollie's football games when he was younger.

"You're quiet." Steph remarked to Ollie, piercing his

thoughts.

Kendall had started up a stream of chatter as soon as they'd turned onto the motorway and Steph had just noticed that Ollie hadn't said a word, not even to complain that Kendall was annoying him.

"He's sulking," Kendall chipped in enthusiastically. "He thinks Keeley is going to run off with someone else at Jordan Jones' house party."

Ollie wished Kendall was closer in age to him, so he could punch her. She was freakishly intuitive about things like this to the point where he suspected that she knew the PIN code to his phone.

"Shut up." He hissed, glaring at his annoying little sister.

"What party is that?" Steph asked, turning around in her seat to look at her son. "Dana didn't mention a party. I thought she and Barry were going to the pub."

"There's no party," Ollie mumbled. "Kendall's full of-"

"That's enough!" Darren barked, cutting Ollie off. "Watch your mouth."

This is going well, Steph thought sarcastically to herself. They hadn't even been in the car half an hour and everyone was at each other's throats. What a joy this trip was going to be.

Darren felt his mood darken further as he churned the miles towards his brother-in-law's. He had agreed to this trip in a rare moment of agreeableness, or more accurately, a not-so-rare moment of guilt. Steph was always making him feel guilty; even when she didn't say anything. He had made plans for New Year's Eve, but Steph had insisted that he could go out any time. She'd even added "like you always do". Darren had declined the usual New Year gathering with his work colleagues in favour of a party at an old friend's, thirty minutes out of town. He had planned on bringing a friend and making a night of it. The work crowd had been disappointed, especially Gemma, who seemed to have developed a bit of a 'thing' for Darren.

He wasn't bad for his age. He had started to see his physical condition decline in his mid-thirties, but he'd made an effort to work twice as hard at the gym to keep the muscles and fight off the fat. His hairline had started receding, but he camouflaged it well with a permanent tan (courtesy of the sun beds) and a buzz cut. He probably got more attention from women now than he had when he had been in his physical prime at twenty. He put a lot of it down to confidence. He'd definitely grown more confident with the years, whereas Steph had seemed to go the other way.

He glanced at Steph from the corner of his eye and felt a stab of remorse for the way he treated her. He had been the one to pursue the quiet, curvy red-head back in their twenties. She could be such a good laugh, but she'd suffered heavily with depression after their happy-accident Ollie had been born and, for years, Darren had struggled to relate the attractive, quick-witted woman he'd fallen in love with to the slightly over-weight, passive wife pottering around their home. He would never leave her and the kids though. He loved Steph, in his own way, and her vulnerable fragility tugged on his heartstrings. He wanted to make her happy, but, now as he drove the family to their destination and he thought bitterly back to his plans-gone-to-waste, he wondered if maybe he was flogging a dead horse and had been for years.

Something lit up in the space between the car's handbrake and the car stereo catching Darren's attention. His keen eyes made out a name illuminated against the backlit screen of an iPhone resting in the central console between the driver and passenger seat. He felt a wave of panic rise from the pit of his stomach. He glanced to the side and, in a rare stroke of luck, Steph was oblivious to the received message; her face buried in a bag-for-life as she rooted around for whatever snack Kendall was demanding from the back seat. Darren discreetly shifted in his seat and reached forward to retrieve the phone. The moment his fingers closed around the soft, silicone case, he realised with a start that it was Steph's phone, not his. He withdrew his hand quickly, but not until he'd flipped the phone over, plunging the lit-up screen into darkness. He patted his own jacket pocket, feeling the reassuring weight of his own phone safely ensconced in its rightful place. He wondered if he'd read the name correctly in the darkness of the car. There was only one reason he could think of that she would text his wife. Darren could feel his heart rate increase as his body responded to the fight-or-flight alarm going off in his brain.

Shit, shit, shit. Darren tapped the steering wheel nervously. His head was fixed firmly looking straight ahead, but his eyes darted to the sides, waiting for Steph to pick up the phone and open the message. Darren tried to think rationally but reacting under pressure had never been his forte.

"Do you want a drink?" Steph's voice cut into his panic.

Darren was so caught up in his own thoughts that he had to ask her to repeat herself.

"Drink?" Steph said again, holding up a bottle of water.

"No thanks." Darren glanced away. He needed to do something quickly, but what?

Steph took a sip from the bottle of water before screwing the lid back on and placing the bottle in the cup holder between their seats. Darren watched her from the corner of his eye as her hand hung precariously close to the source of Darren's anxiety.

"Did I tell you about that protest?" Darren burst out suddenly. He'd meant to start a conversation to distract Steph from looking at her phone, but it had come out sounding loud and unnatural in his panic.

Steph regarded him with a frown of confusion but tried to look interested out of politeness.

"No," She replied. "I had heard a little bit from Dana, but we try not to talk about it as Barry is doing her head in with it all."

"What's Keeley's dad had to say about it?" Darren addressed Ollie in the back of the car. "He's pretty vocal online."

Ollie cringed. "I don't know. We're not all sat around talking about the village. We've got actual lives."

"Ollie!" Steph scolded him, worried that this would set Darren back off into his bad mood. "Don't be cheeky."

Darren laughed at his son's retort; grateful for a distraction. "He's right. All anyone at the pub talks about is who's slagging off who on the community group."

"It might be all fun and games," Steph said coolly. "But it'd be different if you were on the receiving end of some of those posts."

Darren frowned at her tone. Was there something specific she was referring to? His mind was whirring in overdrive. After some busybody had snapped his badly-parked car at the back of the flats, he'd been careful to check the page paranoid that he'd get another mention. This took him back to the matter at hand. Why the hell was she texting his wife?

With a jolt of realisation, Darren identified that they must have spoken before for Steph to have saved her number. He felt his skin prickle as he broke out in a sweat at the thought of the potential consequences. Steph had been acting strangely; a lot more assertive than she usually was lately. He needed to read that message. Forewarned was forearmed. He stared ahead, desperately racking his brain for an idea, but all coherent thought was lost in the swirling mists of panic that he was about to be rumbled. A sign for a service station flashed up and it came to Darren in a flash of genius. He said nothing as he swung the car onto the slip road and he was entering the car park before Steph had even noticed his detour.

"Why are we stopping?" She asked.

Andrew and his family were only an hour and a half away. The kids were old enough to sit out the journey without any toilet breaks.

Darren pulled into a parking space, switching the engine off and pocketing his keys and the phone simultaneously as he swung out of the car.

"Need a pee!" He called back crudely, not looking back as he swung the door closed behind him.

Darren dashed across the forecourt of the service station as quickly as he could; conscious of the added weight of Steph's phone feeling like it was burning a hole in his pocket. For a moment, he'd thought that she was going to notice and stop him. What would he have done then? He'd have had no choice but to laugh at his error and hand it over. He was half-expecting her to notice the missing phone and come charging after him. He didn't dare turn his head to look back at his family patiently waiting for him in the black Nissan Qashqai. It was only when he was inside the building and he had shut the cubicle door behind him in the privacy of the men's restrooms that he dared pull the phone out from safekeeping.

He pressed on the message notification and typed in the same PIN code Steph used for everything from their bank account to the house alarm. The phone unlocked and took him to a string of messages. His heart sank when he saw there had been a string of about eight messages going back to before Christmas, but as he scoured the content he exhaled in relief. He'd been adamant that she'd been messaging to cause trouble and was sticking her nose in to something that was none of her business, but he wasn't mentioned in any of these. From what Darren could make out, Steph had reached out to Tina Cleary via her online business page responding to an advert and they had exchanged numbers and moved the conversation over to texts to discuss Steph taking on some work for her.

Darren was still suspicious though of Tina's motives. Was she planning to say something? He would be furious if she was taking advantage of Steph and was really biding her time before she shared her opinions about Darren's occasional indiscretions. Darren leant against the door as he read back over the messages. He would have to play it by ear. He marked the message as 'unread' and returned to the car.

"Sorry," He grinned sheepishly as he drew his seatbelt across his broad chest. "I grabbed your phone then by mistake. You've got a message."

Steph took the phone from him, without saying anything, and read the message.

"Anything interesting?" Darren asked, trying to keep his voice light and casual.

"No." Steph shook her head. "Nothing interesting."

It was Darren's turn to feel confused now. He'd just seen the string of messages about Steph starting work after about fifteen years of being a stay-at-home parent. Surely this was the kind of conversation she'd want to share with him. Darren regarded his wife suspiciously. Steph caught a glimpse of his expression and hurriedly looked away. She had wanted to talk to Darren about her potential new job, but it felt like such a big step to her that she couldn't bear the thought of it falling apart and Darren pitying her. It felt nice to have plans of her own that didn't revolve around Darren or the kids, and she just wanted to nurse it to herself for a little longer.

Steph tapped out a brief reply to Tina. Steph didn't really know the woman that well, she wasn't even sure how old she was or whether she had kids, but she'd seen her around and, on occasions, serving behind the bar at The Crown. It was only when they'd exchanged a few messages that Steph had connected the owner of Sparkles Cleaning with the pretty, slim brunette from the pub.

It's funny, Steph mused to herself, that she'd seen Sparkles Cleaning advertised on local noticeboards, social media and had fliers through the door, but she'd never known that the friendly barwoman was also the face behind the pink bubble logo. Steph was already excited about the prospect of getting back into work and getting to know Tina better. It would be great to start having a purpose and earning a bit of money herself. Steph received an immediate reply to her message and responded with a date to meet up in the new year.

Ollie watched, from the back seat, as his mother accepted the phone wordlessly from his dad. His mum turned away and Ollie watched their body language intently. He could have sworn that his dad had picked that phone up deliberately. Ollie wasn't stupid; he'd seen the phone light up and his dad swiftly turn it face-down. He had taken the shady gesture as confirmation that his dad was receiving messages from a woman, especially when he'd made an unscheduled pit-stop and rushed off seemingly to reply to whoever he was cheating with. Darren handing the phone over to Steph however, added a new dimension to Ollie's suspicions. Why would his dad be checking up on his mum? She was hardly going to be flirting with anyone. Ollie turned this thought over several times in his head trying to make sense of what he'd seen. Although she had been making more of an effort lately, wearing nicer clothes and make-up. Ollie wondered, feeling slightly panicked, whether his mum had decided to play his dad at his own game. Oh God, imagine how embarrassing it would be if they both got new partners. Ollie cringed at the thought. It was like they were determined to ruin his life.

Ollie wanted to text Keeley, but they'd not even got to his Uncle's house yet and he didn't want Keeley to think he was needy or emotional, bombarding her with messages the moment they were apart. She was just so easy to talk to. He knew that he could trust her if he confided in her about his suspicions about his parents. She was so clever and fearless; she'd know straight away what to do. She'd confided in him that her mum had given her a weird sex talk after "finding" a condom at the house. Ollie would have been mortified, but Keeley had made a joke out of it.

"I even felt sorry for my mum!" She'd laughed, covering her mouth with her hand like she always did now she had braces. Ollie found the gesture adorably endearing, and his heart had fluttered watching her. "My mum was so awkward. She's the cutest though!"

If Keeley could handle *that* conversation and the ribbing about her stuck-up dad, she would know how Ollie should handle his parents. Ollie decided then and there that he would confide in her about his fears. Just as long as their relationship survived being apart for the party of the year.

Dana Simons had no idea that her home was playing such a pivotal part in some of the local teenagers' New Year plans. Jordan had debated on whether to run the party by his mother, as he hated to lie to her, but the risk that she would say no was just too big.

The whole idea of a party had come about in a moment of panic, when he was put on the spot about his New Year's plans, and he couldn't lose face by cancelling. He'd invited some of his friends from school along, but only the ones who could be trusted to keep up his pretence and to not trash his mother's house. The bar that Barry had installed in a little cabin at the end of the garden would be Jordan's plan's saving grace, as he hoped he could keep people out of the actual house, meaning his mother and Barry would be none-the-wiser when they finally stumbled home.

Jordan led back on his bed and stared into space thoughtfully. He really liked Felicity; more than he'd liked a girl before. He desperately wished he had been truthful to begin with, but it was too far along now, and he couldn't see an alternative.

Jordan had thought about coming clean. At least to his mother. Growing up as an only child, Jordan had always been close to her and she did give the best advice. Jordan shook his head, as if chasing these thoughts away. She had enough on her plate as it was, he decided. She'd seemed particularly stressed over Christmas, which was out-of-character for Dana. Jordan had noticed the subtle changes in her; snapping at little things and spending more time in her bedroom with the door closed. Jordan thought she was struggling with having two smaller children around all the time. Barry had two weeks off for Christmas and his ex-wife had jumped on the free childcare. Dana hadn't had much time off and coming home from work exhausted to a messy and noisy house was clearly stressing her out. Jordan liked Barry, but he thought he was being selfish and insensitive to Dana. He used Dana's early nights as excuses to go out to the pub every night, usually when the kids had gone to bed but occasionally before. Jordan had even got up himself to make his step-sister a drink of water when he heard Chloe, who was sweet but a bit of a spoiled brat, shouting for his mum at 10 o'clock one night. He would never have dreamed of ordering his parents to make him drinks at that age. His mum would have told him to make it himself and given him a clip around the ear.

Jordan hoped that when the school holidays were over, everything would go back to normal. His mum was having the attic converted and Jordan thought that the added space, plus another room to style, would brighten up the weary look around her usually sparkling eyes.

Jordan had heard Barry and the kids come in, while he was lounging on his bed deep in his own thoughts. He wasn't meeting Felicity for another couple of hours and he slid off his bed, planning on going downstairs and making an effort with his step-family.

"Hello, mate," Barry greeted him, struggling to see over the armload of bags and boxes he was carrying in from the car. "We've been spending our Christmas money."

Jordan glanced into the living room at Tyler and Chloe, who were bent over their tablets, oblivious to their dad acting like their personal porter.

"Need a hand?" Jordan offered politely.

Barry dumped the shopping on the sofa and put his hand on his back, stretching. "No, thanks. That's the last of it. Has your mum gone out?"

Dana was off work today, but she'd stayed in bed this morning claiming she had a headache. Jordan had noticed she'd got up and gone out not long after Barry and the kids had left for the shops. Jordan had gone to make a sandwich an hour earlier, but the cupboards were shockingly empty considering it was Christmas. There wasn't even any bread. He'd texted his mum asking her to pick some up, and she'd replied that she would do a food shop on the way home.

"She felt a bit better," Jordan said loyally. "I think she went food shopping."

"Thank God for that," Tyler chipped in from the opposite sofa. "There's never anything nice to eat here."

Jordan bit his tongue and walked out of the room, feeling a little annoyed as if Tyler was personally criticising his mother. Barry seemed to not notice his son's cheekiness, or, at least, did a good job of ignoring it. Barry followed Jordan into the kitchen.

"What you after?" Jordan asked, watching Barry rummage around in the fridge and then the cupboards.

"A can," Barry flashed Jordan a self-conscious grin. "Town was hectic. Those kids have done me in today."

"You won't find anything in here," Jordan told him, glancing surreptitiously at the clock. It was only 1 o'clock. They must be stressing Barry out as much as they were his mother. "Isn't your bar stocked?"

"Only spirits," Barry said. "Bit early for a whiskey."

"Just a bit." Jordan made a mental note to himself to check Barry's stock levels and text his friends to bring their own booze.

Barry straightened up from his crouching position in front of the cupboards, looking agitated. "Will your mum be home soon?"

"Not sure," Jordan shrugged. "Shall I text her to get you some cans?"

Barry opened his mouth as if to reply and then closed it

again. Jordan watched him, waiting for him to speak.

"You off out?" Barry asked finally.

"Not until three." Jordan replied.

Jordan saw Barry's face light up. "Any chance you can watch the kids while I pop to the chip shop for us?"

Jordan nodded his head in agreement. Barry seemed to relax and took everyone's order before heading off in the car to pick up lunch. Jordan didn't mind watching the children. They were easy enough with their heads permanently buried in their phones or tablets. Jordan sat on the opposite sofa and scrolled through his social media feeds to pass the time. It was only when his mother appeared, struggling in with her bags-for-life that Jordan realised Barry had been gone for over half an hour.

Jordan greeted his mother and slipped his feet into a pair of trainers to help her carry the shopping in from the car.

"Thanks, love," She said appreciatively, as she started to unpack the groceries. "Barry gone to the pub, has he?"

"No," Jordan shook his head. "He's gone to the chip shop. He should be back in a minute. Want me to phone him to get you something?"

Dana stopped what she was doing and frowned. "The chip shop?"

Jordan nodded, confused by her reaction, pulling his phone out of his pocket poised to message Barry with his mum's order. "Do you want something?"

"No," Dana said, a little firmly. "I've eaten."

Jordan shrugged and went back to helping unpack the bags. It was another fifteen minutes before Barry finally pulled up onto the drive and walked into the house, brandishing the paper-wrapped parcels.

"Thank God!" Tyler sighed, getting up to take a place at the table. One thing Dana put her foot down about was the kids not eating on her lovely sofas.

"You were ages, Dad." Chloe tossed her iPhone onto the sofa as if it was a cheap, plastic child's toy.

Jordan wolfed down his chips and got up to disappear back to his bedroom. As he passed the kitchen, he heard Dana hissing at Barry quietly. Jordan was so surprised to hear any cross words coming from his usually bubbly mother that he almost stopped and stared.

"I saw your car," Dana was whispering, in a stressed-out tone. "So you can forget about lying."

Jordan caught Barry's crestfallen expression and almost felt sorry for him. "I just stopped in because I saw Gary's car-"

"Phone him," Dana cut him off. "Text him. Write a post on social media. Don't leave Jordan here, doing your job, while you sneak around doing God-knows-what."

"I'm not sneaking around." Barry protested a little too loudly.

They both turned automatically towards the kitchen door, suddenly aware of the presence of their children in the house. Jordan quickly ascended the stairs, narrowly avoiding being seen, and missing the rest of the conversation.

He sunk back onto his bed, feeling even more troubled than he had earlier. One thing was for certain though, if Barry was messing around his mother, Jordan would make sure he paid for it.

Chapter 14

Jim wasn't usually one for New Year's Eve, but he was quite looking forward to this evening. He hoped that it would be a pleasant gathering to make up for the hostile atmosphere at home over the Christmas period. He was relieved to discover Laura had made plans for the night when he tentatively broached the subject. As much as he was struggling to maintain a civil relationship with his wife, Jim would have felt guilty if Laura had been expecting Jim to stay in with her like they usually did, and he didn't want a cloud hanging over him, ruining his night.

Jim watched disdainfully as Laura primped and preened in their bathroom and noticed that the feelings of hurt that had been plaguing him since he'd stumbled upon proof of her dishonesty had been replaced by a mild resentment and a great deal of indifference towards her. For all he was aware, Laura could be lying about her plans and spending the evening with a fancy-man. Jim was done with wasting his precious time worrying about Laura's fidelity. It had taken her a remarkably short amount of time to go from tearfully protesting her innocence to behaving stubbornly cool towards him. Jim wondered whether the frosty home environment was a manipulative ploy of hers to force him to leave, allowing her to be free to pursue her 'other man' and ensure she kept the home he'd worked so hard to pay for. She could think again if she thought he was leaving empty-handed. Laura had caused this so ethically she should be the one to leave. Jim sniffed derisively at this thought.

Jim felt a prickle of anger directed towards his wife and

decided to postpone getting ready himself until Laura had left. He wandered back down to the living room, to put some distance between them, and browsed through the latest batch of notifications from the Oak Village Community Group. The traffic on the group was heavy for a village of only a few hundred people, but there had been a lull in posts over the Christmas period, presumably as people spent time socialising or out-of-town with family. Jim had noticed there had been a branch-off group created dedicated to the Little Cedars traffic and impending road improvements. Despite the melodramatic protestations of Barry Simons that had whipped some naïve residents into a frenzy, the local authority had sensibly given the go-ahead to starting the much-needed work on the top road, although they had vetoed the original proposal for a dual carriageway and opted instead for single carriageway widening and a sensible traffic light control system along the entire stretch. Kate had informed him, confidentially of course, that this was due to the Birch Grove to Finchester by-pass being inevitable in the next few years when the budget allowed. Being party to insider information, Jim had deliberately not joined the traffic group. It seemed the fate of the road was already determined, and no amount of protests would change it. Jim had read one of Barry Simons' posts that Barry had screenshotted and shared to the Oak Village group in a bid to recruit more members to his own page and had even commented on the long-winded paragraph hoping to educate Barry and his blind followers. Despite the tense history between Barry and Jim, Jim was always willing to be the bigger person, but Barry's response to Jim's helpful comment had been extremely condescending. The man made Jim's blood boil. Between his arrogance and his ignorance, Jim was having a hard time keeping his cool with his vile neighbour.

Jim had been irritated by the rival traffic page to begin with, but the lack of moaning about the traffic on his own group had been a positive movement, and Jim was pleased to see there had been a definite surge in community spirit as the complaints decreased. Obviously, there was still the usual issues of poor parking, dog mess and noise complaints, but there were also some great stories of neighbours helping each other out, tracking down missing parcels and missing pets.

Jim heard Laura's footsteps on the stairs, and he got to his feet. If she'd been any longer, he would have risked being late for his own friends.

"What time do you think you'll be home?" Laura called through from the hallway and Jim walked out to respond to her.

"Not sure." He replied civilly.

Laura frowned. "I told you I was staying at Gina's. A taxi back would be over £60. I don't feel comfortable leaving Keeley too late."

Keeley, hearing her name and sensing an opportunity, appeared at the top of the stairs.

"Mum, I'll just sleep over Ellie's." Keeley called down. "Her mum said it's fine."

Laura looked torn. Keeley had given her the impression that she was staying in, until Laura had told her that she was staying at Gina's and Keeley had started to make noises about going to Ellie's house and helping her babysit. Laura felt the faint stirring of suspicion in the back of her mind at Keeley's sudden change of plan, but she was running late as it was and didn't have time to do the usual detective work.

"There we are." Jim said, looking pleased. "No need to rush back."

"Right," Laura glanced between her daughter and her husband uncertainly. "Call me if anything changes, Keeley."

Keeley descended the stairs to kiss her mother. "It'll be fine. Have a lovely time."

Laura gathered up her bag and jacket. "Happy New Year, both."

Jim mumbled something that sounded like he was returning the sentiment and made his way upstairs to get ready for his own gathering. He had sensibly booked a taxi which would pick up those of the group that lived locally, and he showered and dressed in record time. The taxi beeped its horn from outside, and Jim was almost out of the door before he remembered Keeley.

"I'm going now!" He called up to her. "Are you ok to lock up or do you want me to get the taxi to drop you to Ellie's?"

"No!" Keeley replied. "I'm not ready yet. I'll lock up. See you tomorrow!"

Jim shut the door firmly behind him and hopped into the taxi, giving the driver the address of the first pick-up. Martin and Caroline lived a few minutes away from Oak Village and then it was a quick stop at Kate's cottage before they made the journey to the restaurant to meet a few other like-minded acquaintances for a civilised dinner and drinks to bring in the new year.

"This is lovely," Kate commented as they settled into a cosy nook for drinks as they waited for their table to be ready. "Have you been here before, Jim?"

"A few times," Jim replied, taking Kate's coat for her chivalrously. "It's definitely one of Finchester's best kept secrets."

Jim had been impressed when Kate had suggested The Walnut Tree restaurant at The Manor Hotel and Spa as the venue for their New Year gathering. Every time he discovered another shared interest between himself and his friend, Jim felt validation for their growing affiliation. Jim took a seat next to Martin and the newly-arrived John, enjoying the high-brow conversation about politics and current affairs.

The bar area of the highly-rated restaurant was starting to fill up and Martin took advantage of the chatter as the noise levels started to rise, glancing surreptitiously around him to check the ladies in their company weren't listening.

"How's it all going between you and Kate?" Martin raised his eyebrows suggestively. "Are you two official?"

Jim spluttered on his mouthful of wine, and Martin chuckled as Jim took a moment to regain his composure.

"Oh no!" Jim responded quickly. "We're just good friends. It's nothing like that."

"Really?" Martin, who was an active member of the local community council with Kate, gave Jim a knowing look. "Apologies! It must be my misunderstanding."

Jim wanted to press Martin for more details on how this 'misunderstanding' had come to light, but he didn't want to give Martin the satisfaction or the potential gossip, so instead he smiled in what he hoped was a mysterious manner.

'Keep them guessing.' He thought to himself, secretly delighted that anyone would pair a woman as well-bred and sophisticated as Kate with him.

John was leaning forward in his chair, hoping Jim or Martin would continue this thread of conversation. John was a slightly-overweight, balding accountant in his early fifties and he had always held a torch for the attractive and eloquent Kate Evett. Following Kate's divorce, John had been newly divorced himself and had always hoped to develop his friendship with Kate into something more romantic. Kate had politely rebuffed John's advances, insisting it was too soon following Colin's death despite the Evetts having divorced. John had gone on to marry Alison, but as he regarded his wife sat across the table, deep in conversation with Kate and Caroline, John had to admit that Kate was far more attractive. He often found himself admiring her petite-but-shapely figure and her elegantly-styled ash-blonde hair. After a few too many jars, Martin had commented on Kate's allure in confidence to John, so John was confident that it wasn't just him who harboured illicit thoughts about their friend. Neither man had mentioned the slightly-inappropriate conversation they'd shared again, but John hoped that Martin's conversation with Jim would draw out something a little more exciting than their usual topics of economies and the bloody news.

Much to John's disappointment, a slim, pony-tailed, young woman dressed in a white shirt and black tie interrupted the group, expertly sliding their unfinished drinks onto her tray as she escorted them over to their now-ready table.

John and Martin exchanged a disappointed look, and John hoped that there would be ample opportunity to corner Jim later when they'd all had a few more drinks to loosen their tongues.

Jim was delighted when Kate took charge of the seating arrangements and directed him to the seat between herself and Caroline.

"Let's mix it up!" She insisted beaming around the small table at her close friends. "None of this out-dated; boys on one side, girls on the other. Martin, over here please."

Jim enjoyed every moment of the evening. The food was delicious, the wine was flowing freely, and it felt great to be amongst like-minded folk. They were debating the merits of switching from wine to brandy, at the end of their meal, when they were interrupted by a waitress.

"Awfully sorry to ask you," She smiled apologetically. "Can we ask that you enjoy your drinks in the bar area please? There's been some issues with the booking system and we need this table."

Jim opened his mouth to protest. How crass of an establishment of this calibre asking paying customers to leave their table like they were at a fast-food outlet! Before he could formulate an appropriate response, Kate was challenging the waitress in a polite-but-firm manner. They had made reservations for 8.30pm, purposely to enjoy lingering over their drinks and into the New Year. The restaurant was specifically picked for it's later-than-average dining times, with the last reservations being taken at 10.30pm to suit the continental travellers that the hotel attracted. The young woman, who looked barely older than Keeley, calmly waited for Kate to finish before firmly insisting that the party adjourn to the bar area.

Jim, keen to step in and resolve this issue for his friends, stood his ground as he watched Kate's irritation grow as the young waitress refused to back down. "We won't be moving until we've finished our evening. This is extremely rude of you."

"Sir," She replied. "There are a party of diners waiting for this table. I'll take your drinks out to the bar area."

"No," Jim's eyes narrowed at the presumptive rudeness of the waitress. "This is the most awful service I've ever received. Fetch the manager."

The young woman flushed angrily. "Fine."

She stormed from the restaurant and Jim watched, from the corner of his eye, as she spoke rapidly to an older woman. The woman patted the waitress on the arm, as if consoling her, and they exchanged a few more words. The group had started to rise from their seats when the younger woman had started to speak, and the two couples hovered uncertainly, looking to Kate and Jim for guidance.

"What seems to be the problem?" The older woman glanced around the group as she spoke before settling her gaze on Kate, as their spokesperson.

"Are you the manager?" Kate's smile was strained and did not reach her eyes.

"Yes." The woman confirmed. "I believe my waitress explained the situation and you wanted to hear this from myself?"

Kate leaned towards the woman, consciously lowering her

tone. "My friends and I spend a great deal of money at this hotel. I'm sure you can find another table that's more suitable. You may also wish to invest in better-trained staff."

The woman closed her eyes momentarily as if she were offering up a silent prayer for patience. Kate's nostrils flared at the gesture, and Jim placed a supportive hand on Kate's arm.

"Unfortunately, that won't be possible." The woman replied. "Now, let me take your drinks over to the bar area."

The younger girl darted over with her tray poised, but the woman took it from her.

"I'll take care of this," She said quietly. "Go on. You're late as it is."

The younger girl smiled gratefully as if relieved to be out of this drama and left. Jim watched as the woman started to load the tray with their drinks. He was surprised that Kate had backed down so easily, but, then again, the restaurant was quite crowded, and Kate was too refined to cause a scene. It was a different story once they were escorted to the bar area, and the group realised they were expected to squeeze around a tiny table on impossibly high bar stools. Jim looked around him, but it seemed it were the only available area for their group.

"This is absolutely ludicrous!" Kate exclaimed, forgetting her manners in dismay at the proffered substitute. "You expect us to teeter on bar stools for the next two hours?"

The manager rubbed her fingers in a circular motion around her temples, as if to communicate non-verbally that Kate was giving her a headache. "It's all I've got. Take it or leave it."

Jim gasped at the blatant rudeness of the woman. "How dare you? We will be lodging a formal complaint about our treatment."

"I'll not bother trying to help anymore then." The woman replied dryly and walked away.

Jim's mouth fell open with shock and he could see Kate was enraged at their treatment. Martin, Caroline, John and Alison were all looking extremely uncomfortable, aware that other diners had started to look in their direction.

"Kate?" Jim addressed her in a low tone. "Would you like us to leave?"

A splotchy red rash had started to colour Kate's chest and her neck. Her hands were trembling with restrained fury, and Jim's priority was removing her from the scene as tactfully as possible.

Thankfully, Alison stepped forward. "Shall we adjourn to ours? For a highly-rated restaurant, their wine choice is frankly poor, and I could do with something a bit more palatable?"

The evening felt soured and Jim sensed Kate was still feeling tense and unsettled after the incident. Back at Alison and John's house, John kept the drinks flowing and, slowly, Jim felt himself start to relax.

Not long after midnight, Jim felt his phone vibrate in his pocket. He glanced at the phone and saw Laura's name flashing up on his screen. She was probably calling to stress about Keeley, Jim thought. There was also a string of notifications for his online group.

"Put your phone away!" Kate ordered, topping up his glass.

Jim smiled back at her and turned the phone off. He was entitled to one night to himself.

Keeley waited upstairs until her father had left the house. Jordan had told them to bring their own booze and Keeley had pilfered half a bottle of gin from the cupboard, topping the original glass bottle up with water. Her dad was ridiculously square and she wouldn't put it past him to 'sniff-test' any drink bottles that he caught her transporting out of the house. The moment the coast was clear, she grabbed her bag, left her window open just enough so she could get back in undetected if need be and headed over to Jordan's.

Keeley had become quite good friends with Jordan, since she'd been going out with Ollie. Jordan had asked her to come over earlier, being as she lived next-door, to help him stash anything he didn't want broken.

Jordan swung the door open to her. "Hi, Keeley. Got drink?"

"Gin!" She held up her bottle proudly. Jordan and Ollie were in the year above, and Keeley was keen to ensure she didn't look like a child.

"Nice." Jordan nodded approvingly. "I don't want anyone coming in the house, except to use the toilet. Will you carry some stuff out to the bar?"

"Yeah, 'course," Keeley said. "Ellie is coming a bit early, is that ok?"

"It's fine." Jordan agreed, sloping off into the kitchen and coming back with bags of mixers and disposable glasses. "Can we stash some of the stuff from Barry's bar in your garden? I don't trust the boys not to smash glasses."

Keeley regarded Jordan with surprise. He was acting really stressed about this party. She had only been invited because Ollie was one of Jordan's best mates, and when Ollie had to cancel at the last minute, she'd expected Jordan to withdraw her invitation. He always seemed so cool and grown-up. She would have assumed he wouldn't want a Year 10 cramping his style, but he'd told her to bring a friend instead.

Jordan saw Keeley's look and he gave her a sheepish grin. "My mum would go nuts if stuff got broken. Oh, and make sure your friend knows that you've got to pretend we're all in sixth form."

"Why?" Keeley asked, taking a bag from him and following him out to the garden. "Why are you even having this party? You look stressed?"

Jordan opened the door to the cabin. Keeley looked around what was essentially just a large shed with glass-panelled double doors. Inside, a wooden counter divided the shed, with one third of the space dedicated to a serving space and a shelf of glasses and mini-draught pump. Four bar stools in a kitsch pink PVC lined the counter on the other side, and there was a cosy sofa taking up the rest of the floor space. Jordan unloaded the glasses and bottles and started to stack glasses back in the bag to take them away. "I kind-of told Felicity I was in sixth form when we met."

"Shit." Keeley's eyes widened. "How old is she?"

"Sixteen," Jordan replied quickly. "Same as me. But she's seventeen in June, I'm seventeen in September. It makes a difference though, yeah?"

"I guess." Keeley nodded. "So, we're in sixth form. Got it. Why have this party though?"

"Felicity can get into bars in town," Jordan shrugged. "It's easier for girls. I'd look like a mug getting turned away, so I told her I always have a party. I didn't think she'd want to come, but she was working until 10pm and didn't want to meet up with her friends later. I didn't really have a choice but to go ahead with it."

"What are we going to do when your parents come back?" Keeley asked thoughtfully.

"That's the only tricky bit," Jordan admitted. "I really need the boys out by 1am. Most of them will have to get home before their parents anyway. Hopefully, my mum will be drunk and won't notice Felicity has stayed."

Keeley laughed at Jordan's plan. She didn't know whether she would have dared to carry out the same plan, but, then again, she needed to sneak herself and Ellie back into her own house tonight. It was either that or stay out all night. She took the bag of confiscated spirits and glasses from Jordan and tentatively lowered them over her own garden, behind a small bush. When she had completed the mission, she headed back to the bar. Jordan poured a generous measure of the gin into a cup and passed it to her.

"Cheers!" Keeley glugged down the foul-tasting liquid, trying hard not to grimace. She instantly regretted trying to show off with a hard spirit. She should have snuck out a bottle of white wine and watered it down with lemonade.

Keeley soon realised that the trick to drinking spirits was to knock them down quickly. By the third cup, she could swallow the drink without feeling like she was going to throw-up, although her head was spinning a little and she was definitely a bit tipsy. Keeley was having an amazing time though. Jordan had only invited a few of the boys, and she and Ellie were the only girls there. Keeley had no intention of cheating on Ollie, but it was nice to be the centre of attention. Felicity was lovely. She'd arrived alone in a taxi. Keeley had expected her to be a bit stuck-up; she was so pretty and sophisticated. Keeley assumed that she would have been stuck to Jordan's side all night, but she was laughing loudly, playing drinking games, and when she wanted to go into the house to use the toilet, she dragged Ellie and Keeley in with her.

"Ugh!" She pulled a face at her reflection in the long mirror in the hallway. "I wish I'd had time to get changed."

Felicity was wearing a tight white shirt and black skirt over tights. She had told the girls that she had been roped into waitressing for her mother, who was the manager of a restaurant. Keeley thought she looked beautiful, but she waved away Keeley's compliments modestly.

"I've still got a bottle of tequila," Felicity confided in the girls. "Let's do some shots now. I want to catch up with you lot."

Keeley glanced at Ellie. She was already feeling pretty wasted, but when Ellie headed into the Simons' kitchen and found three shot glasses, Keeley felt like she couldn't say no. She tossed back the first shot, and then a second. The moment the alcohol hit the gin, Keeley clutched her hand to her mouth.

"Are you going to be sick?" Felicity looked horrified. "Quick! Get in the bathroom!"

Keeley managed to make it to the toilet, throwing the lid up just in time as a burning cocktail of gin and tequila came spilling violently from her. Keeley's head was spinning, and she tried to get to her feet before feeling a second wave of nausea. She sunk back down into a crouch, resting her head on the cool edge of the toilet and closing her eyes to try to stop the room whirling around her.

She could hear voices in the hallway and was semi-conscious of Ellie telling her she had to leave. Something about someone complaining about teenagers carrying crates of lager into Sycamore Street and Ellie's mum kicking off. Keeley opened her mouth to reply but instead of words, a second round of vomit spilled out.

A head appeared around the door, but Keeley felt too ill to acknowledge it or even feel embarrassed that she was lying on the bathroom floor, make-up smeared down her face.

"Leave her." She heard Felicity's voice.

"I just want her to get her dad to remove that post," A male voice was saying. "If my mum sees it, I'll have to go home."

Keeley didn't know or care what they were talking about. She just wanted the spinning to stop and to go to sleep. She was conscious of more voices in the hallway and the sound of the door opening and closing several times.

"Keeley." She felt strong hands pull her up onto her feet,

and she wobbled unsteadily before resting her head on the firm shoulder of her rescuer.

"Mmmmm," She mumbled. "You smell nice."

"Keeley!" The voice was sharper this time, edged with frustration. "Everyone has gone. You need to sober up and go home."

"Happy new year." Keeley slurred, struggling to keep her eyes open.

"Seriously," Jordan's tone was tinged with panic. "My mum just phoned because everyone is naming and shaming the boys on your bloody dad's page. You need to leave."

Keeley frowned as she tried to digest this information. "He's such a knob. I hate him."

Keeley took a step back to try to stand unaided, but the floor felt wobbly and she crashed into a shelf laden with fragranced candles and sea-shells, bringing down the glass shelf which shattered on the tiled floor.

"You're going to have to call someone," Keeley heard Felicity hiss to Jordan. "We can't leave her like this."

"Who?" Jordan barked back. "Her mate has left her. She only lives next-door. Shall we try and put her to bed?"

"What if she's sick?" Felicity sounded concerned.

"She's been throwing up for an hour," Jordan replied. "She won't be sick anymore."

Between them, Jordan and Felicity managed to get Keeley up onto her feet and over to her front door. Felicity rooted around in Keeley's bag, and Keeley sunk to the floor as she watched her.

"Where's your key?" Felicity asked Keeley, speaking slowly to Keeley as if she were a child.

"I didn't bring it," Keeley replied, vaguely recalling that she'd let herself out through the front, and her key was still sat in the lock of the back door. "I'll go through the window."

Keeley tried to point in the direction of her bedroom, but everything was still fuzzy and distorted and she gave up trying.

"I'll have a look and see what she means." Jordan offered, and dashed off to scour the perimeter of the house, glad to be leaving Keeley as he was terrified she was going to vomit on him.

Keeley felt another wave of nausea and struggled to a sitting position just in time to launch a fresh stream of vomit onto the lawn. Felicity jumped back, out of the danger-zone, and waited for Jordan to return.

"Hi!" Felicity turned towards a voice in the street. "Everything ok?"

Felicity saw a short, curvy blonde woman, hovering at the end of Jordan's driveway.

Great, Felicity groaned to herself. All the neighbours would be out in force no doubt.

"Few too many," Felicity forced a cheery laugh. "Just getting her home."

To Felicity's horror, the woman marched up the driveway and crouched down over Keeley.

"Oh, Keeley," The woman said sympathetically. "It's Dana, Jordan's mum."

Felicity's heart sank. They hadn't had time to clean up the mess they'd made, let alone the shelf Keeley had just smashed to bits. What a way to meet his mother.

"Where's her mum or dad?" Dana addressed Felicity this time, when it became clear that Keeley wasn't capable of a coherent response.

"I don't think they're in," Felicity said. "I'm sorry, I don't know her. I just saw her coming in like this. Her friend just left her, so I was checking to see if she was alright."

Dana surveyed the girl and then Keeley thoughtfully. The Oak Village social media page had been going wild with comments after someone had snapped a picture of some year eleven boys carrying crates of booze into Sycamore Street. Dana had phoned Jordan but got no answer and had decided to nip over to check while Barry was side-tracked with his mates. Dana felt almost sorry that she had seen Keeley now, as she'd been having a lovely night. They were all heading back to Gary's to continue the party, but she could hardly leave the girl in this state.

"I'll have to phone her mother." Dana said. "Has she got her phone?"

Felicity retrieved Keeley's phone, wondering what was taking Jordan so long. She used Keeley's thumb to unlock the screen and handed the phone to Dana. Felicity loitered awkwardly as Dana relayed the situation to the girl's mother. There was a back-and-forth exchange, and Dana finally hung up the phone.

"Her mum is at a party," Dana explained. "She'll get here as quickly as possible, but she might be a while waiting for a taxi. Can you help me carry her into mine?"

Felicity cringed in horror, but grudgingly agreed. As she was practically dragging Keeley back across the threshold, Jordan appeared.

"Only way in is up on the garage roof!" He exclaimed in exasperation. "I jumped up and had a look. Shall I try and open the door from the inside?"

Felicity heard him before he came into view and his face froze in a mask of horrified disbelief as he saw his mother and his girlfriend man-handling the inebriated teenager back into his house.

"Jordan!" Dana gasped, stopping abruptly. "What the hell is going on?"

Felicity wanted to be anywhere else in the world right now. She really liked Jordan, and this was not how she had planned on meeting his mother.

Chapter 15

Keeley threw herself onto the bed and covered her face with her pillow. Life sucked enough without her parents kicking off, everyone in school hating her, being grounded and that incessant drilling noise whining from next-door.

In a way, she was glad she couldn't remember much about New Year's Eve. Ellie had filled in some of the blanks via email, as Keeley's dad had not only grounded her but had confiscated her phone too. Keeley had never felt more humiliated than the vague memory of vomiting in front of all those year 11 boys. She hadn't spoken to Ollie, even though he was meant to be home today. Jordan was bound to have told him how Keeley ruined the party and trashed his house. There was no way he would ever want to speak to her again.

Keeley had to face up to everyone tomorrow when she went back to school. She was seriously considering faking an illness. She didn't know whether being phone-less was a blessing or a curse, as she couldn't see how badly she was being slated online.

"I'm grounded. I've got no phone! Help me!" Keeley had emailed Ellie last night when she had finally begun to feel human again.

"I'm not gonna lie," Ellie had been brutally honest. "All the boys were furious because someone posted a picture of them on the page. Half the village are slagging our mums and dads off for letting us drink, and the other half are saying it's a disgrace to post pictures of kids. Logan's mum reckons she's going to sue your Dad for not taking the picture down. My mum knew I was with them. I'm grounded. The comments are going off!"

Oh, great. Keeley had stared at Ellie's words morosely. That was another reason for her dad to get mad at her. Keeley vaguely remembered her mum getting home and profusely apologising to Dana. Dana had been lovely, and Keeley was building up the confidence to apologise to her properly. Keeley knew her dad wouldn't be happy, as he'd had a blazing row with her mother about it, blaming Jordan Jones for Keeley's descent into underage drinking. Keeley didn't care what he said. She had no phone and no friends, thanks to him and his Oak Village Community Group. She liked Dana and she was going to make her own amends for the broken shelf, one way or another.

Keeley wished her parents had gone back to work today, but there was an extra bank holiday. Her dad was still stomping around the house, complaining about the noise of the building work next door. Keeley hadn't slept much last night; partly due to sleeping on and off all day New Year's Day and partly because her mind had been working overtime conjuring up worst case scenarios for her life from now until she was old enough to leave Little Cedars. She was glad Jordan's parents had started their work bright and early and disturbed her dad. He was a selfish, horrible man, and Keeley hoped they woke him up every morning. It would serve him right.

A gentle tap on the door interrupted her thoughts, and Keeley rolled onto her side to watch her mum creep into the room.

"Are you feeling better?" Laura asked gently.

Keeley wished her mum would lose her temper at her. Keeley knew she had ruined her mum's night out, forcing her to pay over-the-odds for a taxi home to pick her up and then hold back her hair all night as she coughed up the last of the vile drinks. Keeley could handle the shouting and the slamming doors of her dad, but her mum's calm, concerned approach seared Keeley's conscience, making her feel guilty and awful.

"I'm ok." Keeley nodded, looking down at her lap. "I'm really sorry, Mum."

"I know you are." Laura sat down on the edge of the bed. "Do you want to talk about it?"

Keeley shook her head.

"I'm going out for a run," Laura told her. "I won't be long. Your dad is here if you want anything."

"I won't." Keeley said coolly at the mention of her father.

Laura sighed, and took Keeley's hand in hers. "He'll calm down. He's just worried about you getting in that mess at your age. Anything could have happened."

"He was so concerned, he rushed home." Keeley couldn't help herself from spitting her response out sarcastically.

Laura's mouth set into a tight line at this. She'd tried to get hold of Jim when she couldn't get a taxi as soon as Dana had called. He'd ignored her calls and texts; finally rolling in at 9am, claiming he couldn't get a taxi until after 4am so had stayed at John's house. Laura was furious about this, but aside from a few cross words with him, she'd been too wrapped up in Keeley's plight to dwell on it.

"You need to go and apologise to Dana," Laura said, ignoring Keeley's comment. "I bought some flowers and a bottle of wine. They're on the kitchen table."

"Thanks," Keeley nodded her gratitude. "I'll shower and go over."

"Good girl." Laura gave Keeley a quick hug and got to her feet. "I'll see you in a bit."

Keeley thought about putting off going around to Dana's until her mother had got back, but she decided that she was procrastinating, and, after a quick shower, she tiptoed downstairs, hoping to avoid her father, and get the apology over and done with.

With the wine and the flowers in her hand, she pulled open the front door and her father's booming voice almost made her drop the bottle.

"Where the hell do you think you're going, young lady?" Jim demanded.

Keeley didn't turn around. "Mum said I could."

Without waiting for his response, she darted out of the front door, pulling it closed behind her, reckoning that, as angry as he was, he wasn't likely to follow her outside and make a public scene.

Usually, Keeley would have been right, but Jim had been brooding on Keeley's embarrassing antics since he'd walked in yesterday morning to an earful from Laura. He'd also suffered the backlash from not monitoring the online content on New Year's Eve. A group of angry parents were threatening legal action over a photo of their children that had been up on the page for over twelve hours, before Jim had seen it and deleted it. Jim personally felt that naming-and-shaming the delinquents, strutting around the estate with alcohol, and their negligent parents was the penalty they deserved. The law, unfortunately, was not on side and he had deleted the post, but the angry messages kept coming. All this, mixed together with the incessant drilling noise from next-door and the weeks of passive-aggressive behaviour of his neighbour, created a cocktail of fury that burst from Jim in a rare loss of control.

Keeley's closed fist was poised to knock on the Simons' door when she heard her father burst through their own door. She turned towards him, her stomach knotted but she managed to keep her expression impassive, refusing to show him any signs of fear.

"This is the last straw!" Jim spat venomously. "You get back in here now!"

Keeley dropped her raised arm to her side. She didn't want to obey him, but she could hardly knock on the door with him yelling on the doorstep like a crazy person. She was loath to give him the satisfaction of following his order and she stood for a moment, weighing up what to do for the best.

Jim, blood still pumping through his veins at an unhealthy speed and anger clouding any rational thought, read Keeley's hesitation for disobedience and stepped forward across the border to pull his wayward daughter back. He misplaced his step and a sock-clad foot met the cold, wet, day-old remains of Keeley's vomit just as Dana Simons, on her way out to escape the building noise, swung open her front door.

She jumped in surprise as she was greeted by a pale-faced Keeley, clutching a supermarket bouquet, and the strangled cry of Jim, hopping back from the herbaceous border, his face contorted in disgust.

"Oh!" Dana exclaimed, clutching her hand to her bosom. "Keeley. Jim."

"Dana," Keeley's blood ran cold with panic. "Sorry. This is a bad time. I'll come back."

"No, it's fine," Dana said flustered, not sure whether to acknowledge Jim or ignore him. "Do you want to come in?"

"No, thank you," Keeley said, holding out the gifts. "I just wanted to say I'm so sorry for everything. I'll pay for any damage, and anything I can do to make it up to you-"

"Oh, sweetheart," Dana ignored the proffered peace-offerings and pulled Keeley to her in a warm embrace. "I know you didn't do it on purpose. We've all been young and silly. I'm just glad you're ok."

Jim saw red at Dana's response. He forgot his sick-covered foot and angrily strode forward.

"This is unbelievable!" He growled. "Of course, you're going to excuse her stupid, reckless behaviour. If it wasn't for your son, she wouldn't have had access to alcohol. It's typical of you people!"

Dana stepped back, surprised by his unbridled rage. She felt a surge of anger that he was attacking her capability as a parent, but as much as she would have loved to let rip with some home-truths, Dana couldn't bring herself to drag his poor daughter into any crossfire.

"Keeley," Dana drew herself up to her full five foot one and turned her body, just enough to make it clear she was ignoring Jim. "I think it's best if you go in now, as I'm on my way out. Thank you for the flowers and the wine. Pop over for a coffee another time?"

"Yes," Keeley nodded. "Thank you."

Dana patted Keeley's arm gently and turned back into the house with the gifts. She gave Keeley a sympathetic smile and pulled the door closed behind her, hoping that the girl's punishment for reaching out to her wasn't too harsh.

Dana walked upstairs to where Barry was helping Gary and his labourer get started on the preparations. The landing was covered in dust already, and they were only emptying the attic and securing some of the floorboards. Dana was finding it hard to visualise how they were going to manage to live here whilst the work was being done.

"Never guess what's just happened!" She released the rant she'd been holding inside. "Can you believe it?"

"The man is a tool." Gary chipped in. "So what if the kids pilfered booze from here? They would have got it somewhere else. My parents had a cabinet full of watered down bottles of whisky and vodka, thanks to me and my sister growing up!"

Barry laughed at this, but Dana frowned.

"They got that booze from here, did they?" She asked. "I saw that the boys brought lager and assumed it was a bring-your-own party."

Barry shot Gary an annoyed look. "I wasn't going to say

anything as I didn't want you kicking off at Jordan. Poor lad was in enough trouble as it was."

Dana gave Barry a cool stare, letting him know that she wasn't happy but would continue this conversation when Gary wasn't present.

"What time are you finishing, Gary?" She asked.

"Another hour," Gary replied. "And I'll be out of your hair."

"I'll be back in an hour," She addressed this to Barry. "Make sure you are home."

She turned away, but not before she'd seen Barry shoot Gary an amused look. He'd be laughing on the other side of his face when she was done with unleashing the months of pent-up irritations she'd been trying to suppress. The past few weeks had all but tipped her over the edge, and Dana was determined to get this resolved once and for all.

She quickly put the flowers, still in their cellophane wrapper, into a vase of water, and grabbed her bag and keys. She had intended to do a quick food shop, but she found herself driving on auto-pilot to Steph's.

"Hey," Steph greeted her. "Good timing. We've only just got back."

Dana moved through the hallway, which was surprisingly free from the usual clutter. Steph directed her into the kitchen, where Steph was emptying their bags into the washing machine.

"You're on the ball." Dana commented. Steph was notorious for leaving washing baskets until they reached mountain proportions.

Steph grinned, aware of the reason for Dana's remark. "New year, new me."

"Oh really?" Dana took the coffee jar from Steph, indicating for Steph to keep working on her laundry pile while Dana made the coffee. "Did you have a good time with your brother?"

"Yeah," Steph nodded. "It was lovely. I'm glad I put my foot down. Kendall loved it, too, but Ollie and Darren weren't impressed, missing the Oak Village celebrations."

"Did you see the drama?" Dana handed Steph a mug. "Darren should be glad that Ollie was away from it all."

"I saw it!" Steph finished what she was doing and took a seat at the table. "Some of the comments! You'd think those kids were taking drugs and torturing baby animals the way some people kicked off."

"They were at my bloody house! I'm glad that didn't come out on the page!" Dana admitted. "I nipped back to check on Jordan, but they'd all been summoned home by their irate parents after the picture was put up. The only ones left were Jordan's girlfriend and Keeley."

"And there was Ollie acting like he'd missed the party of the year." Steph said.

"Did he know about the party?" Dana asked. "Jordan swears it was a last-minute thing, but I don't believe him. He's taken his punishment pretty well though, so I think he knows he was in the wrong."

"Ollie denied there being a party," Steph said carefully, conscious of not wanting to make things worse for Jordan, who she thought was a lovely kid. "Thing is, we used to get smashed down the river when we were in year 11. I'd rather my kids be at someone's house than dangling off a river bridge. I just wouldn't want them trashing my house."

"That's just it, isn't it?" Dana agreed. "I would have let him, if he'd asked. I'm worried though that they've got their booze from my house. Keeley was practically unconscious in the garden, when I got home. Our relations with him-next-door are frayed enough as it is, and now he's blaming us for supplying the booze."

"He'd find someone to piss off in an empty room," Steph responded dryly. "The picture clearly showed the boys with enough lager to sink a ship. You're hardly to blame for unknowingly giving them a warm, dry roof for a few hours."

"I know, I know," Dana sighed. "It just feels like it's one more thing in a long-line of stress."

Steph squeezed Dana's hand sympathetically. "Everything ok with Barry?"

"Yes and no," Dana admitted. "I feel like he's taken advantage over Christmas. He's so lenient with the kids and he's at the pub every day. He's even undermined me with Jordan. I should be pleased that he treats Jordan the same as his own kids, but they have no rules or respect, then he's sneaking off to the pub for a break with no concern for me."

"Have you said anything?" Steph asked, feeling sheepish as this is what she'd put up with for years with Darren in some ways.

"I've just been snapping," Dana said. "I'm going to have it out with him tonight."

"Good luck," Steph told her. "You'll get it sorted. Barry adores you."

"I hope so," Dana smiled gratefully. "How's everything going with you and Darren? Any better since you've put your foot down?"

Steph shrugged. "I think we're getting on better. I've been making a conscious effort to stand up for myself. Saying that, he did shoot off the minute we were through the door though 'to work'. I guess it's early days."

"Good for you," Dana said, meaning it. She could see the subtle changes already in everything from the hallway free of the usual clutter to the way Steph sat up a little straighter, rather than her usual self-conscious slouch. "Are you still looking for a job?"

Steph smiled mysteriously. "I've got something up my sleeve. I've been dying to share it, but I don't want to jinx it."

Dana reached for Steph's empty mug. "Come on, then! Barry can bloody wait his turn!"

By the time Dana got back to the house, Barry had left. Dana slammed the door behind her, in an unusual display of annoyance.

"Is that you, Mum?" Jordan called down the stairs. "Barry said phone him when you're back."

Dana sent Barry a short message, ordering him to return.

"I know you're grounded," She said to Jordan as he sloped

into the kitchen. "But I'm giving you a day off for today only."

Jordan eyed his mother suspiciously. He had a feeling she wanted him gone so she could argue freely with Barry. Jordan wasn't worried, as despite his size, Barry was the gentlest bloke he knew, but Jordan didn't want his mum falling out with him over Jordan's behaviour. He said as much, and he watched his mother's eyes fill up with tears at his sentiment.

"It's nothing to do with anything you've done," Dana told him. "Right, do you want a lift to Felicity's or to your dad's?"

"No, it's fine," Jordan insisted. "Text me when I can come back."

Dana promised she would and gave Jordan a warm hug before he left. She paced the kitchen anxiously until she heard Barry's car pull into the drive. He came into the hallway armed with a huge bouquet of roses and a hangdog expression.

"Don't!" Dana held a hand up to him. If he started apologising now, he'd tug on her heartstrings and she'd back down.

Barry nodded glumly, and carefully led the bouquet down, pulling out a stool in the kitchen for Dana to sit on.

Dana talked and talked. Barry never once tried to interrupt her, intuitively knowing that his wife had suppressed her true feelings for some time. Some of her comments were hard to swallow, but he bit back the instinct to defend his actions. As difficult as this was to hear, Barry was very much aware that it was easier than the alternative of losing Dana.

"I'm sorry," Dana summarised when she had finished saying everything she wanted to, and the weight of her burden had evaporated, leaving her feeling hollow. "But, as much as I love you, I can't live like this. I understand we've got different parenting styles, and you probably think I'm too strict. I don't want military obedience, I just want us to have some semblance of order. And as for what happened New Year, I take full responsibility for Jordan's actions, but the amount of alcohol that the kids drunk here, we're lucky someone didn't die. Nobody should have that much in their house, unless they're running on off-license. We could both do with cutting back."

She finally fell quiet and looked up at her husband, waiting for his excuses or him to turn the blame onto her. She was shocked to see tears shining in his dark eyes and Dana instinctively moved to comfort him, crushed that she had clearly gone too far.

"No," Barry shrugged off her attempt to console him and struggled to his feet. His head was bowed, and Dana thought sadly to herself like he looked like he had the weight of the world on his shoulders. "I'm the one who should be apologising. I promise I'll make this up to you. Everything you're saying is true."

He was quiet for the rest of the day, and Dana waited, nervously, for him to make his excuses and go to the pub, but he stayed in the house and offered to make dinner that evening. After they had eaten, Barry pulled her close to him on the sofa.

"Are we ok?" She asked, breathing in the clean, masculine scent of him.

"Of course," He kissed her gently on the forehead. "I love

you."

Dana felt her heart expand in her chest at his words, and sliding one hand behind her back, discreetly crossed her fingers for luck, offering up a silent prayer that this really was a new start for them.

Chapter 16

Kelly Russell had missed the drama of New Year in the village. She had been the life and the soul of every celebration at the pub for the last few years, but she'd been let down by a friend a few days before New Year. She was absolutely furious, as her friend had spent weeks convincing her to ditch the usual festivities and when she'd finally relented, despite the amount of convincing she'd taken, she'd received a flippant text cancelling.

Kelly could have admitted that her plans had been cancelled, but she'd given Evan such a convincing story, slating The Crown's New Year's party, that she couldn't slink back to the pub without losing face or arousing suspicion. Not that Evan would notice, she thought bitterly, as she crawled through the roadworks on her way to drop Sophie to school. Even with two weeks off work, Kelly had barely seen him over the holidays. He had been out with the kids every day but was still maintaining his usual work-out routine, disappearing for hours in the evening.

Kelly was surprised that it even still bothered her. He had always been a gym junkie; that was how they had met. It had gone from two or three times a week to practically every day in the last year or two. She gritted her teeth as she watched the temporary lights change back from green to red when nothing in front of her had been able to move because some idiot had blocked the crossing. She glanced at the clock, realising that she was going to be late at this rate. She gave a frustrated blast on her horn out of sheer annoyance.

"Mum!" Sophie shook her head in disapproval at Kelly's gesture.

Kelly made a face in response. The lights changed again, and a pitiful two cars slid through before the vehicle two-cars in front of Kelly obediently stopped.

"Aaargh!" Kelly groaned in frustration. "Bloody stupid driver!"

"It would have been quicker to walk." Sophie said helpfully.

Kelly bit back the sharp retort that formed on her lips. It wasn't Sophie's fault that they had left the house late, she reminded herself. Looking at the worse-than-usual traffic, they would have been late if they'd left on time. The sign on the side of the road announced that the roadworks would be in place for the next four months as part of the continuous improvements along the Little Cedars road. Kelly thought she would prefer for Sophie to miss four months of school than sit through this.

"This will be the third time I've been late," Sophie continued seemingly oblivious to Kelly's stress. "This term."

"I know." Kelly said through gritted teeth.

The roadworks had made the awful traffic a million times worse and coupled with Kelly's lack of motivation in the morning plus a heavy dose of January blues, Kelly just couldn't seem to get her act together. She had genuine reasons for being late twice last week; once Sophie had forgotten to remind Kelly that it was violin day, then Kelly had been going straight to a potential lead, but had forgotten her sales pack.

"It's so embarrassing when you're late," Sophie pulled a face. "I have to walk into assembly when everyone's already sat down."

"We won't be that late." Kelly said optimistically.

The lights changed and, spurred on by Sophie's emotional blackmail, Kelly accelerated quickly across to the other side, driving so close to the vehicle in front that she almost slammed into it when they braked abruptly. Kelly's BMW was hanging across the crossing now, and she was on the receiving end of several angry driver's horns. Kelly flipped a middle finger in response to one of the culprits.

"That's so rude!" Sophie gasped. "A man did that to Dad on the motorway and Dad said that's what people with no manners do."

Kelly rolled her eyes but said nothing. She had an appointment for a lead at 9.30, and it wasn't looking likely that she'd get there in time. Kelly edged forward in the traffic, but she could see that the road ahead was bumper-to-bumper past the turning for the school. She was torn whether to text the woman now to reschedule or to brave the traffic and hope for the best.

The frustrating thing was she really needed this sale. The business had started off great, but leads had started to dry up before Christmas, and Kelly had seriously overspent during the festive season. Evan was so anal about paying off the credit card in full each month, and he'd been furious to see she'd racked up about £2000 in clothes, gifts, nights out and food. Kelly didn't know why he was being so dramatic. It wasn't like Evan didn't have savings. He had threatened to lower the credit limit to stop Kelly going over-budget, and she'd hastily promised she'd pay back some of the bill. The only problem was she hadn't really made much money lately. She'd given herself a few weeks off for Christmas with the family, and then, January was notoriously slow.

None of the few leads she'd had this month had come to anything, and she had been pinning all her hopes on this one today. Kelly felt she needed this one for confidence. She needed to hold her nerve and increase her marketing. She promised herself that, if the traffic would just hurry up, she would nail this meeting and spend the rest of the day working on her social media campaign.

The traffic showed no signs of shifting, and she felt herself growing more and more anxious as the clock ticked past 9am, marking Sophie as officially late. Sophie was fidgeting in her seat and Kelly sneaked a sideways glance at her daughter, wanting to tell her to sit still, but reading the concerned expression on her face and knowing, with motherly intuition, that Sophie was close to tears at the stress of another late mark in the register. Kelly felt her chest tighten with helplessness and guilt that she couldn't fix this for her sensitive daughter. Jacob had always been a completely different kettle of fish to Sophie. He was more like Kelly and could confidently walk into any room with his head held high. Kelly toyed with the idea of calling Sophie in sick; her attendance record was excellent, and she was top of her class so a day off wouldn't hurt. Kelly would have suggested this if she didn't have this appointment lined up. This made her feel like even more of a failure; subjecting her daughter to her social anxiety for a lead that probably wouldn't come to anything.

Kelly tried to distract Sophie for the rest of the painfully slow journey, but, when they finally pulled up at the school, Sophie grabbed her backpack and darted off with a worried look etched on her serious face, without waiting for a kiss goodbye from her mother. Kelly felt tears prickle the back of her eyes and an overwhelming urge to call Sophie back and give her the day off school, so she didn't have to walk into school late again.

Sophie would be fine, she reasoned, annoyed at herself for being uncharacteristically emotional. The tears were threatening to spill over and ruin the flawless 'natural' make-up look she had spent so long perfecting this morning. It was probably good for Sophie to have to face her fears, Kelly told herself. It probably built resilience. Or would give Sophie a deep-rooted social complex that she never got over. Kelly turned up the radio, trying to distract herself from her mum-guilt, but, as quickly as she blinked away the tears, they would re-surface. There was an uncomfortable lump in her throat that she couldn't shift, and Kelly felt suddenly very overwhelmed.

What the hell is the matter with me? She asked herself in frustration. She had gone from being an emotionally impenetrable warrior to prone to bursts of self-pitying tears or uncontrollable rage in the last year. Kelly could trace the change back to when her doctor had advised her to come off her contraceptive pill back in July, which she'd been on since Sophie was born. She'd suffered, in the past, from awful pre-menstrual stress, and the pill had seemed to level her out. The doctor had wanted her to take a break from the medication though, especially when she'd been honest and admitted that she rarely slept with her husband anymore. Kelly couldn't cope with these outbursts much longer, and she vowed to give herself one more month before she marched back to the surgery and demanded a new prescription.

She watched the clock tick the minutes away as she drove the short distance to her appointment. Her Sat Nav proclaimed that she would arrive in the nick of time and, as if the heavens were looking down on her, the traffic was moving steadily in that direction.

"Please, please, please!" She prayed aloud, as she watched another set of temporary lights in front of her go green.

The car in front, clearly a risk-taker like her, sailed through on amber and Kelly put her foot down, nipping past despite the light now being firmly stuck on red. She pulled a sharp left into the turning she needed and arrived at her destination at 9.30am on the dot.

Feeling delighted with herself for conquering the odds, she grabbed her bag from the footwell of the passenger side and checked her phone for the right house number. Kelly fluffed up her hair in the reflection of the car window and walked confidently to the door of number 23. She knocked on the door and waited.

After a few moments, Kelly knocked again, but harder this time.

The door to number 24 opened and a man, about Kelly's age, dressed in a smart, navy blue suit, stepped out of the house. He gave Kelly the once-over and, seemingly liking what he saw, gave her a friendly smile.

"She just left for work," The man said good-naturedly. "Can I help?"

Before Kelly had time to answer, a beautiful, younger woman joined the man on the doorstep. She looked immaculate in a tailored coat over dress trousers, with an expensive leather bag on her arm. She glanced at Kelly and her lips curled up slightly in a sneer.

"We don't buy from cold-callers." She said crisply, before locking the door behind her and marching towards a shiny black Range Rover, with the man at her heels.

The wave of emotion that had been threatening to submerge Kelly all morning finally hit, and she hurried back to her car, feeling dejected. She managed to hold it together until the luxury vehicle was out of sight and promptly burst into tears.

She was still sniffing as she pulled back into the space behind her house half an hour later. Kelly sat in her car for a few moments, trying to regain her composure. One of the neighbours seeing her looking a red-faced mess would be the icing on the cake of this awful morning. She had been sobbing loudly sat in the stop-start traffic, but at that point, she couldn't have cared less who saw her. Now that her emotional reserves were drained, Kelly felt a little silly and self-conscious. She just wanted to get back in her house, fire off a shitty text to that stuck-up time-waster and get back to the drawing board.

Her phone buzzed, and she reached over to check it. It was her so-called 'friend' who had begged her to go out of town for New Year, before letting her down when she'd finally agreed against her better judgement. Kelly ignored the message. She knew that, as well as the hormones, the traffic, work, money and her life in general, part of her outburst could be attributed to feelings of frustration and anger hanging over since the New Year's incident. She had pretended she didn't care and that she had had a better offer, but she'd ended up sharing a bottle of bubbly with her mother-in-law, watching Big Ben on the television. Her face reddened at the memory of the humiliation.

Feeling a fresh wave of upset, Kelly got out of the car, slamming the door loudly behind her. She let herself into the house, throwing her branded bag of sales and marketing aides onto the floor and giving it a little kick for good measure. She was seriously considering quitting this latest business partnership. The only reason she hadn't already was because someone had made a flippant comment about all the different "schemes" she'd been involved in over the years, and Kelly hated to lose face. Image was everything to Kelly. Her everyday make-up routine took an hour, and even her gym hairstyle took a good twenty minutes to perfect. There was nothing about her life that wasn't perfectly orchestrated and to be seen to fail publicly was her worst nightmare.

Kelly reached for her phone and started to browse through social media, searching for inspiration. The first thing to catch her eye, though, was a rant about the morning traffic. Kelly didn't usually get involved in the moaning Oak Village posts, except for to 'like' any of the comments that were clearly poking fun at the complainant, but this post was by one of Kelly's friends, not one of the usual knickers-in-a-twist brigade.

"Thanks a lot to whichever idiot in the council signed off on the worst planned roadworks ever! An already hideous journey has been doubled because of those pathetic traffic lights. Really helpful to those of us who have no choice but to do a school run. Second week in of four months… Looks like I'll be losing my job at this rate!" Lisa Harris had written.

There were a lot of comments agreeing with Lisa and

sharing their own frustrations. Kelly's finger flew over the keyboard as she added her own stressful morning to the growing thread, embellishing her tale for dramatic effect. As she waited for the responses, she browsed some other posts, and something caught her eye. Before she could click on it, a notification popped up that "Jim Burbridge also commented on Lisa Harris' post".

Kelly found her lips pursing in disapproval before she'd even read what he had to say on the matter. Her eyes scanned his patronising comment and she felt her blood start to boil at his condescending tone, advising that "some of the commenters on this thread are overreacting a little. Unfortunately, exaggerations and drama make for a more interesting read. A few weeks *slightly* increased journey time for much needed improvements that will save commuters hours in the long run. There is a group dedicated to the traffic which you may find more appropriate for your comments."

Kelly scowled at the paragraph of text. She knew that he was referring to her with "some of the commenters". The fact that she had exaggerated about her journey time and the consequences was irrelevant though. He was only defending the roadworks because he was the one in favour of them in the first place. Kelly had heard that he worked for the council; he had probably planned the whole disastrous debacle. He was probably too busy counting the bonus he'd got to care about how ordinary people's lives were impacted.

Kelly's temper was already flaring as she started to type out a response, but before she could finish, Barry Simons beat her to the punchline. Kelly sat back, satisfied that she didn't have to dirty her hands.

"Funny that the person defending the roadworks is the person who was so keen for them to go ahead. Obviously, you can't be seen to badmouth your employer, but to call these women liars is disgusting behaviour. I personally timed my journey this morning, and I can corroborate their claims. At least an added thirty minutes, and that was before the school run rush. I can only empathise with those who will have to contend with this, and hope their employers are more understanding. There is indeed a group to discuss any traffic concerns, however, as residents of the village, they have the right to share their experiences on either platform."

Kelly clicked on Barry's response and added her own watered-down two-cents. "Well said, Barry. Such a shame that your sensible concerns weren't listened to or this could have been avoided. You clearly have experience and knowledge of this, rather than a hidden agenda (like some people). If you're ever running for council, you've got my vote!"

Kelly watched as the thread grew and grew, with more people responding to Barry than to the original post. Kelly had heard about the incident on New Year's Eve when Mark Something-or-other, who lived on the corner of Sycamore Street, had snapped a picture of a group of youths carrying crates of booze to a house party. There had been more outrage about the teenagers' rights to privacy than about the under-age drinking. Kelly had heard that there were legal threats made to both the poster, an older man who lived alone, and to Jim, as the sole administrator of the page. Judging by some of the responses to Jim's comment, there were some parents still baying for his blood. Kelly felt a twinge of satisfaction at Jim getting his comeuppance. She'd be livid if someone slated her child on a public forum too.

Feeling more upbeat than she had earlier, as if the public disapproval of Jim was a sign from the universe that karma will prevail, Kelly was ready to start planning her own strategy for how she was going to get her life back on track.

Evan watched his colleagues start to pack up and leave for the day through the glass in the door of his office. Part of him wanted to join them; he was exhausted after a sleepless night and putting in a few more hours followed by an hour in the gym was the last thing he felt like doing.

Weary, he rested his elbows on his desk and buried his head in his hands. The moment his eyes closed, he felt the seductive warmth of sleep tempt him. He opened his eyes quickly and stretched in his chair, before standing up.

The hours he'd been working were ridiculous, but Evan had been planning for partnership for years, hence the move to this firm. He had been open about his ambition to Chris and Jane, and this had been the foundation for his move. His previous employer had been a family-run business, and despite Evan's excellent track record, the daughter of his boss had been given a partnership, and it was likely that the next on board would be a family member, and so Evan had felt he had no choice but to leave.

His sole ambition had been to start his own company. He would love it if one or both of his children went into the legal profession, and a family law firm would have been his ultimate dream. He had known from a young age what he wanted to do, but Jacob and Sophie hadn't shown any interest, although there was still plenty of time. He had had to get real about changing his long-term plan from his own company to making partner. Unlike some of his colleagues, his parents had been far from wealthy so there was no loan or inheritance, and the cost of supporting his own family made living without a guaranteed salary impossible. Ricer and Wallis were a good company though, and Evan thought a lot of Chris and Jane. It was definitely more likely that he'd achieve his dreams here than he would have done at his previous employers. It was hard work, but Evan was determined to do well and give his family the life they deserved. Growing up without much money, and not having the newest football kits and trainers that his school friends had always had, had been a huge motivator in Evan's working life. He wanted his kids to have everything he didn't and be able to make life comfortable for them when they were grown up.

He got up, seeing that the office was now almost empty, and went out to the small kitchen to make himself a rare cup of strong coffee. He was very careful about his diet, and tried to stick to water during the day, but he'd been tossing and turning most of the night, and he needed a shot of caffeine to stay focussed.

He was surprised to see Laura in the kitchen, head hidden as she rummaged through a cupboard.

"You're working late." He said.

Laura jumped, startled by his voice, and banged her head on the shelf of the cupboard.

"Ow!" She exclaimed.

Evan rushed forward in concern. "Are you ok?"

Laura emerged from the cupboard, removed her glasses and tenderly rubbed her forehead. Evan could see her eyes were watering from the impact. "I didn't hear you come in."

Laura leant back against the kitchen worktop, feeling dazed from the blow.

"Let me have a look." Evan came to Laura's side and gently peeled her hand away to reveal a golf-ball-sized lump.

He touched it gently and Laura winced in pain.

"Do you feel dizzy?" Evan asked, lowering his head and peering into Laura's eyes.

Laura flushed slightly at the intensity of Evan's gaze. He was so close that she could see the hazel flecks in his brown eyes and she looked down self-consciously. She did feel a little bit disorientated, but she didn't want to make a fuss.

"I'm ok." She said. She wanted to stand up straight, but his body was angled across hers and she couldn't move without bumping into him.

There was a heavy silence and Evan quickly backed away, as if aware that he was crowding her. He opened the small communal fridge and turned back to Laura, brandishing a cooling gel-pack.

"Here," He held it gently to her head. "This might help."

Laura felt the cool pad start to soothe her sore head and involuntarily closed her eyes at the sensation. She reached up to take hold of the pad, but it was a clumsy manoeuvre as Evan's hand was large and Laura's face wasn't, and for a moment their hands were touching. Laura was surprised to feel a little sizzle of something stir within her, but she quickly suppressed it. She firmly took hold of the pad.

"Dare I ask how long that's been in there?" Laura pulled a face, trying to make a joke to break the tension she felt.

"It came free with the fridge," Evan smiled in response. "I can almost guarantee that it's never been used."

Laura smiled, and then winced in pain again.

"You need to sit down." Evan instructed before gently steering Laura to her desk.

"I'm fine." Laura protested, but she let Evan guide her and took her seat gratefully.

"Why are you still here?" Evan asked, returning to his earlier comment. "Everyone has gone home, and you should have too."

"Just tying up a few loose ends." Laura shrugged.

"I was making a coffee," Evan said. "Fancy one?"

"That's what I was doing," Laura told him. "There's good coffee stashed at the back. The supermarket stuff out on the counter isn't the best."

"I'll bring it out to you," Evan offered. "Stay where you are."

He found the hidden designer coffee and carried two steaming cups over to Laura's desk. He paused, planning to return to his work, but decided against it and swung another chair around to join Laura.

"Thanks." She said, accepting the coffee gratefully. She'd discarded the gel pack, but her head still looked sore and tender.

"It's the least I could do," Evan grimaced. "After I've caused your head injury."

Laura smiled. "Don't be so dramatic. It's fine."

Evan took a sip of the coffee. "This is good stuff."

"You don't usually drink coffee." Laura remarked. "Need a boost?"

"I try to stick to water in the day," Evan admitted. "I'm running on empty today."

"Me too." Laura nodded. "What's up with you?"

"I couldn't sleep at all last night," Evan said. "I need to perk up, finish my work and hit the gym or I'll be falling asleep on the bench."

"Why don't you just give it a miss?" Laura asked. "One day won't hurt."

"I might." Evan said, but Laura could tell he didn't mean it. "What's up with you anyway? You're staying late *and* drinking coffee. That's practically unheard of."

Laura tried to smile, but Evan could see her dark eyes fill up with unshed tears.

"Laura!" He leaned forward, horrified that she was on the verge of tears. "Is your head really hurting? I think you need to see a doctor."

"No, no!" Laura waved away his concerns, but her face started to crumble. "It's not my head. Honestly, it's-"

Tear started to fall from her eyes and she abruptly stopped speaking, trying to mop up the tears with her fingertips.

"Oh, Laura." Evan reached behind him from a tissue, and not thinking about what he was doing, started to dry Laura's eyes for her.

The intimate gesture startled Laura and jerked her from her own emotional outburst. She reached for the paper tissue, covering Evan's hand for the second time that day, but this time deliberately, spurred on by some primitive part of her brain that she couldn't control.

Evan felt Laura's long, warm fingers cover his own, just as her eyes met his with a questioning look. His eyes moved to Laura's full, pink mouth and he felt a bolt of longing, moving his face closer to Laura before he realised what he was doing. Laura moved closer without realising she was doing it, but at the last moment, so quickly it wasn't clear who had come to their senses first, they pulled away. Laura quickly turned her head away, but not before Evan had seen her eyes widen in horror. He was equally horrified and shocked at his momentary lapse in control. He pushed his chair back creating space between them and awkwardly held the tissue he was still holding out to Laura. Laura took it and, smiling self-consciously, folded it in her hands.

"Sorry, I'm so tearful," She said, deciding that not acknowledging what had almost happened was the best action. "I've not been sleeping great either, and it messes with your head after a while, doesn't it?"

"Oh totally." Evan agreed, gratefully accepting Laura's unspoken agreement to ignore the near-miss. "Tiredness is the worst. I remember when Jacob was a baby and he had colic. I was so exhausted, I didn't notice I was wearing pyjama bottoms in the supermarket until an old lady pointed it out."

Laura gave a genuine laugh at this. "I remember driving around for miles to try to get Keeley to sleep and then sobbing in my car on my driveway when I realised that the moment I took her car seat out she'd wake up."

Evan grinned, and felt normality settle again between them. "How come you're not sleeping well? Everything still up-in-the-air at home?"

Laura's expression turned serious again. "Pretty much. Everything has kind-of snowballed. I know I mentioned we hadn't been getting on, but it's got to the point where there's nothing we agree on. Keeley, the neighbours, his posts on that bloody online group. I think I've gone past the point of being upset and I'm just exhausted by it all. I can't keep doing this."

Evan nodded sympathetically. "What are you going to do?"

"He won't move out," Laura shrugged. "I don't want to, but you know as well as me that I can't make him. I know the general consensus around the village is that he's an arse, but he's always had his good points. I just don't know what's happened to them."

She fell quiet, realising that she did know when Jim's positive traits had started to diminish, towards at her at least. She hadn't told anyone, not even the friends who she'd confided in about her arguments with Jim, about the condom he'd found in her bag. It was just too embarrassing, and if they believed her innocence, it would cast doubt on Keeley's honesty. Laura wasn't willing to throw Keeley's reputation under the bus for sympathy from anyone. She thought about telling Evan the truth. It felt like a heavy burden and keeping it a secret made it feel like she was the one in the wrong. Laura opened her mouth to speak at the same moment as Evan's mobile phone started to ring.

Evan looked at the screen and flashed Laura an apologetic look before excusing himself. He answered the phone, walking into his office and pushing the door behind him. The door didn't shut all the way and Laura couldn't help but hear Evan's side of the conversation.

"Sorry, I lost track of time." There was a short pause before he lowered his voice. "The office manager is still here. Can you come a little later?"

Laura glanced in the direction of Evan's office and he must have noticed her, as he walked over and closed the door quietly.

Laura frowned at Evan's strange behaviour. It sounded like he was making arrangements to meet someone at the office. Nobody should be seeing clients after hours. Before Laura had chance to puzzle over the overheard conversation, Evan walked back out of his office.

"Sorry about that," He smiled casually, no sign of guilt on his face. "Some clients expect us to be on call twenty-four hours a day. What were we saying?"

He picked up his coffee but didn't take a seat, hovering over her desk expectantly.

Laura shook her head. "I don't remember. Thanks for the coffee, but I've got to run."

Evan's face fell a little, but he nodded. "Is your head feeling better?"

Laura nodded. "It's fine."

She hurriedly packed up her things, returned the gel-pack and the cup to the kitchen and made for the door. "You're the last one here. Are you ok to lock up?"

Evan thought this was a strange thing to say, being as he was usually the last person in the building, but he nodded. He watched her car pull out from the car park, and replayed his phone conversation in his head, realising she must have overheard him. He exhaled noisily in exasperation and annoyance at himself. Not only had he almost kissed a colleague in a moment of craziness, but she now probably thought he was operating some dodgy side-line from the office. Or worse.

He cursed his stupidity. He could definitely blame today on tiredness.

Chapter 17

Laura silenced her alarm clock, and rather than jumping out of bed like she usually did, she rolled over on to her side and screwed her eyes shut. She drifted back into a semi-conscious slumber for the next hour, but a banging noise woke her with a start. She rolled back over to check the time and groaned in annoyance.

It was the first week of March and she'd been sleeping in the spare room since January. She'd purposely booked today off work and had been hoping to catch up on some much-needed rest. Between the erratic hours of the Simons' building work and the stress at home, Laura felt in a permanent zombie-like state.

Reluctantly, she slid out of bed, feeling with her feet for her slippers and slipped a dressing gown around her shoulders. Jim must have turned the heating off before he went to work, she realised as she shivered and padded downstairs. Laura caught sight of her reflection. Her eyes were shadowed with dark circles, her skin was pale and ashy, and her hair looked greasy and limp. Despite the distinct lack of exercise, she'd actually lost weight and she looked away uncomfortably from the image of her hollow, sunken cheekbones in the large hallway mirror.

"Happy birthday to me." She muttered aloud as she switched the kettle on.

This was also part of the reason she'd booked the day off work. Jane wrote down all the staff's birthdays on her office calendar and had brought up Laura's birthday the previous week.

"Where shall we go for your birthday drinks next week?" She'd asked, and Laura had felt herself recoil.

The last thing she wanted to do was celebrate her birthday, especially not with her colleagues. After the weird incident where Evan acted like he was going to kiss her, Laura had severed all social ties with him. The conversation she'd overheard him having in his office had rang enough alarm bells that Laura had raised the question to Jane in a tactful way, not to cause trouble for Evan, but she'd just needed to know that all was above board. Jane had assured her that she was aware that Evan helped a 'friend' who was a law student some evenings in the office.

"She lives locally," Jane had explained. "I think you were on holiday when she came in for a week, but Evan's sorting out a summer work placement too. He's a good one."

Despite Jane's plausible explanation, Laura thought about how "friendly" Evan had been to her and wondered if maybe he had a string of women, including twenty-something students and gym bunnies that he "helped out"; all while his poor wife was juggling the weekday chaos of the children alone. Laura curled her lip in disgust at just the thought of this. She had put a stop to their "running club" and, paranoid that he might see her out-and-about, she hadn't been running since. Jim had been going out more and more, and Laura had gradually stopped going to her fitness classes at the Leisure Centre. She was so exhausted from keeping up a cheerful pretence in work that she barely had the energy to make dinner for herself and Keeley when she came home from work before she would hide away in the spare room reading or watching television. Laura knew that she had fallen into a vicious circle; the lack of exercise left her feeling sluggish and lethargic, and the constant exhaustion stopped her reaching for her gym kit and trainers.

In a panic, she'd pretended to Jane that her daughter had booked her a spa day on her birthday and she's forgotten to book it off. Jane had, of course, insisted that Laura take the day off and Laura had made tentative noises about rescheduling a work's night out.

Keeley had left a card and present on the living room table, and Laura smiled fondly at the sentiment. She sat down and opened the card carefully, feeling tears spring to her eyes at Keeley's message. If it wasn't for Keeley, Laura would have packed up and left weeks ago. The atmosphere in the house was unbearable and Laura knew that the tense, icy-cold relationship with Jim was making her unwell. She couldn't go on much longer like this, despite her initial resolve. It wasn't that she was stubborn, or that she thought she had more right to the house than Jim, but it would look like an admittance of guilt if she left. Keeley didn't have the best relationship with Jim and Laura expected that Keeley would want to come with her if she left. Laura had enough savings to rent somewhere small, but she wouldn't be able to buy anywhere until they'd divided their assets, and it all just felt too overwhelming and final for Laura to make a decision.

She felt utterly dejected and miserable as she made herself a coffee and carried it back up the stairs. Laura rooted around in her wardrobe for a pair of earplugs, popped them in and crawled back into the spare bed to sleep her birthday away.

She came around several hours later, disorientated and

unsure how long she'd been asleep for. Blinking, Laura struggled to a sitting position and removed her ear plugs. The house was still silent, and she assumed that she couldn't have been asleep too long if Jim and Keeley were still at work and school. Laura showered and changed quickly, not wanting Keeley to see that she'd been led in bed all day. Keeley was sensitive to the atmosphere between her parents and Laura didn't want Keeley worrying about Laura's emotional wellbeing.

Laura noticed she had a few messages from friends wishing her a happy birthday, and she quickly responded to them before she noticed a message from Evan.

"Happy birthday. Hope you're having a good day. Miss our sessions. I know you said you were just too busy, but I'm hoping I didn't freak you out. Miss you. Evan." He had typed.

Laura felt irritated by his persistence and she thought about ignoring it, but instead replied. "Thanks. Just want to keep things professional from now on if you don't mind. Take care. Laura."

She put the message to the back of her mind and continued getting ready. Laura had promised Keeley that they would go out for food that evening. She'd planned to leave earlier than usual to avoid the uncomfortable pretence of Jim making an excuse to Keeley why he couldn't come. The lack of card or gift from him this morning was expected, but Laura still felt hurt by the cold snub.

They decided on forgoing their usual go-to restaurant for something slightly fancier and headed to The Walnut Tree.

"What are the desserts like?" Keeley asked as they battled

the traffic towards the motorway.

Usually this stretch would have been relatively clear at this time of day, with congestion in the opposite direction only, but ever since the roadworks had started on the Little Cedars road, everywhere was chaos and there'd been no improvement despite regular complaints from frustrated commuters. Laura, along with countless others, had just accepted that any journey was going to take at least twice as long for as long as the roadworks were in place.

"No idea," Laura replied. "I've never been here before."

They pulled up into the gravel car park and crunched their way to the main doors. Laura had made reservations and they waited in the bar area until their table was ready.

"Fancy a wine?" Laura joked to Keeley as she ordered them drinks.

Keeley grimaced at the memory of her awful misadventure with alcohol. She was glad her mum was able to joke about it. Her dad was still livid about it, two months on.

"I'm going to pop to the ladies." Laura said, placing the drinks down on the table. "Look out for the waitress."

Keeley picked up a menu from the side and read it as she waited for her mother to return.

"It's Keeley, isn't it?" A voice interrupted Keeley's thoughts and she looked up surprised to see Jordan's girlfriend, Felicity.

"Hi." Keeley said in surprise. "I didn't know you worked here."

Felicity smiled a little coolly. "Didn't you? Who are you here with?"

Keeley sensed a little animosity and realised she probably owed Felicity an apology for ruining her New Year. "I'm so sorry about New Year. I did tell Jordan to apologise and thank you for looking after me."

Felicity smiled, but this time with warmth. "Don't worry about that. We've all been in states!"

"I'm so embarrassed." Keeley admitted.

"There's really no need to apologise for that," Felicity shrugged. "Are you having food?"

"Yes," Keeley nodded, grateful that Felicity hadn't made her feel bad about that awful night. "It's my mum's birthday. I'm just waiting for her."

Felicity's face hardened. "Look, Keeley, I like you, but your parents are certainly not welcome here. There's no way my mum would accept a booking from them after how rude they were."

"What?" Keeley's mouth fell open in surprise. "What are you talking about?"

"I'm sorry if you didn't know," Felicity had the decency to look uncomfortable. "They were really rude to me and my mother New Year's Eve. I only knew they were your parents when I showed Jordan the spiteful review your dad posted. My mum has seen them a few times at the pub together and your mum has been quite rude there, as well. They're not welcome here. You'll have to leave."

Keeley was absolutely gobsmacked. She was too surprised

to even think about the logistics of what Felicity had said. She couldn't imagine her mum being rude, but she could picture her dad doing everything Felicity had said.

"Oh God," She responded mortified. "Felicity, I'm so sorry."

Felicity could see Keeley was genuinely shocked and touched her arm lightly. "I'm sorry to be so blunt, but I didn't want to cause a scene when my mum sees yours."

"No," Keeley nodded gratefully. "I'll go. I'm so sorry."

Keeley wanted the ground to open up and swallow her. She grabbed her and her mother's bag and turned towards the direction of the toilets. Her mum was just coming out when Keeley reached her.

"Everything ok?" She asked, concerned at Keeley's panic-stricken face.

"Mum," She whispered urgently. "We've got to leave."

"Why?" Laura grabbed Keeley's hand and swung her around to face her. "What's happened?"

"You and dad," Keeley said in frustration. "I know it probably wasn't you, but the manager and her daughter remember how rude you and Dad were New Year, and they won't serve us."

"What?" Laura shook her head in confusion. "What are you on about?"

Keeley could see the few people in the bar start to turn and look at them. "And they said you drink at the same pub as them, and you've given the mum some attitude. Please, Mum, can we just leave?"

Laura was staring at Keeley, worried that she was having a breakdown. She knew Keeley had more than her fair share of teenage stresses, but she hadn't realised that things had gotten that bad.

"Let's go outside," Laura said, struggling to keep her tone calm. "You can tell me properly."

Keeley nodded. Her heart was pounding in her chest, her mouth was dry, and she just wanted to get away.

Before she could slink out of the door, Felicity rushed over, a look of horror etched across her pretty face.

"Oh my God, Keeley!" She gasped, clasping her hands to her mouth. "I'm so sorry. You didn't say your parents were divorced!"

Felicity took Keeley's hand and pulled her back before addressing Laura. "So sorry! When Keeley said she was with her mum, I just assumed you were the horrible blonde woman. Keeley, you should have said!"

Laura was even more confused now, but she allowed herself to be led back into the bar area.

"Your table is ready," Felicity gushed. "And Keeley said it was your birthday. We'll organise some extra-special desserts from us."

"Thank you," Laura said politely. "But can I ask what's going on?"

When Laura finally pieced together what had actually happened, she was absolutely furious. She tried to keep her composure in front of Keeley, as Keeley was clearly shaken up by the incident.

"Who was he with?" Keeley asked, her small voice pierced the silence as they drove home.

"Oh, love," Laura felt a rush of emotion at the damage they were doing to their daughter. "It was probably just his awful council friends. Don't worry about it."

Keeley nodded and fell back into a mournful silence.

Laura's heart sank when she saw Jim's car on the drive and the lights on in the house. She followed Keeley in through the door.

"I'm going to go up to bed." Keeley said quietly.

Laura felt like her heart was breaking as she watched her daughter, head bowed, disappear to her room. Jim glanced up at Laura as she walked in.

"Happy birthday." He said civilly.

Laura smiled coldly. "I'll be looking for somewhere else to live tomorrow. I imagine Keeley will come with me, but it's her choice."

Jim looked startled for a moment, but he turned away from her. "That's your choice. I don't expect my daughter to be exposed to your new boyfriend."

Laura felt her temper flare up, but she managed to keep her tone calm. "Fuck off, Jim."

She turned away and walked up to her bedroom, shutting the door firmly behind her. Laura vowed that whatever happened, she would be out of this house tomorrow. She couldn't live like this anymore. Laura managed to turn the volume on the television up in time to drown out the sound of her sobs as she cried herself to sleep on her forty-fifth birthday.

Barry Simons raised a hand in greeting to Laura and her daughter as they got out of their car on the driveway, but neither seemed to notice him. He shrugged it off and climbed into his own car, gunned the engine and reversed out of the driveway.

He had been feeling stir-crazy in the house these past few weeks. The attic conversion had nearly been completed, but there was still plumbing, electric work and plastering to be completed before they even got around to the tedious tasks of decorating. In a way, he was glad of the distraction. Barry had taken heed of Dana's stresses and had made an effort to stay in more. He had been to the pub once or twice in January but had made a concerted effort to avoid it in February; to prove to himself that he could more than anything.

Dana was constantly on the verge of tears over the state of the house. Upstairs was like a building site and one of the kids had put their foot through a bag of plaster that had been left on the landing when they stayed last weekend. The vacuum cleaner, after weeks of picking up dust and debris, had finally given up and Dana had been close to packing a case and going to stay in a hotel for the duration of the works.

Barry was aware that he was struggling to maintain his usual cheerful disposition. He felt like his nerves were shot and his temper was constantly bubbling up under the surface. He'd lost his temper with the children, after the plaster incident. Chloe had been so upset that she'd demanded to go home to her mother. Barry had immediately felt like the worst parent in the world and he had managed to smooth the situation over, but it had stuck in his head. The worst part had been, his guilt about yelling at the kids combined with Dana stressing over the broken cleaner, had made him feel uncharacteristically hostile towards Dana. If she hadn't made such a fuss about him being out, he'd have been to the pub and wouldn't have been so pent-up and on edge. With a clear mind, he would have disciplined the children and encouraged them to help him clean up the mess, rather than lose his rag and cause the whole house to descend into chaos. Barry acknowledged that his thoughts were irrational and not remotely productive, but he couldn't help that they were the first that came to mind.

Barry hadn't had the best week in work. They'd lost out on the top road contract to another company, but they'd been more interested in chasing the big earner of the planned dual carriageway to care at the time. The bidding for the contract had been postponed, and Barry had had to report to his bosses today that their rival company had successfully won several medium-sized jobs in the area over their bid. Barry was frustrated with himself that he hadn't seen the competition was serious. They'd been the number one in their district, and many other areas in the country, for years, but it seemed like some smaller companies were gaining reputation and nipping at their heels. Barry's first thought had been that it was his fault; he was too stressed and somehow this had impacted his bid. He recognised the warning signs in his train of thoughts. He knew that he was looking to make excuses for himself, but even recognising the behaviour, it was hard not to just give in.

Barry drove across the village to the supermarket. Lindsey

had texted him, asking if he could have the kids tomorrow after school as she had an emergency doctor's appointment. He didn't feel that he could say no, seeing as it was an emergency, but he had a meeting over in Barnchurch and had had to ask Dana if she minded getting them. If work hadn't been such a nightmare, he would have postponed his meeting, so he didn't feel like he was burdening her, but she had insisted it was fine. He was planning on buying something quick and easy to make for their tea, to ensure that Dana didn't have any hassle when they refused to eat something as simple as Spaghetti Bolognaise.

Dana had gone out to meet her friend, Steph, and Barry eyed her car outside The Crown enviously. He drove on to the supermarket. Despite it being late, the journey took longer than the usual ten minutes due to the useless traffic lights in place. He filled his basket quickly and, as he packed his shopping into the car, received a text from Gary seeing if he fancied a beer.

He'd seen a lot of Gary lately as he'd completed the work in his house, but, without their regular pub nights, Barry hadn't had a chance to have a proper catch up with him. Barry owed Gary a beer for the great job he'd done on the house, and Dana was out anyway. Barry paused, staring at the message, feeling tempted to give himself a day off from his new lifestyle. Dana was at The Crown though, and Barry had made a big deal about how he was "having a few months off".

Barry could practically taste an ice-cold beer, but his resolve was strong, and he started to type out a response to Gary declining. Although, he paused half way through the message, it would be rude after everything Gary had done for him. He'd already proved to himself that he didn't *need* to go to the pub. He could make do with quiet evenings in and a glass or two of wine in the house. He tapped out a reply to Gary and got into his car waiting for a response.

"Pick me up and we'll pop up the Newton instead." Gary replied immediately.

Barry felt some of the tension of the last week melt away and he made his way to Gary's house. Within twenty minutes, they were sat at a table in the cosy Newton Inn with two pints on the table in front of them.

"Nice to have a change of scenery." Gary said, sipping his pint.

"It is," Barry agreed. "Thanks for agreeing to come here. I've got a bet on with Dana that I can stay out of The Crown and I'm not losing."

This wasn't technically true, but Barry didn't want Gary to think he was under the thumb.

Gary laughed. "To be honest, it's nice to have a change from the usual faces and the same old moaning."

They chatted easily about work, football and life, sinking a few more pints. Barry felt more relaxed than he had in weeks and was just thinking about buying the next round when Gary looked at his phone in alarm.

"Oh, for God's sake," He muttered. "Not again."

"What's the matter?" Barry asked.

"Emma's just messaged to say the dog has got out through the back gate again and they're all kicking off on the village page about it." Gary groaned in annoyance. "I can't stop her doing it, but she's not going to hurt anybody. Emma's fuming at me now, as that Jim has advised people to call the warden, so Emma's gone out to look for her."

"He's an arsehole," Barry said. "People should mind their own business."

"I might have to go," Gary grimaced. "Let me just try to call Emma and see if she's managed to find her. I don't want her getting picked up and sent down the pound."

Gary got up and wandered outside to use his phone. Barry looked through the post on his own phone and felt the familiar annoyance that Jim Burbridge provoked in him.

The original post had been delivered in a friendly tone, but the comments were like a witch hunt before Jim had stepped in with his cold and condescending message that he had "reported the dog to the warden and advises others to do the same", claiming that the owner has had numerous chances to secure their animal.

Gary came back into the pub, looking pale. "I'm going to have to go, mate. Emma can't find her. I'm worried the warden has had her or some busybody has taken her down as a stray. She's so placid, she'd go off with anyone."

Barry gulped down his pint quickly and got to his feet. He drove Gary back to his house and got out of his car ready to help him search for the animal. At that moment, Gary received a message on his phone. His face lit up and he held the phone out to Barry to show him.

"Your Dana has got him!" He exclaimed in relief. "She saw her waiting outside The Crown and took her home for safe-keeping when she saw the mob mentality online."

"Oh, thank God for that." Barry said relieved. "Jump in. We'll go and get her."

Gary quickly called Emma, and Barry could hear he was getting an earful. He grinned sheepishly at Barry as he hung up.

"In trouble now, are you, mate?" Barry grinned back.

"She's in a mood with me anyway because I bought Kelly Russell a drink last Friday," Gary shrugged. "This is the excuse she needs to have a proper kick off."

Barry parked his car on the drive and went into the house. Dana was stood at the back door, watching the big dog run around the garden.

"Thank you!" Gary said gratefully to Dana. "I was terrified she was going to end up in the pound. I'm going to board that gate up first thing. I don't know how she's getting out all the time."

"She's a clever girl," Dana said, stroking the dog's soft head. "There's some spiteful people about so I got her to jump in the car with me. You should be careful though, Gary, anyone could have pinched her."

"I know." Gary nodded. "Thank you. I really am grateful."

When he had left, Dana turned to Barry and regarded him suspiciously. "Have you just driven home like that?"

"Like what?" Barry asked innocently.

"Drunk." Dana said slowly. Barry could see the

disappointment on her face.

"I'm not drunk," He protested. "I had one with Gary. Don't make a big deal of it."

"You've had more than one," Dana scowled. "Look at the parking on that!"

She pointed through the kitchen window to his car, parked at an angle, on the driveway, and Barry felt a surge of irritation.

"I parked it quickly because Gary was in a rush!" Barry burst out in frustration. "Honestly, I can't win!"

Dana's eyes narrowed, and she looked like she was weighing up her next comment, but instead she said nothing, sitting down heavily at the table as if she were too weary to continue. Guilt flooded Barry and he crossed the kitchen to wrap his arms around his wife.

"I'm sorry." He said finally, not able to bear the hurt on Dana's face.

"It's fine," Dana shrugged. "I'm overreacting."

"You're not." Barry said, and he took a breath as if ready to pour out everything he'd been holding inside. He opened his mouth to speak, but he felt tongue-tied and the words wouldn't come, so instead he went out to the car to bring in the shopping.

Dana made polite small-talk with Barry when he came back into the house, but there was a definite tension that even Barry, in his tipsy state, could sense. They cautiously tiptoed around each other and, by the time Dana made her excuses and went up to bed, Barry felt scrambled and miserable.

He sat alone, in the decadently decorated living room that Dana had put her heart and soul into, and fidgeted mindlessly with his phone, trying to distract himself from the same thoughts that kept tumbling to the front of his mind. His eyes caught sight of the online post that had led him to rush home, causing that heart-wrenching look of sadness on Dana's beautiful face. Even seeing Jim's name made Barry's sadness flare quickly to anger. Barry's melancholy thoughts twisted into something darker.

Barry heard the front door open and Jordan walk in.

"Jordan!" Barry called. "Can you show me how to do something?"

Jordan loped into room and Barry explained what he wanted. Jordan took the phone from him and Barry tried to concentrate on what Jordan was telling him.

"What are you doing this for?" Jordan asked, looking over Barry's shoulder as he furiously tapped away.

"Because he deserves it," Barry told his stepson emphatically. "We're all sick of him."

Chapter 18

Tina wished that time would slow down. She had seriously over-committed herself this week; spreading herself thinly to try to get everything done and please everybody. Thankfully it was Friday, and she had just one job to get done, some emails to look through and then everything else could wait until Monday morning.

Even as she thought this, she remembered with a shudder that she'd agreed to cover a shift Sunday evening at the pub. Her heart filled with dread, but she forced herself to think positively before the overwhelmed sensation had time to take hold.

"It's a few hours of easy work," She promised herself. "And it's not for much longer."

Tina walked into what she referred to as "Robbie's room" but had been serving as her office. She fired up the laptop, and rooted around for her reading glasses, pleased that she'd woken up early enough to start making a dent in the admin she'd been letting pile up. She crosschecked, with her online banking, what payments were still outstanding, sent out some reminders and processed some payments quickly. Once she was done, she meticulously double-checked everything until she was satisfied that all was as it should be.

She grabbed a jacket and a bag of supplies and headed out to her only job for the day, wishing she didn't have to go.

This constant juggling would all be a thing of the past soon, she thought happily, as she braved the chilly spring morning to her client's house. She stopped at the shop on the way, using the ATM to draw out some cash and buy a few of the essentials she'd need, and as she dropped her purse back into her bag, she noticed a new message on her phone.

Tina noticed the name of the sender first and, assuming it were a personal message, read it as she stood in the doorway to the store. It was only when she'd digested the message, Tina realised, with horror, that it had been sent to her business page.

She re-read the message, feeling sick to the stomach as she comprehended that she would have to respond one way or another.

Tina stared at the phone in her hand, as if gaping at it would help her to think of a solution. She wished she'd just been honest from the start, but she'd had her reasons; mainly the desire for an easy life. Tina had poured her heart, soul, blood, sweat and tears into turning what had been a part-time job to fund her life into a successful business that employed three local workers. She was finally in a position where she had found someone to buy the business, leaving her free to concentrate on her real ambitions. It was typical that the moment she was in a great space, something like this would happen and rain on her parade.

Her first thought was to send a quick, informal message explaining that she'd verbally agreed the sale already, but Tina knew that it was likely that everyone would find out that she was the founder of Sparkles once the new owner was in place and the lies would just cause hurt and bad feeling. Resolutely, Tina dropped her phone into her bag. As much as it would pain her, she knew that she needed to have this conversation over the phone or face-to-face; a flippant message wouldn't do. Her hesitation had taken a few minutes of her time, and she picked up her pace, wanting to get the job over and done with now she had another task added to her list.

Tina reached her destination and, her brain was so addled from the shock of the message, it took her a few minutes to work out what was different about the four-bedroomed semi-detached home. She stopped in her tracks at the end of the driveway, surveying the scene in confusion, before she realised what it was.

It was the car on the driveway. Someone was home. Tina knew it wasn't Laura's car and she proceeded with hesitation. Sometimes this happened, and a client was unexpectedly home, but Tina had reservations as she'd never really had any interactions with the husband, although she'd heard enough about him from friends and customers to feel wary.

Instead of unlocking the door with the key in her pocket, Tina knocked loudly and stepped back to wait. It took a few moments for Jim to answer the door, looking uncharacteristically dishevelled and red-eyed.

"Yes?" He eyed her suspiciously.

"Hi," Tina pasted on a cheerful smile, despite his unfriendly greeting. "I'm booked to clean today. Is it convenient?"

"Who do you work for?" He asked slowly as if verifying her story.

Tina wondered whether he was ill; he seemed confused and disorientated. "Sparkles."

Jim frowned at this. "Who booked you?"

Tina fought the urge to sigh. "Your wife. Laura. I've been coming every week for the last year or so."

That seemed to trigger some recognition.

"Laura doesn't live here anymore," He said coldly. "She should have informed your employers that you were no longer needed."

"Right," Tina said awkwardly. "She's paid up until this week, so would you like me to-"

"No," Jim cut her off. "In fact, I'm horrified to learn she's had this company in my house without my permission. A good friend of mine had jewellery stolen by a colleague of yours. I'm not accusing you, of course, but you can see why I'd be cautious."

Tina was gobsmacked at his audacity. "That's a lie."

"What?" Jim looked surprised at her response as if he hadn't expected her to speak back.

Tina was too incensed at his accusations to process that his wife had seemingly moved out and maybe he was acting out of character. "That someone stole from your friend. I own the business, and I've had nothing reported to me about any of my employees."

"Well, you would say that." Jim looked down on Tina from the doorstep, his lip curling up into a sneer before slamming the door in her face.

Tina was livid. She'd heard all kinds of rumours and gossip about what a horrible man Jim Burbridge was, but she'd never expected him to be a spiteful, vindictive liar. Her hands were trembling with rage as she marched out of the street.

Tina still felt shaken up as she unlocked the door and let herself into her home. She had been working hard on trying to focus on the positives in life, and she told herself that, despite the upset, she now had two hours back in her day and no longer had to fit that house into an already packed week. Tina sat down at her desk, but she was too wired, after the confrontation, to be able to focus on anything that required brain-work. She got back up, dragged out her own cleaning supplies and blitzed her apartment until it was sparkling.

By the time she had finished, she felt calm enough to sit back down and tackle the last of her to-do list. This thought reminded her of the message she needed to reply to. Frustrated, Tina got back up for the second time and took her phone from her bag. Before she could even think about starting to compose an apology, she noticed her online business page had a new review.

Her blood turned to ice as she read the spiteful, fabricated words in disbelief, her rage growing by the moment until she was physically trembling with fury.

She knew that there was nothing she could do to delete the lies from Sparkles' profile, and she realised, with horror, that not only was this embarrassing, but it could potentially cost her the sale of the business. It didn't take long for the tears to come, at this thought, and she wept with sheer frustration that, after years of struggling to get by, she was going to be knocked down at the final hurdle.

Tina hadn't thrown herself down on her bed and wept

devastated tears since her teenage years, but she felt overwhelmed with unspent anger. She sobbed at the injustice until she felt purged of her tears and ready to take constructive action.

She pulled herself up into a sitting position, and rubbed at her red, puffy eyes. She wasn't going to take this lying down, and she had an idea of how she could fix this.

Kelly woke up on Saturday morning with her phone still clutched in her hand. She blinked groggily and gently lowered the phone onto her pillow, flexing her stiff fingers to loosen them up. She felt someone stir next to her, which surprised her as she usually woke up alone on Saturdays. Her legs were hanging out of the blanket, and she drew them in, tangling them with her sleeping partner's own limbs to warm up.

"Evan," She mumbled sleepily. "What time is it?"

"Early." He grunted in response.

Kelly closed her eyes again, but then remembered the reason that she'd gone to sleep clutching her phone like a life raft and opened them again. She checked her phone with nervous anticipation and felt the familiar deflated sensation when there was no message in her inbox. She sighed, and rolled onto her back, staring up at the ceiling.

Since she'd made her mind up to quit the money-saving business venture, she'd been frantically searching for something to fill the void and pay the bills. She'd seen this great opportunity advertised online and had immediately felt like her prayers were being answered. This was different than all the various schemes and franchises she'd been involved in. It was local, it was established and more importantly, it would be all hers. She'd have employees and responsibilities. She would be honour-bound to make it a success, for the sake of the staff, which was a huge 'plus' to Kelly. She knew that she had dropped more than one previous venture the minute the going had got tough, but this would be different, and she knew she would put her all into it. All that was standing in her way was the response from the owner.

Kelly hadn't mentioned it to Evan yet. He had looked annoyed when she had explained that she was finishing her latest venture, and he may not have said "I told you so" but Kelly was more than capable of reading between the lines. She sat in bed for a few moments, allowing herself the luxury of daydreaming about owning her own company. Since she'd decided that this was what she wanted to do, Kelly had felt a renewed optimism and sense of purpose. She was even willing to help out herself when her staff took leave or were sick. Kelly held the daydream to herself like a comfort blanket and checked her phone once more, just to be on the safe side.

Kelly slipped out of bed, unable to fall back asleep with all the thoughts and plans rushing around her head and wandered downstairs to make her morning smoothie. She cleaned up after herself, rather than leaving the ingredients and utensils littered across the worktops as she usually did and decided to make a start on the kids' packed lunches for their activities, despite this being Evan's job. She heard an alarm go off upstairs and wandered up to wake the children.

Begrudgingly, they began to rise. Kelly was surprised to see

Evan had snoozed his alarm and fallen back into a deep sleep. She bent to shake him awake, before changing her mind, switching his alarm off and dressing herself. He hadn't been himself for ages, Kelly thought as she arranged her hair in a messy bun on top of her head in the bedroom mirror, he never slept in. This might do him some good.

The children both looked shocked when Kelly made them breakfast and told them she'd be taking them to their various activities today.

"Is Dad dead?" Jacob asked, widening his eyes in mock horror.

Kelly couldn't help but laugh at his cheek. "No, he's having a lie in. Now, hurry up!"

Kelly was surprised at how much time was wasted sitting around between drop-offs and pick-ups and decided to use the time that Sophie was swimming to use the gym at the Leisure Centre. She did a quick thirty-minute set but was so anxious about not being late for the end of Sophie's lesson that she was ten minutes early. Kelly was adamant that today would run smoothly and neither of her children would have reason to criticise her Saturday takeover to Evan and give him the satisfaction of thinking she couldn't cope.

The only downside to a spontaneous workout was Kelly hadn't brought any clean clothes and would be stuck in her sweaty workout gear for the rest of the day. She was doing her best to calm the redness of her skin with the only make-up she could find in her bag, when a familiar voice spoke, surprising her.

"Hello stranger."

Kelly cursed her enthusiasm. She hadn't seen Darren for ages. It was typical that when she did, she was looking like a hot mess.

"Hi," She clicked her compact shut and looked up him, twisting her mouth into a friendly smile. "How are you?"

"Good," Darren wasn't much taller than Kelly, but he was quite muscular and easily twice her width. "I messaged you the other day."

"Oh God," Kelly pulled an apologetic face. "I totally forgot. Everything has been so hectic."

For good measure, Kelly leaned forward and touched his bicep gently.

"What's been going on?" Darren asked sounding concerned and leaning into her touch.

Kelly felt the familiar satisfaction that her subtle flirting had worked on Darren.

"Oh," She widened her eyes and removed her hand, stretching both arms up over her head to adjust her hair. She hid a smile as Darren predictably ran his eyes over her curves. "I've had a nightmare with work. I'm buying a business and everything's just chaotic."

"Wow," Darren's eyes settled back on her face. "What kind of business?"

Kelly gave a secretive smile. "All will be revealed. How's things with you anyway?"

"Good," Darren nodded. "I haven't seen you at the pub for a while."

"Busy," She gave him a flirty wink. "I'll be there tonight."

"Me too," Darren's face lit up. "Are you going out with Tina?"

"Not tonight," Kelly shook her head and made a sad face. "I'll probably be on my own."

"I'll buy you a drink." Darren promised.

"I might let you," Kelly grinned in response. "I've got to go and get my daughter. It's been nice to see you. Hopefully catch up soon!"

She sashayed off in the direction of the swimming changing rooms and frowned slightly at their exchange. He had a cheek, she thought to herself. Bloody men.

It was late afternoon by the time Kelly arrived home with the kids. She was surprised that she still felt upbeat and energetic, despite having spent the whole day ferrying the children around and still not having received a message from the business seller.

Evan was sprawled across the sofa, watching football, when Kelly walked in. He smiled appreciatively at her.

"Thanks for today," He said. "I had the best sleep."

"Good," Kelly bent down and gave him a rare kiss on the lips. "You needed it."

Evan looked delighted at her gesture and pulled her down next to him. Kelly laughed as she tumbled onto the sofa, and Jacob made a disgusted noise at his parents' show of affection and stormed upstairs. Evan and Kelly exchanged amused glances, and Kelly got back to her feet.

"Aw." Evan held out a hand to her. "Come and watch the football with me."

"I'm going for a shower." Kelly smiled in response.

"Do you want to do something later?" Evan asked unexpectedly.

Kelly nodded tentatively. "Like what?"

"Shall we all go for food over the pub?" He offered.

Kelly regarded her husband for a moment. If he was going to be flirty and good-natured every time he had a lie in, she thought she'd get up early every Saturday from now on.

"Yes," She agreed. "See if your mum if she wants to come, too."

Evan looked surprised, but Kelly had left the room before he'd had time to say anything else. Evan's good mood boosted her own positivity, and Kelly found herself in a remarkably upbeat temperament for the rest of the day. Evan drove over with the kids to pick Pam up for the evening, giving Kelly time to have a bath and take her time blow-drying her hair into loose, bouncy waves around her shoulders. She wasn't ready when Evan beeped the horn outside, so she sent them over ahead of her, finished getting ready and drove herself to The Crown.

"You look beautiful." Evan complimented her as she walked into the lounge and took a seat at the table.

Kelly flushed with pleasure at his comment and wondered whether this new start in her career was just what their marriage needed. She chatted animatedly to her husband and Pam, enjoying the quality family time. As they were finishing their meal, talk turned to the online Oak Village Community page. Pam was a member of the Little Cedars group, a larger online community for the whole suburb, and they often compared characters and posts that overlapped.

"Did you see that nasty man getting..." Pam looked to Jacob when she couldn't think of the right word. "What's the word you say, Jake? When someone gets reprimanded?"

Jacob smiled at his grandmother. "Roasted, Nan?"

Pam looked pleased and Kelly hid a smile at her hip mother-in-law.

"Which nasty man?" Kelly asked, looking interested. "I haven't looked at the page for a few days?"

Pam's eyes lit up at the prospect of having fresh gossip for her daughter-in-law. "I'll show you."

She got out her phone, but the page wouldn't load. Evan offered his phone and Kelly leaned over Pam to help her find the post. Her eyes widened in surprise that Jim Burbridge had left a review on Sparkles, the cleaning company's business page and shared the review to the online community group. The business, as well as several loyal customers, had responded, criticising Jim.

Kelly noted that Barry Simons had been particularly vocal in his defence of the business and his criticism of Jim. Their rivalry was a common topic in the village now, but even Kelly couldn't believe the level of public hostility between the men.

Pam waited for Kelly to finish catching up on the drama. "Can you believe it?"

Kelly shook her head, re-reading the comments in silence. She knew people tended to be more outspoken online than in person, but this thread was really something else. Kelly felt a little uneasy at the post and she used her thumb to swipe the app closed on Evan's phone. She was just about to hand it over to Evan, when she caught sight of his messages. She wasn't snooping; they were open underneath his internet application and had popped up when she had closed his social media.

It was the name "Laura Burbridge", the third message down, that caught Kelly's attention and the first line of text "Thanks. Just want to keep things professional…". Kelly felt her heart quicken but kept her face neutral.

She angled her body away from Pam, so Pam couldn't see what she was reading. Kelly reached over and drained her glass of wine.

"Can you pour me another please?" She asked sweetly, hoping to divert attention away from her for a moment to give her time to read Evan and Laura's chain of messages.

She read the thread backwards, reading Laura's curt response first. Her stomach dropped when she read Evan's unsolicited message.

"Happy birthday. Hope you're having a good day. Miss our sessions. I know you said you were just too busy, but I'm hoping I didn't freak you out. Miss you. Evan."

She felt a rush of hurt, followed by anger. She scrolled back through the messages and saw, with shock, that he'd been regularly meeting up with that woman before Christmas. Sometimes two or three times a week. Her heart was racing now at the discovery, but she stayed tight-lipped. Her children and her mother-in-law were present. She closed the thread and, wordlessly, handed the phone back to Pam to return to Evan.

"Are you ok?" Evan had noticed his wife turn pale.

Kelly nodded, taking her wine and draining half of the glass in one go. "I'm just shocked at those comments."

Evan regarded Kelly suspiciously but said nothing.

"Are we going yet?" Jacob interrupted.

"Are you coming back to ours?" Evan asked Pam.

Pam looked at Kelly expectantly. "Oh, I'm sure you two would like some time to yourselves."

"No, it's ok," Kelly said. "I'm meeting a friend in a minute here. You can keep Evan company at the house."

Evan looked surprised, but he got to his feet. "Come back to ours for a coffee, and I'll drop you home later."

"Get me another bottle of wine while you're at the bar." Kelly called to Evan, purposely not making eye contact.

Evan returned with the wine, and Kelly picked the bottle up, ducking his kiss and walking towards the bar.

"Don't drive home." Evan warned her, and she gave him a cool smile as her family left.

Once her family were safely out of sight, Kelly felt the adrenaline start to course through her body. She stayed in the lounge area, not wanting the distraction of people around her while she was processing this discovery. Her hands trembled with the shock as she poured herself a drink from the new bottle. She sat and thought about what she had read. There could be no 'innocent' explanation for it. Something had clearly been going on between the pair of them and Laura had ended it for whatever reason. Kelly felt sick, but she kept drinking, letting the alcohol numb the hurt.

Her mind raced with the revelation and she thought about how she was going to confront Evan. A rational voice inside her head told her he would deny it. Evan was far from stupid, and he'd have an innocent excuse. Kelly wished she'd had longer to go through the messages to gather the evidence, but it was too late now. She suddenly realised what she needed to do to get the truth. Kelly pushed the half-finished wine away and got to her feet. She noted, in the back of her mind, that she was a little tipsy, but she dug out her car keys and made her way into the car park.

The cold air of the March evening sobered her up a little and she drove the short distance to Barry Simons' house. She knew the Burbridge family lived next door, and she pulled her car up outside. Barry's house was at the end of the cul-de-sac, and Kelly looked between the house adjoining his and the one on the other side trying to work out which was the right house.

It was dark now, and she got out of her car to take a proper look. Barry's car was missing from his own driveway, revealing a heap of discarded building supplies outside the garage door. This jolted Kelly's memory. There had been a building dispute, she remembered, which suggested that the Burbridges lived in attached house to Barry's.

Without giving herself time to plan what she was going to

say, Kelly marched up the driveway and banged sharply on the door.

Chapter 19

Keeley heard her alarm go off and slipped out of bed quickly. She never set her alarm on the weekend. During the week, it took three snoozed alarms and her parents yelling at her for her to rise, but today was different. Keeley wanted to be up and out of the house.

She dressed quickly, not daring to shower and risk waking her father. She debated exiting via her emergency window route, but she decided she didn't want to risk her means of escape being discovered. Instead, she crept down the stairs and out through the front door.

Keeley had nowhere to be or nothing to do, but since her mother had left the day after her birthday, Keeley had felt trapped in the house. Her mum had assured her that it was only temporary, speaking to her for the first time like an adult.

"Keeley," Laura had said, looking weary and exhausted. "I can't stay here another night. I'm going to stay with Gina and I'll find somewhere as soon as I can."

Keeley had wanted to cry and beg for her mother to stay, but the pain in Laura's dark eyes stopped Keeley from making any tearful demands. Keeley knew, instinctively, that if she'd shown any weakness, her mum would have abandoned her own needs and stayed for her. She couldn't ask her mum to keep sacrificing her own happiness.

"It's ok, Mum," Keeley had replied bravely. "You've got to do what's right for you. Just don't take too long, ok?"

They had both been fighting back tears at this point. Keeley had offered to stay off school and help her mum move some things out during the day. They were both aware that once Laura left the house, it was likely that Jim would do all he could to prevent her coming back and taking anything else. Laura had declined Keeley's offer, and Keeley was secretly glad as she didn't think she could keep up the courageous façade for much longer. The moment she'd got to school and away from her mother, Keeley had promptly burst into tears.

Thursday evening had been weird. Keeley had felt a stab of sympathy for her dad, looking dishevelled and miserable. He'd brushed away her one attempt to talk about it and he hadn't thanked her for leaving him a plate of bolognaise. Keeley had noticed the plate untouched on the counter when she was making her breakfast Friday morning, and in a moment of anger at the situation, had thrown it, plate and all, straight into the bin.

Keeley had spoken to her mum several times over the course of the two days. It didn't go unnoticed to Keeley that, even in her mother's lowest moments, she was still her mum's priority. Keeley was both elated and saddened when her mum texted her to tell her she'd found somewhere to live. Laura warned her that it wasn't big, and it was only temporary, as a friend of Gina's had an empty flat on the Oak Fields estate. Keeley was happy that her mother wouldn't have to sofa-surf with friends, and Keeley was happy that she wouldn't be stuck with her gloomy and bad-tempered father, but it felt very final.

Keeley had lived in Sycamore Street all her life. She couldn't imagine waking up in a different room or making breakfast in a different kitchen. More than that, she'd lived with both parents all her life. Her mother hadn't said anything about the separation, except for that they'd hadn't been getting on for a long time and 'this was the right thing to do'. Keeley knew that Laura finding out about the extent of Jim's relationship with Kate was the key driver, but her mum refused to discuss this with Keeley. Keeley felt torn between outraged anger at her father and sympathy for the pitiful figure who was too proud to admit he was wrong. She also felt a heavy dose of guilt at the realisation that she hadn't even considered staying with her dad.

"He's still your dad," Laura had warned her, when they had talked on the phone last night before Keeley went to sleep. "Of course, I want you to live with me, but you live with Dad too."

Keeley had wanted to say that she didn't want to live with her dad, but she'd heard these words in her head and had thought that they sounded childish and petulant. She certainly wouldn't be living with him if he moved that woman in, Keeley thought, her temper flaring up again. She hadn't voiced any of these thoughts to her mother though.

"When do you think the flat will be ready?" Keeley had asked instead.

"I can get the keys tomorrow," Laura had told her. "I'll get the basics and hopefully move some stuff in Sunday."

"I'll help you." Keeley had offered, and they had made plans to see each other Sunday.

In Keeley's head, tonight would be the last night she spent in her family home. She had already started to discreetly pack up some things that she needed to take. She was conscious of not hurting her father's feelings, but he had shown no concern over how she felt since her mum had moved out.

Keeley's eyes stung from a combination of the cold morning wind and the tears of sadness prickling up behind them, and she brushed them away with her fingertips. She had wanted to get up and out of the house, to avoid the uncomfortable atmosphere, but it wasn't even 9am on a Saturday morning and none of her friends would be awake for hours. She realised, with annoyance, that she hadn't thought this through very well and it was colder than she had expected it to be. She should have just stayed in bed, feigning sleep.

Keeley walked out of the village and along the top road, having to cross several times because of the road works. She walked in the direction of Birch Grove, with no purpose in mind except to do something until she *actually* had something to do. She had plans to go into Finchester with Ellie shopping at midday and then she was going to the cinema with Ollie and some others this evening, otherwise she'd have offered to help her mum. She kept walking until she reached the turning for the supermarket. Keeley had been walking for about forty minutes, and she decided to kill some time wandering around before she walked back to call for Ellie. She was hungry and tired, and she eyed up the instore café wishing she had the confidence to sit in there on her own.

She could see the security guard watching her suspiciously and, fearful that she was going to get pulled in for suspected shop-lifting, Keeley left the store.

As she turned onto the main road, the rain started. She walked back slowly, past the point of caring that she was soaked to the skin, willing the time to hurry up until she could knock for Ellie. If she timed it right, Ellie's mum would offer her tea and toast, Keeley thought to herself. There had been no bread in the house when Keeley had tried to make a snack last night. Two days without her mum and the standards had already declined.

Keeley reached for her phone to check the time for the millionth time that morning. There was a message waiting from Ellie, and Keeley's heart lightened that this meant Ellie was awake. She automatically quickened her pace, but her spirits sunk when she saw that Ellie was ill and cancelling their plans.

Keeley couldn't help the wave of self-pitying tears come, and she was grateful of the hood on her coat shielding her sorry state from any passers-by. She cried all the way home, head bowed. The sight of her driveway empty of her dad's car cheered her temporarily, but then she wondered why he hadn't phoned her asking where she was. This made Keeley feel even more sad and lonely. Her own father was too involved with his own affairs to wonder why she had left the house abnormally early.

All Keeley wanted to do was to make something to eat and climb back into bed. She noticed with frustration that not only was there no bread, but they were out of milk. She stripped off her soaking wet clothes, wrapped herself in a towel and got back into bed, feeling too tired to venture out to the shop after her early wake-up and her fruitless walk, but too hungry to sleep, and as she thought about how hungry and tired she was, and how her dad didn't care, and she was losing her house, she felt anger start to replace the sad feeling running through her veins.

At some point, her furious thoughts slowed down and she

drifted into an uncomfortable slumber. She woke, with a start, to hear a noise downstairs, and she sat up to listen.

The voices were muffled, and she couldn't make out any words. Keeley heard the front door shut and then there was silence again. Awake now, the feelings that she'd escaped in her sleep came flooding back to her. She sat in her bedroom until she could no longer ignore her hunger, and slipping on pyjamas, she made her way apprehensively downstairs.

"Have you just got up?" Her dad addressed her disapprovingly. "You've wasted half the day."

Keeley glanced at him from the corner of her eye. He was dressed in his usual weekend wear of jeans and a jumper, but his face was unshaven, his sandy hair uncombed and his eyes looked bloodshot and tired. If it hadn't been for the judgemental tone of voice he'd used to greet her, Keeley thought that she'd have almost felt sorry for him.

She opened her mouth to reply that she had been out, but then shut it again, deciding that it was none of his business what she chose to do. Instead, she opened the cupboards, searching for something she could eat. She took her food up to her bedroom and stayed there for the rest of the day.

It was about 5pm when she could no longer bear the four walls of her bedroom. Keeley showered, dried and straightened her hair and was applying her make-up when her dad called up to her. Keeley got up from her cross-legged position in front of the bedroom mirror to see what he wanted, but as she pulled the handle of her door, something inside her made her pause. There was no rational thought behind her actions, more of an intuitive reaction to the strained tone of her father's voice, and she walked back to her bedroom window and unlatched it, so that it could be opened from the outside.

Keeley walked down the stairs and her dad was stood in the hallway, brandishing a sodden, muddy carrier bag.

"What the hell is this?" He asked, his face red with indignation.

"I don't know." Keeley shrugged insolently. "Is that all you called me down for?"

"Is that all I've called you down for?" Jim repeated her words, struggling to control his temper.

"I told you," Keeley said enunciating every word slowly, despite knowing this would provoke his anger. "I don't know."

"I'll tell you what it is!" Jim burst furiously, and he started to pull glass bottles of alcohol from the bag one-by-one lining them up in the hallway. "It's years of poor discipline and disobedience! You've been allowed to run wild for years and, I'm telling you, it stops now!"

Keeley had started to walk back upstairs but she stopped and watched him remove the alcohol bottles from the bag. It was only when he tossed a stack of tumblers down and they fell and shattered, she realised with horror that this was the bag from Jordan's step-dad's bar. It must have been sat behind the bush in her garden, unnoticed since New Year. She struggled to keep her face neutral.

"They're not mine." Keeley repeated, but she felt a prickle of fear run through her spine.

"Clean that up." Jim spat, pushing the broken glass with the toe of his shoe. "And then you can get to your room and stay there. This ends now."

"It's not mine!" Keeley yelled furiously. "I've told you. You threw it there, you can clean it up!"

"Do you think I'm stupid?" Jim shouted back, and he stepped across the glass so close that for a moment Keeley thought he was going to strike her.

Keeley took another step up the stairs, unconsciously increasing the distance between them. The adrenaline was pumping around her body, but she was stuck between fight-and-flight mode. She didn't answer him, but she stayed frozen to the spot.

"I'm speaking to you!" Jim shouted. "It's your alcohol. I'm pouring it all away, but you can clean that glass up."

"It's not mine!" Keeley finally triggered by his aggression screamed at the top of her lungs.

"You're a liar." Jim lowered his tone this time. "Now clean it up."

"You're a liar!" Keeley screamed, her barriers finally down and the anger and hurt rushing out. "You lied to mum and I can't wait to leave this house like she did."

"She's the liar!" Jim retaliated, forgetting in his blind fury that he was speaking to his daughter. "She has been carrying on all this time."

"No, she hasn't!" Keeley screeched. "You're the one who's been seen out with that hideous old cow!"

Jim blanched at her words but recovered quickly. "Ask your mother. She started all this with her dirty affair."

"You're a liar!" Keeley screamed. She had never been angrier. Keeley had never been in a physical fight in her life, but her father's venomous accusations had her shaking with rage and it took all her restraint not to fly from the stairs and claw her father's selfish face.

"Of course," Jim sneered at his daughter. "You would believe anything she said. A woman of her age carrying protection and thinking I'm stupid enough to believe it wasn't hers. She disgusts me."

Keeley fell silent as what Jim was saying took a few moments to connect in her brain. She stared at Jim as she remembered the awkward conversation her mother had had with her months ago. Keeley was adamant that her mother was innocent in this break-up, and just the memory of her sweet mother bumbling through the cringeworthy conversation made Keeley's defences rise. Suddenly, the most important thing to Keeley was protecting her mother from Jim's disgusting accusations.

"Oh!" Keeley exclaimed, her mouth turning up into a sneer to match her father's. "Are you still banging on about that condom?"

Keeley spat out the word 'condom', feeling a twinge of satisfaction when her father visibly recoiled.

"That wasn't Mum's." Keeley continued, her tone heavy with spite. "That was mine."

Even as the words came out of her mouth, Keeley regretted them. Jim looked as though he were going to burst in anger and Keeley's bravado died on her lips as a balloon of panic inflated in her chest. Keeley turned and ran the short distance up the stairs, slamming her bedroom door and dragging the chest of drawers in front of it.

She sat on the bed, breathing heavily and angry tears spilling their way through her freshly-applied make-up. She could hear her father stomping around downstairs. Keeley glanced at her phone at the same moment there was a knock at the door. She heard Ollie's voice at the exact moment she saw the missed calls and the message from him, "I'm outside". Keeley suppressed the wave of nausea and got to her feet in a blind panic.

She dragged the chest away from her door as quickly as she could, but she could already hear her father's angry tone. Mortified, Keeley flew down the stairs and took in the scene with her heart in her mouth.

Ollie was stood at the doorway, his mouth opened in shock, as Jim launched a tirade of abuse at the teenager. They both turned to stare at Keeley and Jim put his arm up against the hallway wall, barring her exit.

"Get back upstairs." He hissed at Keeley, before turning his attention back to Ollie. "You need to get from my property. My daughter is under-age and the first thing I will be doing is calling the police."

"Dad! No!" Keeley rushed forwards trying to duck his arm, and Jim pushed her back roughly.

Ollie stepped forward, crossing the threshold instinctively, to help Keeley, but Jim, shocked at his own reaction, stepped aside. Keeley seized the opportunity, hurrying past her father with urgency. She seized Ollie by the arm and dragged him from the house.

"Get back inside!" Jim shouted as if Keeley's movement had

snapped him out of his daze.

"I'm never coming back!" Keeley shouted, tears falling from her eyes.

"I mean it!" Jim stood on the doorstep, making no attempt to follow them. "I'm calling the police."

Ollie turned to Keeley, his face stricken with panic. "What's going on?"

Keeley shook her head through her tears. "Come on. I'll tell you."

They raced out of the street, Keeley clutching at Ollie's hand and crying wild tears of fear and anger. It was only when they got to Ollie's estate, Keeley realised that she didn't have her phone or her purse. She dropped onto the curb and buried her head in her hands.

"It's ok." Ollie wrapped his arms around her. "You can stay with us."

"I need my stuff," Keeley sniffed. "I want my mum."

"We'll get it later," Ollie promised her. "I really think we need to tell my mum what's happened in case he does phone the police."

Guiltily, Keeley pushed aside her own feelings and got to her feet. She felt awful that she'd unwittingly caused problems for Ollie.

"He won't," Keeley told him. "I'll go back and sort this."

Ollie regarded her doubtfully. "Just come back with me. Let him cool down."

Keeley took Ollie's hand and they made their way to his house in silence. Keeley knew Ollie would try to talk her out of going back, but this was her fault. She had caused Ollie to bear the brunt of Jim's wrath, and she would put it right.

Dana had been looking forward to a child-free weekend with her husband, but as she watched Barry gathering up his wallet and his keys, she resigned herself to a night in alone watching the television. She could pop over The Crown or see if Steph fancied company, but her heart wasn't in it.

The atmosphere at home had been tense since Barry had driven home Wednesday, stinking of beer. After their heart-to-heart at the start of the year, Barry had taken Dana's words literally and implemented a self-imposed ban on nights down the pub. Dana had just wanted him to spend a bit more time at home, but he'd taken it to the extreme. She wished she hadn't said anything as, between the disruption of the attic conversion and life in general, he had been uncharacteristically bad-tempered. His usual easy-disposition had disappeared, and he was bordering on obsessive in his online feud with Jim Burbridge. Dana had been close to having it out with him but remembering how literally he had taken their previous conversation, she had decided it was wiser to keep her mouth shut and say nothing. If Wednesday's events were anything to go by, it seemed that he would agree to whatever she said and then go on doing what he wanted behind her back anyway. It was the realisation that she couldn't trust him that hurt the most. It had almost been a relief when he mentioned casually that he was planning on going to the pub that evening. Maybe now that it was out in the open and Barry wasn't hiding his whereabouts, his personality would return to normal.

Dana tucked her feet up underneath her on the giant sofa and reached for the remote control to browse the choice of films. She could sense Barry loitering in the hallway, but she purposely ignored him.

"I'm going now." He said finally.

Dana glanced over her shoulder and smiled to show she wasn't in a mood. "Have a nice time, love."

"I won't be too late." He said before leaving.

Dana rolled her eyes at his last remark and turned back to the television. There was a film starting at 7pm that she quite fancied watching. She glanced at the clock; she had half an hour to kill until it started. She got up and walked into the kitchen, searching for a takeaway menu in the pile of leaflets above the microwave.

As she browsed the delivery choices, a sudden loud noise startled her. She realised, with surprise, that it sounded like Laura and Jim next-door were having an argument. They weren't usually the type to raise their voices, but Dana had heard on the village grapevine that he'd been seen out-and-about over the last few months with the blonde, older lady from the council. Maybe it was all coming to a head. Dana couldn't help but to strain her ears to try to make out what they were saying.

After a few minutes of standing still in the kitchen eavesdropping, Dana was still none the wiser. The voices went quiet and Dana, half-disappointed, half-amused at her own nosiness, walked over to the fridge to see if anything in there appealed to her. She was inspecting the calorie content in a microwavable meal-for-one when the shouting started just as abruptly as it had ended. There was an ear-piercing scream and the slamming of a door. Dana's heart quickened at the sound and she turned instinctively towards the kitchen window, just in time to see Keeley Burbridge hand-in-hand with Ollie Rees running past her house. Dana stepped back from the window, not wanting to be caught nosing. She stood at the window for a few more moments, realising she hadn't seen Laura's car for a few days and wondering whether she should call Steph to see if Ollie was ok.

She took the ready meal from the fridge and placed it next to the microwave, as she weighed up whether she should get involved or not. Dana had always been the type to act first, think later, but the last few tense months living with Barry's mood swings had taught her to be cautious rather than risk upsetting any more apple-carts.

She'd had more than one screaming episode with Jordan in their time, she mused to herself. He had always been a good boy, but it was par for the course with teenagers. Dana decided she'd send a text rather than call Steph, and she spent a few minutes composing a text before sending it.

Dana had spent so long deliberating that it was almost time for her film to start, and she hurried back into the living room. Dana loved romantic comedies, but Barry would always fall asleep or start fiddling with his phone every time they watched one of "her" film choices. It would be nice to actually enjoy a film without feeling guilty that he wasn't enjoying it or getting irritated at his constant fidgeting. She nestled into the plump cushions and started to watch the film, adamant that she wouldn't dwell on the atmosphere between her and Barry.

As Dana watched the light-hearted romance start between the main character and the unattainable lovable rogue onscreen, she felt herself start to relax. She loved a love story.

'That's my problem,' Dana thought to herself, as she watched the main character jump to another conclusion. 'I think too much'.

She had been watching the film for about half an hour when her phone buzzed with Steph's response. Dana reached for the remote to pause the film and was relieved to see that Ollie and Keeley were with Steph.

"Keeley had a bit of a row with her dad," Steph replied. "She's here with Ollie. They're both fine but thanks for looking out for him x."

Dana felt better at Steph's response. She hadn't wanted to stick her nose in, but they were just kids and she would want someone looking out for Jordan. And Barry's children, of course. Dana grimaced slightly at the thought of a teenaged Tyler and Chloe, and then quickly berated herself for her pessimistic thoughts. She had married Barry and his children were part of that deal, she reminded herself. She needed to stop being so down on them.

Dana remembered that she still hadn't eaten, and she wandered back into the kitchen. She picked up the cardboard sleeve, checked the instructions and popped the film-covered carton into the microwave. She didn't usually eat microwave meals, but Barry and his kids loved them. Dana realised that this was just one of many differences between how she and Barry had lived before they blended their homes.

A car pulled up outside, and Dana glanced out of the window, wondering for a moment if Barry had had a change of heart and come home. The car was parked in front of Dana's driveway and Dana peered through the blind, seeing that it was a white sporty-looking car, not Barry's huge 4-wheel-drive. A slim woman exited the car, looking shiftily from house-to-house. This caught Dana's attention and she watched as the woman stepped into the streetlight.

It was dark outside, but Dana was pretty certain that she recognised the woman as Kelly Russell. Dana frowned, wondering whether she was coming here to see Barry for some reason or another, but the woman walked past Dana's drive, and the beeping of the microwave diverted Dana's attention back to her meal.

Gingerly, Dana tried a forkful of the steaming lamb moussaka. She had expected it to taste bland and like a budget airline meal, but it was surprisingly quite good. She spooned the dish from the plastic container to a plate and carried it into the living room. Dana wondered whether she should take the same approach to other differences between her and Barry's lives. If the ready-meals that she had snubbed for the last year were this tasty, and surprisingly low in calories, then maybe some of his other non-conventional habits were worth trying too. As she thought this, she bit into a boiling hot piece of meat and she hurried back into the kitchen for a glass of water.

For the second time that night, she heard raised voices coming from next-door although not as loud and alarming as Jim's argument with his daughter, thankfully. As Dana waited for the mixer tap to run cold enough to fill her glass, she glanced towards the window and saw the same woman strutting back to her car. She called something back over her shoulder and as she did, Dana caught sight of her face in the streetlight. She was 99% sure that it was Kelly and Dana wondered what trouble she'd been causing next-door. It had gotten to the point that Dana didn't even look at the online Oak Village page any more, such was the stirring and bitching. Kelly always seemed to be involved, one way or another. Dana was relieved to see her get back into the car and drive off. She could really do without getting caught up in the latest village drama.

Dana finished her meal while she was watching the film, but her mind kept drifting back to the differences between the way her and Barry lived their lives; parenting being the big one. Dana felt like she tried her hardest to accommodate Tyler and Chloe, but maybe she'd been harbouring more than a little resentment over the undisciplined way Barry and his ex-wife had chosen to bring their children up. Dana realised, in a moment of clarity, that she had unconsciously been waiting for his children to adjust to their new household and magically turn into replica Jordan's somewhere along the line. She had to admit to herself that this was never going to happen.

Dana sat up straighter at this thought. She paused the film and wandered out to the kitchen, deciding that if she was going to spend the evening philosophising, she would need a glass of wine to accompany her deep thoughts. She noticed that another car was now outside the house, and the registration plate showed the vehicle belonged to Steph's husband. Dana hoped that this would be the last of the drama for the evening, as Darren had a notoriously short temper and the last thing she wanted was for it to come to blows. She poured herself a glass of wine and glanced at the clock. It was a little after 8.20pm, and Dana sipped her wine in the kitchen, nervously listening for any raised voices that would indicate that she would need to intervene before Steph's husband got himself into trouble.

Dana had finished the whole glass, and there had been no audible sounds of a commotion. She couldn't sit here eavesdropping for the rest of the evening, she thought irritably. She wasn't the neighbourhood babysitter. She refilled her glass, intent on going back to finish her film. As she debated whether to grab a bag of kettle chips to go with her wine, she saw someone hurriedly cross the driveway and get back into the car.

Dana did a double-take when she realised who it was. She debated rushing to her front door and calling out, but before she could decide what to do, the car had driven off. Dana felt a stab of annoyance that she'd just wasted nearly fifteen minutes of her evening worrying about other people, when they didn't even have the decency to fill her in on what was going on. It felt like the story of her life. All she wanted to do was finish the film.

She placed her glass down heavily on the glass coffee table, spilling a little, and jabbed at the play button on the remote control. She had been watching for ten minutes when her phone started ringing and she paused the film for the third time, feeling irritable at the constant interruptions. She saw it was Jordan and her exasperation was replaced by immediate concern.

"Everything ok, love?" She asked.

"Mum," Jordan sounded upset. "I'm really sorry to do this, but I can't get a bus. Can you pick me up from Finchester please?"

"Of course!" Dana replied. "What's the matter?"

"Felicity and me have broken up," Jordan admitted glumly. "I'll wait outside the McDonald's?"

"Oh, love!" Dana sighed. "I'll be there as soon as I can. It'll probably take twenty minutes though, so go and sit inside."

"Thanks, Mum," Jordan said gratefully. "Love you."

Dana immediately forgot her own frustrations and grabbed her car keys. She locked the front door and jumped into her car, reversing off the drive a little less carefully than usual in her haste to reach her son. As she paused to pull on her seatbelt, Dana noticed a lone woman, on foot, cross Dana's driveway in the direction of the Burbridge's house. Dana wondered for a moment whether Laura was back, but the figure was too short to be Laura, and Dana accelerated away, her mind turning back to her son.

Finchester was less than twenty minutes away on a clear road, but the roadworks in place meant that it took her the best part of fifty minutes to make the return journey despite there being nothing on the road on a Saturday night. Jordan was quiet and forlorn, offering only short responses to Dana's concerned questions. As they pulled back into the driveway, Dana turned to look at her son.

"I really am sorry," She said. "I thought it was going well."

"It was." Jordan shrugged. "Mum, I told her I was in sixth form."

"Oh, Jordan!" Dana gasped.

"I know, I know," Jordan shook his head sadly. "It's my own fault. Thanks for coming to get me. I'm just going to go to bed."

Dana unlocked the door and watched, with concern, as Jordan made his way up the stairs. She was disappointed that he'd lied to his girlfriend, but she felt her heart ache at his sadness. The first heartbreak was always the hardest.

She switched her film off, suddenly not interested in finding out what happened, and took a large sip of her now-warm wine, before tossing the remains into the sink. She wanted to go up and speak to Jordan, but she knew she needed to give him time and space. Dana switched off the lights downstairs and poured herself a glass of water to take up to bed when she heard the familiar roar of Barry's car on the driveway.

She debated scarpering up the stairs, too tired to deal with any atmosphere, but his key was in the door before she could make a move.

"Hi," She called. "You're early. I was just going to bed."

"Already?" Barry walked into the kitchen, glancing at the clock. "It's only 9.30."

"I'm shattered." Dana replied. She couldn't help herself from adding. "You drove home?"

"Yeah," Barry nodded, and Dana noticed he looked pale-faced and seemed stone-cold sober. "I didn't drink."

This caught Dana's attention. "You didn't?"

Barry reached for Dana's hand and the anxious look in his eyes froze her to the spot.

"Dana," Barry said. "I need to tell you something."

Chapter 20

Tina Cleary had been away all weekend, visiting Robbie in Plymouth. The coach journey seemed to take forever, and she'd only just made it back to The Crown in time for her Sunday evening shift. She had the foresight to text her boss to tell him she might be late, but luck was on her side and she ducked through the heavy wooden doors with minutes to spare.

Tina swung her backpack from her shoulder and underneath the bar for safe-keeping. She took off her leather jacket and knotted her hair into a ponytail; securing it with the elastic from her wrist. The lounge was empty now after the lunch period and the bar had not yet started to fill up with the usual evening crowd. Tina busied herself with a few odd jobs, making the most of the quiet time, not daring to pull out her books until she'd done some work.

The door opened as Tina was wiping down the tables, sending a blast of cold air into the small bar. A voluptuous blonde woman moved through the narrow doorway, her husband holding the door chivalrously for her. Tina looked up, surprised to see Barry Simons and his wife, Dana. They both looked fraught and, instead of making his way straight to the bar, Barry settled his wife at a corner table, helping her to remove the dark-coloured shawl she was wrapped in.

Tina pasted on a cheery smile, addressing Barry. "We haven't seen you for ages! We were about to put up 'Missing' posters!"

She expected the usually jovial couple to laugh at this, but Barry looked embarrassed and Dana just smiled politely.

Tina tried again to engage Barry in conversation as she took his order at the bar.

"Are you ok?" She asked solicitously.

Barry shook his head. "It's awful, awful news."

"What's happened?" Tina asked in concern. She finished pouring the drinks and gave Barry his change, waiting for him to reply.

The door opened into the bar and Barry turned towards the noise, distracted from Tina's question. Kelly Russell and her husband shuffled into the room, closely followed by another couple. Kelly's face was devoid of her usual make-up and Tina could see her eyes were red and puffy as she navigated her way around the tables to the bar. Her husband, Evan, followed her and Tina was surprised to see Barry hug Evan in an unusual display of affection.

"We can't stay long," Evan was muttering to Barry. "My mum is with the kids. We just needed to get out of the house."

Tina turned her attention to Kelly. "What's happened?"

Kelly opened her mouth to speak but her lip wobbled, and her eyes filled with tears. She waved a hand at Tina, indicating that she needed a moment.

Tina turned her eyes towards the other couple. Darren and Steph Rees wore identical strained expressions to Barry and Dana, and Steph was sniffing into a crumpled tissue. Dana was up out of her seat and had pulled Steph into her arms.

Darren stood, a little awkwardly, next to his wife and her friend. He glanced over at Tina and Kelly at the bar before looking away sharply

"Kelly?" Tina asked again, ignoring Darren, panic rising in her chest. "What's going on?"

"Jim Burbridge." Kelly managed to choke out, her voice breaking. "He's dead."

Tina felt the blood drain from her body and her legs wobble underneath her. "What? Are you sure?"

Kelly nodded. "His body was found in the house this morning. Police have been there all day."

"Oh my God!" Tina clutched her hand to her mouth in disbelief. "Does anyone know what happened?"

"Scenes of crime have been there," Kelly sniffed. "They only do that if it's unexplained or…"

She trailed off, too upset to continue. Evan moved to her side and took her arm gently.

"I can't stay here," Kelly leaned against her husband for support. "Can we just go home?"

"Of course," Evan said, his eyes full of concern. "Let me just speak to Barry."

Tina watched as Evan moved to Barry's side and they spoke in low voices. Kelly stared into space, her eyes full of unshed tears.

"How are his family?" Tina asked Kelly.

Kelly shrugged. "I don't know. The wife was the one who found him. They weren't there."

"They had separated." Tina said automatically.

"How do you know?" Kelly turned to look at her sharply, surprising Tina.

"I clean for them," Tina replied. "Well, at least, I did."

"Oh!" Kelly nodded, her eyes narrowing. "Of course. You're Sparkles."

"Kelly," Tina reached for her friend's hand anxiously. "I meant to tell you-"

"It's fine." Kelly moved out of Tina's reach and waved her hand dismissively. "I know Evan's been helping you with your degree and you're selling the business. It's fine."

"Sorry I didn't tell you," Tina said lamely. "I meant to phone you Friday, but things happened, and I just forgot."

"It doesn't matter," Kelly said coolly. "There's a man dead."

Tina felt shocked at Kelly's coldness towards her, but she knew it was to be expected.

"I know," Tina nodded. "But I should have told you and I'm sorry."

Kelly nodded her head once in acknowledgement. She regarded Tina thoughtfully for a moment.

"One thing, though," Kelly said, struggling to keep her voice level. "Who's buying your business?"

Tina swallowed nervously. "Stephanie Rees."

Kelly's eyes widened, and she stared at Tina in disbelief. "Darren's wife?"

Tina nodded, and they both turned to look at the older woman, who was sat with Dana Simons.

Tina waited for Kelly's reaction, but none came. Tina felt sick at both the news of Jim's death and Kelly's frosty response to Tina's own deceit. An immediate explosion from Kelly would have been preferable, now it would be a case of waiting to see what she would do. Kelly turned away from Tina, without saying any more, and moved to Evan's side. She took his arm, and they said their goodbyes to their friends.

Evan glanced back at Tina, as he swung the door open for Kelly, with an apologetic look. Tina met his eyes, but before she could react, he was gone, and she looked down at the floor, feeling sick and helpless.

Dana wished she hadn't come to the pub, but she had just wanted to get out of the house. Every time she looked out of the window, she could see the police cars and the forensic officers going back and forth into Jim's home.

It wasn't the police tape and the official-looking investigators that triggered her to burst into tears every time she looked, despite the surreal nature of the scene in their little cul-de-sac, but the sight of Laura's abandoned Kia, two wheels on the pavement, as if she had only meant to "pop" in the house.

Dana couldn't imagine how awful it must be to find your husband's dead body. Just the thought of it sent shivers up her spine. In a way, she was glad Laura hadn't knocked their door when she made the grim discovery, but, at the same time, Dana's heart ached with sympathy at the thought of Laura waiting with the corpse. Dana hadn't realised until she had spoken to the police officers that came making door-to-door enquiries that Laura and Jim had recently separated, but Dana thought that that would have made her feel even worse if she were Laura.

Dana had been overwhelmed with shock when the officers had come to her door at about 10am that morning. She'd had a late night, talking with Barry into the early hours, and they were both still in bed when the door had knocked. The officers, a young woman in her twenties and an older woman, about Dana's age, had taken her into the kitchen and put the kettle on for her. It was only when they had started to gently question Dana that she had realised, with horror, that she was a potential witness to a murder.

Her feelings ricocheted between heartfelt sadness for the family of Jim and nauseous horror that a murder had been committed yards from her home. The officers had asked her to accompany them to the station to make a statement, and Dana felt drained and exhausted from hours going over the sequence of events she had witnessed.

She sat still, in the corner of the pub, nursing the drink Barry had bought her. Steph sat next to her, clutching her hand for comfort. They had spoken briefly earlier; Steph finding out about the horrible, horrible circumstances from Ollie and immediately calling Dana. Steph had been, understandably, tentative about visiting Dana at her home. The thought of visiting the house adjoining the murder scene while officers were still finger-printing and doing God-knows-what seemed disrespectful, but as they sat in the cosy pub, surrounded by the fraught faces of their neighbours, Dana suddenly felt that this seemed just as morbid and distasteful as a meeting place.

She watched as Kelly and Evan Russell, seemingly feeling the same, left within minutes of arriving. Kelly looked pale and tearful, and Dana wondered whether this was because the police had already called around to see her.

"Do you have to go back to the station?" Steph spoke quietly, interrupting Dana's thoughts.

Dana shook her head. "I don't think so. They said they'd let me know if they had any other questions, but I was there for hours. They were very thorough. I-"

Dana had meant to say that she didn't have anything else she could tell them, but that wasn't true, so she shut her mouth instead.

"Dana," Steph started hesitantly. "I-"

Dana felt her chest contract in panic at Steph's words, and she spoke quickly to silence Steph. "It doesn't feel right that we're here, does it?"

"Oh." Steph looked taken aback by Dana's hurried exclamation. "No, I suppose it doesn't."

"How has Keeley been?" Dana continued, glancing across the room at Barry, who was now speaking with Tina.

"In shock," Steph looked saddened. "The poor girl. She's with her mum now. They're staying with a friend."

"Has Ollie been ok?" Dana asked. "It must be awful for him."

"He's been upset," Steph told her. "Understandably. He's so young. It's hard enough to know what to say when you're our age. He's still shocked, isn't he, Dar?"

Darren had sat down on the edge of the table, and was staring uncomfortably into space, but now the subject had turned to the children, Steph attempted to bring him into the conversation.

Darren nodded, and got to his feet, pushing the half-finished pint away. "I think I'm going to get back to him, Steph. I don't like him being on his own. You stay here."

Steph got to her feet as well. "No, I'll come."

Darren tried to protest but Steph was adamant that she wanted to go home. Dana felt relieved when her friend had left, and she sat alone in her thoughts for a few moments until Barry joined her.

Dana noticed that he didn't have his usual pint in his hand. "Do you mind if I go home?"

"That's fine with me," Barry gave a sigh of relief. "Feels wrong to be in here."

"I know," Dana chastised herself for suggesting it, given the circumstances. "Let's go."

They walked the short distance back to the house, dropping their heads in respect as they approached the house. There was still a police car parked outside, alongside Laura's car, but the house was in darkness now. Dana shivered as she thought of Jim's body lying in the house all night while they slept next door.

"I'm really sorry for dragging you out," Dana said as she

boiled the kettle once they were back inside. "I didn't think when I suggested meeting Steph."

"It's fine." Barry said. "I needed to get out of the house."

They both fell quiet, consumed by their own thoughts. Dana carried the coffee through to the living room and was just about to take a seat when there was a knock at the door. Dana and Barry exchanged concerned looks.

"I'll get it." Barry said, and made his way slowly to the hallway.

Dana stayed frozen to the spot.

"Hello. Sorry to call so late." A voice floated through the space towards her. "Is it Mr Simons? I'm Detective Constable Rhodes. As part of the ongoing investigations into the incident, we would like to ask you some questions. Are you able to accompany us down to the station please?"

Dana's blood ran cold and she rushed into the hallway. Barry was nodding, and reaching for his jacket, his face solemn and tense. He tried to smile reassuringly at Dana.

"Shall I come?" She asked, her voice sounding high-pitched and unnatural to her ears.

"No need, Mrs Simons," The officer told her politely. "I see we've had a full statement from you already."

"I'll call you to pick me up." Barry told Dana firmly, his eyes warning her gently to not make a fuss. "Jordan's here. You'll be ok."

Dana swallowed and nodded. She hadn't even thought about being in the house on her own. She stood helplessly in the hallway as Barry followed the officers to their unmarked car, shutting the door softly behind him.

Chapter 21

The moment Kelly was safely across the road from the pub, she unchivalrously dropped Evan's arm. Despite their heart-to-heart yesterday, and Evan's insistence that nothing had happened between him and Laura, there was a lot that had been left unsaid.

Evan flinched at her deliberate release of his hand. It seemed that the shock of the news of Jim's death had only caused a temporary truce between them. Kelly had been crying on and off since they had heard the news that afternoon, and when Evan, as shocked as her at the news, had instinctively comforted her and they had gone out, as a united front, to meet with their neighbours at the pub, Evan had assumed that they were both agreeing to a cease-fire.

Kelly picked up her pace, walking several steps ahead of him. Kelly didn't want Evan's comfort, yet at the same time she yearned for him to chase after her, begging for forgiveness. She had that many emotions tumbling inside her that Kelly wasn't even sure why she was crying anymore; sadness, guilt, anger, hurt or fear.

'Probably all of them.' Kelly thought wryly, swiping away at the fresh tears with the back of her hand.

Evan called out to her and she ignored him. He jogged the few steps between them, reached out and grabbed her arm, swinging her to face him.

"Are we ok?" Evan asked.

"We're fine," Kelly shrugged, not meaning it. "You were

only carrying on with other women for the last year. It's fine."

"I wasn't 'carrying on'," Evan said in a frustrated tone. "I explained last night."

Kelly stared at his face, searching for any indication that he was lying. She was usually an expert at reading people's body language, but in an ironic twist, her husband had been spinning her bullshit for at least a year and she'd been none-the-wiser. Evan had been gobsmacked when she'd accused him of cheating with Laura. Kelly was far from naïve but even she had believed the look of disbelief on his face. She had had to admit to "seeing" the messages on his phone, and as predicted he'd had a perfectly innocent explanation, but nothing could have prepared Kelly for it.

Kelly may have been more than a little tipsy, but she had remembered the wording of his sleazy text message to Laura perfectly, and she had spat it at him venomously.

"I miss our sessions! Hope I didn't freak you out! Do you think I'm stupid?"

Kelly had seen the realisation hit Evan, and his expression changed from confused to a look of weary acceptance.

"Kelly," He had leaned forward, seizing her wrists with his hands and looking pleadingly into her eyes. "I need you to listen. Laura is just a running buddy. I go running with people from work, that's all that means, but when I said I freaked her out, now that's something I should have told you a while ago."

Kelly had tensed at his serious tone, but she realised, with a pang of sadness, that she had been expecting some revelation since Evan had started "working late". Probably even longer than that, if she were honest with herself. She expected him to tell her all the clichés; it wasn't working, he'd met someone else, it wasn't her, it was him. Kelly hadn't been expecting him to confess he'd been spending a great deal of this time with her so-called friend.

"You know how I moved to Ricer & Wallis because I want to be a partner?" He started, and she nodded, letting him continue. "The majority of what I told you is true; I have been taking on extra cases. I've also been supporting some local law students and arranging work placements, which is great for my profile with Jane and Chris."

"Just get to the point." Kelly interrupted, feeling sick at the thought of what was to come next.

"Ok," Evan said. "Maybe not "some" local students, one of them. Tina."

"Tina?" Kelly had felt her blood start to boil. "You've been hanging around after work with Tina Cleary? She doesn't even go to university. She's a bloody cleaner."

"She's not," Evan had protested. "Well, yes, she has got the business and she still does a couple of jobs, and the bar work, but she's a second-year student. Juggling the business and Uni can be a struggle so I've just been helping her with a few things."

"Let me get this straight!" Kelly had exploded. "You and my "mate" have been lying to me. I bet you did a bit more than help her with her books. Why else wouldn't she tell me?"

"She didn't want to tell people about her degree," Evan explained. "She was worried that she'd have to drop out *because of finances, and she didn't want to jinx it."*

"Aww." Kelly had replied sarcastically. "What a lovely story. It's lovely you've got so much in common. Is that how you fell in love?"

"You're being ridiculous." Evan had sighed. "Nothing has happened between us. It's just work, and it's good for my profile at work."

"Whatever," Kelly had reached for the door handle and gotten out of Evan's car. "Do what you like. I don't care."

Evan had hurriedly got out of the car after her. "Kelly! Where are you going?"

"I'm going for a walk," She had given him a warning look, which told him she seriously needed some space. "Go and drop your mother home."

Kelly had stormed off, wishing she hadn't bothered calling him to pick her up from the pub. When she had eventually gone back to the house, Evan had tried to speak to her about their argument, but Kelly had insisted on going to bed. She'd purposely slept late in the morning, and he'd woken her up to the news of Jim Burbridge's death, causing both of them to forget their own troubles.

Seeing Tina had brought all the hurt rushing back to Kelly. Kelly felt humiliated that Tina had been laughing behind her back all this time, not only being the reason that Kelly's husband was staying out late, but also having Kelly unknowingly try to buy her business. Everyone in the village probably knew that it was Tina's; everybody except Kelly.

Kelly felt hurt and betrayed by Tina. Kelly had gone out of

her way to befriend her when she'd moved to the area and started working at The Crown. Kelly had offered her business advice and taken her on nights out, and all the time the little cow was scheming on Evan. Kelly realised, with horror, that Tina had her fair share of dirt on Kelly too, and it was only that, and of course the sombre atmosphere in the pub, that has held Kelly back from having it out with Tina.

Evan stared at Kelly, waiting for a response, and Kelly felt the fight drain out of her.

"I just want to go home." She said in a sullen voice.

Evan sighed, realising it was going to take a lot more to earn her forgiveness, and they walked on towards their home in silence. As they turned the corner into their street, Evan could see a dark car parked outside the house. The outdoor security light was on, illuminating two strangers talking to Pam on the doorstep. Kelly and Evan both quickened their pace, and the strangers turned towards them.

"We're looking for Mrs Kelly Russell?" The taller of the two, an attractive blonde woman, dressed in a dark coat, held up an identification badge. "My name is Detective Sargent Parker. We have some questions to ask regarding the death of Jim Burbridge. Are you able to accompany us to the station to help with our enquiries?"

Kelly's legs almost gave way underneath her, and Evan steadied her, his own face draining of colour with shock. Evan opened his mouth to protest, but Kelly silenced him with a gentle hand to his arm, as she regained her composure.

"Of course."

"I'm coming." Evan said hurriedly.

"That's fine." The Detective said calmly, opening the car door and indicating to Kelly that she should get in.

Evan stood, speechless, as Kelly turned her head away from him, lowering herself into the car. Pam's face was a picture of surprise, but she recovered quickly, breaking Evan's trance, handing him his own car keys.

"Drive down, love," Pam told him. "I'll stay with the kids."

Evan wanted to insist that Kelly get out of the car, and get in his, but she was purposely looking away from him, and the officers were preparing to drive away. His professional brain kicked in, starting to override the shock of his wife being taken in for questioning over a murder.

Why had she got in the car without asking any questions? He wondered. It was like she had been expecting it. She had been at home last night, so she couldn't be a suspect.

But she hadn't. Evan's inner voice reminded him. He had left her in the pub at 7.30pm, and he had picked her up just before 8.30, when they had had that awful confrontation about Laura and Tina. She'd stormed off again and been gone for at least half an hour. Evan's blood ran cold.

Kelly had had a public spat with Jim, but so had a lot of their neighbours. She wasn't capable of murder. A little voice reminded Evan that he'd given Kelly a lot of reasons to be in a fit of rage last night. She would never hurt anyone deliberately, but when she was drunk and emotionally-wounded? Evan tried to silence the terrifying thoughts and accelerated sharply, hoping to catch up with the unmarked car.

Detective Sargent Victoria Parker took the vending machine coffee gratefully from her colleague. It had been a long day, and it wasn't looking any closer to ending.

"Have we got the results of the autopsy?" She asked her Inspector as she flicked through a pile of paperwork, pen poised to start making her own notes.

"Not yet," He replied. "I don't think they're going to reveal any surprises though."

DS Parker nodded her head. She didn't think so either, but they needed to dot the I's and cross the t's, as always. When the team had got the call from the first response officers, she'd assumed it would be a cut-and-dry case. It was rare to have a murder in middle-class Suburbia and when these things did happen, it was usually domestic.

The trembling wife had been waiting on the doorstep, the door pulled almost closed behind her to hide the body lying in the hallway. DS Parker believed that the woman was in genuine shock and had sent her to be treated before she could give a statement. She had seen a lot of liars in her time as an investigator, but Laura Burbridge's account of her whereabouts and her husband's background had struck her as truthful. There were signs of a break in upstairs; a bedroom window ajar and a chest of drawers dragged out of it's original position, plus there were miniscule fragments of broken glass and mud in the hallway and stair carpet. Circumstantially, it didn't look great that the victim and his wife had separated within the last few days, but as long as her alibi checked out, DS Parker was keeping an open mind that Mrs Burbridge wasn't the killer.

DS Parker scanned Mrs Burbridge's statement, picking out the key strands that the team were currently exploring. Initially she'd felt dismissive when the wife had mentioned the "a spot of bother" on the victim's social media group for the local village, but there were several print-outs on the desk in front of her and just a glance at some of the conversations told DS Parker that this was going to be a long night trying to unwind this tangled mess.

Detective Constable Rhodes came into the room and dropped another sheaf of paper down next to her.

"What's your thoughts on this?" DC Louise Rhodes asked, taking a seat next to her Sargent.

"Is this from the neighbour?" DS Parker responded, picking up the statement and reading the top line. "He had a solid alibi. The follow-up should be back on that pretty quickly but keep him in mind. The only witness we had was his wife, as the other immediate neighbours are away for the weekend, and the rest of the street didn't add anything. We've got a confirmed sighting of the daughter and her boyfriend leaving the street from the old lady at number 3, and nothing else."

"How did you get on with-" DC Rhodes leafed through some notes looking for the name. "Kelly Russell?"

"She's still in," DS Parker stated. "She's taking a break. Her husband is out in reception pacing the floor. He's making me feel tired just looking at him. I'm going back in now to go over her statement with her."

"I'll go through the social media, shall I?" DC Rhodes

offered.

"Please," DS Parker nodded in agreement. "It's making me cringe to read how some of these people speak to each other."

"That's the internet for you." DC Rhodes chuckled. "Wasn't like that in your day, was it?"

DS Parker laughed at her cheek. She opened the door and crossed the hallway, past reception, to the interview room. Kelly Russell's husband was still on his feet and he looked at DS Parker expectantly for news, his face etched with worry.

"We shouldn't be much longer," DS Parker said politely. "Kelly's just going to read over and sign her statement."

"I'm not happy about her not wanting a solicitor," Evan said. "She's had a shock. She's not thinking straight."

The fact that Kelly hadn't wanted a solicitor, even though by the neighbour's account of the evening she was potentially the last person to see Jim Burbridge alive, combined with Kelly's demeanour led DS Parker to feel confident that the woman was innocent. Of the murder, at least. Her statement was another story, and DS Parker wasn't surprised that the woman didn't want her husband present.

"She'll be along shortly." DS Parker replied politely and left him standing in the reception area waiting for his wife.

Kelly smiled courteously as the officer came back into the room. DC Elliott had brought them all fresh coffee, but DS Parker left hers untouched, her bladder already full-to-bursting.

"We'll verify this as quickly as we can," DS Parker advised

the woman sat opposite her. "I'll need you to check the information you've given us is correct and sign it before you leave."

"Is this confidential?" Kelly sat forward looking worried.

"We'll need to speak to the people that saw you including the, uh, gentleman you were with," DS Parker explained. "And it is possible that this statement will be used in any trial as you were one of the last people to speak to Mr Burbridge."

Kelly couldn't hide the look of fear on her face and DS Parker wished she could shake some sense into the woman. The silly girl was one piece of evidence away from being arrested on a murder charge. She should be sighing with relief that she had an alibi.

"He's got a wife." Kelly said in a small voice.

"We'll be discreet." DS Parker replied, starting to feel exasperated with the woman.

It was gone 11pm, and DS Parker had been working flat-out all day. They had a room full of paper, naming potential leads that had been generated by the wife, the neighbour and now the neighbour's husband and this woman. DS Parker also had the unsavoury task of interviewing the daughter and her boyfriend, which she was dreading. The kid's dad had just been found brutally murdered, and the girl had obviously been in pieces. DS Parker was grateful that there had been other people who saw Mr Burbridge before his death, as it meant they didn't have to rush in and interrogate the poor, traumatised kids immediately, but it would have to be done.

DS Parker had two teenagers of her own and no matter how long an officer had been doing a job, there was always that "too close to home" moment that cropped up occasionally and stuck in your throat for a while afterwards.

When she had finished in the interview room, she managed to sneak a bite to eat, and made her way back to the room where her team were working.

"How are we doing?" DS Parker asked as she walked back into the room.

"This is a minefield." DC Rhodes groaned, fanning herself with the sheaf of internet print-outs.

"Have we still got access to the group?" DS Parker asked. "It might be sensible to keep an eye on it, see if anything else comes up."

"I've got Mr Simons' rival group here," DC Cooper volunteered. "It was only up since Wednesday, which checks with his statement. It's pretty childish stuff, but there's nobody who's jumping out at me as wanting to kill the victim."

"How quickly did he shut it down?" DS Parker asked, leaning over his shoulder.

"An hour or so after he heard about the death." DC Cooper replied. "Out of respect, he said."

"Cross check the names of the commenters with the ones we've already got from the witness statements." DS Parker instructed. "I've got more interviews lined up for the morning and I need someone to work the alibis. You'll have to call it a night soon."

Chapter 22

Steph woke up on Monday morning, after a sleepless night tossing and turning, and was surprised to see Darren had got up before her. She slipped on a dressing gown and walked downstairs to let the dog out, but neither Darren nor the dog were anywhere to be seen.

Steph checked that the dog's lead was gone, paranoid that Darren had simply let him out and forgotten about him, but the lack of blue harness hanging from the coat rack confirmed that Darren had in fact taken the dog out for once, without being nagged to do so.

In the past, Steph would have been delighted at this display of consideration, but it wasn't just her new attitude towards Darren that left her feeling indifferent to the gesture. She had been in a constant state of worry ever since hearing the news of Jim Burbridge's death. Her first priority had been to hold her own emotions in check to be there for her son.

Steph had already decided to let Ollie stay home from school today. He'd had a big shock, and Darren had mentioned that it was likely that the police would want to speak to him at some point. Steph felt sick at the thought of the investigation, and she busied herself in the kitchen, trying to silence the constant whir of thoughts in her mind.

The sound of the door opening, accompanied by the dog's paws clattering across the floor, interrupted Steph's thoughts.

"Hi." Darren greeted her, taking his shoes off at the

doormat instead of trampling mud into the floor as he usually did. "Kids up?"

"Not yet." Steph replied, and turned back to the worktops she was wiping down, not feeling like making conversation.

"Is Ollie going in?" Darren asked, stepping around her to fill the kettle.

"I'm not going to wake him up," Steph said. "I think he needs a day off."

Darren said nothing, and Steph didn't care whether he agreed with her or not. Ollie had had a shock. He needed a few days to process his feelings.

"I'm not going to work." Darren said, after a few minutes of silence.

"Why not?" Steph looked surprised at this.

Darren shrugged. "I just want to be home in case Ollie needs to speak to the police."

"I can go with him." Steph said sharply.

Darren looked surprised at Steph's tone. He gently placed a mug of tea next to her and left the room with his own. Steph heard him walk up the stairs and assumed that he'd gone back to bed now he'd given himself the day off work. She was surprised when Kendall and Ollie came downstairs, without her nagging them to get up.

"How are you?" She asked Ollie concerned. "I don't want you going in to school today."

"I'm fine," Ollie told her. "I don't mind going in."

"I'd prefer you to stay home." Steph told him, and he shrugged, looking like a younger, skinnier version of his father.

Steph got herself ready to drive Kendall the short distance to school. She hadn't even looked at any social media since she'd heard the news, but sitting in the awful traffic, Steph wondered if even the serial complainers in the village would keep their comments to themselves today out of respect. Part of her wanted to check to see what people were saying, to see if there had been any arrests or any developments, but she was a bundle of nerves and the other part of her couldn't bear to look.

She wanted, more than anything, to speak to Dana. She had tried talking to her last night, but Dana had started talking about something else and then Darren had wanted to get back to the kids and the moment had passed. Steph knew she'd be in work now, so there was no point driving around, and even if she wasn't, Steph didn't think she could physically drive into the street, knowing that the poor man had been led dying in his own home.

Steph shuddered at the thought, feeling her chest constrict with panic. She didn't want to go home and be trapped in the house with Darren either. Once upon a time, he would have been the one that she wanted to turn to, but she might as well have been living with a stranger. He had said very little about the death, except to show his concern for Ollie.

Keeley had stayed with the Rees' Saturday night, and had had no inkling that anything was untoward when she had left Sunday morning to be picked up by her mother at the end of the street. Steph had thought that it was a bit strange, at the time, that the girl's mother hadn't wanted to speak to them. She would have been concerned that her teenage daughter had slept over her boyfriend's house, without permission, and would have wanted to know the in's and out's. Obviously, Steph had made Ollie sleep downstairs on the sofa, but when Keeley had received a phone call from her mother, she had darted off with a quick "thank you" to Steph, and they'd heard nothing until Ollie had phoned Keeley later in the day.

It had taken Steph a few hours plus a conversation with Dana to believe that what Ollie relayed was true. If it hadn't been for the presence of the children and Darren, she would have crumpled in shock on the spot. She still didn't know what to do. Every time she forced herself to think about what had happened, she was overcome with a sense of panic. The only remedy was to distract herself. Her family needed her right now; she couldn't fall apart.

She circled back to the house, not wanting to but having nothing else to do. Her phone pinged with a reminder. She stared at it confused for a moment, before remembering that she had arranged to meet Tina to discuss the business sale today. Steph sat in the car, trying to pull herself together enough to compose an apologetic message asking to postpone the meeting. Steph knew that it was likely that she would have to cancel her plans all together. At some point, what happened was going to come out, she thought to herself. There was something so clear and final about this thought, after almost twenty-four hours of fragmented, irrational thinking, that Steph was finally overwhelmed by a wave of panic and she gave in, sobbing so hard that she felt like she couldn't breathe.

A gentle tap on the car window startled Steph, and she

jumped to see a woman stood awkwardly on her driveway, smiling down apologetically at her. Steph hurriedly wiped her eyes and got out of the car.

"Is everything ok?" The woman asked politely, and Steph looked at her, confused as to why a stranger had noticed her outburst and was enquiring after her.

"Yes, thank you," Steph managed to respond. "Just had some bad news."

Steph walked towards her house, mortified by the audience, but she realised that the woman and a man, who she hadn't noticed loitering awkwardly at the bottom of the driveway, were following her to the door. Steph turned towards them, muddled and disorientated after her breakdown.

"Can I help you?" She managed to ask, before it dawned on her that they looked like plain-clothes police officers. They must be here to see Ollie.

"We're looking for Mr Darren Rees." The woman said. "Is he home?"

Steph stared at them for a few moments in confusion. "Darren?"

"Yes," The woman nodded, starting to look slightly wary. "Is he home?"

"He should be." Steph opened the door, before turning back to them. "Are you the police?"

"I'm Detective Sargent Parker," The woman said. "And this is DC Cooper."

"I thought you'd want to talk to my son," Steph frowned. "Why do you want to speak to Darren?"

"Just part of an investigation," DS Parker said. "Why would we want to talk to your son?"

"His girlfriend's dad was found dead." Steph stared at them, certain that they were wrong, and they had meant to ask for Ollie. "We thought you'd need to speak to him."

DS Parker couldn't believe that her team hadn't connected the dots and warned her that a man on their list to interview was the father of one of the minors they needed to interview. She glanced at DC Cooper and he had the good grace to colour slightly, giving her all the evidence that she needed as to who's fault this was.

"We also need to interview your son, Mrs Rees," DS Parker recovered quickly. "Are you able to escort him to the station this afternoon? We understand how difficult this can be for young people, and we have specially-trained team to support."

"Yes, of course," Steph nodded. "What time?"

At that moment, Darren, hearing voices on the doorstep, opened the door.

"The police want to talk to you, Dar." Steph said emotionlessly.

Darren looked surprised. "Me?"

DS Parker stepped forward and explained who they were and what they wanted.

"Am I under arrest?" Darren asked, scratching his head and

looking more confused than worried.

"No," DS Parker shook her head. "It's just as part of our investigations."

"Well, why can't you talk to me here?" Darren said, pulling the door open wider.

Steph hovered uncomfortably between the police and her husband, unsure what to do.

"Is there any reason that you can't come down to the station?" DS Parker asked, trying to hide her exasperation.

"Is there any reason you can't talk to me here?" Darren countered.

DS Parker could tell that this man was going to be difficult. It would probably serve him right if she explained what she needed to talk about in detail, in front of his wife.

"Darren," Steph suddenly interrupted, looking cross. "Can you just go and answer their questions? They said you're not under arrest, and you need to think how Ollie would feel hearing them ask you questions about Keeley's family."

"How do you know that's what they're going to want to talk about?" Darren snapped at his wife, annoyed by her siding with the police.

"What else are they going to want to talk about?" Steph shrugged.

"I don't know anything about the family, except Keeley!" Darren exclaimed. "That's why I don't get what they could possibly want."

"Mr Rees," DS Parker said levelly. "We've conducted a number of interviews, as you can imagine, in relation to the death of Jim Burbridge. You may have information regarding the whereabouts of people who were in contact with Mr Burbridge."

"Oh." Darren nodded his head thoughtfully. "Is that all? Ok, I'll get my keys."

"You can come in the car with us." DS Parker nodded to the dark car parked on the street.

"I'd rather not," Darren wrinkled his brow. "No offence."

"We'll follow you," DS Parker nodded her consent. "We'll see you at 1pm if that's ok, Mrs Rees?"

Steph was too shocked to speak, and simply nodded. She felt her heart was racing so fast that it could burst through her chest, as her mind spun over what the officer had said. Darren left, without any further fuss, and Steph went back into the house, feeling like she was going to faint.

'They know!' Her brain screamed at her and she leaned against the bannister of the stair for support.

"Mum!" Ollie came padding down the stairs. "Are you ok?"

Steph forced herself to pull herself together. "Yes, yes, I'm fine."

"Sure?" Ollie regarded her with concern, and she nodded her head.

She took a moment to regain her composure, and once she was sure of her voice, she told him that they would need to go and speak to the police that afternoon. Steph was almost certain that she'd be called in, but she didn't mention that, or Darren's interview, to their son.

Ollie looked remarkably calm about the request. "Keeley's had to go down, too."

"It's just procedure." Steph reassured him.

"Give me a shout when it's time." Ollie said nonchalantly and disappeared back to his bedroom.

Steph walked into the living room and sank down onto the sofa. She was so scared that she didn't even feel she could cry. She wasn't even scared for herself; it was the thought of leaving the children that was terrifying her.

"You're being silly." She told herself. "It was an accident. They'll know it wasn't deliberate."

She tried to calm herself with these thoughts but a little voice in the back of her mind taunted her, and no matter how hard she tried, she couldn't silence it.

DS Parker clapped her hands together emphatically as she briefed her team.

"We've got a few more lines of enquiry, thanks to the 'Disgusted of Tunbridge Wells' brigade." She told the tired faces of her team.

They'd been working methodically through pages of print-outs of comments and messages to the victim's online community group, and a few names stood out as having reasonable grounds for a grudge. DS Parker couldn't believe that she'd been so confident that this would be a cut-and-dried domestic. She hadn't counted on the residents of Oak Village being such a bunch of trolls.

"Here's an updated list of interviews," She passed the list to DC Elliott. "Good work on checking the alibis. We've got Barry Simons' confirmed. There's a small window that isn't accounted for, but we'll bank that for now. Have we got an update on the wife?"

DC Cooper spoke up. "Similar situation. Her story checks out, but there's a window between 8 and 9 that she said she was at the apartment on the Oak Fields estate cleaning. We just need a witness to confirm this. Nobody has had time to go out to do door-to-door yet."

DS Parker frowned at this. "It's important we get that confirmed. As a separated spouse, she's the most likely suspect."

"I've got a question," DC Elliott chipped in. "There's an exchange between the neighbour and a woman that was posted to both of the village online groups. If you look at this one, it looks like comments have been deleted as some of the conversation doesn't make sense."

DS Parker took the print-out and nodded. "That woman is on the list. We'll raise it with her."

"Do you want Mr Simons back in?" DC Cooper asked, pen poised to add to the list.

"Not yet," DS Parker shook her head. "See what comes out of this next lot of interviews."

DC Rhodes opened the door, interrupting the Sargent's train of thought.

"How did the interview go with the daughter?" DS Parker turned to her colleague sympathetically.

DC Rhodes looked uncharacteristically anxious. "There's something in the statement I need you to see. It might be nothing, but…"

"For the daughter?" DS Parker frowned, feeling her heart sink.

DC Rhodes nodded and wordlessly handed her Sargent the paper copy. DS Parker sat quietly pouring over the signed statement, searching for what was concerning her colleague. It was a lengthy and thorough interview, and DS Parker took her time, ensuring that she was fully digesting what she was reading.

A tap on the door interrupted them, and DS Parker flicked her head at the constables, signalling for one of them to deal with the disruption. She came to the discrepancy in the statement at the same time as a shadow fell over her. She looked up to see DC Cooper nervously clutching yet another ream of print-outs. She hadn't forgotten about her near-embarrassment at the Rees' that morning and she ignored him, out of annoyance.

"Oh, I see!" She looked up, seeking DC Rhodes' eyes. "The phone!"

DC Rhodes grimaced as she nodded in agreement. "She said she left the house with nothing, yet after her mother called the emergency suite, the first thing she did was get hold of her daughter. She didn't know where she was, but the daughter picked up straight away. She didn't have to phone around friends or parents. It just made me think."

DS Parker tapped her pen against the table thoughtfully. As the mother of teenagers, she knew that her sons were permanently attached to their phones. How likely was it that Keeley had gone back to the house for her phone? They'd have to get her back in. The boyfriend was scheduled to come in, with his mother, in the next half an hour. He might have more to add. She'd wait for his statement first.

DC Cooper cleared his throat, and she realised that he was still hovering next to her. She looked up at him questioningly.

"Autopsy and forensics both in." He said nervously.

DS Parker scanned the papers quickly. It all read as she suspected; blunt force trauma to the head, time of death approximately 9pm. They had a positive match on the murder weapon, as suspected a heavy liquor bottle, but it had been wiped clean of prints. There had been several empty bottles of alcohol in the recycling bin by the back door, alongside a set of broken glass tumblers. Forensics had found significant amount of spirits in the sink and drains, indicating that Jim had emptied the bottles, which was consistent with the daughter's story. They had lifted four sets of prints from the bottles in the recycling bin; two were unidentified, one belonged to the victim, but the fourth shocked DS Parker.

"I must be losing my touch," She said frustrated. "I need Barry Simons back in. We've got a match for prints."

Chapter 23

For the first time in years, Barry slept through his alarm and Dana had to shake him awake. She debated letting him sleep, but she knew he would be angry at himself if he missed work.

He'd been having trouble sleeping for the last few nights and had reluctantly taken a few herbal tablets, which had surprisingly knocked him out cold. Barry felt his mind start to wake, relishing the blissful moments of nothingness before he became fully conscious and the darkness of the last few days settled over him.

He struggled to open his eyes, dreading the day ahead before it had even begun. He was a strong man, who had spent a great portion of his life working long hours in all weather conditions without complaint, yet it was now that he was waking up in a beautiful house, next to a loving wife, to drive to a well-paid job, that he could barely summon the energy to lift his head from the pillow.

He had thought he'd already hit rock-bottom, but as he lay in his bed, feeling weary to his bones, he realised he'd been premature in his assumption. This was the lowest he had felt, emptier and more hopeless than when his first marriage had broken down, and he'd been drinking himself to death in a lonely and desolate house that wasn't a home. Meeting Dana had saved him; her gentle positivity had lifted him and provided him with the strength to put himself back together. He'd been proud of how he had turned his life around, mentally congratulating how he had narrowly avoided his drinking habit spiralling out of control and tearing his life apart.

Dana had spooked him when she had brought up the time he spent at the pub, and although he didn't let her know, he had been shaken by her words and his own realisation that maybe he didn't have it all under control. He had reacted, with arrogant confidence in his will-power, ceasing his daily pub visits to prove to himself, rather than Dana, that he had control over his drinking.

He didn't stop drinking though, because he didn't need to. Alcohol had never been the problem, he continued to tell himself. He didn't need to drink, and he continued to reward himself with just one or two drinks, stopping shy of over-indulgence to prove himself right. If he had a problem, he wouldn't be able to stop, and he could stop.

His moods grew darker, the longer he abstained, and he blamed work, the kids or Dana for the way he felt. It was with deep shame and regret that Barry acknowledged that he'd enjoyed having an outlet for his frustrations in his ongoing dispute with Jim Burbridge. There were only so many times that he could lay the blame for his changed disposition on his loved ones before he would have been forced to own his temper, so having a nemesis had been perfect. Jim Burbridge had upset many people in the village, and this allowed Barry to feel justified and almost vigilante in actions that, if Barry had been feeling himself, he would have dismissed as childish and spiteful.

He wished he could find some way to repent for the way he had treated Jim. Barry wasn't so hypocritical that he would ever claim that he and Jim would have ever been best friends, but the tragedy of the man's death left Barry overwhelmed by regret and guilt. He had no idea what had happened to Jim, or what he was going through, to cause him to act in a condescending and rude manner, but what Barry did know was that no matter how Jim had behaved, Barry should never have reduced himself to the same level.

He'd told himself he was sticking up for his wife when he had publicly ridiculed the man over the traffic problems, that in all honesty were not Jim's fault and simply bad luck due to the poor planning of the contractor. He was "standing up" for the people of the village when he had enlisted Jordan's help to create a rival online community to replace Jim's, when really Barry knew he had projected the frustration and fear that he felt, after he had found himself cheating his own self-imposed pub ban, onto Jim. He was "defending" a young business owner when he worked collaboratively with Tina to publicly discredit Jim. Barry wasn't saying that Jim was right or blameless. His death hadn't made him a martyr, and the review he had left the poor girl was spiteful and potentially damaging. It didn't make Barry's actions any less heinous. As Barry had said countless time to his own children: two wrongs did not make a right.

He had deleted the rival community group, out of respect, as soon as he had thought to, not long after he heard about the death. The group that Jim had created single-handedly was still a live, harrowing record of the unpleasant and uncharitable way in which the community had treated both Jim and each other. Barry had looked at it, just once, out of morbid curiosity. He would have loved to remove his own hostile comments, but it seemed wrong to try to erase the words when they could never be righted with Jim himself.

Barry hadn't been surprised that the police had wanted to speak to him in relation to the unexplained death of his neighbour. The tension between the men was no secret, and Barry knew his name would have come up in conversation with any of their neighbours. The police had to do their job and Barry was glad that he had already admitted everything to Dana so that his alibi came as no shock to her.

It was only Dana, gently waking him, her face etched with concern for him, that motivated Barry to rise from his bed. A little part of him, the part that he recognised deep-down as destructive, wished he hadn't confessed to her. He had taken the first step in getting his life back on track, but while only he knew, he could back out at any time. By confiding in Dana, he had committed himself, and somehow the thought left him feeling desperately trapped. If he failed, she already knew and then what?

Barry pasted on a smile and made a joke about his herbal-induced coma. Dana's mouth turned up into a smile at his humour, but the worry remained in her eyes, and he looked away, unable to bear her pain as well as his own.

"Are you sure you're up to going in today?" She asked.

"I'm fine," Barry reassured her. "Are you?"

Dana nodded and then shook her head. "I don't know. It's all so surreal."

"I know," Barry placed a comforting hand on her arm. "Why don't you stay home today? You've had a shock."

Dana shook her head quickly. "I don't want to be here on my own."

Barry stared at her for a moment, surprised by the extent of her fear. "You know that it wasn't a random thing. Someone didn't just walk in off the street and-"

"I know!" Dana cut him off with a shudder. "I know that's probably the case. I just feel creeped out and, don't forget, I was here. I saw people. I gave the police names."

"And everything you gave them was helpful," Barry said calmly, taking her in his arms. "The police will be able to build a picture of Jim's movements that night which will help them find out who hurt him and bring them to justice."

"But what if they don't?" Dana asked, the panic clear on her face.

"They will." Barry repeated firmly. "But I'll come home from work early so you're not here alone, and if you still feel uneasy, we'll just move."

Dana opened her mouth to protest, but Barry silenced her with a kiss.

"We'll leave together," Barry said firmly. "I'll be back here at 2pm sharp."

Dana nodded, feeling silly but grateful.

He kept true to his promise and moved some meetings around to ensure that Dana wasn't coming home to an empty house. Barry felt marginally better for getting up and going through the motions of working. The normality of his day was a welcome distraction to his own turbulent emotions. He avoided going into the main office, not feeling up to having to discuss the death that was no doubt the main topic of conversation in the town.

Dana arrived home a little after him, her relief to see him

evident on her face. They ate a light, late lunch together and Barry could sense by Dana's quietness that there was something else playing on her mind.

"Everything ok, love?" He asked.

"I was just wondering," She admitted. "What happens next?"

"The police said they'd confirm my, uh, alibi and let me know if they had any more questions," Barry replied, relieved that that was all that was on her mind. "It should be straight forward enough."

"Not that," Dana said, nervously looking away from him. "I was talking about the…"

She trailed off, and Barry placed his cutlery down on his plate, his appetite suddenly diminished.

"To be honest," Barry cleared his throat, hoping he sounded confident. "I think I was over-reacting a little. I was just feeling a bit out-of-sorts and I don't really think I need to go again."

"But last time," Dana protested. "You said it helped."

"I can't even think about this right now," Barry said decisively. "There's people with real problems. Like them, next-door. I'll be fine."

"You were serious about it, Saturday," Dana said. "What's changed?"

"What's changed?" Barry looked at her in disbelief. "There's a full-scale murder investigation going on. I might be innocent of that, but my behaviour towards the man was shameful. I just can't do this right now. My head feels like it's going to explode!"

"And drinking is going to help, is it?" Dana's face turned to stone, and Barry could feel the disappointment radiating from her in waves.

"I'm not drinking." Barry held his hands out, gesturing at the glass of water in front of him. "I haven't drunk since I went to that meeting!"

"It's been less than 48 hours." Dana retorted in frustration.

"And I'm cured already!" Barry shot back sarcastically, getting up sharply from the table, the legs of his chair scraping noisily across the tiled floor. "It's a miracle!"

He stormed from the room, feeling his heart racing at the rare argument between them. He went into the kitchen and was reaching for a can at the back of the fridge before he was aware of what he was doing. His hand closed around the cold metal and he recoiled at the recognition. The first action he had taken, when upset, angry, tired, stressed, had been to reach for a drink. He paled, his heart still beating hard in his chest, and his mind torn between popping open the can in a show of defiance or throwing the whole drawer of cans into the bin.

Dana followed him into the kitchen, carrying their unfinished plates. She glanced at him, stood in front of the opened refrigerator, but averted her eyes quickly. Barry wished she would say something to provoke him, but she didn't. She wouldn't, he realised. That wasn't Dana. She looked small, in her bare feet, and her vulnerability softened his heart.

Resolutely, he withdrew his hand from the fridge and shut the door, turning to his wife.

"I'm sorry," He said, his eyes heavy with remorse. "There are meetings on Tuesday's and Saturday's. I will go."

"It's up to you," Dana said quietly. "Whatever you do, I'll support you. If you want me to come, I'll come."

She had stayed up after he had fallen asleep Saturday night, reading up on alcohol addiction and how best she could support him. It was new territory to her, but she was adamant that she would be there for him, every step of the way.

"Thank you." Barry nodded. "If I go for a shower, can you get rid of all this?"

He gestured at the fridge, embarrassed, and Dana nodded quickly, feeling her eyes tear up in sympathy. Barry hurried from the kitchen and Dana set about completing the task, quickly and as quietly as she could. She spared nothing, and she used a washing basket to gather up the empty bottle and cans. She took it out to the garden, intent on draining the outside 'bar' of every last drop, when she heard the front door knock.

She hesitated, not wanting to pause in her mission, but she slid the basket discreetly onto the floor, pulling the door closed, and quickly made her way back into the house. The person knocked again with an air of authority and urgency, causing Dana to jog the last few steps. She knew before she opened it that it was the police.

"Hello, Mrs Simons." It was the same woman who had interviewed Dana, accompanied by a colleague, and Dana looked at her expectantly, waiting for her to tell her that they had apprehended the murderer.

"Is Mr Simons home?" She continued. "We have some further questions for him."

Dana was surprised that they wanted to speak to Barry, and not her, for more information, but she darted up the stairs and Barry, cutting his shower short, dressed hurriedly and came downstairs.

"Everything ok?" He looked concerned as he greeted the officers.

"We have a few more questions," The Detective said, looking serious. "We need you to accompany us down to the station."

"I've told you everything." Barry frowned. "Can't you just ask me here?"

"We need you to come down to the station." The woman repeated firmly.

Dana blanched at her tone. She had been worried when he was taken in yesterday, despite knowing that he was innocent and that he had a room full of witnesses who could confirm that he had attended a support meeting for alcoholics during the time the murder was committed.

What about the period after? Dana's mind started to panic. He was in the house with her. What if they didn't believe she'd told them everything? They must know when people are lying. This is their job. They must have sensed she was lying. Oh, God, this was her fault.

Dana felt her pulse race but fought to keep her expression

calm.

"Shall I come down?" She asked Barry.

Barry was looking more concerned than he had yesterday, as if he'd expected to be called in for questioning then, but this visit had caught him off guard.

"You'll probably just be waiting around," He told her. "Why don't you go and see if Steph fancies some company? Jordan will be home in the next hour."

Dana nodded, but she watched him walk down the driveway to their waiting car with a growing feeling of guilt and fear.

Tina exited the bus on the top road and walked the short distance back to her home. She had planned on using the library to start working on an assignment after her lecture, but her head wasn't in it.

She had felt sick with worry all weekend that Jim Burbridge's review was going to cause the buyer to pull out of the sale. Without the money, she would have to take another job and she was already struggling to keep up with her workload. She knew that her final year was going to be even more challenging, and so continuing to run the business was absolutely out of the question. Even with Barry valiantly agreeing to her plan to discredit Jim's review, and the loyal customers and friends that jumped in to defend her, Tina had still wondered if it would be enough. She had her heart set on the business going to Stephanie

Rees. Tina felt a responsibility to the staff that she employed and would rather fold the business and support them in getting jobs elsewhere than see them exploited by someone who's only aim was to squeeze maximum profit, not build on a reputable and ethical local company.

It didn't seem important now, Tina thought to herself as she walked home. The man was dead, and Tina felt awful. She had openly bad-mouthed Jim Burbridge online the day before he died. If a poor review accusing a company of employing thieves didn't put off potential buyers, then surely the business insinuating that the reviewer was having an affair as well as being an outright liar would do the job.

Tina had reacted in temper and desperation, but Jim's untimely death had her feeling remorseful. She should have risen above the review. It was one bad comment amongst more than a dozen fantastic ones. Tina had tossed and turned in bed last night, unable to sleep, consumed with guilt at the way she had handled the situation. The worst part was acknowledging why she had flown off the handle. She could tell herself all she wanted that it was fear over the losing the business sale, but as the sky grew lighter, Tina's mind had replayed the conversation with Jim over and over, eventually forcing her to acknowledge what had triggered her to lash out.

She had known exactly who he was talking about when he referred to "his friend". Tina had an encyclopaedic memory when it came to her business. Between the three women she employed and the few jobs she picked up herself, Tina had had close to fifty customers over the lifetime of her business, and very few who hadn't lasted. She had the highest standards for herself and her team, ensuring she got feedback on every cancellation. If she really thought about it, she could probably recite them all and that's how she had known who Jim was referring to.

Even the thought of the woman ignited a spark of anger in Tina. Years of pent-up fury had been misdirected at Jim, and Tina couldn't excuse her behaviour once she had faced up to the true motivation behind her need to react to his comments. He had been a casualty of Tina's need for retribution. It had brought back all the feelings of hurt, confusion and helplessness that she'd genuinely thought that she'd come to terms with.

Tina shook her head, trying to chase away the thoughts. She knew better than anyone that she was only hurting herself when she clung on to the past. It was today and tomorrow that counted. What was done, was done. She needed to forget it all and move on.

"Even if the business doesn't sell," Tina told herself as she picked up her pace. "I'll make it work."

She was deep in thought, and lost in her own head, when she suddenly became aware of footsteps behind her.

"Tina!"

She turned, startled, and stopped to allow Darren Rees to catch up with her.

"Hi." She said politely, unsure why he had called out to her. They were hardly on the best of terms.

"Hey," He said breathlessly, having ran the last twenty yards to catch up with her. "How are you?"

Tina shrugged. "Alright. You?"

"I was hoping to run into you." He admitted and Tina, feeling self-conscious stood talking to him in the street, inclined her head in the direction that she was walking in an unspoken command that they walk and talk.

"What's up?" She asked, trying to sound disinterested.

He paused, as if weighing up how to go about this conversation, before going ahead and asking directly. "Why are you messaging Steph about the business?"

"Because she wants to buy it." Tina replied. "Why else would I be messaging her?"

"I don't know," Darren responded looking at Tina's face and trying to ascertain that she was telling the truth. "I just got the impression that you didn't like, well, you know."

"That I didn't like you and Kelly messing around?" Tina replied bluntly. "No, I can't say I did. But if you're asking whether I was going to say anything to your wife, then the answer is no."

"Right, ok," Darren had the decency to look embarrassed. "There was nothing really going on, it was just a laugh."

"Whatever," Tina shook her head. "Look, Darren, it's none of my business and it's done, and nobody needs to know."

Darren groaned at her response and Tina frowned at his reaction.

"What's happened?" She asked, praying that he hadn't already said something to his wife, citing Tina as a party in the know about his little indiscretions with Kelly Russell, and further damning the sale that was clearly not meant to be.

"I've just been called to the police station," He told her. "Kelly went to Jim Burbridge's the night he died. She met me afterwards, just to talk, and I've had to give a statement."

"Oh God!" Tina exclaimed, horrified. "Hopefully that'll never have to be used in court."

Darren looked like he wanted to cry, and Tina felt the tiniest sliver of pity for him, despite her disapproval of both his and Kelly's behaviour. This silly dalliance being revealed would hurt too many people; Evan, Steph and all the kids.

"Does your wife know?" Tina asked hesitantly.

"I've just come from giving my statement," Darren said. "I'll have to tell her something. She'll want to know why I was called in. Our Ollie was witness to Jim and his daughter having an argument on the day it happened, so he's got to give a statement too."

"What are you going to do?" Tina asked.

"I don't know," Darren admitted. "I can't drop this on her now. It was stupid of me, and I've learned my lesson. She doesn't need this on top of everything."

Tina nodded in agreement. "You'll just have to say that you bumped into Kelly and that's all it was."

Darren looked pleadingly at Tina. "You won't say anything?"

"No!" Tina exclaimed. "I don't want anyone knowing I knew this! I really wish I didn't!"

"Right," Darren looked shame-faced. "I'm really sorry."

They had reached the turning to Tina's street and Tina walked on, without saying goodbye to Darren. She bristled with annoyance that he had sought her out to ask for her confidence. She tried not to be judgemental of him and Kelly, but it rankled her that she had been unwittingly dragged into their mess. She didn't feel she had the right to feel the same way about Kelly, but that was a little more complicated. A bit like their friendship.

Kelly had struck up a friendship with her when Tina had moved to the area and started working in The Crown. For unknown reasons to Tina, Kelly had been persistent in pursuing an acquaintance with her, despite them not having much in common. Tina had tried to keep Kelly at arm's length, not approving of her flirtatious nature. She had even watched Kelly fluttering her eyelashes at Robbie, which would have been the final straw for Tina, had she not been feeling a little guilty herself about the attention she was receiving from Kelly's husband.

Tina's head ached with the tangled mess of thoughts, feelings and regrets, and she swiped open the door to her block, wanting nothing more than to lie down in a dark room. She wondered what reason Kelly had for going to Jim's house. Probably something to do with the bloody online community group. It crossed Tina's mind that the police might even want to speak to her, after all she'd had a public run in with him. If they were working off a list of people who had disputes with Jim, Tina supposed that they'd get around to her eventually.

Tina paused on the landing of the second floor to fish her keys out of her bag at the precise moment the middle flat door opened. Tina did a double-take when she was faced with Laura Burbridge and her teenaged daughter.

"Hi." Laura said politely.

Tina could see the dark circles around her eyes behind her thick-rimmed glasses. Her face looked sallow and lined, and Tina felt a rush of empathy for what the woman must be going through.

"I'm so sorry about your loss," Tina said, wanting to hug her but sensing Laura's discomfort at their meeting. "How are you?"

"We're ok." Laura glanced at her daughter behind her.

Tina followed her gaze before looking away quickly. Keeley's eyes were downcast, and she purposely didn't look up at Tina. She looked like a shadow of the girl that Tina had seen out and about in the village; her thin body swamped under an over-sized hoodie, her hair greasy and lank, her eyes puffy and red.

Tina nodded dumbly. "Are you staying here?"

"For now," Laura said shortly, before turning away and locking the door. "I'm sorry, we're in a rush."

Tina stepped aside and let them pass, feeling heavy with unease as if she had intruded into their personal grief. She made her way quickly to her apartment and it was only when she was led on her sofa, curtains closed and lights off, that she wondered, with horror and shame, if Laura had read her accusations of Jim's affair online.

Chapter 24

The Detective Inspector had requested to speak to DS Parker in private, and she handed over the latest statement that she was working on to DC Rhodes and made her way to the meeting room.

She'd slept for less than three hours in the last thirty-six, she had reams of paperwork to get through and for every question answered, another dozen seemed to crop up. She knew that DI Jones wasn't happy that they hadn't made any arrests, but there was honestly nothing more she could do until they'd worked through the evidence they already had.

DS Parker knew that the DI had got his hopes up that a fingerprint match for Mr Simons would lead to a confession or enough evidence for an arrest, tying up the case quickly but it was purely circumstantial. The murder weapon and the body were clear of any evidence of his involvement. Mr Simons had claimed that his teenage stepson and Mr Burbridge's daughter had taken alcohol from his house on New Year's Eve, and DS Parker had added this to the growing list of things to check.

"How are we doing?" He asked as she stepped into the little meeting room.

DS Parker let out the exasperated sigh that she'd been hiding from her team all morning. "Struggling. Every avenue is throwing up more names, and we don't have the resources to get through them quick enough."

"Agreed." He nodded, and surprised relief flooded through

DS Parker's stressed body. She had assumed that the Inspector would lead this case, but he'd stepped back and let her get stuck into a lot of the decision-making. She had been fearful that he was regretting that decision and was calling her in to let her know that he was taking over due to her lack of progress. "I've got another three heads at your disposal. I don't need to tell you what you need to do."

"Thank you." DS Parker responded gratefully. "Are you still happy to lead any suspect interviews?"

"Yes," He nodded. "Thoughts on Barry Simons."

"Honestly?" DS Parker sat forward in her chair, keen for his opinion. "I don't think it was him."

"Me neither." The DI agreed. "Talk me through your reasoning."

DS Parker contemplated this for a moment. The science behind an investigation came so naturally to her that a lot of the time it felt like she was acting on intuition.

"The victim was killed by a blow from an object that was on hand. Not something that was premeditated." DS Parker summarised. "The victim had had many run-ins previously with Mr Simons and none had escalated into violence. He's a big bloke and I think if he had been provoked to violence, he seems the type who'd have used his fists. His alibi checks out; he was at a support meeting in town and then there's footage of his car outside the supermarket which places him exactly where he says he was."

DI Jones sat back thoughtfully. "What else?"

"I would have had the wife as a key suspect if I hadn't met

her." DS Parker continued. "Recently separated, her having moved out of the family home despite her insisting that this was her choice. The blow to the head with a bottle would be more likely from her; a smaller female overcome with rage. Her alibi was checked immediately and there's only the smallest of windows that she could have done it."

"Last seen alive by Kelly Russell at about 7.30pm." He nodded. "The neighbour, Mrs Simons, sees another woman heading to the house at 8.45pm on foot. The description doesn't match the wife. Is there a mistress?"

"I wondered that." DS Parker nodded. "The scene is typical of it being a domestic, but nobody has volunteered anything, there is no record of him talking to any women on his phone and the wife just claimed they'd been growing apart for years."

"Kelly Russell." DI Jones said pensively. "How do you feel about that one? She was the last person to see him alive, and she claimed she was looking for his wife, not him."

"If she's lying," DS Parker said. "She's good. She was more concerned about having to name her alibi, in case her husband found out. She insists that she didn't step into the house and forensically nothing tells us that she did."

"You know what I'm going to ask." DI Jones smiled apologetically.

DS Parker nodded resignedly. "We got what we could from her yesterday, but we couldn't go in hard, given the circumstances. She was still in shock and we're hoping to get more from her today."

"Thoughts?"

DS Parker grimaced. "It's more likely it was the daughter, in a fit of rage, than the wife, the neighbour or Mrs Russell unfortunately."

"Agreed, unfortunately." DI Jones said. "Did the boyfriend bring up anything new?"

"Nothing." DS Parker advised. "He claimed he thought she had her phone when she left. We've asked her to come back in, and we'll raise the discrepancy in her statement. In the meantime, we've had more door-to-door enquiries out today, just in case we missed anybody yesterday."

"Well done," DI Jones told her. "I want you to know I wouldn't have done anything differently."

"Thank you." She said relieved. "I'm hopeful that we'll get an arrest by the end of the day."

She stepped back into the corridor, bracing herself to jump back into the sea of paperwork and motivate her swamped team.

"Updates?" She called out as she stepped back into the room.

DC Rhodes waved a piece of paper in her direction. "Do you want the good news or the bad news?"

DS Parker couldn't help but smile at her humour. "You'd better give me them both."

"Good news is we're up-to-date with all checks on alibis," She grinned. "Nothing dodgy to report- it all checks out. Bad news is the wife and the daughter have just turned up for you."

DS Parker held back a sigh. She wasn't looking forward to this.

"But," DC Rhodes wasn't finished. "There's an old dear in reception who says she has information regarding the case. Do you want me to deal with her?"

"Does she have a name?" DS Parker asked, almost glad of any postponement to her interview with the victim's poor daughter.

"Mrs Morgan." DC Rhodes said.

"I'll see her first," DS Parker knew she was probably procrastinating but she couldn't help it. The longer she could go on without finding evidence that the victim had been murdered by his teenage daughter, the better. "Has Cooper taken them down to the support team?"

"Yep," DC Rhodes nodded. "Can I do Mrs Morgan with you?"

"Come on then." DS Parker thought she could do with Rhodes' incessant banter to help her through what was likely to be a grim day.

DS Parker made herself known to an older lady, who was in her fifties and hardly an "old dear" as Rhodes had put it. They took her into a room and DS Parker went through the formalities before Mrs Morgan began.

"It's terrible news, isn't it?" The woman started with a gleam in her eye. "A murder. In Oak Village."

"Terrible." DC Rhodes had a tendency to encourage dramatics and DS Parker gave her a reproachful glare.

"Not surprising though," Mrs Morgan continued. "Standards have gone right down since they threw up all those houses. It used to be a lovely, little place. I didn't used to bother locking my door."

"My mum always says that." DC Rhodes nodded encouragingly.

DS Parker started to regret letting her come. This was a murder investigation, for goodness sake.

"Mrs Morgan," DS Parker cut in before the woman could get further in her reminiscing. "You had information regarding the night of the death?"

"Yes," Mrs Morgan agreed grandiosely. "I was out early yesterday at Church and then we went to visit my daughter for the rest of the day, so I didn't know anything about it until I saw Angela at the post office this morning. I was so shocked! But then I thought, well, actually, I did see something, and I said this to Angela, and she said I should definitely tell you, even though it's only a little thing. And I thought about it, and I didn't like to bother you with something trivial, like a busybody-"

She showed no signs of slowing down her monologue and DS Parker cut in.

"No, it's important that people report even the littlest things," She said. "What did you see?"

"I was in the kitchen and a big, dark car drove into the street at about 8.20." Mrs Morgan finished, looking slightly dejected that her story had been cut off before she could give it a proper build up.

There were thirty-two semi-detached houses in Sycamore Street. DS Parker imagined that a few cars would be driving in and out over the course of the evening.

"What number house do you live in?" DS Parker asked, not feeling very hopeful about Mrs Morgan's information.

"Number 6." Mrs Morgan told her. "I was feeding the cat. And then I let him out after his dinner, say fifteen minutes later, and I saw the same car drive out."

DS Parker prayed that DC Rhodes wouldn't comment on the length of the cat's meal.

"And," Mrs Morgan continued, looking pleased with herself again. "I knew that it wasn't one of the neighbours as it had one of those personalised number plates, and we've seen that car before, me and Angela."

"What was the registration?" DS Parker asked.

"I don't know what the numbers were meant to be," Mrs Morgan admitted. "But it spelt Dazza- as in D,A,Z,Z,A."

DS Parker's heart skipped with excitement. She'd seen that registration when Kelly Russell's "friend", Darren Rees, had insisted on driving himself down to the station this morning. She sat up straight in her chair and nodded at Mrs Morgan.

"Right," DS Parker said assertively. "I'm just going to need a few more details from you."

"Excuse me," Laura spoke quietly and politely to the young

man on the reception. "We're waiting for Detective Sargent Parker?"

"She's just with someone." The man said with an apologetic smile. "If you could take a seat, someone will be along shortly."

Laura sat back down next to her daughter, feeling sick with worry and exhaustion. She reached for Keeley's hand, and Keeley passively let her. After Laura's initial shock had worn off, her immediate thoughts had been for Keeley. As grim as the image of Jim's lifeless body was, Laura knew that she would eventually come to terms with it as long as she knew her daughter was alright.

Laura had felt relief pierce her horrified state when she had discovered that Keeley had stayed the night at the Rees' house, but this soon turned to fear for Keeley's psychological wellbeing when she processed that this unplanned sleepover had been the result of a blazing row between Keeley and her father. Laura's own last conversation with Jim had been surprisingly civil, but she couldn't imagine what the long-term effects for Keeley would be having to live with the guilt and regret of her last words with her father being in anger.

The police had been great, and there was a trained grief counsellor on hand for Keeley as well as a team to support her during the invasive interviews. Laura knew they had to do their jobs, but she had hoped that they wouldn't need to speak to Keeley more than once. They needed to be alone to process what had happened. Keeley hadn't cried yet and, with each passing minute that she stayed silent and vacant, Laura found every breath harder to take, as if an invisible band were tightening slowly around her chest.

It had been a whirlwind, yet it had seemed to happen in slow-motion. Yesterday seemed like no time had passed, yet it seemed like a lifetime ago. How could Jim have been so alive one minute, and so dead the next? Laura felt the bile in her empty stomach rise up, as her thoughts invoked the haunting image of his cold, lifeless body. She forced herself to swallow and waited for the nauseous feeling to pass.

"Mrs Burbridge?" The friendly-faced woman who had attended Keeley's interview with her yesterday appeared in the corridor.

Laura stared at her blankly for a moment as her overworked mind tried to place her, before she remembered and got to her feet.

"Hello, Keeley." The woman offered her hand, and Laura was relieved to see Keeley shake it politely, although she remained silent. "If you'd like to follow me down to the family room. Your mum can come in if she likes until we're ready to start."

Laura and Keeley followed the eccentrically-dressed woman to the room. The woman, whose name still escaped Laura's memory, chatted in calm, measured tones just filling the silence.

"Sorry, Detective Sargent Parker is just running a little behind," The young man that Laura had spoken to earlier interrupted them. "She won't be much longer."

Laura wondered whether that meant that they had found the killer. She mentally crossed her fingers, hoping it did. She needed this to be over.

After what seemed like an eternity waiting, DS Parker and the officer, who had interviewed Keeley yesterday, appeared, apologising for keeping them waiting, and Laura went out to the corridor to wait again. She watched the hands on the wall clock move around at a snail's pace, feeling helpless that she couldn't shelter her daughter from having to relive that awful night. The suffocating feeling increased until Laura felt she could no longer control her overwhelming desire to knock on the door and take Keeley away from it all, but no sooner had she risen to her feet to succumb to the compulsion, the door swung open and a pale-faced Keeley emerged.

DS Parker asked to speak to Laura for a moment, and she went into the room, but they had nothing more to tell her than reminding her of the processes they were following and the support available.

"Will you need anything else from us?" Laura asked anxiously.

"Hopefully not," DS Parker smiled sympathetically. "We'll keep you updated."

Laura and Keeley made their way back to the car, and it was only once they were on the road back to the village that Keeley spoke.

"Mum," She said in a small voice. "I think I've said something I shouldn't have."

Laura turned to look at her, forgetting about the road in front and causing the car to swerve wildly.

"Mum!" Keeley exclaimed as they both jolted back in their seats.

Laura swallowed nervously. "Sorry. What do you mean?"

"They asked me more questions this time," She explained. "I just couldn't think straight yesterday."

"That's ok," Laura comforted her. "You were in shock. They will understand. That's why they asked you to come back today."

"I told them what we argued about." Keeley said quietly.

Laura stared ahead, eyes fixed on the road. "That's good. You should always tell the truth."

"They asked me about how I got my phone." Keeley continued.

Laura's chest tightened but she kept her face impassive.

"Did you not have it when you left?" She asked carefully.

"No, Mum. I didn't have anything. I just ran out." Keeley sounded worried. "Ollie's Mum went over to speak to Dad and she got it for me."

"That's ok." Laura said, unsure of why this was relevant.

"They didn't know she went there," Keeley shook her head frantically. "I could tell by their questions. They didn't know."

"That's good," Laura said. "She might be able to tell them something important."

"No, Mum!" Keeley exclaimed. "You don't get it! She was really, really angry at Dad."

"She was?" Laura glanced at Keeley's agitated face. "Why?"

Keeley opened her mouth, and before she had time to form the words to tell her Mum everything that had been said, the floodgates finally opened, and Keeley burst into hysterical tears.

Back at the sparsely-furnished flat, Laura did all she could to placate Keeley and reassure her that neither she nor Ollie's mother had done anything wrong. Keeley had eventually calmed down slightly, and Laura sent her into the one bedroom that was furnished to lie down. Finally alone, Laura sunk onto a chair and buried her head in her hands. Knowing that Keeley had known about the source of the start of her and Jim's marriage breakdown, and that this had been the main cause of Jim and Keeley's fight, made her feel responsible. Laura could only imagine how angry the usually quiet and mild-mannered Steph Rees had been, genuinely believing that Jim was serious about pressing charges on her almost-sixteen-year-old son.

Jim may not have done it, and there may have even been no grounds for prosecution even if he did, but Laura could imagine how, as a mother, Steph's first instinct would have been to protect her son. She sincerely hoped Ollie's mother hadn't lashed out in temper, but all Laura knew was that someone had. It was out of her hands, Laura thought to herself. Keeley had done the right thing, and they could only hope that Jim's killer was brought to justice.

She looked around the strange, foreign place in which they were living, feeling glad that they had somewhere, but wishing that it felt like home. They had only basic furniture, no kitchenware or food, and Laura realised, with a sense of dread, that at some point she would need to go back to the house to pick up the documents that would be needed for Jim's arrangements as well as their belongings. The officer had said something about when she could go back, but, for the life of her, Laura couldn't recall what had been said.

Laura crept into the bedroom and was comforted to see Keeley had fallen asleep. Laura wondered whether she should try to pop out to the shop, but she didn't think she could face going anywhere local and running into anybody she knew. On the other hand, she didn't want to go further afield and leave Keeley alone for too long either. Laura found herself walking back and forth, like a caged animal, in the small living space, unable to make a decision or to relax. She decided that she'd have to face the neighbours at some point and, scribbling a quick note in case Keeley woke up, Laura slipped on her shoes.

She had only managed to get as far as the front door of the apartment block before her fear that she would bump into someone she knew was realised. Laura gave Tina a polite-but-standoffish smile, hoping she was giving off the vibes of somebody that didn't want to make conversation.

"Hi." Tina clearly wasn't picking up the vibes as she stopped square in the middle of the doorway, obstructing Laura's exit. "I'm glad I bumped into you."

Laura paused, wishing she wasn't so conditioned to be good-mannered so she could just rush past as if she hadn't heard her. She waited for Tina to expand on her statement.

"Laura," Tina started uncomfortably before bursting out. "I don't know whether you saw, but I said some really horrible things, and I don't expect you to forgive me, but I just want you to know they weren't true, and I was lashing out about the review, and I'm so, so sorry."

Laura stepped back in surprise at Tina's outpouring. They

had never had more than a polite conversation with each other, despite Laura employing her services for over a year, and she'd always struck Laura as quite introverted. Hearing an unexpected apology tumbling out of Tina's mouth felt as surreal as the whole situation.

"I'm sorry," Laura said slowly. "I've really no idea what you're talking about."

Tina took a deep breath. She hadn't meant to offload an apology onto Laura in the middle of the communal hallway, but the thoughts had been flying around her head since she'd seen Laura and her daughter earlier, and it had all just came spilling from her mouth as if she had no control over her brain. Tina wished she'd just kept her mouth shut. The poor woman had enough on her plate and Tina felt guilty that she was hurting Laura by raking up the past, all to try to alleviate her own conscience.

Laura was looking at her now in confusion, and Tina had no choice but to explain.

"I'm sorry," She started again cautiously. "I'm not sure if you even saw it, but there was a review that Jim left on my page. I'm afraid it wasn't very good, and I reacted quite badly. I just wanted to apologise, that's all."

Laura looked taken aback, but she nodded slowly. "I was aware that there were some comments about a review that was left. I saw it Friday evening, but I don't recall seeing anything you'd written. To be honest, I think everyone is as bad as each other online, but I appreciate your apology. Thank you."

Tina frowned, a little confused. Hers had made up the bulk of the comments on the post but, then again, Laura had had a lot going on, and Tina was just grateful that Laura had accepted her apology graciously.

"Thank you," Tina said gratefully. "If there's anything I can do for you or your daughter, please let me know. My mother died, in not very nice circumstances, when I was seventeen, so I understand how hard it will be for you both."

"I'm so sorry to hear that," Laura said. "I had no idea."

"My brother was only twelve," Tina continued, keen to make amends with the courteous woman. "And it was very hard for him. He had some really great support through counselling. I've got the details somewhere and I've got some books, too. Obviously, when you're ready."

"Thank you." Laura felt a lump in her throat. "I've been so worried about how Keeley will get through this. That would be really helpful."

"Whenever you want to talk," Tina found herself blinking back tears. "It's hard, but you will both get there."

Instinctively, Laura reached out and hugged the girl. When she moved away, Tina smiled shyly back at her and Laura felt a rush of gratitude for the much-needed hope that Tina was offering her.

Chapter 25

DS Parker glanced at the clock. She had known she would be pulling a late one today, but after the latest developments, she would gamble a month's salary on her not getting home tonight.

She ducked into a quiet room and made a quick call to her partner and children. The "suspicious death of a local man" had been splashed all over the community and regional news today, and they had expected a call from her; knowing that this would take over her life until there was an arrest.

She needed to get the new 'persons of interest' in for interviewing, and the sooner, the better in her opinion. They had spoken to both parties already today, which could cause complications if they were unwilling to come back in voluntarily. DS Parker preferred to keep arrests to the bare minimum, but this sudden progress was too much of a coincidence to leave until tomorrow.

Impatiently, she called the DI. It was very likely that there would be an arrest, if not two, made today, and he would need to know what was going on. All aspects of this investigation would be under the microscope at some point and DI Jones was putting faith in her. She needed to get this right.

While she waited for the DI to come in, she called together the team to brief them on the next steps.

"Can I get a rundown of what's confirmed and what's still outstanding?" She called, feeling the familiar heady buzz of when a case was close to cracking. She could probably reel it off herself, but it was always wise to double and triple-check all the little details. "Rhodes, give me the timeline."

"Victim's wife moves out of family home Thursday 2nd March," DC Rhodes said confidently. "Victim goes to work as normal but takes Friday 3rd off as family emergency. Daughter is at home with him. She advised that, apart from staying off work, nothing out of the ordinary happened. Daughter confirmed he was out, at unknown location, between 1000 and approx. 1600 hours, Saturday 4th. Unknown caller to the house. Between 1800 and 1830 hours, victim argues with daughter over alcohol found in garden and then about victim's wife having an affair with undisclosed person. Daughter's boyfriend arrives, and daughter flees house, leaving bedroom window open and chest of drawers in middle of room."

"Daughter's alibi?" DS Parker probed.

"Seen fleeing house by neighbour, Mrs Dana Simons," Rhodes continued, without pausing. "Confirmed by boyfriend's mother, Mrs Stephanie Rees, that Keeley Burbridge stayed at their house and did not leave until her mother called her the next day, by which time body had been discovered."

"Next?" DS Parker prompted.

"Neighbour, Mrs Simons, identifies Mrs Kelly Russell outside the house at approx. 1930 hours. Mrs Russell is confirmed as being at The Crown pub immediately before this from 1730 hours. She then meets with Mr Darren Rees at approx. 1945 hours. He confirms that they talk in her car outside the pub until approx. 2015. Mrs Russell calls her own husband and he meets her at the pub and drives her home."

"Do we have that confirmed?" DS Parker frowned, contemplating the connection between Darren Rees and Kelly Russell in a fresh light.

"No," DC Rhodes admitted. "We only have Mr Rees' testimony that they were together from 1945- 2015. We can get the CCTV from the pub if necessary."

"Ok," DS Parker nodded. "Hold that thought. Anyone else?"

"Mrs Simons identified an unknown woman outside the victim's home at 2045," DC Elliott chipped in, keen to not give all the limelight to DC Rhodes. "Another neighbour, Mrs Sharon Morgan, identified Mr Rees' car in the street between 2020 and approx. 2035."

"What else do we have?" DS Parker grabbed a pen and made a few notes to herself.

"Victim's daughter left house without phone, and between 2100 and 2200, the boyfriend's mother, Mrs Stephanie Rees, hands phone to Miss Burbridge." DC Rhodes shot a satisfied look at DC Elliott.

"Known disputes with victim?" DS Parker went back to her original notes.

"Mrs Laura Burbridge, recently separated. Both suspected each other of an affair, according to daughter. Mrs Burbridge claims both untrue."

"Any chance she could have done it?" DS Parker asked.

"Body temp, amongst other things, puts estimated time of death between 2100 and 2300 hours. Mrs Burbridge has no alibi between 2000 and 2100, so it's possible." DS Parker said when no-one spoke. "She claims to have been at a flat in the Oak Fields estate that she is renting from a friend. We have nothing that ties her to this forensically and no identification at this point. Next dispute?"

"Barry Simons, neighbour." DC Cooper offered. "Public disputes on the social media group over traffic and a review Mr Burbridge left for a local businesswoman."

"Any chance?" DS Parker asked.

"Alibi confirmed until 21.30. Alibi from 21.30 is his wife and step-son." DC Rhodes pulled a face. "Finger prints on bottles similar to murder weapon but confirmed that these belonged to Mr Simons by victim's daughter. A bit circ'."

"Circ'?" DS Parker frowned at the young woman.

"It's short for circumstantial." DC Rhodes confirmed.

"Ok," DS Parker shook her head. "Please don't make up words. There's enough jargon to get through as it is."

DC Cooper smirked at DC Rhodes and, not for the first time, DS Parker wondered why she hadn't gone into primary school teaching instead; similar behaviours to deal with, better hours.

"Other persons of interest?" DS Parker asked.

"Mr and Mrs Rees." DC Rhodes redeemed herself. "New information from the daughter gives them a motive as Mr Burbridge was making threats to report the son for, ummm, underage relations. Both had a window of opportunity and neither have disclosed this when giving testimony about other suspects' whereabouts."

"Good work." DS Parker said approvingly. "The matter of

Mrs Russell slightly complicates this, but we can bring in both Mr and Mrs Rees, and see what comes from this before we bring her back in. We'll be looking to take samples from both to match unidentified evidence from the scene. Absolutely anything else before we prepare to bring them in?"

"Only the deleted comments thing." DC Cooper shrugged. "Tech are taking forever on this."

"Ok." DS Parker nodded. "I'm just waiting for social services to get back to me, as we're potentially leaving the Rees' children alone if we take both parents in. I'd be hesitant to do so, but I don't feel this can wait. Elliott, you're coming with the DI and I. Cooper and Rhodes, argue amongst yourselves on who's going home tonight and who's staying."

Steph had spent the afternoon pacing the house, anxiously awaiting the sound of the front door. Despite listening intently for the familiar jangle and creak, the sound still startled her, and she dropped the cutlery in her hands onto the kitchen worktop with a clatter.

Kendall, too young to fully comprehend the tension in the house, tutted loudly from her seat at the kitchen table before turning back to continue spooning yoghurt into her mouth, eyes firmly fixed on the YouTube video on her iPad.

Steph rushed into the hallway, leaving the assorted silverware scattered across the counter. Darren was removing his shoes and jacket, and he turned to his wife slowly with a sheepish smile.

"What happened?" She asked. "I've been trying to phone you!"

"Sorry, love," Darren said gruffly, not making eye contact. "How did it go for Ollie?"

"Fine," Steph replied. "Why did they want you? What happened? I've been worried sick."

Darren bit back a sigh of exasperation. "That's a bit dramatic. It was only to give a statement to say I was in the pub and saw Kelly What's-her-name there."

"All day?"

"Well, no," Darren admitted. "But I had to hang around for ages, because they had loads of people they needed to see."

"You weren't there when we went down." Steph said accusatorily.

"I popped to work on the way back. Had a few things to take care of." Darren brushed past her into the kitchen. "Are we having dinner?"

"Nobody feels like it." Steph replied coolly.

She had been planning on putting something quick on even though neither she nor Ollie were hungry, but Darren's selfishness had flipped a switch in Steph, and she felt her blood start to boil. Her mind had been spinning wildly, unable to switch off, leaving her drained and running on empty. Steph stared at the back of Darren's head as he lumbered around the kitchen, seemingly without a care in the world, and she felt the nervous energy inside her whirling into a tornado of rage. She needed to get out, the still-rational part of her brain told her. She was ready to burst, and she couldn't afford to lose control of herself. Not now.

Steph wanted desperately to jump in her car and drive far away from here and from everything that was going on. She wanted to silence her own thoughts. She needed distance and calm to decide. She just needed everything to stop, her mind screamed at her, and Darren was making it worse.

Steph knew that, as much as she wanted to, she couldn't run now. The love and responsibility for the children had her trapped here, and the reality of this made the four walls of her home feel heavy and oppressive. The panic started to take over and, more fearful of losing it in front of the children, Steph stumbled blindly to the back door, seeking the cold March air on her skin and in her lungs.

She pulled the door closed gently behind her and leant against the doorframe, taking in mouthfuls of the crisp, fresh air, willing her body to not betray her. Everything inside her screamed that she needed to confess, but she couldn't bring herself to. Not for herself. She would be happy to accept any punishment in exchange for the release of the guilt that was slowly pushing her to the brink of madness. But she couldn't do that. Not when Ollie and Kendall needed her. She had pulled herself back from the depths of her own despair on more than one occasion because, while her children were reliant on her, failure was not an option. The thought of being away from them, of not being there to carry out the thankless, mundane tasks that shaped them and supported them, of missing picking up on cues and clues of when they needed her love the most, made Steph's heart hurt with an agony that was harder to bear than the torment of her guilty conscience.

This would be the penance, she told herself. She felt like she would never feel peace while she was carrying this secret. She wanted to grab Darren by the shoulders and scream her truth at him. She wanted him to recognise that he had failed her children and that it was because of his selfish ways that she would hand their lives over to him over her dead body. She wouldn't be carrying this hideous, awful shame if she thought for a minute she could trust him to give them even half the love and attention that she gave them. Being their mother felt like Steph's life purpose. His selfish, moody ways had drained away at Steph's small reserves of confidence over the years, but she acted as a barrier, shielding the children from his negatives. They only got to see the flashes of fun, loud Dad, and Steph would rather live forever with her burden, than leave them vulnerable to the emotional abuse she had suffered.

Steph had never put a name on the toxic impact of living with a thoughtless, temperamental partner, that lived self-centredly in his own world where any attempts to coerce him into compromising could lead to weeks of sulking, resulting in Steph tiptoeing on eggshells and resigning herself to keeping her mouth shut, sinking deeper into her own misery.

She blamed herself for letting it happen. She should have left him years ago while she was still reasonably young enough and energetic enough to carve out a life for herself. Instead she had stayed, feeling the weight of the little criticisms and manipulations slowly tilt the balance of power until she felt financially and emotionally caged in her marriage.

It was horrible irony that she had just began to fight against the status quo. She had taken the first shaky steps in rebuilding her shattered confidence, starting small with physical changes; her hair, her make-up, the nourishment she gave to her weary body. These small changes had started to snowball, and she had found confidence to stand up for herself in little ways, like insisting on spending time with her family for the first time in years. The most exciting development had been, for Steph, the decision to go back to work, and even more exhilarating had been the plans to own her own business. She had felt truly alive for the first time in years and, in her heart, she knew part of the excitement was the realisation that this path would eventually carry her away from the prison of her marriage.

She had an opportunity to change her life, to escape the worthless feeling and build something for her children and for herself, and all because of a horrible twist of fate, she could feel it slipping away. She could live with settling for a miserable existence, hoping that when her children grew up that maybe their own accomplishments and happiness would give her enough satisfaction to see out the rest of her days. She couldn't bear the thought of their formative teenage years being darkened by Darren's oppressive nature. The crushing helplessness was torture.

When Darren had been called in for questioning, Steph's first reaction had been fear. They knew it was her, and they were grilling Darren about her whereabouts. She had felt sick walking into the station, sitting outside the room where they questioned Ollie. She had felt a nauseous sense of acceptance when an officer had asked her to confirm some information. Her mind had screamed 'This is it!' but she had simply been questioned on Ollie and Keeley's whereabouts, and had answered their questions before being dismissed to take Ollie home. She came home, feeling even worse. She had been given her opportunity to tell them everything that had happened. She was ashamed that she couldn't do it, but her instincts had been to protect her children. The thought of Ollie sat alone in the corridor, not understanding why his mother didn't come back, was too painful. Darren would have turned up eventually to collect him, but there would be nobody to support the children to come to terms with the emotional blow of what their mother had done. Ollie would be ostracised from his friends. Kendall and Ollie would go through their life, with not only the stigma of their mother's crime, but without the unconditional love and support that all children needed to grow.

Steph steadied herself, with one hand on the back door and one against the garden fence. She had made her decision when she had walked away without confessing her involvement. There nothing more she could do except wait. It felt like it was in the hands of the universe now.

She chided herself for wasting what could be the last of her freedom on her obsessive worries. She could be doing something constructive so that, if the worst happened, she had some kind of support in place for the kids.

"Think, think, think." She told herself, and the desire to act suddenly felt urgent.

It would have to be Dana. Steph cursed herself for backing out of speaking to her when she had the opportunity. Dana was her best friend; the kindest, nicest person Steph knew. Steph didn't want to burden her, but she was the only one she could trust. The children's wellbeing was more important than Steph's own conditioned desire to keep her troubles to herself. Steph knew she couldn't ask Dana to have the children, if the worst happened. Darren would never allow it for one, but both Barry and Dana had an air of natural authority about them. If Steph could just explain to Dana the full extent of her concerns, Dana and Barry would be sure to keep an eye on the children's wellbeing, no matter how disgusted they might be in Steph's own admission.

Steph felt her confidence waver at the thought of having to relive the events out loud. It would put Dana in a horrible position, but Steph had an overwhelming desire to act now to secure some kind of guidance for her children if the worst happened. She forced herself to concentrate on taking one step at a time; go into the house, put your shoes on, drive to Dana's. The smallness of her thoughts seemed to calm her pounding heart. She could do those things.

She walked into the house and wordlessly slipped her feet into her boots.

"Where are you going?" Darren asked.

"Dana's." Steph stared straight ahead, willing herself to keep moving before she lost her resolve.

Just one foot in front of the other. She reached out, curling her fingers around the handle of the door. She yanked it down and pulled her arm backwards, ready to take the next step across her threshold. A shadow fell across her and she blinked, unsure of what she was seeing, so involved in the execution of her plan.

"Mrs Rees." The blonde female detective was stood on her porch. A cluster of officers, plain-clothed but their authority discernible, waited several steps back and it took a moment for Steph to process their presence.

The officer started to speak, but Steph could only hear the rushing of her own blood in her ears and feel the horrified acceptance that she was too late. They were here. It was over.

Chapter 26

Evan sat in the traffic lights, watching them turn from red to green again, and inched forward a couple of car lengths before he braked to wait the next turn. He usually missed the rush hour 4-6pm traffic but, after the events of this weekend, he was making a concerted effort to be home at a normal time.

It had taken all his resolve to peel himself away from his desk at 4.30pm and fight the ingrained habit of being the first in, last out, but suddenly his career dreams seemed unimportant compared to his home life. It was bitterly ironic that he had poured all his efforts into his career to build a life for Kelly and the kids, yet it was these late nights that had created the gulf between him and Kelly to the point where they'd stopped communicating.

He had, foolishly, agreed to keeping Tina's confidence and Kelly was so used to leading a separate life that she hadn't even confided in him that she had visited Jim Burbridge's home on the night of his death. That had been the real moment of truth for Evan. He could understand that she'd been distracted Saturday night when they argued over Evan's text to Laura and then, Evan's admittance of the time he spent with Tina, but for Kelly to not mention the coincidence of having visited the Burbridge's home on the night of Jim's death. Evan couldn't believe that things had got that bad between them.

Evan had known that he couldn't justify "hope I didn't freak you out" without explaining how he stayed on late at the office to tutor a student. He had thought that telling Kelly it was Tina would alleviate any concerns that she had over him having an affair, but he could see, in hindsight, how that had made it worse. Part of him had wanted to throw a few accusations at Kelly in retaliation, but he had held back, mostly out of fear that once they were out in the open, there was no going back.

Kelly had refused his help at the police station, claiming she didn't need a solicitor and she didn't want him looking over her statement. She had insisted there was nothing to worry about, but had told him, a little sheepishly, about her visit to Laura, which had filled Evan with guilt and horror that his actions had resulted in his wife being placed at a crime scene. As soon as they were back at the house, the tears she had been in all day disappeared and she was back to her usual snarky, upbeat self, offering to drive Pam home and heading straight to bed to ignore him.

Evan was at a loss on what to do. The whole incident had highlighted that what he'd thought to be just a few cracks between them was, in fact, much deeper than that; a scuffed, worn surface hiding a hollowness beneath, as if their familiarity and friendship had eroded away from the foundations up and he had been walking around on the precarious exterior, ignorant to the nothing beneath.

Kelly had withdrawn from him and he was desperate to try to fix it, if it wasn't too late. The traffic lights changed again, and he crept forward, almost making it to the turning before the lights flicked through their sequence, and he sat, frustrated, at the red light, just minutes from home.

He finally crossed the junction, his mind preoccupied on where to start in the battle to fix his marriage, when he noticed a familiar figure alight from the bus in front of him, stepping into the road and pausing waiting for an opportunity to safely cross.

Without thinking, he pulled his car to the side of the road and opened his window.

"Tina!" He called.

Her head turned in his direction, and Evan could see a flicker of indecision cross her face before she stepped back onto the pavement and walked the short distance to him, with an air of resignation.

"Alright." She greeted him cautiously.

He knew immediately that she knew Kelly knew, and he felt his heart sink. He hadn't wanted to betray her confidence, but Kelly was his wife. He hadn't had a choice. He opened his mouth and said as much.

Tina waved a hand dismissively. "It doesn't matter. I shouldn't have asked you. It was wrong of me."

They fell into an uncomfortable silence; Tina stood awkwardly on the pavement and Evan twisted to look up at her from his seated position in the car. Evan felt a pang of guilt at the dejected slump in her usually-dignified stature. He couldn't help but feel fond of Tina. Her optimism and ambition, in the face of the rough start she'd had, reminded him of his own younger self.

Like Tina, he'd grown up with an absent father and a mother that had struggled to pay the bills and keep food on the table. She had defied the odds to improve her lot, and she'd done it through tougher circumstances than Evan had ever faced. As much as his loyalty lay with Kelly, he couldn't walk away from Tina when she seemed so down.

"Can we talk?" Evan asked tentatively, indicating that she could get in the car.

She paused for a second, before glancing around nervously, and sliding into the vehicle. Evan pulled out and drove in the direction of their street.

"Where've you been?" He asked, buying time as his mind searched for the right words to say to her.

"The police station." Tina said.

Evan turned his head sharply to look at her. "The police station?"

Tina nodded, and Evan realised that being stuck in a game of piggy-in-the-middle between him and his wife was the least of her concerns.

"What happened?" He asked. "Was it about the review?"

Evan had seen Tina and Barry tag-team Jim on the online Oak Village group on social media. The whole village had seen it. He felt a rush of sympathy for her. No doubt she felt awful, now that the man was dead.

"Yes," She said simply, before turning to look at Evan earnestly. "I honestly felt so guilty about what I said. I thought I'd be one of the first the police would want to speak to."

"You were far from the only person who publicly criticised Jim Burbridge," Evan said. "I don't think there's a person in the village he hadn't annoyed with that group. Even the miserable whingers had criticised him over the way he didn't block other residents who were rude to them on their incessant online rants. I'm surprised the police have even had time to come knocking for you."

"They didn't," Tina admitted. "I saw Laura. I had to apologise for what I'd said. Even if he hadn't died, it was still out-of-order. She didn't know what I was talking about. I went back to check, and nearly all my comments had been removed. It's probably Jim who did it, but then I thought, why wouldn't he remove the whole thing? Anyway, it didn't feel right so I went down the station."

"What did they say?" Evan asked.

"The police?" Tina shrugged. "Nothing much. I just told them what the comments said and had to give my own whereabouts."

"Your own whereabouts?" Evan knew that it was most likely just for procedure, but he wanted to convey his support for Tina. "I hope you feel better for going. It was brave of you."

Tina looked uncomfortable. "It wasn't something I particularly wanted to speak about, but it's done now."

Evan was aware that Tina's mother had died in unexpected circumstances, and although she'd never spoken openly about it to him, Evan had googled it out of curiosity. There was very little in any news archives, but Evan knew there had been some police involvement. He imagined that any police interview would bring back memories of her own mother's death. It must have been traumatic for her.

"I'm sorry you had to go through that," Evan said. "You did the right thing."

Tina looked surprised at Evan's comments, as if she hadn't expected him to understand the depth of her turmoil. "Thanks."

Evan sensed that she was on the brink of saying more on the subject, and he looked at her expectantly, curious to know what she had been through, but she turned away, gazing out of the window.

"Is Kelly ok with you?" She asked finally.

Evan shrugged, disappointed that she had changed the subject. "Not really."

"I'm really sorry." She said again. "I'm sure it'll be fine."

"I'm not sure," Evan admitted. "I didn't realise how bad things had got."

"No?" Tina made a face of polite interest, but she didn't look surprised.

"You've probably spent more time with her over the last year than me," Evan said. Tina could see the questioning look in his eyes and she prayed he wasn't about to ask her what she thought he might. "Has she, has she met someone else?"

Tina struggled to keep her face neutral, but Evan could see the shadow of doubt cross her face.

"We're not that close," Tina said objectively. "I think this is a conversation you need to have with Kelly."

Evan felt his heart sink, as if her refusal to deny his claim confirmed what he had suspected. She was hiding something. Tina saw the hurt on Evan's face, and she felt a surge of pity for the man. He had been good to her. She seriously doubted whether she'd have made it through the course so far without his help. Tina reached for his hand and squeezed it, reassuringly.

"Go home, Evan." She told him. "You can fix this. She loves you."

Evan was horrified to feel tears fill his eyes at the genuine concern in her voice. He blinked them away and gave her hand a squeeze in return.

"You're very wise," He smiled. "For a youngster."

Tina laughed, relieved that he had broken the tension with a joke, and the hearty sound lifted Evan's own bleak mood.

"I've had to be." She smiled, and without warning, she kissed him chastely on the cheek and slid out of the car. "I'll see you."

Evan nodded, watching her walk away, without a backward glance; her dark ponytail bouncing with every step. Her familiar dignified posture had replaced the slumped shoulders of less than twenty minutes ago, and he marvelled at her ability to bounce back.

It filled his heart with hope. If a twenty-four-year-old could find it in her to fight her way up through the disadvantages and tragedy of her life, and not only build something admirable for herself and her brother, but do it all with genuine compassion and grace, he could fix his own relationship.

Evan watched Tina disappear from sight, and he gunned his engine. He had a marriage to save.

DS Parker stretched her back and rolled her shoulders. Spending the best part of the past 36 hours hunched over evidence had taken its toll on her aching muscles.

DI Jones had commenced his interview and DS Parker had felt a stab of disappointment when he had apologetically told her that he would be interviewing Mr Rees, and she could deal with Mrs Rees. She had hoped that she would be the one to coax the confession from the suspect, but she understood that, as the most senior, it made sense for DI Jones to take the lead. The wife may still have crucial information that would be vital to a conviction if Mr Rees refused to confess. Heartened by this, DS Parker made her way into the interview room.

DC Cooper was sat with Mrs Rees. They were awaiting legal representation, hence the delay. DS Parker was amazed that Mr Rees had proceeded happily, declining legal representation as if he had nothing to fear, and she'd marvelled at the lack of inhibitions of a man that acted without thought. As she waited for Mrs Rees' solicitor to arrive, she kept one eye on the door to DI Jones' interview room, expecting the man to suspend the interview and demand to exercise his right the moment he realised how deeply embroiled he was.

Steph Rees' demeanour was enough for DS Parker to see that the woman was burdened by knowledge of what had actually happened that night. DS Parker felt a sliver of sympathy for the woman's predicament, the choice behind withholding evidence or sacrificing your husband and the father of your children must be torturous.

Rebecca Kinsey, the representative Steph had called, finally arrived. She was a tiny slip of a woman, spectacled and blonde, and Parker and Cooper retreated to give them privacy. DS Parker could see that DI Jones was still engaged in interview with Mr Rees, and she wondered how much longer it would be before the truth was revealed.

As they waited to start the interview, DS Parker mentally calculated how long it would be before they would finish interviewing, processing and tying up any loose ends and she could be home in bed. She was grimacing at the prospect of the next day's early start on minimum sleep when DC Rhodes interrupted her thoughts.

"Still waiting to go in?" She asked.

DC Cooper nodded, glancing at the clock. "Shouldn't be too long."

"Are you finished yet?" DS Parker asked. DC Cooper had offered to assist with the interviews so that Rhodes could get home at a reasonable hour.

"Not quite," She told her. "A lady came in with some information. It might be of interest to you."

"Who was it?" DS Parker asked, distracted as the door to the interview room finally opened and Ms Kinsey stepped out.

"Tina Cleary." DC Rhodes said. "She-"

"Tell me after," DS Parker got to her feet hurriedly, gesturing for DC Cooper to follow her. "We'll work all that through first thing."

DS Parker briskly walked over to the room, and Ms Kinsey

indicated that they were ready to start the interview. DS Parker ran through the formalities and, once completed, turned to Steph Rees with her first question poised on her lips.

"It was my fault!" The red-haired woman exclaimed, not giving DS Parker a chance to ask her question. "I didn't mean to, but he was shouting, and I was so angry and scared."

DS Parker felt her heart sink. She wanted to let the woman finish, praying that this was a horrible, misguided attempt to protect her husband, but her hands were tied by the rules and she was duty-bound to arrest the woman and terminate the interview.

"Mrs Rees," She spoke clearly and deliberately. "I need to-"

The woman spoke again, rushing to get the words from her before DS Parker could finish.

"He had chest pains!" Her voice came out as a strangled cry. "We argued, and he was clutching his chest. I should have called for help, but I snatched Keeley's phone from him and stormed off. I left him to die."

DS Parker saw her confused expression mirrored on DC Cooper's face and struggled to regain her composure.

"Mrs Rees," DS Parker said. Her voice was calm, but her mind was furiously processing what the woman was saying and calculating how much of a risk to the case she was taking by letting the woman speak. "I know this is difficult, but what you are saying is very serious. I need you to tell me, from the beginning, what happened."

Ms Kinsey opened her mouth in protest. "Mrs Rees, we need to terminate this interview."

"No." Steph Rees seemed to visibly relax, as if the weight of her burden was floating away with her words. "I need to tell you what happened."

DS Parker could see the solicitor and DC Cooper's growing discomfort, but DS Parker wasn't worried any more. She knew, instinctively, that Steph Rees wasn't lying to cover up for her husband, but she was equally confident that the woman hadn't taken a glass bottle to the man's head. She needed to let her finish. This was a vital piece of the puzzle in working out who had killed Jim Burbridge.

Hours passed before the detectives were finally assembled together, and DI Jones' face was a picture of frustration. This was the third avenue that had come to no fruition, and they were no closer to solving the case.

DS Parker had felt sick with nerves briefing her superior on Steph Rees' false confession. Fortunately, he agreed that the woman was genuine in her belief and jumping to arrest her would have slowed down the process and sent them potentially miles away from uncovering the truth. DS Parker was shocked that the woman's husband was seemingly innocent. Steph was adamant that, on hearing Jim Burbridge's threats to her son, she had jumped in the nearest car, which was coincidentally her husband's personalised-registration-clad 4-wheel-drive and driven to Sycamore Street at approximately 8.20pm on Saturday 4th March. The man had answered the door to her, but his phone had been firmly wedged between his shoulder and his ear, and he had signalled for her patience while he finished his phone call. This rude gesture had further invoked Steph's anger and, by the time he hung up, she was spitting with rage. Steph had attempted to reason with the man, denying that the teenagers had the relationship that he was claiming they had, but the conversation had quickly soured, with both of them raising their voices. He had clutched his chest in a manner that Steph had panickily described as "as if he were having a heart attack" and she had snatched the pink-cased phone from him, claiming that he had set his own phone down and picked up what was clearly his daughter's during their argument. Steph had stepped over his threshold, at the beginning of the conversation, and she had glanced over her shoulder as she left. She claimed that his face had been an ashy-grey and he had been doubled over, clutching at his chest. Steph confessed to the deep regret and shame she had felt at walking away, knowing that she should have intervened.

DS Parker had wanted to comfort the woman and tell her that that wasn't possible. Laura Burbridge had told the police that her husband had been suffering from chest pains, and despite the glaringly obvious head injury, they had instructed that the autopsy to consider this. From the thorough results, it was hypothesised that Jim had been suffering with anxiety and panic attacks, as his heart was as healthy as a man ten-years younger. She wasn't able to comfort her with any specific details but had assured Mrs Rees that there was further evidence that discounted Mrs Rees' belief that she was guilty of, if not causing, contributing to his death. She had been confused, but as the realisation had begun to sink in, DS Parker had seen the astounded relief on the woman's face. She had finally gone home, but DS Parker's working day was far from over.

"The phone call." She said urgently to her team. "His handset showed no sign of any incoming calls after 10am.

Missing phone records, missing social media comments. His wife claims there was no mistress, but, in the absence of another suspect, I think we've got no choice but to assume the wife did it. She's got a window of opportunity, no alibi between 8 and 9pm plus she would be likely to know his passwords to delete the comments and the phone records."

"I can't drag her in on circumstantial evidence at this time of night." DI Jones shook his head. "Call it a night and we'll call her in in the morning. I'll put an urgent request on that data. If he was on the phone to the wife, we'll have enough to bring her in."

The rest of the team nodded and started to disperse. DS Parker stayed for a little while, head in hands, feeling exhausted and deflated. She had really believed that Darren Rees had killed Jim in a momentarily loss of temper and both his wife and his girlfriend had been protecting him. DS Parker didn't know whether her usual impeccable instinct was failing her, or whether she'd just been temporarily blind-sided because she had felt a genuine empathy for Laura and her daughter. She wearily rose to her feet and made her way home.

Chapter 27

Kelly woke up uncharacteristically earlier than her alarm. She hadn't slept well at all since the revelations of the weekend and, annoyed at her body, she slipped out of bed, noting that Evan had already left for work.

He had wanted to talk about everything that had happened, and he had surprised her when he had been back at the house by 5pm for the first time in years. Kelly was glad of the distraction of the children. Sophie had been delighted that her beloved father was home and had insisted that he take her to her karate lesson, buying Kelly a reprieve from his ambush. She had managed to avoid his desperate need for a heart-to-heart, thanks to Sophie shadowing him until her own bedtime, and then Kelly had played her only card, feigning a migraine and retiring to bed.

She reluctantly admitted to herself that she couldn't keep avoiding him forever, but she had nothing to say to him. He had lied to her and made her look and feel a fool. She may not have been an angel, but she hadn't cheated, discounting the few drunken kisses. Her mind flicked back to the few times that she had almost succumbed, and she felt a flush of shame at how close she'd come, but technically she hadn't, and that was what counted. She was adamant. Her mind was made up. She was terrified of living without him, supporting the kids and giving up her lifestyle, but pride was all she had. Kelly wasn't prepared to lose that for two holidays a year, a flash BMW and a wardrobe full of expensive clothes. She was going to put all the wheels in motion, starting with biting the bullet and getting herself a regular person's 9-to-5, even though it pained her to be dull and boring like the rest of the world. Once that was sorted, Kelly promised herself she'd face up to having the dreaded conversation with Evan.

She knew that she was putting it off, but she had too much on her plate and she couldn't afford to show any weakness. Just the thought of leaving Evan made her heart feel like it was breaking. Kelly took a deep breath and pushed that crucial part of her to-do list to the back of her mind.

'Do the little things first,' She urged herself. 'You're stronger than this.'

Kelly stopped at the bottom of the stairs; the smell of bacon puncturing her thoughts.

"What are you doing home?" She asked, surprised to see Evan looking flustered, juggling a spatula and a wooden spoon.

"I'm taking the day off." He said, frowning over his multitasking. "I thought I'd make my beautiful family a cooked breakfast."

As he said it, he moved a pan too quickly and fat dropped onto the gas hob, sending a flame shooting up. Kelly leapt forward, instinctively, pulling him away from the naked flame and turning off the burner. She took the frying pan from his hand, simultaneously flipping the bacon in the other pan and giving the beans a stir.

"Careful." She said. "You've got too many things on the go."

"Thanks." He said. "Are you doing much today?"

Kelly opened the fridge door, purposely blocking him from view.

"Mmmm," She replied noncommittally. "Few things to do."

She wanted to walk out of the kitchen, but he looked endearingly sweet struggling to cook a simple breakfast and Kelly couldn't help but feel a gentle tug on her heartstrings at the sight of him. She told herself that she was staying out of maturity, and she settled onto a stool, watching him from a distance.

"Go back to bed if you want," Evan offered. "I'll sort the kids out."

"I'm not tired." She replied and stayed seated.

He insisted on taking Sophie to school and, while he was gone, Kelly debated throwing on her clothes and ducking out to the gym, knowing that he had every intention of having the conversation she'd been avoiding. A little voice inside screamed at her to stay put, to hear him out and she slammed plates into the dishwasher in a desperate attempt to drown it out.

Kelly plunged a frying pan into a sink full of scolding hot water and was aggressively scouring at the fried-on residue when she heard a little tap at the back door. Her head jerked up and she immediately recognised the hulking shape. She rushed to the door and pushed her way outside, forcing Darren Rees to step backwards.

"What are you doing here?" She hissed frantically, terrified that Evan would be back at any moment.

"I wanted to tell you," Darren said. "It's over between Steph and me. I want to be with you, Kel."

"What the hell, Darren?" Kelly couldn't believe the bad

timing. "I don't want you to do that!"

"What about everything you said Saturday night?" He frowned, looking confused.

"I was drunk!" Kelly responded sharply. She didn't add that she'd been feeling hurt and rejected, and she'd only reached out to him to soothe her crushed ego. She could recall that she'd become tearful, telling him how much he had hurt her New Year. He'd spent the best part of a year flirting and flattering her, and she'd been feeling stressed and low over Christmas. He'd sweet-talked her into agreeing to spend New Year out-of-town at a friend's party, and when she had finally relented, he'd cancelled their plans at the last minute. She could clearly see now that Darren was a waste of space. She couldn't believe how naïve she'd been, falling for his lines and his lies. She knew that she was just as guilty of using Darren's attention as a distraction from worrying about Evan's growing distance, but she couldn't see it at the time. It was only now, facing the reality of her and Evan's inevitable break-up, that Kelly realised how foolish she'd been.

"Can I come in?" Darren tried again, reaching out and snaking an arm around Kelly's waist.

She pushed his arm away in disgust. "No! You've got a wife and kids. Just go home, Darren!"

"I don't understand why you're being like this." He stepped back and regarded her with clear irritation. "I know you didn't want to go too far while I was still married, but it's over now. Just let me in, Kelly, we can talk."

Kelly stared at him. She'd heard him the first time, but it was only now sinking in that he had broken up with his wife.

Oh, God, this was a mess.

"Why did you do that?" Kelly asked. "We were just having a flirt and it went too far."

"I told you," Darren said. "We were only together for the kids."

"I'm married." Kelly said firmly. "You need to go."

Darren felt his annoyance boil over into anger at her haughty attitude. After a nightmare mix up at the police station, Steph had tipped him over the edge when they had arrived home at midnight and she'd sat him down, with a strength he had never seen in her, and told him that their marriage was over. He'd been too gobsmacked to argue. There was something about her tone which told him she meant it and would not be backing down. His knee-jerk reaction had been to find the nearest, available female to take Steph's place. Kelly was keen and attractive. He had assumed she'd be over-the-moon at his offer, but her visible horror was infuriating. His ego was already bruised and tender, and he lashed out with typical hot-headedness.

"We'll see how long you're married when your husband finds out!" He spat at her, turning and storming back to his car.

Kelly watched him leave, with the horrible understanding that this was her karma. Exhausted, she turned back into the house and her stomach flipped when she saw Evan stood, frozen, in the kitchen doorway, his face drained of its colour.

"How long have you been there?" She asked quietly.

Evan stepped forward and Kelly had to look away from the pain etched across his face.

"A few minutes." He replied.

There was no anger, just acceptance, and Kelly knew she had to do the right thing.

"Sit down," She pulled out a kitchen stool. "We need to talk."

DS Parker's day had got off to a bad start. She had slept through her alarm and was already running late when she jumped into her car, noting with dismay that she'd left the interior light on all night. She turned the key in the ignition and the engine chugged pathetically before giving up on her. She had no idea where the jump leads were, and she frantically dialled DC Rhodes' number.

"Are you in work yet?" She asked. "Can you pick me up?"

She walked down to the main road, using the time to plan her strategy for the day. It was likely that they would have the phone records back by this morning. If they couldn't find anything to indicate that Laura Burbridge was lying, then she didn't know what the next move would be.

DC Rhodes swerved onto the curb and DS Parker gratefully jumped into the car.

"How did it go with the Reeses?" DC Rhodes asked as they neared the station.

DS Parker filled her in on the surprising turn of events.

"Oh!" Rhodes gasped. "That's crazy about his call list being wiped, because listen to this!"

DC Rhodes explained how the local woman, who had publicly argued with the victim, had come into the station volunteering information.

"She noticed her comments had been deleted," DC Rhodes explained. "She lives in the same block that Laura and the kid have moved to, and she felt awful, given the circumstances, about the wife seeing this crap she'd written."

"What did they say?" DS Parker asked, sitting up interested.

"Basically," DC Rhodes wriggled in her seat, as if physically preparing herself for the story she was getting ready to spin. "Jim said something about how he had had to cancel their services after hearing that a good friend had noticed missing possessions, or something along those lines. He basically said he'd tried to discuss his concerns civilly with the business owner and he'd never been spoken to so rudely in his whole life."

"I know this," DS Parker started to tune out. "He wrote it as a review on Sparkles' social media page and he took a what's-it-called and posted it on his Oak Village group."

"A screen shot." DC Rhodes confirmed. "Right, anyway, Barry-the-neighbour called him out saying that he had only ever heard positive things about Sparkles and made a dig, something about how Oak Village had seen Jim be publicly wrong before."

"So what bits were deleted?" DS Parker asked.

"It's all in her statement," DC Rhodes told her. "In short, Tina had said something like 'Your girlfriend is a liar. We cancelled her contract for personal reasons. Tell Kate to get in touch if she'd like to discuss this further but keep your slanderous lies to yourself.'.

"Oh wow." DS Parker was suddenly all ears again. "Who is Kate? And why did she think she was Jim's girlfriend?"

"Apparently, they've been seen around," DC Rhodes shrugged, glossing over this as according to Tina it was old village gossip. "She's a local community councillor that he's friendly with."

"Why hasn't anyone mentioned this?" DS Parker asked exasperated.

"Hang on," DC Rhodes flapped her hand at her, indicating she hadn't finished. "That's not all. It's not in the statement, but as she left, Tina turned to me and said, "I had to come in and say something. I mean, it could be nothing but that's not the first man in her life who's suddenly died." I asked her what she meant, but she looked embarrassed and told me she didn't have a great opinion of the woman and it was probably better if we just stuck to the facts."

"What's her surname?" DS Parker asked.

"I don't remember," DC Rhodes said apologetically. "We're almost at work. Let's get this case nailed, boss!"

DS Parker flew into the briefing room. Suddenly, everything felt like it was falling into place. DS Parker barked out orders. She wanted Laura Burbridge and Tina Cleary in to confirm Kate Evett's connection to Jim. The phone records showed that he had called and messaged the same number regularly over the past six months, including at 8.15pm on the day of the murder, but it was a pay-as-you-go SIM and there was no registered keeper. DC Cooper tried the line, and there was neither an answer nor a personalised voicemail.

She typed Kate Evett's details into the database. She had a clean record, which was expected for a lecturer and a community councillor. The only statement they had ever taken from her was when she had discovered her husband's dead body after she'd returned from work late one evening. It had been classed as 'unexplained' not 'suspicious'. The autopsy had confirmed he'd died of a heart attack, as suspected. There was no police involvement after the initial call and the autopsy, but DS Parker stared at the details on the screen, wondering at the coincidence.

Chapter 28

Laura felt like she had watched every hour on the clock through the night and, fed up of battling her own mind to rest, she finally rose from her bed. She padded into the open-plan kitchen-lounge and looked around, still uncomfortable with the strangeness of her surroundings.

Everything felt surreal, like she was living in a dream. Only five days ago, she had handed over the deposit for a six-month-lease on the flat, optimistically viewing the little home as cosy. For months, maybe even years if she were honest, she had felt like her whole life was an anti-climax. She had tried to ignore the growing voices in her head, screaming that there must be more to life than this. Laura had tried to silence the yearning for something more, the constant itchy-feet, through throwing herself into any distraction; work, running, the gym. She had wondered, on more than one occasion, if she was having a mid-life crisis. It just felt so out of character; once upon a time dependability had been her middle name. She felt ungrateful and guilty for the persistent thoughts. She had a good job, a faithful husband, a beautiful daughter and a lovely home. Laura had tried to block out the overwhelming sense that something was missing. She had been truly, deeply saddened when the realisation hit her that her marriage to Jim was dead, but, with the mourning of almost twenty-five years together, came a little buzz of excitement. This was the start of the rest of her life. She no longer had to sacrifice, burying some of her hopes and dreams over the years to compromise and live a harmonious, dull life as Mr and Mrs Burbridge. Laura had felt a spark ignite within her, and then just as quickly it was extinguished. Sadness and guilt were the only things Laura felt when she looked around the apartment. She had wanted a life without Jim, but not like this.

Laura sat alone in the sparsely-furnished room, staring out of the window, not noticing as the sky changed from inky-black to the dull grey of a cloudy spring morning. Overriding her own emotions was the frantic concern for her daughter. Laura may have lost a husband twice in the space of less than a week, but Keeley had lost her father in the most horrible way.

After coming home from the police station, Keeley had finally broken down and unleashed the torrent of heartbroken tears until she had fallen asleep as if the power of her grief had sapped her of every ounce of her strength. She had finally surfaced, looking deathly pale and fragile, in the early evening. Laura attempted to open up a conversation and then, when that failed, to coerce her into eating. Keeley had stared vacantly into the distance, pushed the thick soup around the bowl without even a drop passing her lips before she'd muttered how tired she was and had retreated to her bedroom.

The rational part of Laura knew that this was probably to be expected, the first part in a long and painful process of mourning. The scared and shaken fragment of Laura's mind, however, was terrified that part of her beautiful, spirited daughter would be lost forever; the tragedy stealing the childlike zest for life years before Keeley should have shouldered the harsh reality of losing a loved one. Laura felt doubly-grieved. She had lost her husband and she was terrified that part of Keeley would be lost forever.

She sat gazing, but not seeing, for maybe hours before she

realised her body was aching from her tense position. She stood up, arching her sore back, and moved over to the window, looking out on the rooftops of the village, wondering whether this little village that she had grown to love as her home would ever feel the same.

Laura had moved here as a happy, young newly-wed. They had thought the little village was just perfect to start a family; close enough to town and the motorway to be convenient, but bordered by nature, the river and the woods. A perfect little place to bring up a family. Everyone knew each other, and the couple who owned the local shop would greet you, asking after your children by name. It had felt idyllic and Laura wondered whether she had been naïve or even smug, thinking that she really did live in the nicest little community. The Oak Village Community group had, if not opened her eyes, certainly shone a light on some of the less admirable qualities of the neighbourhood. Pettiness, bitching, bullying. Laura was aware that people could display these qualities, but she genuinely believed that the majority of people were kind-hearted, and even if they were having an off-day, they would still have more respect than to publicly criticise and belittle their neighbours for all-and-sundry to see. Laura didn't know whether it would be fair to Keeley to stay here. In an age of screen-shots, who knew what could be dredged up in the future. It wasn't so much the online criticism that worried Laura. Jim had given out just as much, if not more, as far as she had seen. Laura hoped that she could help Keeley to erase the last few months of tense arguments and the fateful last fight with her father and encourage her to nurture and cherish the happier times they had had together. The last thing Laura wanted was for someone to pull up a screen-shot some years down the line and point out flaws in Jim's character. That was the problem with the internet, one comment or criticism could be your legacy.

Laura vowed to do all that she could to protect and heal her daughter. As long as she was around to do it, a nagging voice in the back of her mind that she had been suppressing finally cut through all the other thoughts and worries. Laura tried to push it aside. She couldn't worry about this now. The only things she could allow herself to think about were the things she could control, she told herself firmly.

It was a little after 10am when a phone call from the investigators working on the case of Jim's death called Laura asking if she could come in to help with some queries. The officer that Laura spoke with didn't sound any different than usual in her calm, professional tone, but the terrifying doubts came flying back to the front of Laura's mind. She fought to remain in control of her body as panic coursed through her airways, restricting her airflow. Laura had seen enough news and TV shows to know that, in cases like these, it was usually a spurned spouse. She knew that, at some point, the police would, if they hadn't already, suspect her. The thought of being arrested and torn away from her daughter, when Keeley needed her the most, made her blood run cold. Laura tried to remind herself that, if that were the case, the police would turn up at the house and arrest her. Her rational reasoning was no match for the pure terror running through every nerve in her body.

It was times like this that Laura wished that she was from a big, close family. Just knowing that there was a brother or a sister that she could entrust Keeley's care to would be comfort, but there was no-one. Laura's greatest fear, since she had become a mother, had been both her and Jim dying, leaving Keeley with nobody. Laura's parents were both dead, she had no siblings and Jim had just an elderly father and an unmarried brother who both lived hours away and were in no way capable of taking a teenaged girl.

For a fleeting moment, Laura considered taking Keeley and running away. Even as the thought generated, Laura dismissed it instantly, but it stayed there, hovering in the background. She had always wondered what motivated people to take crazy risks but, as the feelings of helplessness and fear spiralled through her, she thought that she could understand.

Laura felt frozen, suspended in uncertainty and bound by her most horrific nightmare being realised. She tried to rationalise, but her panic had taken her past the point of no return. The only thing she could do now was make a plan. Fleeing was out of the question. It would imply guilt, for one, and there were endless outcomes in this scenario, none of them positive. She felt too scared to voice her fear to a close friend, as if saying it would make it come true, but, at the same time, she was terrified that this may be her only time to act. She could almost taste the bitter regret she would feel if she failed Keeley.

The first people that came to mind were Ollie or Ellie's mothers. Laura wondered how she would even begin to frame this to them. What was the etiquette for when you thought you might get wrongly arrested for your husband's death and you're hoping that a friend's parent might promise to look after your grief-stricken, traumatised teenager to stop them having to go into foster care? Laura was very aware that she had no idea of the processes. Would she even be allowed to have a say in where Keeley went? Laura's mind suddenly flew to Tina. She had mentioned having a younger brother at the time of her mother's death. Laura felt sick at the thought of asking her about it, but she needed to hear something positive, how it would get better.

With her heart pounding in her chest, Laura gently woke Keeley. Just the sight of her tousled dark hair and her pale skin against the pillow bought tears rushing to Laura's eyes, but she pulled herself together with a steely determination, telling Keeley she was just popping up to see Tina. Keeley blinked sleepily a few times, and for a moment, she looked the same beautiful, carefree girl she had been before all this happened. Laura watched, feeling uselessly helpless, as a shadow crossed Keeley's eyes and she saw that, in that waking moment, it had all rushed back to her. The pain, beneath her dull dark pupils, was almost tangible.

The agony of not being able to help her child spurred Laura on, and she made her way up the stairs to Tina's flat. She rapped sharply on the door and waited. For a moment, Laura wondered what she would do if Tina wasn't in. She didn't have much time until she was due to go down to the police station and she still needed to arrange for someone to check in on Keeley. From the moment that she had faced up to her darkest fear, it felt like the clock had started ticking and she was running out of time.

Laura was jolted from her thoughts when she heard a rattle and the key turn in the door.

"Oh, hi," Tina's guarded expression melted into a friendly-but-cautious smile. "How are you?"

Laura swallowed nervously. The need to do something, anything, had seemed so forceful and urgent, but now Laura was here, she felt like Tina would think she was acting like she was hysterical or attention-seeking. Even worse, what if Tina thought this was an admission of guilt? Laura wanted to turn on her heels and flee.

Tina, as if sensing Laura's hesitation, pulled the door open wider. "Why don't you come in?"

Laura stepped into the flat and Tina led her through to an identical living space to Laura's. Tina's own home was cosily furnished with soft duck-egg-blue walls, a deep pale sofa covered in a thick throw and inviting rugs that picked up the accents of the décor and subtly served to separate the living area from the kitchen-diner. A large mirror hung from one wall, cleverly reflecting the light, making the room seem more spacious.

"Your home is lovely." Laura said, seeing, even in her turmoil, how a few furnishings could transform a room into a home.

"Thank you." Tina said.

She moved quickly to the kitchen and set the kettle on to boil.

"Tea or coffee?"

Laura stood awkwardly, still at the doorway, and she moved into the room, unsure whether to take a seat.

"Coffee, please." She replied.

Tina gestured towards the sofa. "Sit down. I'll bring it over."

Laura watched Tina move around the kitchen. She had a quiet grace about her and Laura wondered how old she was. She had the young, un-lined face of someone in their twenties, but the way she carried herself suggested she was older. Tina handed Laura the mug and sat down gently opposite her in a wing chair next to the window.

"How are you both?" Tina asked.

"Ok." Laura said, searching for the words she needed to say what she came here to ask. "I wanted to ask you..."

She trailed off and sighed. "I'm sorry. I don't know what I was thinking coming here. I'm all over the place."

Tina smiled reassuringly. "I know that feeling. How is your daughter?"

"Not great," Laura admitted. "She's alternating between sleeping and crying. She hasn't said much."

Tina nodded. "It will get easier."

"Can I ask," Laura said tentatively. "What happened to your mum? How did you and your brother cope?"

Laura felt awful asking, but she was desperate for something to cling to. Tina picked up her mug, wrapping both hands around it for comfort and Laura noticed how young and vulnerable she looked in that gesture, barely older than Keeley.

"We just did," Tina said simply. "We thought that we wouldn't. Every day I felt like I couldn't bear the pain for another day, that it was drowning me. I can remember thinking about all the times that I had been happy, trying to remember that feeling, because I believed, so adamantly, that I would never feel happiness again."

Laura nodded. She knew that feeling. Everything felt grey and miserable. Even the periods of panic that she felt were almost welcome compared to the infinite depth of sadness.

"And your brother?" Laura asked. "It must have been awful. You were both so young."

She wanted to ask what had happened, but that felt intrusive. She couldn't imagine having to tell someone, a stranger, how Jim had died.

"That was the worst part," Tina said. "Feeling his own pain. Feeling helpless that I was meant to protect him, and I couldn't."

Laura felt her heart ache in empathy, understanding Tina's struggle.

"Your dad?" Laura started, but Tina shook her head. Her mouth set in a tight line.

"He was never around," Tina said. "We didn't know where he was. Even if he was alive."

"Oh!" Laura's hand flew to her mouth. "I'm so sorry. I shouldn't have-"

"No." Tina smiled to show Laura she didn't mind. "That's ok. It's a big part of why it was so hard. We hadn't seen him for years, since my brother was a baby. My mum died very suddenly. One moment it was the three of us, the next she was gone."

Tina took a sip of the hot drink in her hands and continued. "She wasn't ill. It was an accident. She was driving back from her job and she was in a head-on collision. She died from her injuries. I had just turned seventeen, Robbie was twelve. It was seven years ago, but I can still remember opening the door to the policeman and just knowing."

Laura felt the rush of tears, and this time she couldn't stem them.

"My mum was still young. She was thirty-five. She hadn't had the easiest life, but she worked so hard to provide for us. She was so much fun, even though she was always exhausted from juggling us kids and her jobs. She was determined that Robbie and I would have an easier life. She wanted us to go to college, have good jobs and our own homes. We were living on the other side of Finchester. We hadn't long moved. She had busted her ass to afford to rent a house in a nicer area. Her biggest fear was that me or Robbie would fall in with the wrong crowd and end up wasting our lives. End up like our father."

"What happened when she died?" Laura pictured a seventeen-year-old Tina and a pre-teen brother trying to get through such an awful tragedy together.

"I was a mess," Tina admitted. "My first reaction was my own sadness, but then they were asking about family and everything. We had nobody. My mum had no living relatives, as far as I was aware. They let us stay with my friend's mum the first few nights. I remember when it dawned on me that this couldn't go on forever and I was so naïve. I genuinely thought they'd let me look after Robbie. I thought there'd be some money."

"Oh, Tina!" Laura felt shaken that Tina had lived her own worst nightmare. "I'm so sorry."

"There wasn't money and they weren't happy for Robbie to live with me on his own," Tina continued. "They tried really hard to find someone where we could live together, but it was hard. I was seventeen. In the end, I told the social worker to just find the best place for him, even if it were without me. It was hard enough to place a twelve-year-old without adding his almost-grown-up sister to the mix. It was only meant to be temporary, because they thought they'd found someone. A woman made enquiries when she heard about my mother's death. She did a swift U-turn when she realised all my mother had left behind was two distraught kids and a bit of debt."

"She wasn't family after all?" Laura asked, trying to imagine the despair Tina must have felt losing her mother at such a crucial stage of her life and then having to suffer being parted from her brother.

"Oh," Tina gave a bitter laugh. "She was family, alright. She was my mum's half-sister. The social worker soon established that my grandmother was dead, and my grandfather was in the early stages of dementia. From what I remember, she was a lot older than my mum and they had different fathers. They were never close, but it was the only living relative we could find. They tried tracing our father and his family, but it was as if they didn't exist. I can hardly remember him ever being in our lives. I couldn't pick him out in a line-up. It's hard to believe, isn't it? You can literally hear a name and find them online within seconds. You don't even have to know their name; a friend's name, where they work, you can track them down. My mum had got rid of everything and they weren't ever married. There were only our birth certificates. I know his name and where he was born. I still look him up sometimes. Robbie went through a period where he really wanted to find him, but we've both agreed, for now, that we're fine as we are."

"That must have been terrible," Laura felt an urge to hug the girl again. "Are you and your brother still close?"

"Very." Tina placed her cup down gently on the floor next to her and her eyes lit up at the mention of her brother. "I worked so hard to make sure I had a place for him to live. It was like an incentive for him to behave in school. He came to live with me after he finished his exams. It was one of the best feelings ever. I supported him through college and he's now in his second year of uni."

"Wow!" Laura blinked away fresh tears at this happy ending. It was just the hope she had wanted, but Keeley didn't have an older sister to protect her or a younger sibling to inspire her to fight against the harsh, unfairness of life. This thought was all it took to tip Laura's emotional exhaustion over and, to her shame, she burst into tears.

Tina rushed over to Laura's side, her face a picture of concern. Laura hadn't wanted to admit her fear to anyone, especially not a stranger but, between racking sobs, she confessed to Tina what she feared the most. For a while, Tina just held Laura in her arms and Laura felt wretched and selfish that she had put this on the poor girl. Laura dabbed at her eyes ineffectively with the tips of her fingers.

"I'm so sorry." Laura apologised, pulling herself together. "I'm just exhausted and not thinking straight. I need to go back to Keeley and I've got an appointment with the detectives..."

"I've got to go in to see the police later too," Tina admitted. "Just a few questions about the Oak Village Community page, but I can go later if you'd like me to stay with Keeley?"

"Do you have a time?" Laura asked.

"They just said to come down about 12," Tina shrugged. "But I can phone them and tell them I'll come later."

"Her boyfriend's mum offered to sit with her if I needed to do anything," Laura said. "I'll call her and see if she can come over, and maybe we could go down together?"

Tina could see that Laura wanted someone to be there, so if anything did happen someone would know to fight for Keeley.

She nodded. "Yes, thank you."

Laura made her way back to her flat and Tina sat, for a while, thinking about what Laura had said. She didn't think she was being dramatic. Laura didn't have a flawless alibi. She would make the obvious suspect. The crime scene was Laura's home so naturally it would be teeming with Laura's DNA. All it would take would be for something or someone to place her at the scene. Tina thought that if it were her, she would be equally terrified.

Tina picked up the empty cups and carried them over to the kitchen. Her phone lay, where she had left it when Laura had knocked the door, and Tina picked it up. With a jolt, a memory flew back to her and she felt her heart skip with hope. Her fingers flew over the keys and she listened, impatiently, to the ringing, praying for the call to be answered.

"Hello?" She was almost breathless with anticipation. "Kelly, I know I'm not your favourite person right now, but there's something I really need you to try to remember."

She crossed her fingers for luck that Kelly had forgiven her enough to hear her out.

Tina exhaled with relief as Kelly started to speak. "Can we talk face-to-face? Half an hour?"

Tina hung up the phone and rushed into her bedroom to finish getting ready. She glanced at the framed photo on her bedside table; her pretty, smiling mother with a toddler Robbie in her arms and an eight-year-old Tina grinning gap-toothed at the camera. Tina offered up a silent prayer that this would work.

Chapter 29

Evan dropped heavily into the seat that Kelly held out for him. He felt like the life had been sucked out of him and he didn't trust his legs to keep working. He lowered his head into his hands, unable to process what he had heard, the snatched words just buzzing around his disorientated brain.

Kelly took a seat opposite him, and he caught a glimpse of her from the corner of his eye. Her face was deathly pale, and her eyes were wide and anxious. Her long, auburn hair was in a ponytail, pulled over one shoulder, and her long fingers twisted the strands repetitively.

"Who was that?" Evan asked, fighting to keep his voice cool and steady.

Kelly pressed her lips together, unsure of how to start.

"He's from the pub," Kelly said. "Darren Rees."

Evan nodded his head. He had thought so.

"How long has it been going on?"

Kelly could hear the hurt underneath Evan's controlled tone and it made her want to burst into tears. "It was just stupid flirting. Nothing has ever happened."

Evan looked at her directly for the first time, and Kelly could see there was hope beneath his steely gaze. "Do you think I'm stupid?"

"No!" Kelly exclaimed. In her passion to make him believe her, she jumped to her feet, sending the stool crashing to the floor. Ignoring it, she went on. "I promise you. It was inappropriate and stupid, and it meant nothing! But, I swear, Evan! I didn't sleep with him."

Evan stared at her, his heart felt like it was breaking but he needed to know the truth.

"But you kissed him?" He said. "And other stuff?"

"No!" Kelly protested again, but then she continued in a small voice. "I did kiss him. I was drunk, and I regretted it. Nothing else though."

"How long has this been going on?" Evan asked coldly.

"There's nothing going on." Kelly insisted.

Suddenly, faced with losing him, Kelly felt like saving her marriage was the most important thing in the world.

"What did he want?" Evan asked.

Kelly looked away uncomfortably. "He's broke up with his wife. He wanted to tell me. I told him to leave me alone."

"He broke up with his wife?" Evan asked incredulously. "He clearly thinks it's pretty serious."

"No!" Kelly shook her head violently. "It's nothing to do with me! I swear to you, it wasn't anything more than flirting and a drunken kiss."

"A drunken kiss?" Evan raised his eyebrow scathingly.

"Ok, more than one." Kelly looked ashamed. "Evan, I don't want to lose you."

The poignant tone in Kelly's voice pierced Evan's heart and

he felt his eyes fill up with unexpected tears. This was all a mess. He had been terrified of losing her due to his own stupidity and had spent the last few days overcome with regret and sadness. And now this.

"Tell me everything." Evan said. "From the beginning."

Kelly felt like she had opened up the floodgates when she started to speak. She withheld nothing; telling Evan how Darren had started flirting with her at the pub, asking her to come to his office to pitch her money-saving deals back around August last year. She admitted that he had initiated conversation through text messages afterwards and she had happily flirted with him keen for a sale but, growing to enjoy the attention. Sometimes they texted regularly and, then, some weeks not at all. Things had never amounted to anything more than texts, except three or four times when they had "bumped" into each other. It had all fizzled out around New Year, but Kelly had phoned him, drunk and low, on Saturday night when she had thought that Evan was cheating on her.

Evan listened to what she was saying, watching her eyes as if looking for clues of any dishonesty. She skirted over the "three or four" meetings and Evan finally spoke.

"You met three or four times?" He asked emotionlessly.

Kelly nodded. Her face serious and still.

"I need to know." Evan pressed her for the details he thought might crush him.

"The time I went to his office," Kelly started nervously. "And then we bumped into him on a night out."

"We?" Evan asked.

"Me and Tina." Kelly gulped, before adding hurriedly. "Tina didn't know anything."

Evan narrowed his eyes thoughtfully. What was surprising him the most was not once had she tried to put any blame on him, like he had thought she would. He had expected her to blame him for any loneliness or lack of attention, or throw his own deceit in his face, and now she was defending Tina, even though this would have been a perfect opportunity to sour Evan's professional relationship with her.

"Go on." He nodded, needing to hear it all.

"I saw him at the pub quite a lot, but we didn't sit together or anything," Kelly said hurriedly. "I saw him out once more on another night out and, like I told you, I talked to him outside the pub on Saturday."

Evan opened his mouth to speak, but Kelly wasn't finished. She delivered the devastating final bombshell, hating herself for having to tell him.

"He came here once," Kelly said quietly. "We just talked in the kitchen."

Evan reeled from the blow. "Did you take him anywhere else?"

Kelly shook her head. "No, I didn't want to."

"But you kissed him here?" Evan asked quietly.

Kelly nodded and looked down at her feet.

Slowly, as if all her adrenaline had been spent, she righted the stool she had sent crashing to the ground but stayed standing next to it. She looked at Evan, her eyes heavy with unshed tears and she waited for him to speak, to shout, to call her names and condemn her for the terrible things she had done.

"I'm going out for a little while." Evan said.

She nodded, understanding that he needed time to process her confession. He turned and left the house without another word. Kelly sat alone in the kitchen, filled with guilt and sadness. She had no choice but to await his decision.

Her phone rang, and she was surprised to see Tina's name flashing up on the screen. She answered hesitantly and listened to Tina's flustered tone. Fearing the worst, that Tina's request to see her had something to do with her disclosure to Evan, Kelly changed quickly and made her way to Tina's. She had realised that she wasn't even mad at Tina any more. Tina hadn't had the easiest life and Kelly respected her need for privacy. It stung a little that she hadn't felt that she could confide in Kelly and it made Kelly question her own character that Tina had turned to sensible, trustworthy Evan rather than her assertive friend.

Kelly was surprised that the tension between them, and Tina's big secret, wasn't the reason Tina had asked to see her so urgently. Kelly waved away Tina's attempt at an apology.

"No, Kelly," Tina insisted. "I was wrong to ask Evan to not mention it. I didn't want anyone to know because I was scared I wouldn't be able to finish it. He only found out by accident when I was looking for work experience. If I was going to tell anyone, it would have been you."

"Really?" Kelly regarded Tina questioningly. "I got the impression that you disapproved of, well, you know."

Tina looked sheepish. "I did a little, but it was just flirting. You didn't do anything."

Kelly sighed loudly, and Tina looked at her sharply.

"Oh, Kelly!" She gasped. "What's happened?"

Kelly filled her in quickly and when she was finished, she sat back in Tina's wing chair.

"I'm so sorry," Tina said genuinely meaning it. She felt that she had been quick to judge Kelly and she had dismissed all the great qualities about her, like her fearless bravery, her honesty and her big heart. "He'll come around."

"I hope so," Kelly smiled sadly. "Anyway, you needed to see me? Everything ok?"

"Not really," Tina said glumly thinking of her poor new neighbour. "But I've got a feeling you might be able to help. You sent me a message, Saturday night. You came to mine, but I was at Robbie's."

Kelly nodded. "Probably for the best, too. It was after Evan had told me about how he'd been helping you and I was furious at you both."

"I'm so sorry," Tina said again. "But you knocked my door? Just before 9?"

Kelly tilted her head inquisitively, aware that Tina was going somewhere with this. "Yes. Probably about ten-to."

"Ok," Tina took a deep breath before leaning forward and

looking at Kelly earnestly. "I need to swear you to secrecy first of all."

Kelly held up her hands in assurance of her confidentiality. "Promise."

"Laura Burbridge and her daughter have moved in downstairs," Tina started nervously. "Laura was here Saturday night between 8 and 9pm before she went back to the friend's house she was staying at."

Kelly frowned, unsure what this had to do with her.

"Obviously you know that her husband was found dead," Tina continued. "They had separated, so she feels even worse, and she's got her daughter, and no other family..."

Tina was too scared to continue any further. If Kelly hadn't seen Laura, then Tina couldn't ask her to lie. She stopped speaking abruptly and looked at Kelly with trepidation.

Kelly looked on at Tina for a few moments as if it was taking a while for what Tina was telling her to sink in, and then a flash of recognition lit up Kelly's face.

"Oh!" She said. "I saw her!"

"You did?" Tina asked in equal parts hope and fear.

She wasn't asking Kelly to lie, but she wanted Laura to have an alibi and the peace that this would bring.

Kelly thought back to her own police interview. "Laura left here at 9?"

Tina nodded. "About that."

"I definitely saw her." Kelly said triumphantly. "Evan and I had argued about a text he sent her."

"Laura?" Tina frowned in confusion.

"They went running together. That's why I went to Jim's- to ask for her version" Kelly explained. "Then he told me about how he'd been helping you with uni work and placements. I was so shocked that I stormed off. I knew you weren't working at The Crown, so I came here. I thought he might have tipped you off, so I sat outside yours and sent you that message when you didn't answer the door."

"You didn't say anything to Laura though." Tina pointed out, dejected by the hole in the story. "After you'd been looking for her."

"He'd already explained all that," Kelly shrugged unperturbed. "I'd had enough humiliations and it was you I wanted to see at that point. I heard a door open and I glanced over the railings because I was sat outside your door on my phone. I didn't want anyone walking upstairs and seeing me, looking like a weirdo."

Tina smiled despite herself. She could actually picture Kelly sat waiting for her with dogged determination. "And you saw her?"

Kelly nodded with so much confidence that Tina forgot her doubts. "I saw Laura walking down the stairs. I thought about calling out to her, but I had been crying, I was a mess. I didn't mind you seeing me like that, but I don't know her."

"Then what did you do?" Tina asked hopefully.

"I waited a few minutes and I went home." Kelly said simply.

They both fell silent for a few moments, lost in their own thoughts.

Finally, Kelly looked at Tina expectantly. "Should I go to the police and tell them this?"

"I don't know," Tina replied uncertainly. "I don't really know whether we wait for them to ask? I'm going down the station with Laura at 12 because we've got to answer some queries."

"You have to?" Kelly looked surprised for a moment before remembering the online comments. "Oh, the Sparkles review."

Tina flushed, embarrassedly remembering another thing she had withheld from Kelly. "I'm really sorry about that as well. I was stupid not to tell you."

"Did you think I'd butt in and try to tell you how to run your own business?" Kelly asked without a trace of bitterness.

Tina opened her mouth to protest, but Kelly smiled.

"I would have," Kelly admitted. "Or I'd have talked you into letting me on board and then lost interest."

They both exchanged sheepish smiles at each other.

"I know how everything you do is for you and Robbie," Kelly said. "I'm glad I didn't get a chance to jeopardise anything for you. In fact, you're my new role model."

Tina couldn't help but wrap her arms around Kelly at her sweetness. She felt like Kelly's understanding had taken a weight from her shoulders. They both laughed, and Kelly got to her feet.

"Can you just mention to Laura that I saw her?" Kelly asked. "If the police need me, they know where I am. It was about 9 and she was leaving."

"What was she wearing?" Tina asked suddenly terrified that Kelly was lying to make amends and would break the law to do what she thought was right.

"Work out stuff," Kelly said without skipping a beat. "Dark trousers, like Lycra or something, and a dark jacket or jumper."

Tina felt reassured by Kelly's confidence and she hugged her again.

"I've got to go," Kelly said, the sadness returning to her eyes. "Wish me luck."

Chapter 30

Kate pulled into the car park of the large supermarket halfway between Birch Grove and Little Cedars. She was relieved she had no lectures to attend today, as she had a meeting with some local business owners about the impact the road improvements were having on their income. She was glad that she had followed her instincts and remained neutral on the matter. The number of complaints about the current roadworks had been phenomenal. It would have been highly embarrassing and, as a community representative, career-destroying if she had indicated any preference for the work being undertaken.

She rooted through her handbag for the shopping list she had written, pushing aside receipts, pens and miscellaneous items, fishing out a small square of paper. She squinted at the paper in confusion. It was written in the familiar cursive of her own hand, but she couldn't recall the moment when she had jotted down this to-do list. Her eyes travelled down the page and onto the last task. Her heart skipped a beat and she scrunched the paper up into a ball, tossing it back into her large handbag.

Kate marched towards the store, selecting a trolley and resigning herself to having to guess what she had needed. She perched her leather tote on the handle bars of the cart and her eyes crept back to the pink note-paper sat amongst the everyday objects that she carried everywhere. She looked away, spying a bin outside the shop's automatic doors and snatched the offending notelet and tossed it into the refuse.

She turned her thoughts, forcefully, to her forgotten shopping list. It frightened her; how forgetful she had been of late. She purposely went out of her way to jot down notes to herself throughout the day, fearful that once out of her mind whatever snippet of wisdom or routine task she had thought of would be impossible to conjure back. She knew that it was, most likely, a side effect of the medication she took to help her sleep. Kate had researched it on the internet and, despite how problematic it was to her everyday life, she was reluctant to mention it to her doctor. He had already mentioned that she needed to stop taking them and she had only so many stashed away for emergencies.

She had tried a lot of different herbal remedies over the last six years and, while some did the job of knocking her into a deep dreamless sleep, it was only ever temporary before the horrid nightmares returned. Kate shuddered at the memory of the most recent one. They were unlike any other dreams, always so vivid and lifelike. They left Kate shaken and disturbed for days afterwards, so anxious that her body would fight the urge to sleep for days until her body was weak and drained. Her work was impacted as well as her physical health.

No, Kate thought to herself decisively. She would take forgetfulness over that any day.

She moved slowly through the aisles of fruit and vegetables, trying hard to recall what she had wanted, despite knowing that the only thing this would trigger would be her own frustration with herself. The trolley felt heavy and cumbersome in her hands and she felt so tired that, for a moment, she considered abandoning the trolley and driving home.

Kate spurred herself on.

"You can't go home," She muttered to herself. "You've got no milk or tea bags."

The thought took her by surprise and she smiled at her sudden memory. It seemed to be the way it worked. The harder she tried, the more she couldn't remember, whereas when she wasn't trying, things just seemed to pop back into her head as if from nowhere.

Feeling slightly uplifted, she strode on with a sense of purpose and stopped at a display of freshly cut flowers to admire them. She reached forward to move the cellophane wrap away from a bouquet of roses and lilies when she was bumped from behind and fell forward a little, just managing to right herself before she damaged the display beneath her. She looked back to see the discourteous culprit and saw a harassed-looking woman yank her own trolley back from her rambunctious pre-school child.

"Sorry!" The woman exclaimed before pulling the child away from the flowers.

Kate tutted and turned away. She had automatically reached for the flowers out of habit, but she didn't want any this week. Lilies had always been her favourite, but today they reminded her of Colin's funeral. She walked away as quickly as she could, wanting to put distance between anything that brought it all back to her.

She was shaking now. Kate watched the tremor in her hands and felt the accompanying hot flushes that came with the strong memories. She kept moving, trying to detach herself from the warning signs that the hideous memories were just moments away from overpowering her senses.

Even in the throes of panic, Kate felt a bitter pang of anger in the pit of her stomach as she always did. She had been forced into a corner by the actions of others, yet she was the one who had lost out, she was the one who had her life turned upside down by the horrific nightmares. She pushed the trolley a little too roughly in temper, banging against a display of reduced produce, and causing surrounding shoppers to look up.

Kate noticed their curious looks and turned sharply into another aisle. She couldn't help but be conscious of the opinions of others. It was how she had been brought up. Kate had always prided herself on her breeding and eloquence, even in the midst of a nervous episode, Kate was acutely aware of how she looked to the outside world. Her mother had been much the same; carrying herself with dignity and poise through family upsets and right through until her death. She had looked most regal at the private hospice where she spent her last few months, insisting that her hair was set even when her whole body was shutting down organ-by-organ.

She was a strong woman, Kate thought. Kate took comfort in knowing that her mother would have sided with her, even if Colin hadn't. It cemented, in weak moments of doubt, that Kate had been right. Her mother had stood by her convictions, even when she knew death was imminent. Kate admired the steely resolve that she had shown, refusing Emily's pathetic attempts at reconciliation after the shame she had brought to the family. Kate's lip turned up in a scornful sneer as she thought of her gold-digging sister, coming back around, sniffing for a second chance when it was clear that Rosemary had just months to live and Emily's father was already permanently confined to a care home, unable to make the most basic decisions any more, let alone any changes to their last wills. Kate had been surprised when Emily didn't turn up to try to contest the will but, then again, she was so ignorant, she probably wouldn't have known what to do.

Kate had inherited everything, which wasn't any grand fortune but was enough to allow her to live comfortably for the rest of her life. She would have fought Emily tooth and nail for this out of principle. Rosemary and Alan Whitby had made their decision to disinherit Emily, despite her being Alan's only biological child, years previously, when they were both healthy and of sound mind. She had been absent for years with no contact, and Kate had been beside herself with rage when the conceited, selfish girl had reappeared, seeking forgiveness and a share of the estate.

This had been around the same time as the cracks had started to show in her previously-blissful marriage to Colin. He had been inconsiderately indifferent of Kate's understandably emotional reaction, dismissing Kate's justified claim that Emily's motive was to worm her way back into the will.

"She probably just wants to make amends," Colin had argued. "Not everything is about money. Her mother is dying. Wouldn't you want to meet your only grandchildren?"

Kate had been shocked and hurt by Colin's refusal to side with her on such an emotive subject. Kate had been there for her mother when she learned of her terminal illness and arranged her step-father's care when her mother was too weak to. Kate had done everything for her parents while still working and running a home. Colin should have been there to support her but, in the end, Kate had learned to keep her thoughts to herself to avoid provoking any more heated arguments.

Kate had ridden out her mother's subsequent death and funeral with quiet dignity. She had refused to speak about the arrangements with Colin, and Kate's mother's death had been the start of a rocky few years until the silence between them increased and the distance between them grew wider, then Colin finally announced it was over.

Kate had been devastated, despite the fact that she had grown used to living almost separate lives. He was working more and more in the city and had bought a little place there when her inheritance had allowed them to pay off their mortgage. They still holidayed together, and Kate had been hoping that Colin's retirement would bring them closer once more. The shame she had felt at the thought of the public humiliation of a divorce was like nothing Kate had ever experienced. She felt like the whole village were talking about her and she grew uncharacteristically suspicious, turning up at the city flat unannounced and calling him at unreasonable hours of the day, determined that there was more to it.

She had felt so ashamed of herself when she had given in to weak displays of emotion. Even now, just recalling the memories left Kate feeling excruciatingly embarrassed.

She tried desperately to redirect her mind from spiralling uncontrollably down memory lane and Kate shoved her trolley into the next supermarket aisle, casting her troubled eyes over the shelves of wine, searching but not seeing anything except the images burned into her mind's eye.

"Why now?" She had asked.

Colin had thrown her a look of derision. "Katherine, you can not possibly claim that you haven't seen this coming?"

The humiliating thing was that she hadn't. They had been spending less time together since he'd gone back to work recently, granted, but they hadn't had a blazing row since the subject of Emily had arisen the previous year. Colin had called her 'cruel' and 'unnatural' when she hadn't shown any emotion on learning of Emily's death. They had had the most awful fight, and in the aftermath, Kate had wondered if Colin would broach the subject. He had suffered a heart attack not long after, while alone in his City apartment and had moved back into their home, taking a prolonged period of absence from work to recover. Kate had been selflessly attentive in helping him to get back on his feet and they had skirted around any subjects that they couldn't see eye-to-eye on. Kate had taken this as a compromise and to hear Colin's scornful tone bought a rush of hurt and confusion to her.

He'd started to move out his belongings slowly, over a period of months, and Kate had maintained a stiff upper-lip and a cheerful public disposition, telling their mutual friends that they were "happily divorced but still close friends". Somehow, the term "separated" bothered Kate, making her feel like she would be viewed as unable to resolve her disputes, whereas "divorced" felt more publicly acceptable, in fact, it was almost fashionable, as long as people believed it was her choice. She couldn't bear the thought of being viewed as a victim.

Despite her outward show of acceptance, Kate was deeply upset by Colin's cold, ungrateful attitude towards her after everything she had done for him.

Even as Kate's mind travelled back through these unwelcome memories, Kate was aware that he had been the one in the wrong, not her. Colin had used her tragic family skeletons to his own twisted advantage, staging arguments that he knew unsettled her and left her emotional and irrational. It was because of him that her sleep was disturbed with the image of his body, twisted and still at the bottom of their stairs. If it were just this memory, of just a corpse, all traces of life gone, Kate thought she could have lived with it, but it was the final throes of his life that haunted her. Hearing his raspy last breaths and seeing the horror on his face as he fought against the finality of his death; it was these grim memories that refused to be forgotten.

They flashed before Kate's eyes in the ordinary, impersonal environment of the superstore and her heart started to race. Her hands gripped at the handle of the shopping cart and she was aware of her own breathing, coming ragged and uneven as she struggled to breathe. In front of her were rows and rows of near-identical glass bottles, but all she could see was Colin's face, his skin changing to an ashy-grey-blue before her eyes. She could hear him struggling to breathe and see clearly the pleading desperation in his eyes.

Like then, she was blind to her surroundings. No longer was she aware of the few shoppers moving around her as she gasped for breath, overwhelmed with the clarity of the images flashing through her mind.

Back then, she had stood staring at Colin as his heart gave up for the second time, but she felt no rush of adrenaline. Kate hadn't been frozen to the spot watching the life pass from him helplessly with fear. It was a vehement hatred for her husband that had stopped her administering first aid and calling the emergency services. She had stepped, coldly, over his body and driven the short distance to work. It wasn't until she returned home, later that evening, after a regular day of lectures and a game of badminton that she sought help. By then, Colin was long gone, and Kate had stood on the doorstep waiting for the ambulance, feeling genuinely shocked and shaken at the discovery, as if she hadn't walked away and left her husband dying in their hallway that morning. It had been very much a normal day just a few months after he had told her he wanted to end their marriage. Kate had recovered from her initial shock and was back in control of her emotions. There had been no tearful outbursts and no late-night phone calls since the early days of Colin's announcement. Kate was proud of the way she had publicly dealt with the delicate matter. She had emphasised to their joint friends that no-one was to take sides, as much as they would be tempted to pledge their loyalties with her, as the divorce was hard on poor Colin, who would remain a dear, dear friend. Colin had remained silent on the matter, aware of the importance of keeping up appearances, but that morning, when he had stopped by the cottage to pick up some more of his belongings, they had argued. Colin had decided that he didn't want to accompany her on the upcoming trip they had booked to Italy. Kate had been, understandably, upset and unkind words had been exchanged between them. Months, or maybe years, of withheld emotion and frustration had come pouring out, but it was Colin's parting shot that was echoing around Kate's head as his sudden spike in blood pressure wreaked havoc on his already-damaged heart.

"We'll see how pious everyone still thinks the wonderful Kate is when they find out how she refused to take in her orphaned niece and nephew!" Colin had snapped at her in retaliation with a cruelty that had made blood run cold.

"Knowing they'd end up in care. You cold bitch."

Kate had felt her own heart contract in terror at the thought of what this would do to her reputation. Her standing in the community meant everything to her. Without her status, Kate had nothing, and she had shouted and screamed at Colin in a wild temper. She had no idea what she said in that final few moments before Colin was silenced forever by the pain in his chest.

"Miss?" A concerned voice pierced Kate's consciousness. "Miss? Are you ok?"

Kate looked at the young man peering at her with worry and then slowly looked around, taking in her surroundings. She nodded vaguely at the man but, in her head, she was still stood in the hallway of her home, watching Colin fight for his life, his eyes begging for her help.

Sweat was beading at her temples and her chest was heaving as she breathed in short, quick breaths. She needed to get out of here. Kate pushed the trolley away from her, grasping her bag to her body tightly. She stumbled, in her panicked haste, her shoulder hitting a free-standing shelving unit and sending a heavy liquor bottle to the hard-tiled floor.

She righted the stand before any more bottles broke free and looked helplessly down at the pool of glass and liquid at her feet. The smell of whiskey assaulted her nose and she looked at the rows of bottles that she had stopped from following suit. Horrified recognition dawned on Kate and she pulled her hand sharply away from the smooth glass beneath her hand.

She rushed out of the shop, not caring that her haste was

attracting attention of passing shoppers. Kate fumbled in her bag for her keys, desperate to get away from here, from the crowds. Her senses, overtaken by her horrible memories, overwhelmed her and everything felt noisy and busy. She drove with pure instinct, not aware of whether she stopped at lights or kept to the speed limit, but, as she did, other fresher memories assaulted her mind and she was rushed back to the journey she had taken Saturday night.

Kate had started the evening, feeling moderately annoyed, when her close friend, Martin, had made a comment alerting her to the online rumours that she had been having an affair with Jim Burbridge. Kate had been upset and embarrassed, immediately calling Jim to demand that he rectify these awful untruths. Jim had been coolly uninterested in her plight, claiming that he had deleted the slanderous comments before hanging up on her. Kate had felt her anger start to rise and had called him back, but, infuriatingly, his voicemail had picked up. In the back of Kate's mind, a horrible recognition had been growing from the moment Martin had held up his phone to show Kate the screenshotted evidence. The picture of the dark-haired girl, in a thumbnail image next to the vindictive words, would have meant nothing to Kate on its own, but the girl's surname combined with the familiarity of the almond-shaped eyes and angular cheekbones conjured up memories of a secret which she had thought had been buried with Colin.

Incensed, Kate had hopped in her car and driven to the village. Very conscious that Jim's insufferable neighbour had been part of the rumour mill, Kate had deliberately parked her car on the next street and nipped through the little walkway to the top of Sycamore Street.

Jim had been surprised to see her, but he hadn't offered an immediate, deferential apology as she had expected. He had been hideously stand-offish, going as far as to tell her that he "couldn't care less about her reputation". Kate was absolutely astounded by the change in the man, who had, for months, been like an obedient puppy, agreeing with everything she said and anxious to please her.

He had told her that his wife had left him, and Kate had shrugged dismissively.

"I'm here to discuss more important matters," She had told him coolly. "I will have to insist that we sever ties. An association with you is potentially very damaging to my standing in the community."

Jim had laughed cruelly at that, ridiculing her and her "sense of grandeur".

They had both exchanged words. Kate had struggled to keep her composure, whereas Jim had hurled insults with an almost- infantile glee. Kate had been taken aback and confused at his lack of restraint, but then the bottle of whisky on the stair had caught her eye.

"Oh!" She had remarked, picking up the bottle and seeing that roughly one third was gone. "You've taken to the bottle. That explains your behaviour. No wonder your wife left you."

The words, as intended, had hit the mark and Jim had exploded, going from frostily cruel to red-hot anger in seconds. He had launched a full tirade of verbal venom at Kate and she had paled, stepping backwards in instinctive fear.

It was the words that he used, Kate remembered suddenly, as she pulled up at her destination. She killed the engine of her car, and sat for a moment, staring into space, vividly seeing Jim's face, twisted with fury.

"You cold bitch!" Jim had shouted, and it was like she was back in the cottage and it was Colin stood in front of her. Kate felt unrivalled levels of fury course through her. He had ruined her life when he had died. Any peace and contentment had been snatched away with his dying breath. She had lived with guilt that she did not deserve. She had not killed him, but she was suffering as if she had. In the day time, anxiety had stolen any enjoyment of her achievements and, in the night time, the horrible images had robbed her of sleep, driving her to the edge of despair over and over again. He had betrayed her trust, taking what she told him in confidence and throwing it in her face. She had been glad that her awful half-sister had died, after all the grief and shame she had caused the family when she had taken up with an unsuitable man and refused to listen to reason. Colin had been visibly disgusted at her words, and even more so when she stated that she did not care what happened to Emily's orphaned bastards.

Kate heard Jim's words and felt his rage, but, when she looked, it was Colin she saw. Colin, who had threatened to destroy her reputation and had abandoned her when she was still grieving her own mother. Colin, who she had given everything to. Uncontrollable anger flew through her nerves and she felt like she could burst out of her own skin with the fury. She didn't feel the heaviness of the glass when she lifted the bottle, it felt so light in her hands. She heard it whistle through the air and she heard the sickening thud that was the thick glass connecting with Jim's skull.

Kate had watched Jim crumple to the floor, stepping back to avoid being pulled down in his fall. She had waited, frozen, for a few minutes, waiting for him to come around before realising that he was dead.

Kate had meticulously wiped down the bottle with a tea towel, before deleting Jim's call records to disassociate herself from the mess he had created for himself. She had felt a sense of calm settle over her as she had left the scene. She certainly didn't feel like she had killed someone, she had thought as she drove home. All those years she had been plagued with guilt over Colin's death that was not her fault, she mused as she stripped off her clothes and piled them into a hot wash at home. Yet she didn't feel remotely guilty about swinging a bottle at Jim Burbridge's head, knocking him dead instantly. What a funny thing the mind was, she thought smiling to herself. She had slept well that night and she had thought that maybe she was cured, but the next night, the nightmares had returned with an alarming alacrity.

Kate hadn't thought about Jim until today, at the supermarket. Her dreams had been plagued with Colin's death still. She wondered about her unnatural reaction, whether she had been driven to madness by sleep deprivation. She alighted from the car and opened the boot to collect her shopping. She stared in the empty space, before remembering she had left the store without buying anything, and she frowned, wondering why everything felt so hazy and strange.

"Excuse me?" A voice startled her, and Kate turned towards a middle-aged blonde woman. "Are you Mrs Kate Evett? My name is Detective Sargent Parker-"

Kate realised, with startling clarity, that she had been waiting for this moment ever since she had walked away from her husband, leaving him to the hands of fate. It felt like almost a relief to her heavy conscience. Almost. Overriding the desire to be unburdened of her horrible secret was the most basic instinct for self-preservation.

Kate recovered her composure and arranged her face into a polite-but-uninterested smile.

"We need to ask you some questions regarding the death of Jim Burbridge. Are you able to accompany us down to the station?"

Kate's heart skipped a beat at hearing the words aloud, but she kept her expression neutral as she answered in a haughty tone. "I don't think I would be much help to your enquiry, I'm afraid. I barely know the man. We haven't spoken in weeks. I'm just off to a meeting, but I can spare you a moment or two if you'd like to step inside?"

Kate glanced around, conscious of any neighbours snooping. The two officers were dressed in plain-clothes, but Kate thought that it was obvious by their look that they were police.

"I'm afraid this can't wait," DS Parker said firmly. "I really must insist-"

"Am I under arrest?" Kate asked sharply with a purposeful edge of sarcasm.

"No," The woman looked annoyed. "Not at this point, however there is a civic duty to assist with police enquiries."

"Sorry," Kate flashed an apologetic smile and touched the

officer's arm lightly in a friendly gesture. "Of course, I'd like to help if I can in any way. I'm just in a frightful rush to get to this meeting."

"What time is your meeting?"

DS Parker shot a sideways glance at her younger female companion, and Kate felt a glimmer of pride at the controlled way she was handling this shock visit. She made a show of looking at her watch.

"Perhaps we could take your contact details?" The woman said before Kate could answer.

Kate held back from beaming brightly that the officers were backing down when faced with her natural air of authority. She would attend the station, but she needed to compose herself and really think about how best to play this. She fumbled with her phone and gave the details to the younger officer, who was poised with a pen and open pad. The younger woman gave a short, sharp nod at DS Parker.

The older woman hesitated. "Mrs Evett, I am going to need you to accompany us down to the station immediately."

The cogs of Kate's mind had been furiously turning since she was greeted by the plain-clothes police and she realised, with self-satisfied glee, that if they had any reason to suspect her, she would have been arrested by now. This knowledge filled Kate with confidence and she shook her head, convinced that maintaining her polite but unfazed demeanour was key to detracting any concern.

"I'll be happy to help in any way," Kate delivered her offer with the professional air of self-assuredness that she saved for her most important council meetings. "I should be free around 3pm."

DS Parker's face remained neutrally calm and she uttered her next words in such a casual, matter-of-fact manner that she was halfway through her script before Kate realised what was happening.

"I am arresting you on suspicion of murder. You do not have to say anything, but it may harm your defence if you do not mention when questioned something which you later rely on in court. Anything you do say may be given in evidence. Do you understand?"

It turned out to be another long day for DS Parker and her team. By the time she emerged from the interview room with DI Jones, she was starving from missing both breakfast and lunch.

"Sarg'!"

DS Parker had been hoping to sneak into the staffroom and pilfer the chocolates somebody had brought in that week, but the voice came from the direction of the room they had been using for this case and she felt morally obliged, as their Sargent, to answer.

DC Rhodes stood in the doorway, a wide smile on her face and a brown paper bag in her hand.

"Charged?"

DS Parker glanced behind her, checking the corridor was empty, while simultaneously putting her finger to her lips in a signal for Rhodes to be quiet. Seeing that the coast was clear, she gave Rhodes the thumbs up and moved quickly over into the room.

"She's still insisting she's innocent," DS Parker said, once they were safely inside the room. "But her story is a mess. She stuck by her claims that she hadn't spoken to the victim for a few weeks even when we matched her number. She contradicted herself a few times, even her solicitor looked like he wanted to gag her. We're just waiting on a match for prints and forensics, as she claims she's never been in the house. I'd bet anything that we get something conclusive."

"Good call on the arrest." DC Rhodes said holding the brown paper bag out as an offering.

DS Parker smiled gratefully. She'd been nervous at making the arrest, but the phone number, the wiped physical records and the comment Kate Evetts had made about not having spoken with the victim were just enough to give her credible reason for suspicion. She was glad her risk had paid off, as she'd walked back into the station to a gift from an Angela Hanigan, allegedly the nosy neighbour of Oak Village, who had a clear iPhone snap of Kate's car parked up on the curb blocking the pavement one street over on the night of the murder. Angela had been unsure how to upload it to social media to complain about the poor parking etiquette, and then, in the ensuing drama of the neighbourhood death, had completely forgotten about it. Her close friend, Sharon Morgan, had been bragging about giving evidence at the post office, which had seemingly triggered Angela's memory as well as her desire to get in on the action.

DS Parker peered into the bag that Rhodes was offering her

and sighed with pleasure at the sight of the take-away baguette and large cookie.

"Oh my God!" She exclaimed. "I literally couldn't ask for a better team. Now, get yourself home. You should have gone home hours ago."

"It's fine," Rhodes smiled a little shyly. "I'm just going to finish logging all this new stuff from today. I'll drop you home when you're ready."

DS Parker opened her mouth to protest but Rhodes shook her head firmly.

"Don't argue," She said, back to her usual sassy self. "I know you'll insist I leave early Saturday. I've got a date."

DS Parker smiled but said nothing. They both knew that she would.

Chapter 31

August 2017

Dana Simons tilted the kitchen blinds to watch the sign being hammered into the ground outside their home.

"Are you ok, love?" Barry asked.

Dana nodded, despite the anxious feeling in her stomach at the twin 'For Sale' signs in sight. It took her back to the feelings of excitement and anticipation when they had bought the house, not even two years previously. Dana couldn't help but feel disappointed that her hopes and dreams for this house to be her forever home hadn't come true. It had felt too-good-to-be-true even then, Dana thought sadly. The day they had gone to view the house, Dana had marvelled at the luxury of a long, well-kept front lawn running adjacent to the driveway. Every room had her 'oohing' and 'aahing' in delight, already picking out tiles and wall colours in her mind. It was picture-perfect and, after years of squeezing her belongings into a tiny two-bedroomed terrace with Dave and Jordan, it felt like she had finally achieved the life that she had dreamed of.

It had been with a heavy heart that they had decided to leave the village. The aftermath of Jim Burbridge's death had been difficult for them both. Barry was still struggling with feelings of remorse for his role in their neighbourhood dispute and Dana had suffered with nightmares, caused by the what-if's of being a key witness to all the comings-and-goings on that horrible night, horrified that she had passed the murderer in the street.

The shock would have been a good excuse, if Barry needed one, to bury his admission and use the distraction to go back to his up-and-down relationship with alcohol, and Dana had watched, almost expecting this to happen. Barry had stayed strong and, with the support group and Dana by his side, he had been tee-total for almost five months.

Barry moved to Dana's side and gently steered her away from the window, wrapping his arms around her and placing a gentle kiss on her forehead.

"We can stay if you want," Barry told her. "I'll live anywhere as long as it's with you."

Dana couldn't help but smile at his words. She'd been racked with worry that they were making a rushed decision, that they would lose money on the sale, that they wouldn't find something so big for the price, but Barry's words silenced the hundreds of stressful thoughts spinning around her head. She knew that Barry was right. It didn't matter where they lived as long as they were together.

She felt a fleeting twinge of annoyance with herself. She'd wasted the time at the house, stressing about making everything look perfect and wanting everything bigger and better, when she should have been focussing on what really mattered: Barry and the kids. She forced aside the feeling with her typical optimism. It was done now, and she could only learn from her mistakes.

She pressed her head against his chest, comfort washing over her as she heard the steady beating of his heart. "I think it'll do us good to have a fresh start."

Barry nodded, relieved. He had meant what he had said; he would do anything to make Dana happy. It was difficult though, driving into the street and seeing the Burbridge's empty house, the feelings of guilt for the way he had actively encouraged a rivalry with his neighbour and the temptation to blur the edges with distractions at The Crown.

"I think so." Barry agreed.

"You better get a move on," Dana said reluctantly, glancing at the clock. "You'll be late."

Barry gave Dana a parting squeeze before assembling his belongings. He had been unwilling to get involved in Dana's idea, still feeling badly scarred from his involvement in the Oak Village Community group, but Dana had encouraged him with her no-nonsense persuasion. He missed manual work and loved socialising; helping to run a group in the wider community to improve their facilities and help neighbours who maybe didn't have the time or the physical strength to maintain their own gardens was a perfect way for Barry to contribute. The only caveat had been that he didn't want anything to do with the social media side of things, which Dana could perfectly understand.

"Are you coming along later?" Barry asked, as he slipped his feet into his old work boots.

"Of course," She beamed at him, her nostalgia over the house temporarily forgotten. "Chloe is super excited about helping out! As soon as Lindsey drops her over, we'll catch you and the boys up. We promised Steph we'd give her a hand with the refreshments."

Dana watched fondly as her husband reversed off the drive

and went back into the house to call Steph to check whether she needed anything else. Dana was proud of how well Steph had taken to her newly-single life. She had been going from strength-to-strength since she'd cut out the negativity that was her soon-to-be ex-husband. Her confidence had increased ten-fold, and she had a natural flare for business. Initially, she had started cleaning alongside her employees, but she'd quickly spotted another niche she could fill and was currently in the planning stages of opening a little café in the village to add to her portfolio.

Dana heard a car pull up outside and she flung open the door eagerly to greet her step-daughter and her mother. Lindsey chatted for a few moments before getting back in the car and leaving. Chloe flung her bag onto the floor and kicked her shoes off, before looking up at Dana expectantly.

"Can I have a drink?"

"Can I have a drink, what?" Dana asked back, trying to look stern but smiling despite herself.

If anything, she had decided, she should feel happy that Barry's kids felt comfortable enough around her to be their true, cheeky, messy selves.

"Can I have a drink, Dana, my beautiful step-mother who I love so much," Chloe grinned, before adding. "Please?"

Dana laughed and hugged the little girl affectionately. "Just quickly then. We need to go and help Steph and Kendall take drinks and snacks over to Daddy's community group."

"Yay!" Chloe clapped her hands together with childish delight. "I love Steph. Did you know she's going to open a café? And she said when I'm big enough I can be her waitress."

Dana smiled happily as Chloe kept up a non-stop stream of chatter as they got ready to drive over. As she reversed from her driveway, her eyes were drawn to the identical 'For Sale' signs planted in her and the Burbridge's front lawns. Before the wistful feeling had time to set in, Dana felt Chloe's little hand reach over and squeeze hers from the passenger seat.

"Don't worry, Dana. I was sad when we said goodbye to our house too," Chloe told her wisely. "But it's the people inside it that matter."

Dana felt her eyes fill with tears at Chloe's sweetness.

"And the toys." Chloe added seriously, causing Dana to burst into happy laughter.

The phone call took Laura by surprise and she stepped into her bedroom to listen. When it was over, she wandered back into the living room.

"Who was that?" Keeley asked, looking up from the open laptop.

Laura turned to her daughter, lowering the phone to her side, deliberating how much Keeley needed to know and how much she should try to protect her. Laura sat down, gently, on the wing chair next to the large window of their second-floor flat.

The last few months had been a wake-up call to Laura about how, no matter how much she tried, she couldn't shelter her daughter from the harsh realities of the world. Laura couldn't help but muse that things had been so much simpler in her youth when the news was something you watched before the soap operas and if you wanted the opinion of your neighbours you'd invite it by knocking their door or inviting them over for a cuppa. She smiled wryly at this thought; she sounded like an old lady.

"It was the detective," Laura told her finally. "They're still a while away from trial. She was just letting me know."

"What else?" Keeley asked razor-sharp at picking up when Laura was holding back.

"Kate Evett is undergoing some assessments," Laura admitted. "To determine whether she is fit to stand trial at all."

Laura watched Keeley digest this. It was better for her to hear this from her mother than through social media posts, Laura knew, but it didn't make it any less difficult to deliver the news.

"What happens if she doesn't?" Keeley asked hesitantly.

"It would be up to a judge," Laura said carefully. "There would definitely be a supervision order, given the nature of the crime."

Keeley nodded, and Laura waited for her to ask more questions, but she remained silent.

"That means..." Laura began, but Keeley waved a hand at her.

"I know," Keeley nodded, returning to the screen on her lap. "Evan showed me all that."

Laura frowned. "He doesn't do criminal."

"No, but Tina is going to," Keeley said confidently. "It's so interesting."

Laura nodded and said nothing, not sure whether to be proud or concerned about Keeley's obsession with all things legal following a week's work experience at Ricer & Wallis.

"It's mad, isn't it?" Keeley continued. "Tina being related to that woman."

"It is," Laura agreed, feeling the familiar pang of sympathy for Tina now that, thanks to social media rumours, it was public knowledge in the village that Kate Evett was the estranged half-aunt of Tina and her brother, Robbie. "What are you working on now?"

"This." Keeley angled the laptop to show her mother the images she had been carefully manipulating for the past few hours. "I'm just sending them back to Kelly now. We like this one the best."

Laura felt a pang of relief at how quickly Keeley had gone back to her laptop after hearing the news, and she leaned forward to look at the images.

"And Robbie designed those?" Laura couldn't help but admire the professional-looking logos, despite her preoccupation with the news about the trial.

Keeley nodded her head and Laura could see the glimmer of enthusiasm in her eyes.

"Honestly, Mum," She enthused. "He's so good! Kelly looked at loads of professional designers and she didn't think any of them were a patch on Robbie. And he's still got a year left of his degree."

Laura was surprised at how quickly Evan and Kelly were working on turning Evan's dream of starting his own company into a reality. Despite everything that she had had going on over the past six months, she hadn't been completely oblivious to the rumours of Kelly's alleged affair with Darren Rees. Laura had ignored any gossip; her mind flicking back to Evan's fleeting attempt to kiss her. Whatever had happened, it seemed neither of them were entirely without blame, and regardless, Laura thought that it was nobody's business but their own. They seemed to have worked through whatever differences they had, as when questioned as to why their beautiful house was on the market and the flash cars had been downgraded, Evan had excitedly announced that he was leaving Ricer & Wallis to start his own company with Kelly's full support.

Laura had been surprised at how taken she was with Kelly Russell, who had gone out of her way to get to know both her and Keeley during a time when neighbours had either been unnaturally awkward or suspiciously friendly, like they were either afraid to speak to them for fear of intruding on their grief or as if they were dying to get all the morbid details of Jim's death to share at the local pub.

"They're both very talented," Laura nodded. "Robbie and Tina."

Laura meant it. They had both suffered not only the tragedy of losing their mother but had been knowingly let down by their only living relative, yet they had stuck together and were two of the kindest, hard-working young people Laura had ever met. She would miss Tina popping in for a coffee and a chat so regularly when they moved; which brought her on to the next topic she was hesitant to raise with Keeley.

"Keeley," She started. "You know that the lease is up here next month?"

"Mmmm." Keeley replied, not looking up from the laptop.

"This was never intended to be forever," Laura continued, trying to choose her words carefully. "And it's your final year in school so there's only a year to get through any commute."

"Commute?" This caught Keeley's attention and her head snapped up to look at her mother.

The house in Sycamore Street had been on the market for a month, but Laura wasn't confident of it being a quick sale, given the circumstances, but she did have enough money to put down a deposit on somewhere more permanent for them. Laura had thought that a fresh start somewhere where everyone in the street didn't know you were the wife and daughter of a murdered man might be good for them and the place they'd known as home wasn't just minutes away; a grim, physical reminder of the tragedy.

"I wasn't thinking of leaving the country!" Laura replied quickly. "I just thought it might be nice for us to go a little further afield than Little Cedars."

"Like?" Keeley tilted her head to the side, regarding Laura suspiciously.

"Birch Grove? Finchester?" Laura suggested. "Or further? I just thought that it's been difficult with everything that's happened and everyone knowing our lives."

Keeley dropped her gaze at Laura's words, but not before Laura had seen the familiar pain in Keeley's eyes. It had been hard, and it still was, but everyday they were able to go a little bit longer between fresh waves of grief.

"It'll be difficult wherever we live, Mum," Keeley raised her head again, with a resilient courage and looked her mother in the eyes. "People will know wherever we go anyway. It's on the internet so unless you want to change our names and move to, I don't know, North Korea, you'd better get used to it."

Laura's eyes widened in surprise at Keeley's brusqueness. She had a point, but Laura was saddened to think that Keeley was so resigned to living with not only the pain of losing her father but the burden of strangers knowing private details of her life.

"I understand that," Laura sighed. "I just thought that there might be too many painful memories in the village."

Laura's mind went immediately to the social media group that had since been shut down, thank goodness. She hadn't looked at it since Jim's death, but she couldn't help but recall some of the spiteful and nasty things that had been said in the past. Laura had heard that another resident, Angela Hanigan, had started a new group a few weeks later but she was still some way away from being able to look at any Oak Village related news without feeling the wretched pain of their loss.

"If you really want to move, Mum," Keeley said gently. "I'll go wherever you want."

"But you don't want to?" Laura asked.

"It's our home," Keeley shrugged. "Good, bad and ugly. This might be where it happened but it's where all our friends are."

"I know that," Laura searched for the right words to phrase what she wanted to say, worried that Keeley hadn't considered everything that could possibly crop up. "I was thinking more of the whole Oak Village online side of things. I know the group that your Dad made is gone but, like you said, it's the internet, who knows if things that people said won't crop up in the future. There were some pretty awful things said by people."

Laura wanted to add that Dana Simons had warned her that any news of the trial was shared on the page by some insensitive residents with morbid curiosity, but Keeley beat her to it.

"I know some of the people talk about what happened," Keeley told her. "And I know people slated Dad on there when he was alive. Tina did, and Barry. I can understand that Tina was just lashing out because of that woman, and I do forgive Barry, because Dad did kind of start it. I told Barry he should have known better. Actually, you all should. Grown adults acting like the words you type aren't exactly as real as the ones that come out of your mouth. If anything, they're more real because they're there forever."

Barry and Dana had both turned out to be good friends in the aftermath of Jim's death and Laura knew, instinctively, that they were acting out of genuine kindness and not looking to redeem any guilty consciences or score any village gossip. Dana had Jordan couriering over Keeley's school work and the family had taken on the task of packing up the house when Laura couldn't bring herself to do it.

Keeley wasn't finished. "Mum, this is our home. I know it's not perfect, but nowhere is. It doesn't matter where we live next, whether it's a big house or this flat. We'd still be sad if we woke up in a twenty-bedroom mansion with individual hot-tubs. And it wouldn't stop people talking."

Laura smiled. "I think we'd be slightly less sad if that were the case."

Keeley grinned. "Ok, well, you find that house and we'll talk."

"I understand what you're saying," Laura said softly, regarding her daughter with awe at her maturity. "When did you get so grown up?"

Keeley smiled, pleased that her mother's comment was a perfect segue into what she had been trying to figure out how to raise.

"By the way," She launched straight into it, sensing that this was the closest to a seamless opportunity that she would get. "Ollie's mum is going to her sister-in-law's birthday party next weekend, and their dad has let her down, again, to have Kendall. Steph says I can stay over and look after her, because she's really naughty for Ollie so she won't leave them together, but I need to ask you?"

Keeley spoke so quickly that it took Laura a few moments before she realised what she was being asked. Laura blinked several times dumbly before she could even begin thinking about how she was going to respond.

"Stay over? At your boyfriend's?" Laura repeated, feeling sick at the thought.

"Oh, Mum!" Keeley blushed. "Don't say it like that! I'll be looking after Kendall. Steph will be home, but they're going to a club, so it might not be until, like, 2am."

"I'll just come and get you." Laura offered quickly.

Keeley gave her mother a stern look. "Mum! That's ridiculous. I'm not going to do anything."

Laura looked away, a little uncomfortably at Keeley's frankness. "Keeley, I'm not stupid."

Laura was surprised to see Keeley's eyes flash with annoyance.

"I'm not!" Keeley exclaimed. "Do you think I would lie to you?"

"Well, no," Laura said quickly. "But I know how it is. You're getting older, and you've been going out with Ollie a while. It's only natural..."

"Mum!" Keeley cut her off. "I'm telling you now, I haven't and I'm not planning to. Can you just trust me?"

Laura tilted her head in confusion. "So, the whole condom thing?"

"It wasn't mine." Keeley said firmly, but a look of shame flashed across her eyes as she recalled the horrible last argument. "I was only defending you."

"Well, it wasn't mine!" Laura insisted.

"Maybe it was Dad's." Keeley shrugged, but Laura shook her head.

"I know him," She insisted. "He would never cheat. And nor would I."

They both fell into a thoughtful silence. Laura took Keeley's hands in hers and they smiled sheepishly at each other.

"Guess we'll never know." Keeley said finally.

"It doesn't matter," Laura told her, and then added to Keeley's surprise. "I trust you and I think it's lovely that Steph's getting out and about. You can stay over."

Keeley's face lit up and she threw her arms around her mother.

"Oh, thank you!" She sang happily. "You're the best."

"Just don't do anything you regret." Laura joked, already wishing she could take back her offer but knowing that she had to trust her daughter.

Keeley rolled her eyes, giving Laura glimpse of the petulant child that was still there beneath the sombre grown-up she'd been of late.

"I'm going down to help out with Dana and Barry's litter pick," Keeley said, changing the subject rapidly as if she sensed her mother had agreed under duress. "Fancy it?"

Laura hid a look of surprise at Keeley's involvement in the newly-founded community group. She hadn't thought that it would Keeley's cup of tea for a number of reasons but, wanting to make the most of any opportunity to spend time with her, Laura agreed.

"It's a nice idea," Laura said, as they strolled through the village down to meet the rest of the volunteers at the river. "Doing something positive for the village."

"There's been some moaning about it already, apparently," Keeley told her. "I guess you can't please everyone."

September 2016

Tina bitterly regretted last night's bar crawl. Kelly had convinced her to "pop out for a few", but a few had turned into a lot, and Tina felt awful.

The sound of her alarm pierced her skull, she felt simultaneously hot and cold, aching and nauseous. She had to get through a full day's work and, for a moment, Tina contemplated calling in sick. There were definitely downsides to running your own business, she thought as she forced herself out of bed in search of water and painkillers.

Tina hadn't planned to go out, but she'd been working the Sunday evening shift at The Crown and Kelly could be quite persuasive, practically begging her to come. Tina was quite fond of Kelly, in her own way, and had let herself be coerced. Classes didn't start for another week in university and Tina had thought that it might be nice to act like a normal student for once. Her brother, Robbie, had gone back to Plymouth ready to start the second year of his own degree after spending the whole summer at home, alternating between sleeping and partying, while Tina worked her ass off covering holidays for her staff and banking enough cash to just about carry her through the next few months.

She hadn't counted on employing people being so expensive and time-consuming, which was part of the reason she was keen to keep a few shifts at the local pub. It was easy, enjoyable work and, on quiet days she could get a bit of reading done plus it forced her to socialise.

This hellish hangover, however, was a definite reminder of one of the arguments in favour of her usual reclusive ways, Tina thought as she finished a pint of water, cautiously stood next to the sink.

She showered quickly, trying to trick her own body into cooperating with the promise that the quicker she moved, the quicker she could be back home in bed. It was just a short walk to her first job and Tina promised her hungover self that she'd stop for food on the way back. Tina checked her messages as she walked, and she cringed when she saw that Evan Russell had texted her last night.

She felt awful that she'd not got around to mentioning her work experience to Kelly, but she was so superstitious with things like that. Tina suspected that it was a throwback to the worst year of her life: her mother's death, not being able to track down their father, being rejected by their only blood relative and being helpless to stop Robbie having to live with a foster family. Tina had stopped getting her hopes up and this had a knock-on effect up until present day. She hadn't wanted to mention she was taking on employees at Sparkles "just in case it didn't work out" and then, exactly the same worries had stopped her from mentioning the fact she'd been accepted onto the Law degree course last year to any of her friends in the village.

Which put Tina in a very awkward situation last night.

She'd ended up doing some work experience at the firm that Kelly's husband worked at, and in a moment of panic, had sworn him to secrecy. He was actually a really nice guy, which made it even worse that Tina had been meeting up with him for help with her assignments and other advice. It had gone past the point where Tina felt she could say anything now, and it had been excruciating listening to Kelly confiding in her, last night, how distant and distracted Evan was, how he was never home. Tina had wanted to confess all, but then Kelly had started telling Tina how she'd been talking to one of the regulars from the pub online and how he was asking her to meet up with him that night.

Tina had been horrified to learn that Darren Rees was the man Kelly was referring to; a notorious womaniser and a married arsehole. Tina had done her best to convince Kelly to forget about him, but with every drink Kelly knocked back, she was more and more adamant that she liked Darren.

"D'you know what?" She had slurred to Tina. "I'm going to go home with him tonight."

Tina hadn't been able to hide her shock. "You can't! He's married!"

"So's Evan." Kelly had countered. "But he seems to have forgotten, so I'm going to forget about him."

Tina had continued trying to reason with Kelly, but Kelly had been oblivious to Tina's concerns, excitedly dragging Tina over to the vending machine in the Ladies' toilets of some sticky-floored late-night bar they had ended up in.

Tina had watched Kelly unsteadily feed coins into the machine until, with a whir, the machine dispensed the cellophane-wrapped packet. Kelly had unwrapped the box and popped the individually-packaged contraception into her clutch bag, except for one which she shoved into the pocket of her jacket.

"Well, if she's going to be stupid at least she's being careful." Tina had reasoned when she admitted to herself that she was fighting a losing battle trying to convince Kelly to listen to reason.

Tina had begrudgingly accompanied Tina to meet up with Darren and some of his work friends, hoping that Kelly would come to her senses. Just when Tina was planning on making her excuses and leaving, she felt a gentle tug on her arm.

"Let's go home, Tina." Kelly had said, and Tina had happily obliged, wobbling together into a taxi.

Kelly had chucked her jacket down on top of Tina's and reached across for Tina's hand in a drunken display of affection.

"I don't think I could really cheat on Evan," Kelly had told her out of nowhere, and Tina had felt her heart skip a beat with relief. *"I'm just really lonely."*

Tina's heart had then surged with empathy for the attractive, older woman and she had given Kelly a massive hug before she'd helped her to her door and walked unsteadily back to her own flat at the end of the street.

Tina replayed the night in her mind, as she unlocked the door to her first customer's house. She slipped her jacket off and hung it over the Burbridge's bannister, which was already teeming with coats and bags. Tina turned to walk into the kitchen, but in her still-delicate state, stumbled on a book, A Guide to Social Media or something similar, on the bottom step and reached out to keep her balance, sending coats and bags raining down on her.

Frustrated and exhausted, Tina sunk down onto the bottom step amongst the mess and put her head in her hands. She fought hard against the tears of self-pity that threatened to spill over. Everything had been getting on top of her lately, she was nervous about her second year, fatigued from working all the hours that she could and, to top it off, worried that Robbie wasn't taking his degree seriously enough. Tina was just one bad day away from quitting everything and getting a normal 9-to-5.

She looked up, trying to force the tears away, and reached for her jacket in the mass of fallen coats. She was done: giving up, going home and getting back in bed to sleep off this hangover before googling full-time jobs. Tina tugged at the jacket to separate it from the pile and upturned a leather handbag in the process. She looked at the mess around her and was mentally preparing herself to clean up the chaos and disappear, texting Laura on the way home with a generic excuse for why she couldn't make it when her eyes were drawn to a framed picture she hadn't noticed before.

It was a candid shot of Laura and, presumably, her daughter; bodies turned towards each other, mouths open in delighted, carefree laughter. There was something about the relaxed nature of the pose that made Tina think of her relationship with her own mother, and in that moment, she knew that quitting was not an option.

Determined, she rose to her feet and replaced the coats one-by-one. Once completed, she turned her attention to the strewn contents of the handbag and replaced them before hanging the bag back up. She retrieved her own jacket last and laid it carefully over a kitchen stool to avoid upsetting the already precarious stack of coats, and as she did, she noticed a shiny packet on the floor by her foot.

She scooped it up, recognising it as a condom packet. She was surprised, knowing that Laura was married, and then chided herself for such judgemental thoughts. She'd been unnecessarily disapproving of Kelly last night. She needed to start minding her own business, she told herself, popping the packet back into the handbag.

ABOUT THE AUTHOR

The Village Online is the second novel by Lily Hayden. Lily worked in Financial Services for fourteen years before quitting her job to write Butterflies, her debut novel.

Lily is passionate about books, travelling, animals and equality. She lives in Wales with her four children, three cats, two dogs and a husband.

Follow Hayden Woods Creative on Facebook, Twitter, Instagram and LinkedIn for up-to-date news and releases.

Praise for Butterflies

"...her thoughts, fears and feelings will have you empathizing and even shouting at her a few times! Some good twists to keep you on your toes..."

"... I felt as though I knew the characters...I think we all need a friend like Lucy..."

"Fab light read that keeps you guessing"

Printed in Great Britain
by Amazon